AMULET

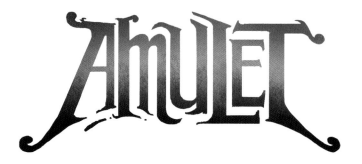

KAZU KIBUISHI

BOOK ONE
THE STONEKEEPER

AN IMPRINT OF
SCHOLASTIC

ISBN 978-0-439-84680-6 (hardcover)
ISBN 978-0-439-84681-3 (paperback)

30   17 18 19

Printed in Malaysia   108
First edition, January 2008
Edited by Sheila Keenan
Book design by Kazu Kibuishi and Phil Falco
Creative Director: David Saylor

Scholastic Inc., 557 Broadway, New York, NY 10012.

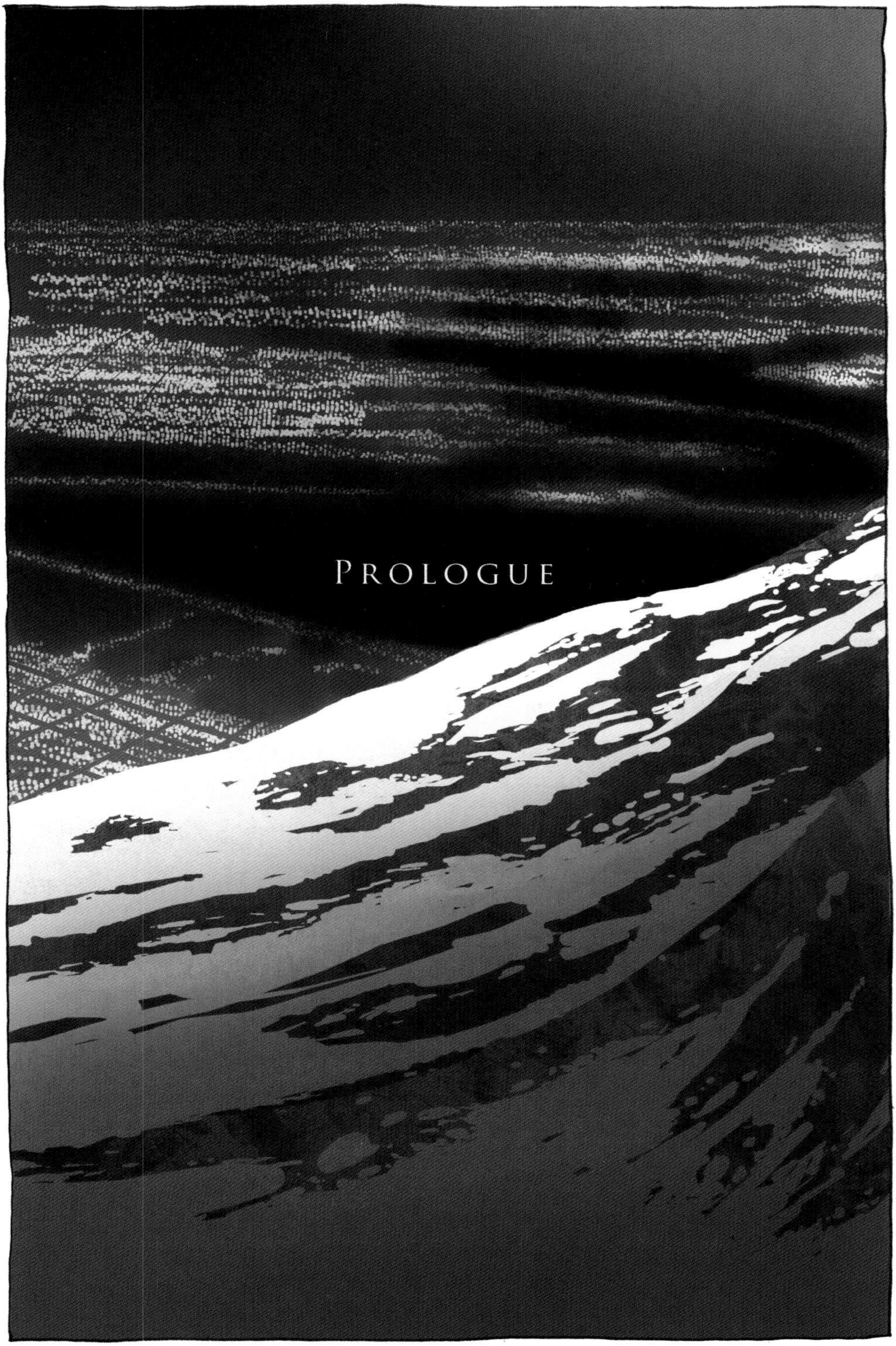
PROLOGUE

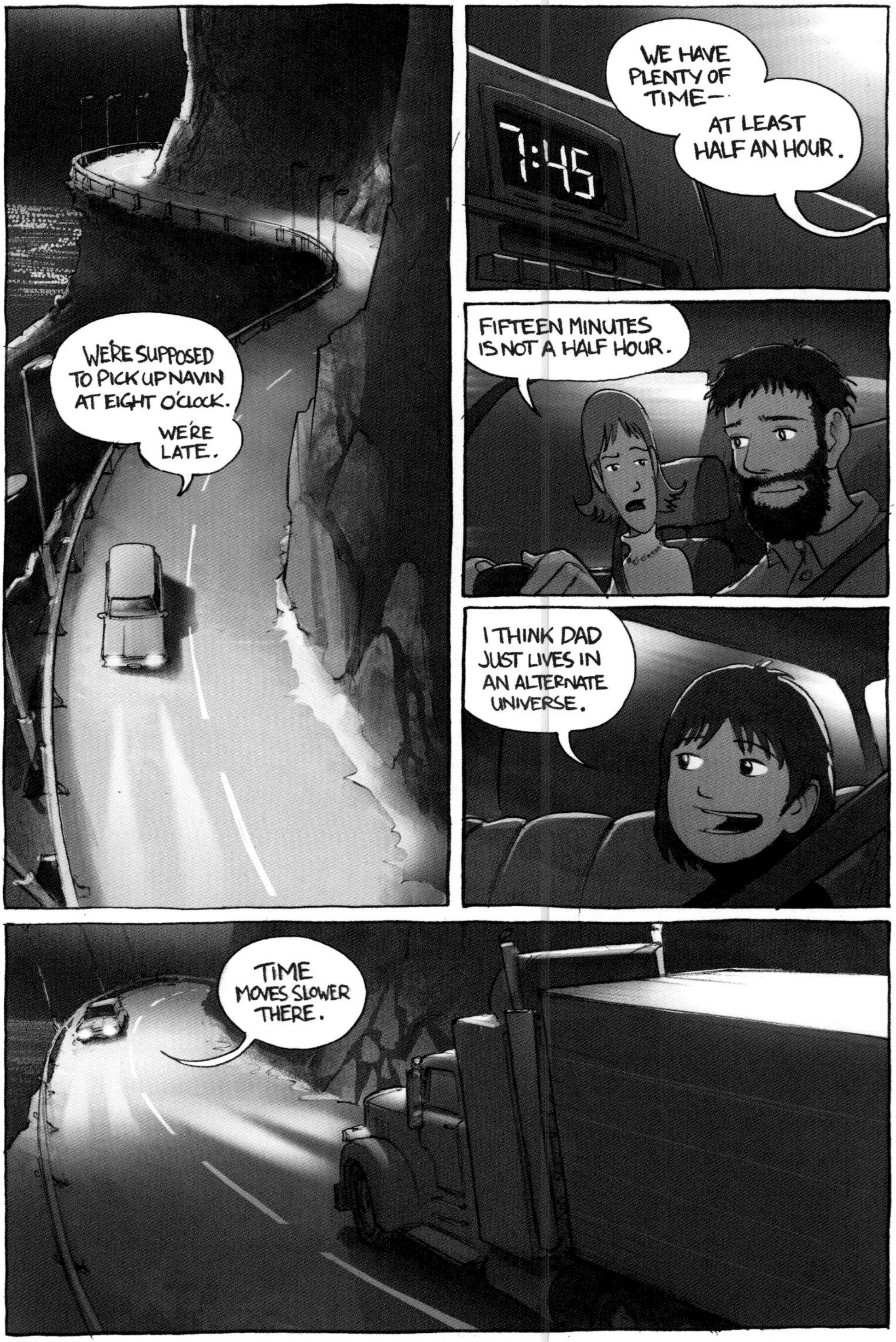
WE'RE SUPPOSED TO PICK UP NAVIN AT EIGHT O'CLOCK.
WE'RE LATE.
WE HAVE PLENTY OF TIME—
AT LEAST HALF AN HOUR.
7:45
FIFTEEN MINUTES IS NOT A HALF HOUR.
I THINK DAD JUST LIVES IN AN ALTERNATE UNIVERSE.
TIME MOVES SLOWER THERE.

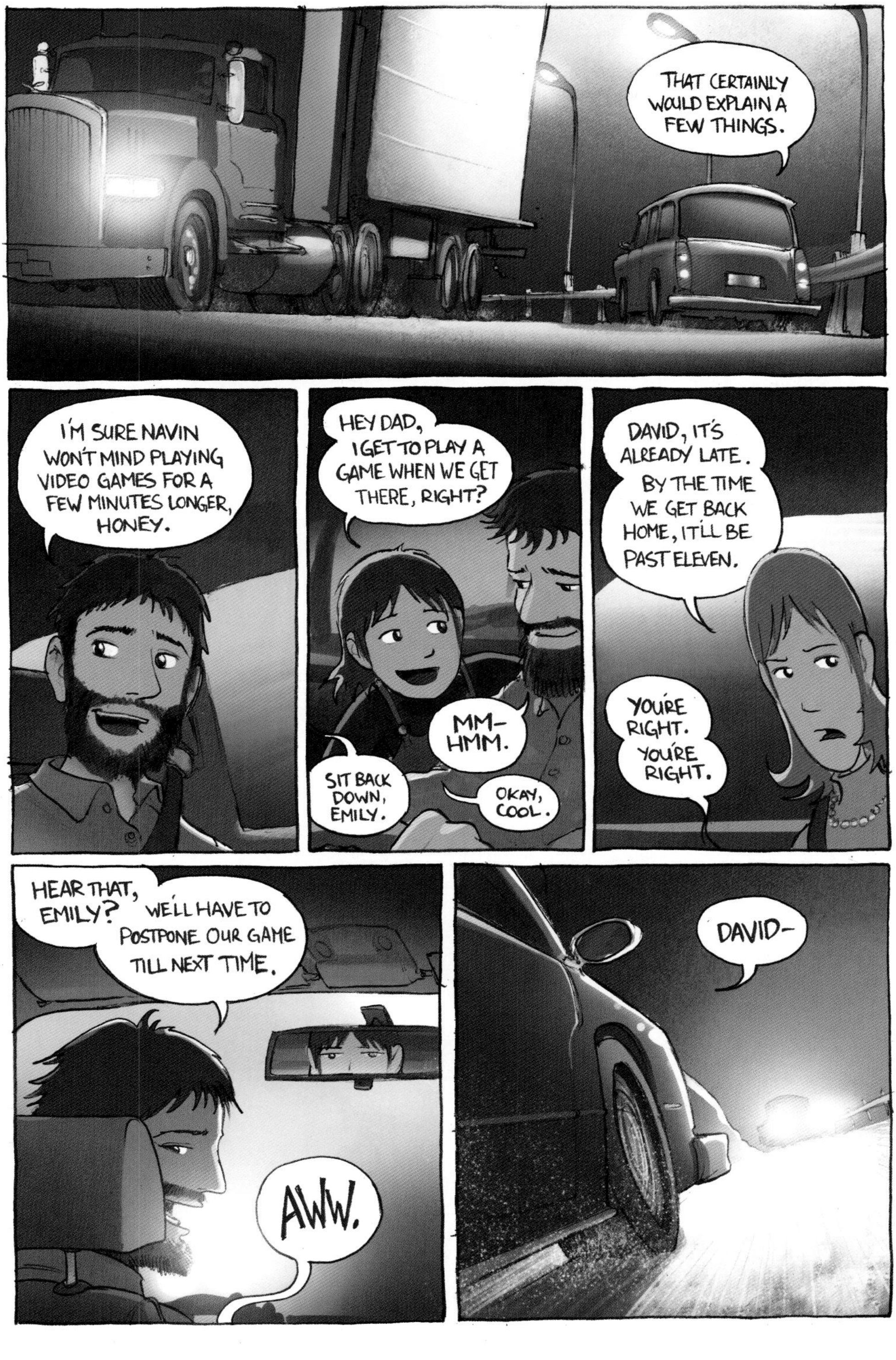
THAT CERTAINLY WOULD EXPLAIN A FEW THINGS.
I'M SURE NAVIN WON'T MIND PLAYING VIDEO GAMES FOR A FEW MINUTES LONGER, HONEY.
HEY DAD, I GET TO PLAY A GAME WHEN WE GET THERE, RIGHT?
MM-HMM.
SIT BACK DOWN, EMILY.
OKAY, COOL.
DAVID, IT'S ALREADY LATE.
BY THE TIME WE GET BACK HOME, IT'LL BE PAST ELEVEN.
YOU'RE RIGHT. YOU'RE RIGHT.
HEAR THAT, EMILY?
WE'LL HAVE TO POSTPONE OUR GAME TILL NEXT TIME.
AWW.
DAVID-

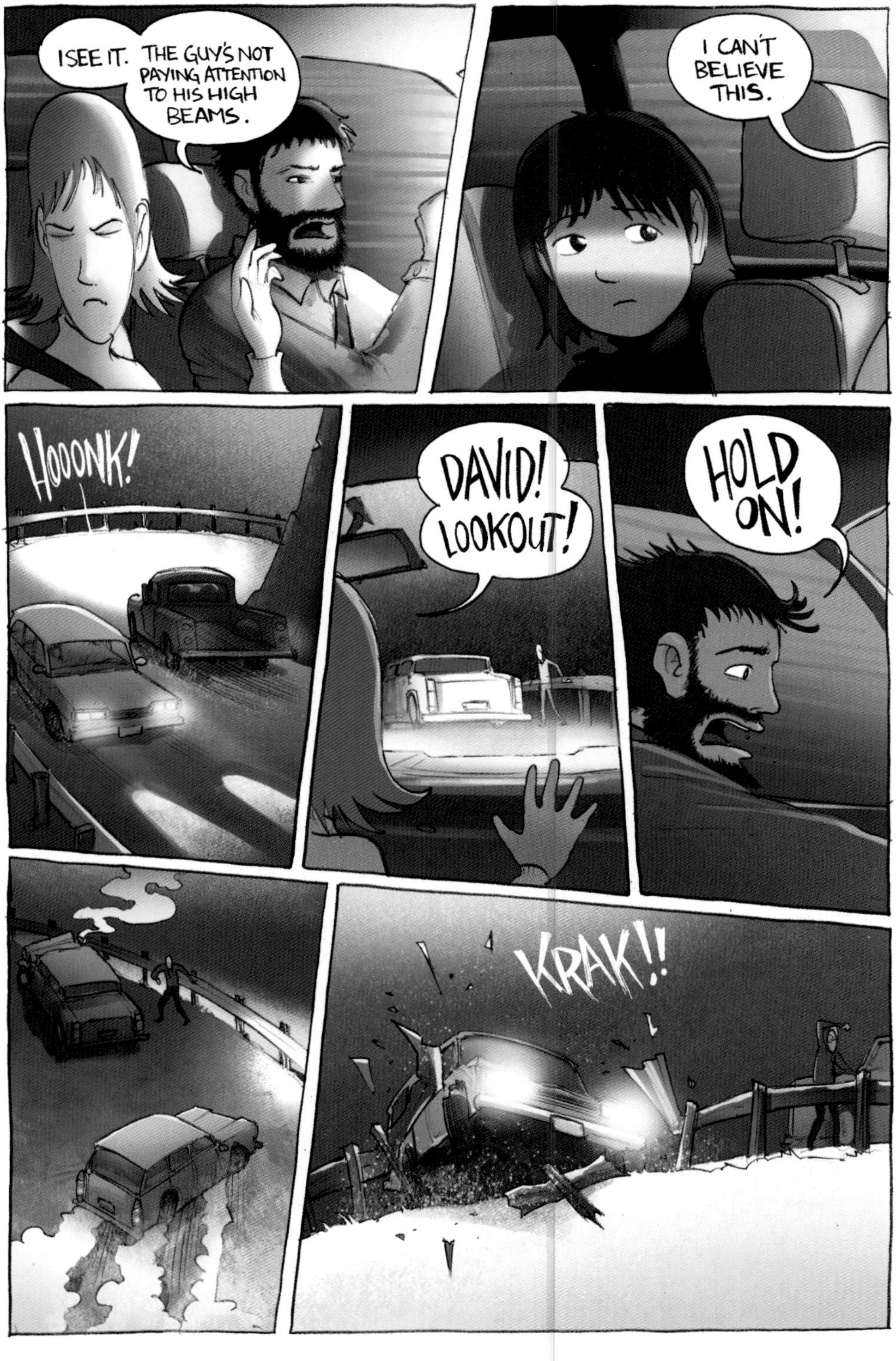
I SEE IT.
THE GUY'S NOT PAYING ATTENTION TO HIS HIGH BEAMS.
I CAN'T BELIEVE THIS.
HOOONK!
DAVID! LOOKOUT!
HOLD ON!
KRAK!!

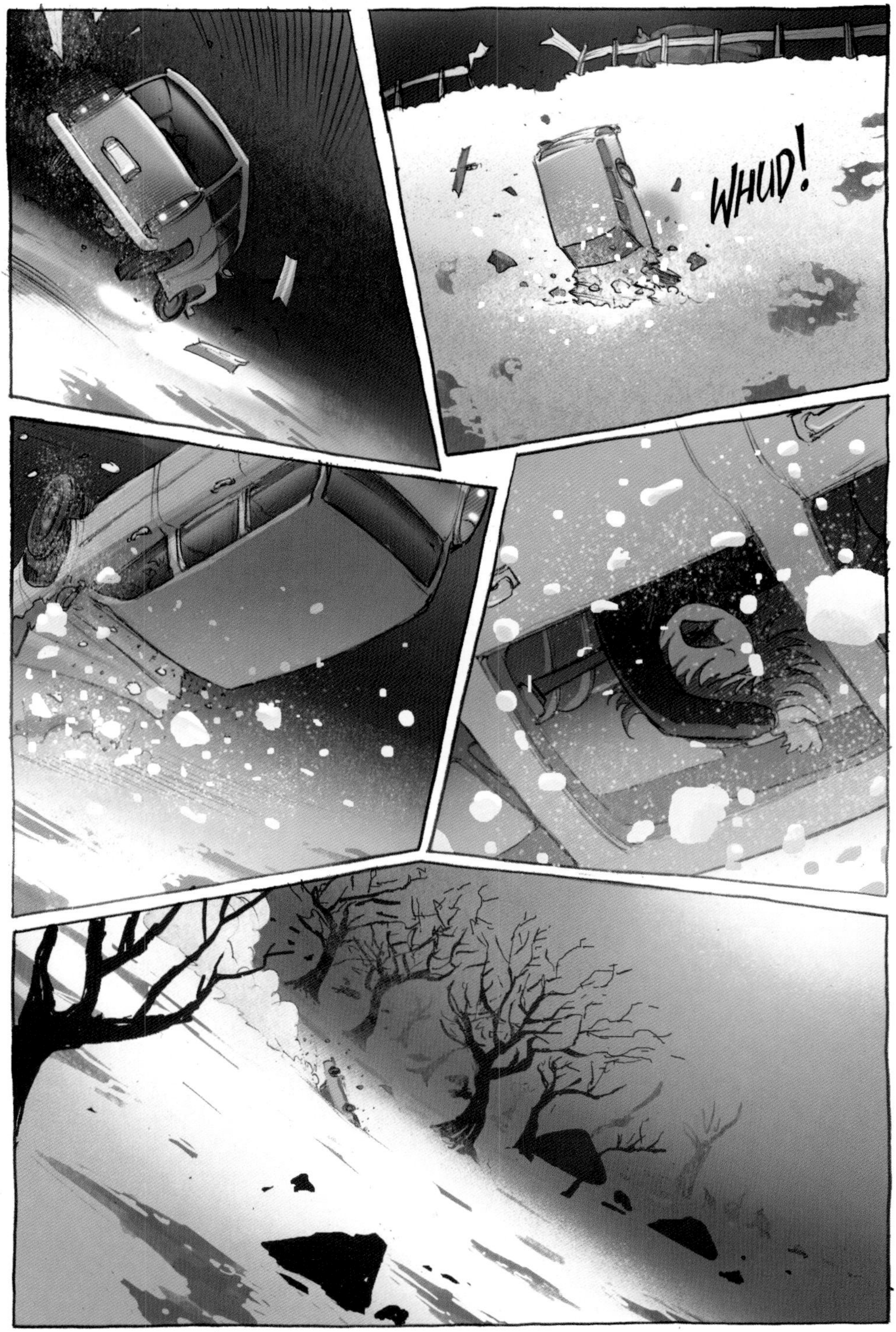
WHUD!

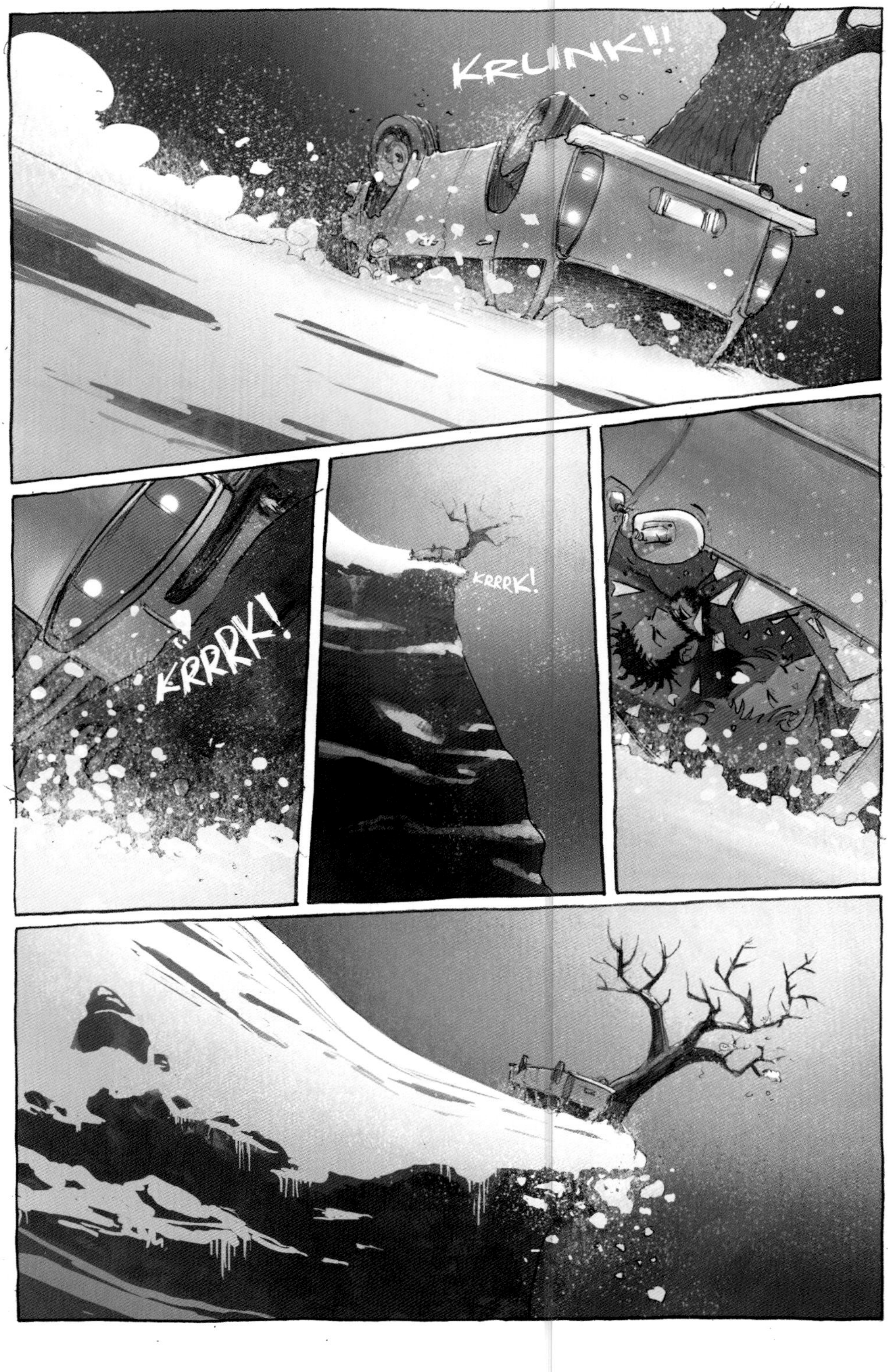
KRUNK!!
KRRRK!
KRRRK!

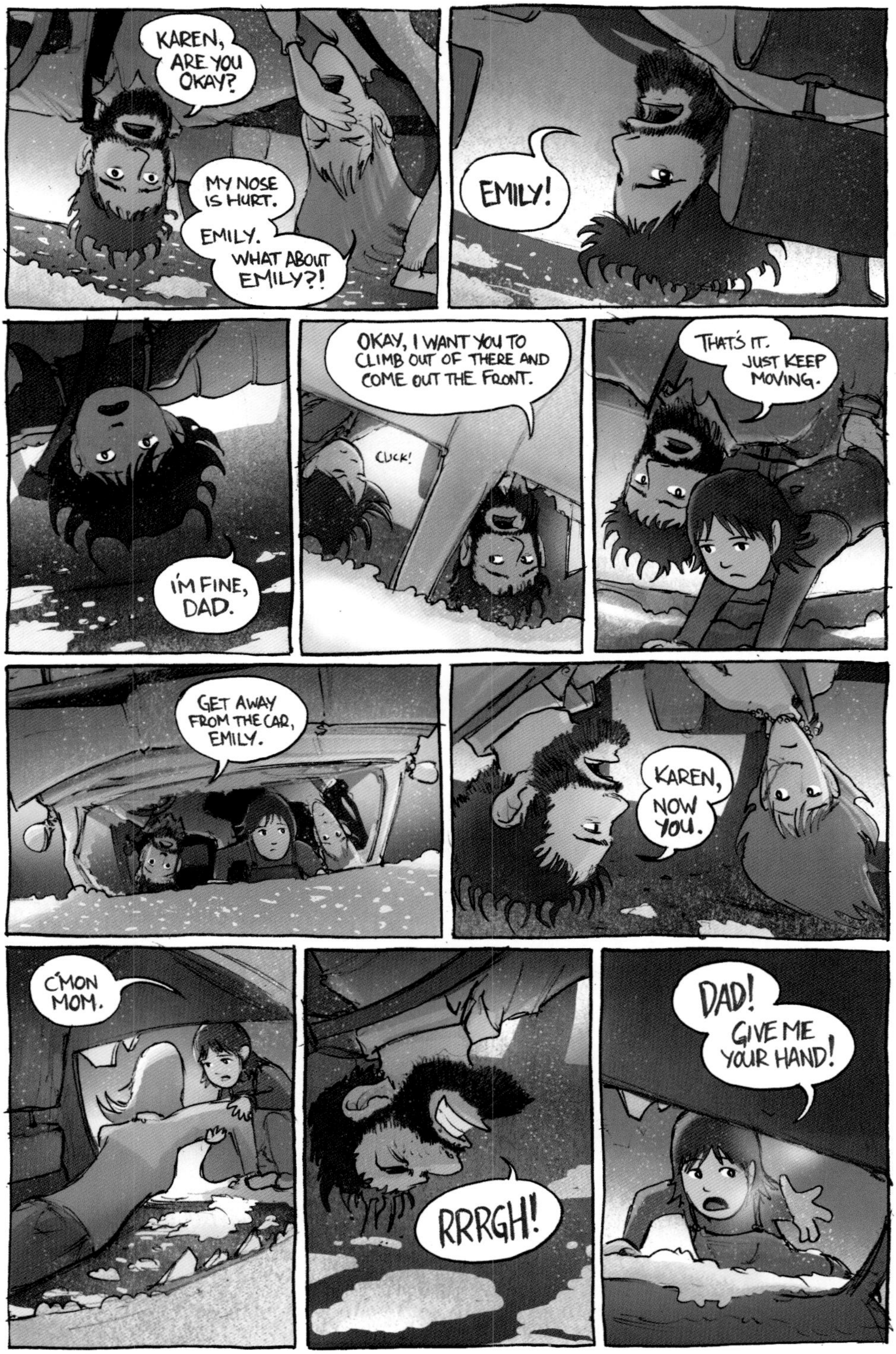
KAREN, ARE YOU OKAY?
MY NOSE IS HURT.
EMILY.
WHAT ABOUT EMILY?!
EMILY!
I'M FINE, DAD.
OKAY, I WANT YOU TO CLIMB OUT OF THERE AND COME OUT THE FRONT.
CLICK!
THAT'S IT. JUST KEEP MOVING.
GET AWAY FROM THE CAR, EMILY.
KAREN, NOW YOU.
C'MON MOM.
RRRGH!
DAD!
GIVE ME YOUR HAND!

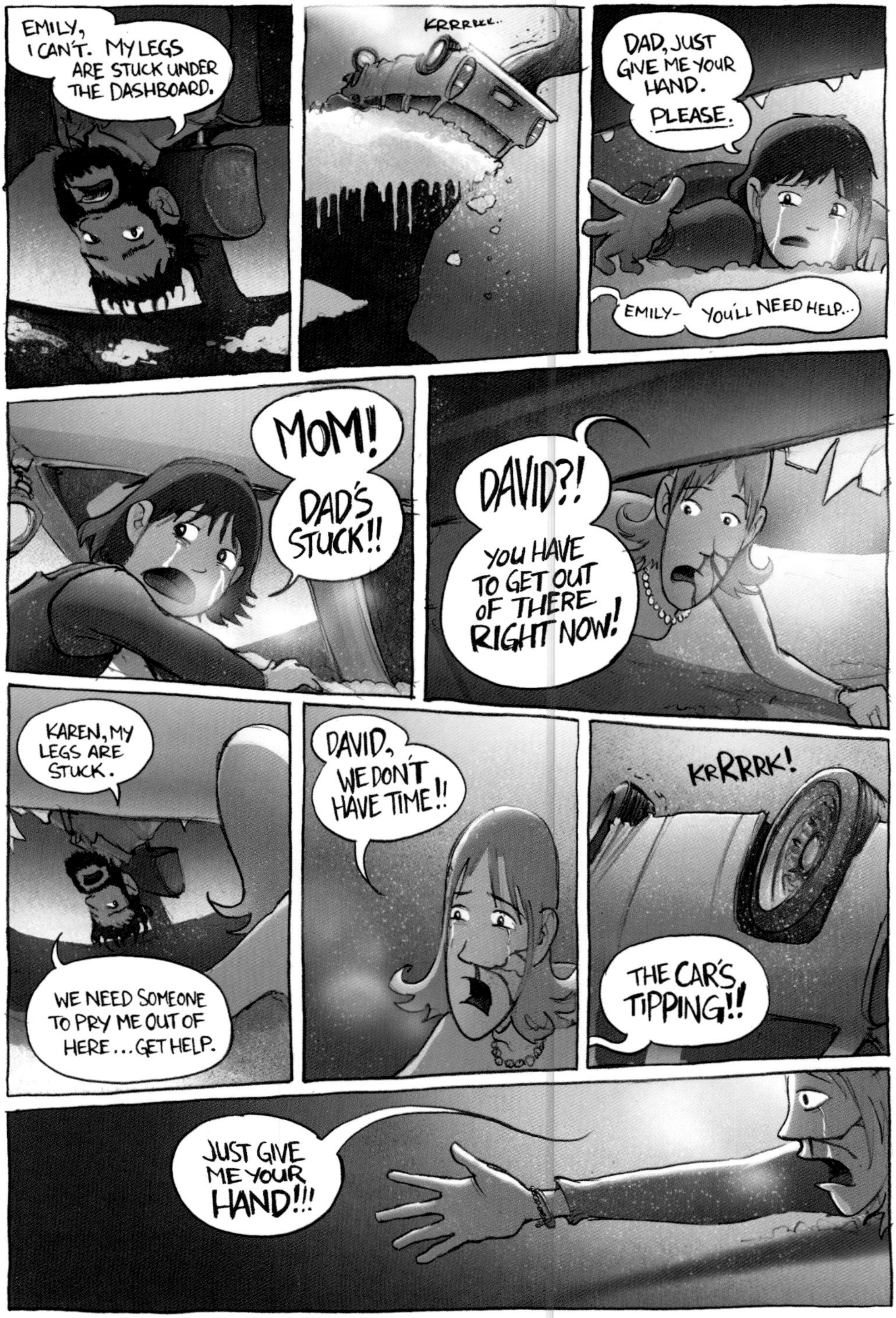
EMILY, I CAN'T. MY LEGS ARE STUCK UNDER THE DASHBOARD.
KRRRRKK..
DAD, JUST GIVE ME YOUR HAND. PLEASE.
EMILY-
YOU'LL NEED HELP...
MOM!
DAD'S STUCK!!
DAVID?!
YOU HAVE TO GET OUT OF THERE RIGHT NOW!
KAREN, MY LEGS ARE STUCK.
WE NEED SOMEONE TO PRY ME OUT OF HERE... GET HELP.
DAVID, WE DON'T HAVE TIME!!
KRRRRK!
THE CAR'S TIPPING!!
JUST GIVE ME YOUR HAND!!!

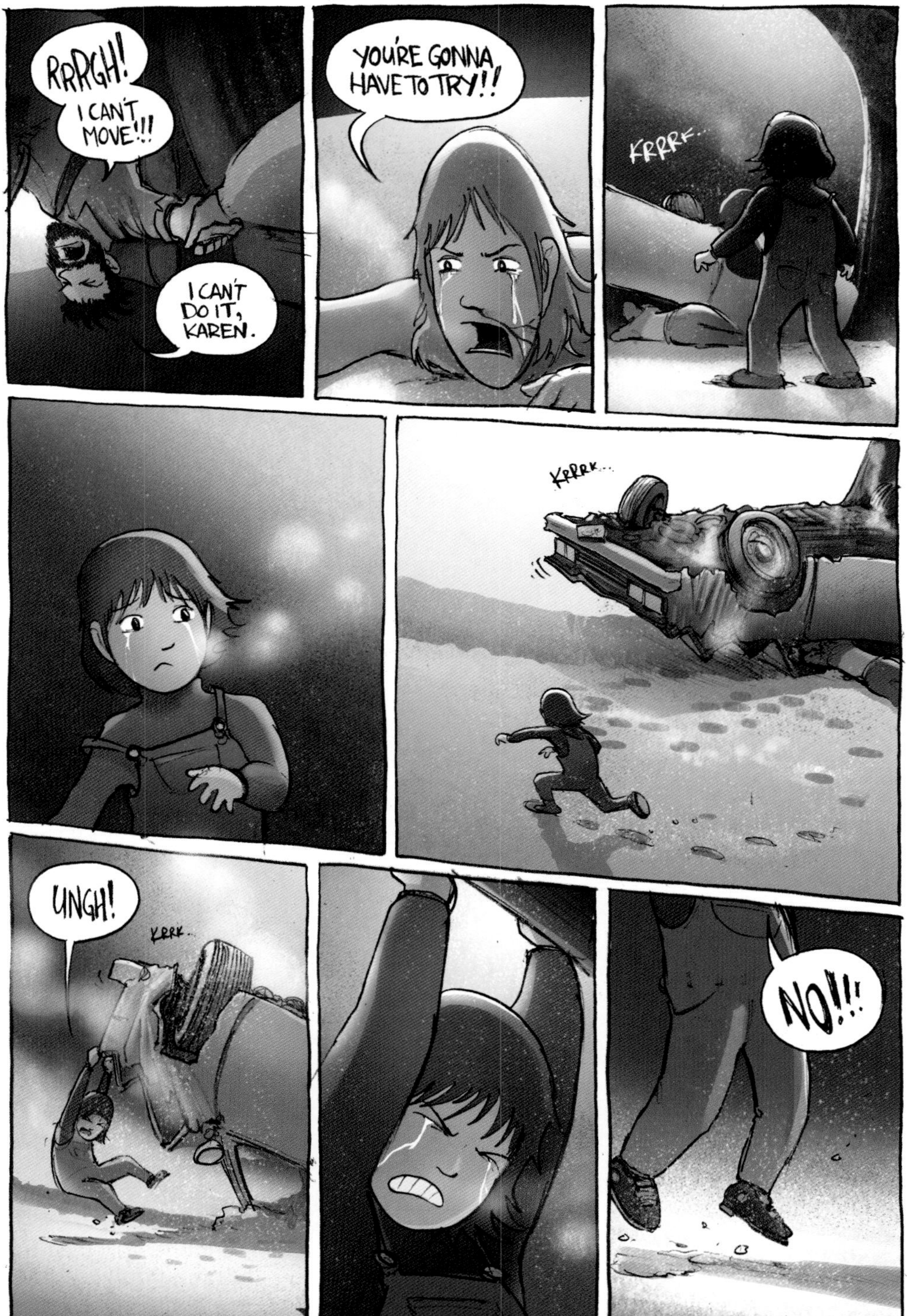
RRRGH!
I CAN'T MOVE!!!
I CAN'T DO IT, KAREN.
YOU'RE GONNA HAVE TO TRY!!
KRRRF...
KRRRK...
UNGH!
KRRK...
NO!!!

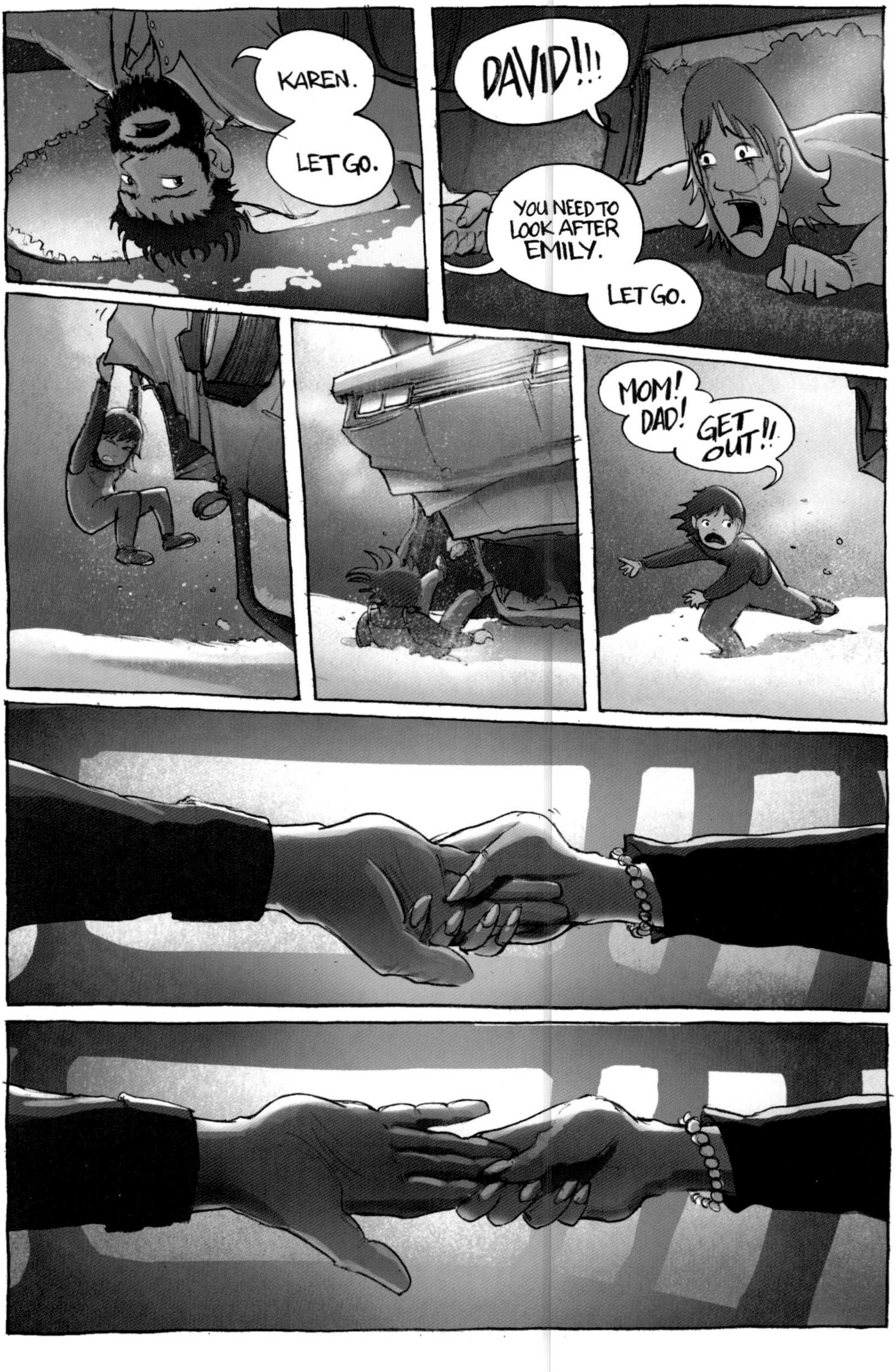
KAREN.
LET GO.
DAVID!!!
YOU NEED TO LOOK AFTER EMILY.
LET GO.
MOM! DAD!
GET OUT!!

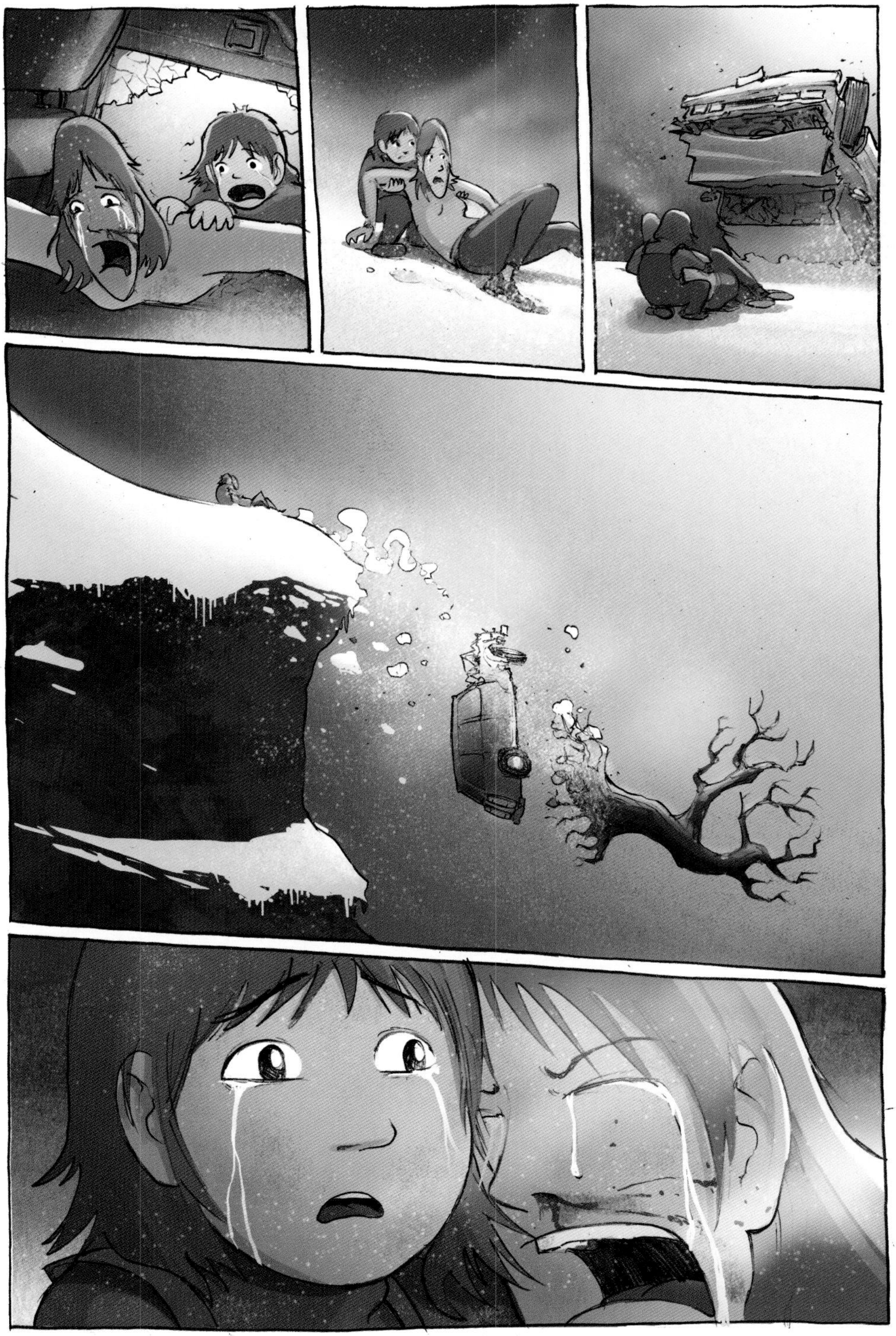

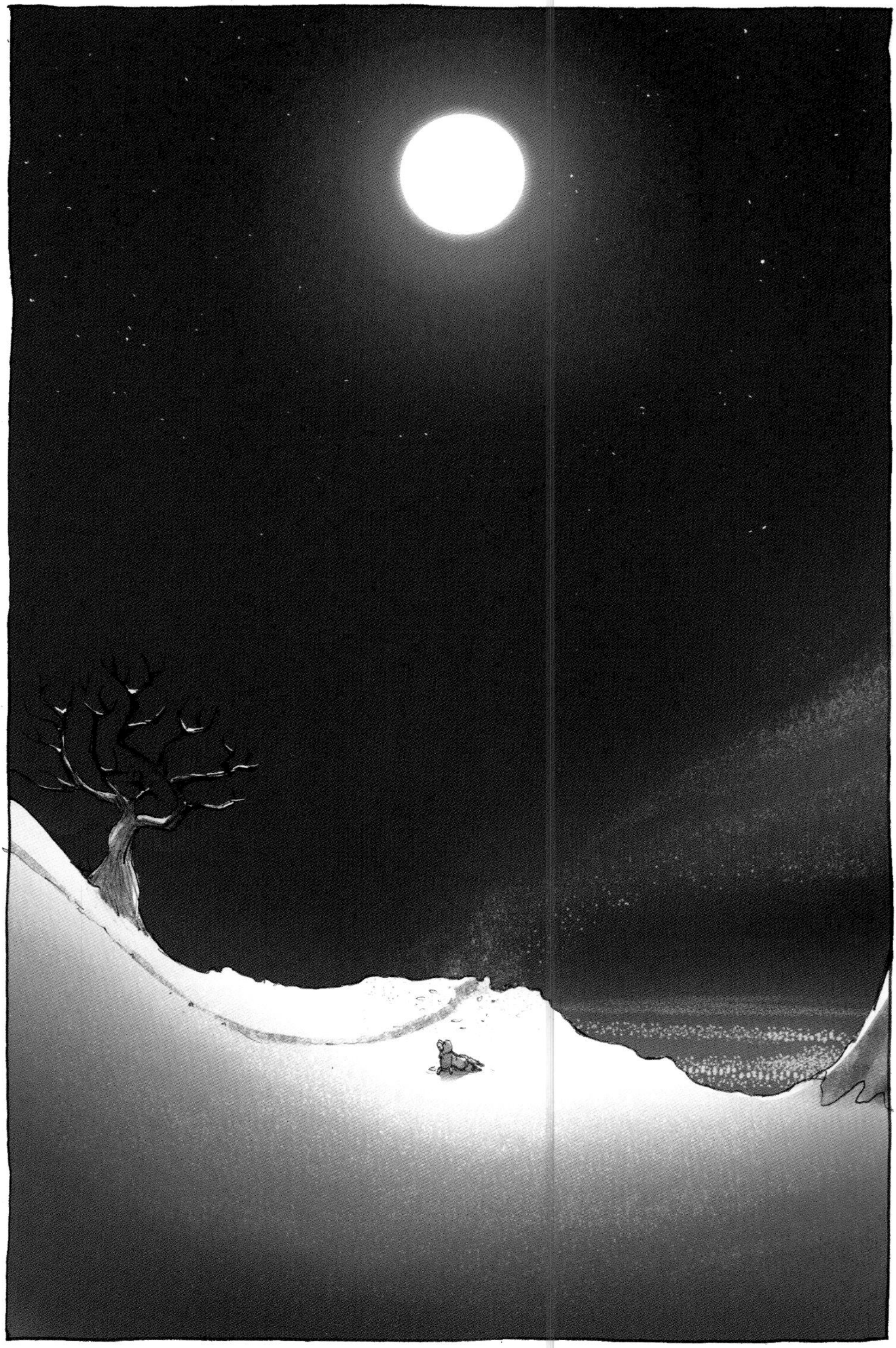

Book One
The Stonekeeper

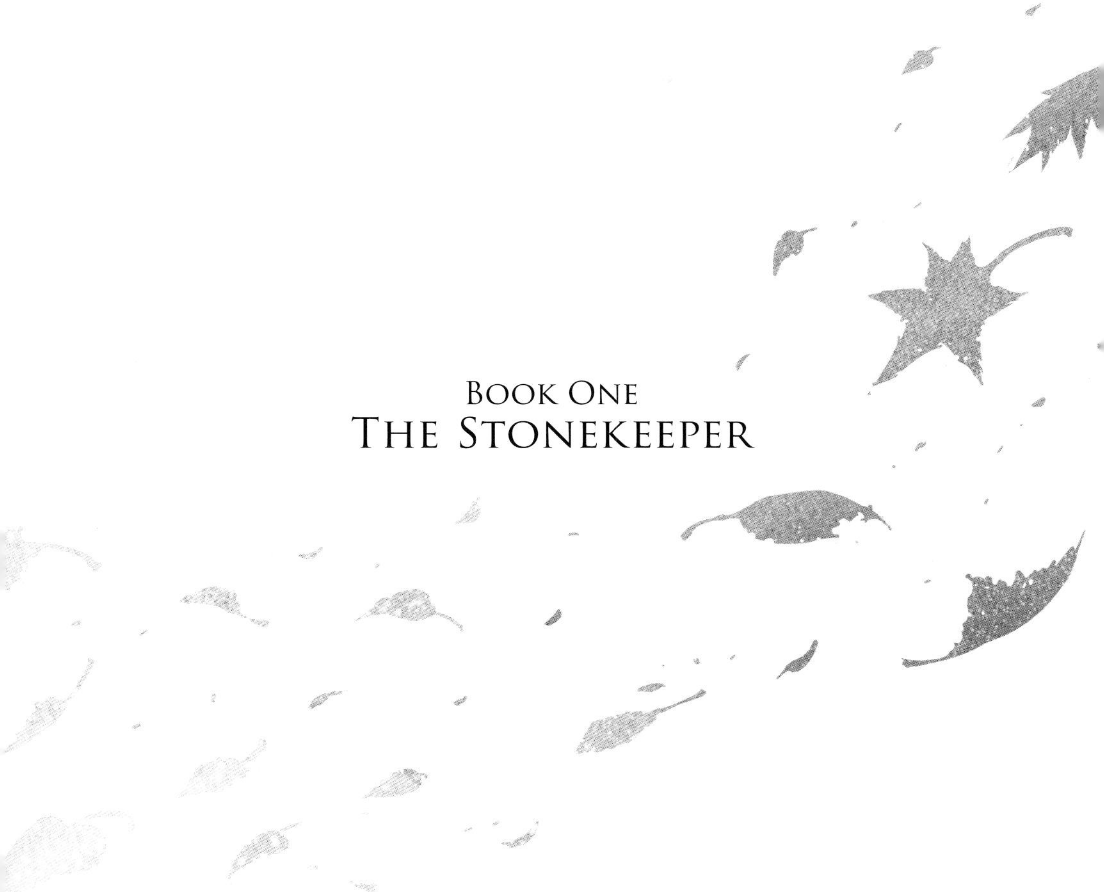

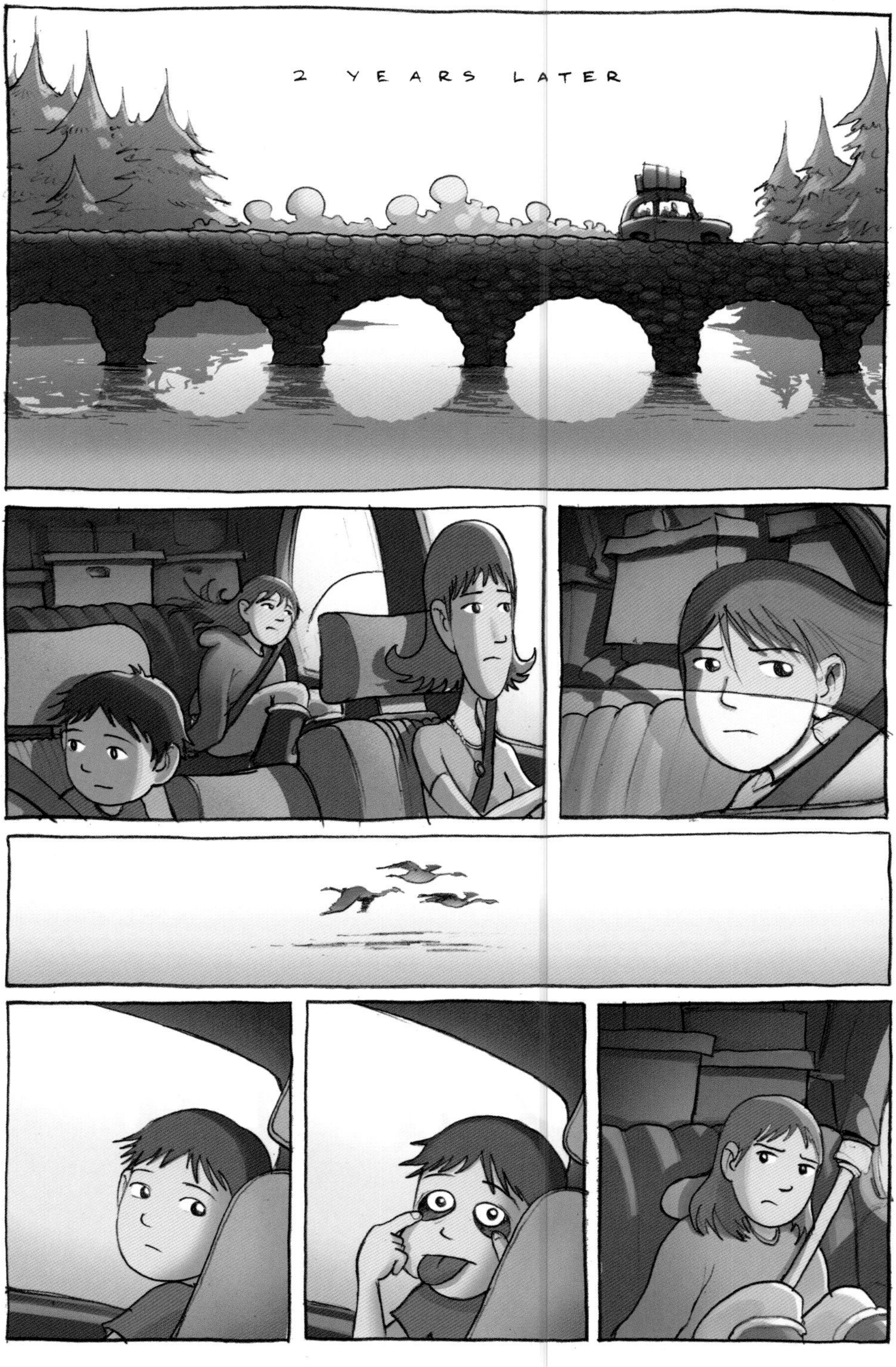
2 YEARS LATER

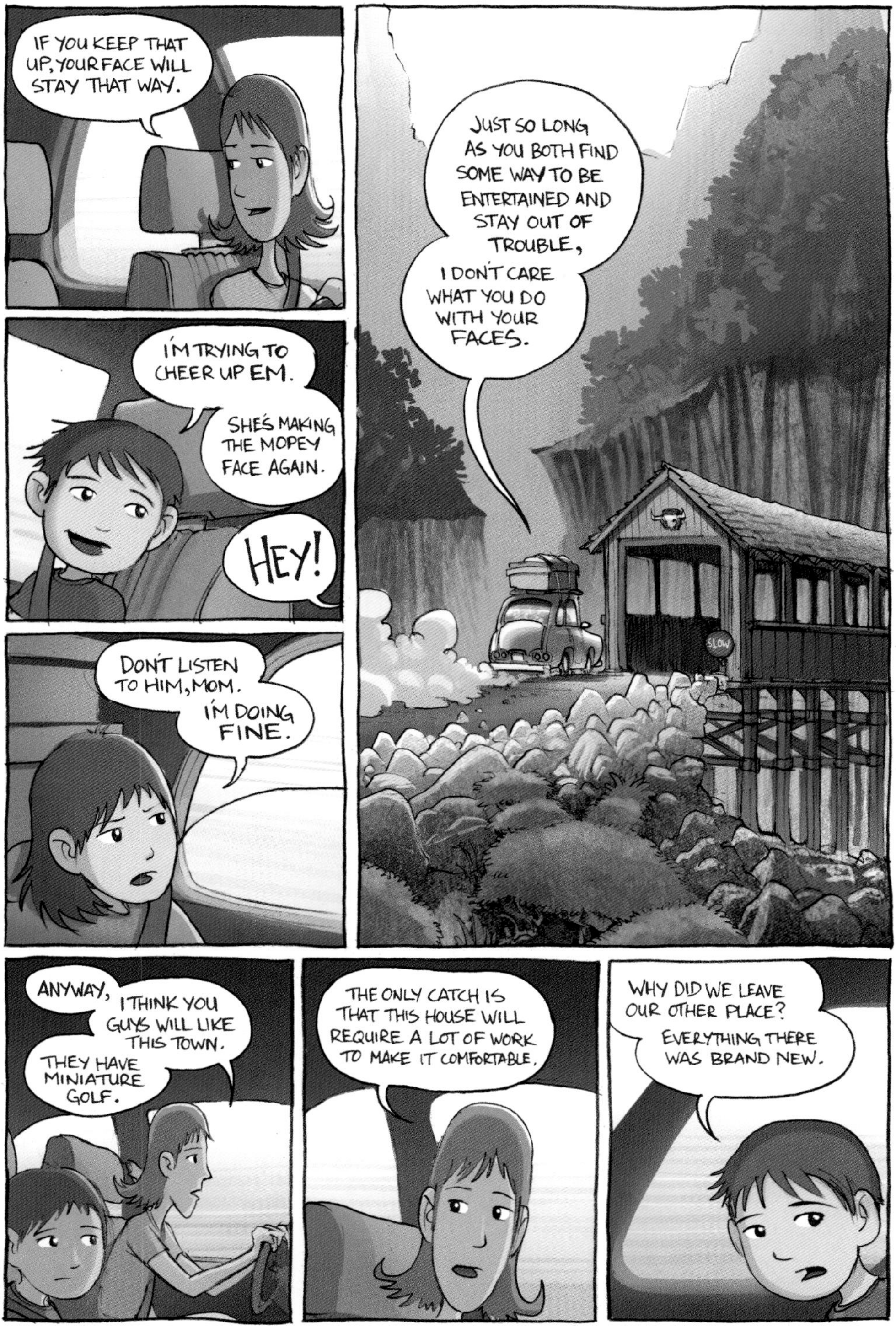
IF YOU KEEP THAT UP, YOUR FACE WILL STAY THAT WAY.
I'M TRYING TO CHEER UP EM.
SHE'S MAKING THE MOPEY FACE AGAIN.
HEY!
DON'T LISTEN TO HIM, MOM.
I'M DOING FINE.
JUST SO LONG AS YOU BOTH FIND SOME WAY TO BE ENTERTAINED AND STAY OUT OF TROUBLE,
I DON'T CARE WHAT YOU DO WITH YOUR FACES.
SLOW
ANYWAY,
I THINK YOU GUYS WILL LIKE THIS TOWN.
THEY HAVE MINIATURE GOLF.
THE ONLY CATCH IS THAT THIS HOUSE WILL REQUIRE A LOT OF WORK TO MAKE IT COMFORTABLE.
WHY DID WE LEAVE OUR OTHER PLACE?
EVERYTHING THERE WAS BRAND NEW.

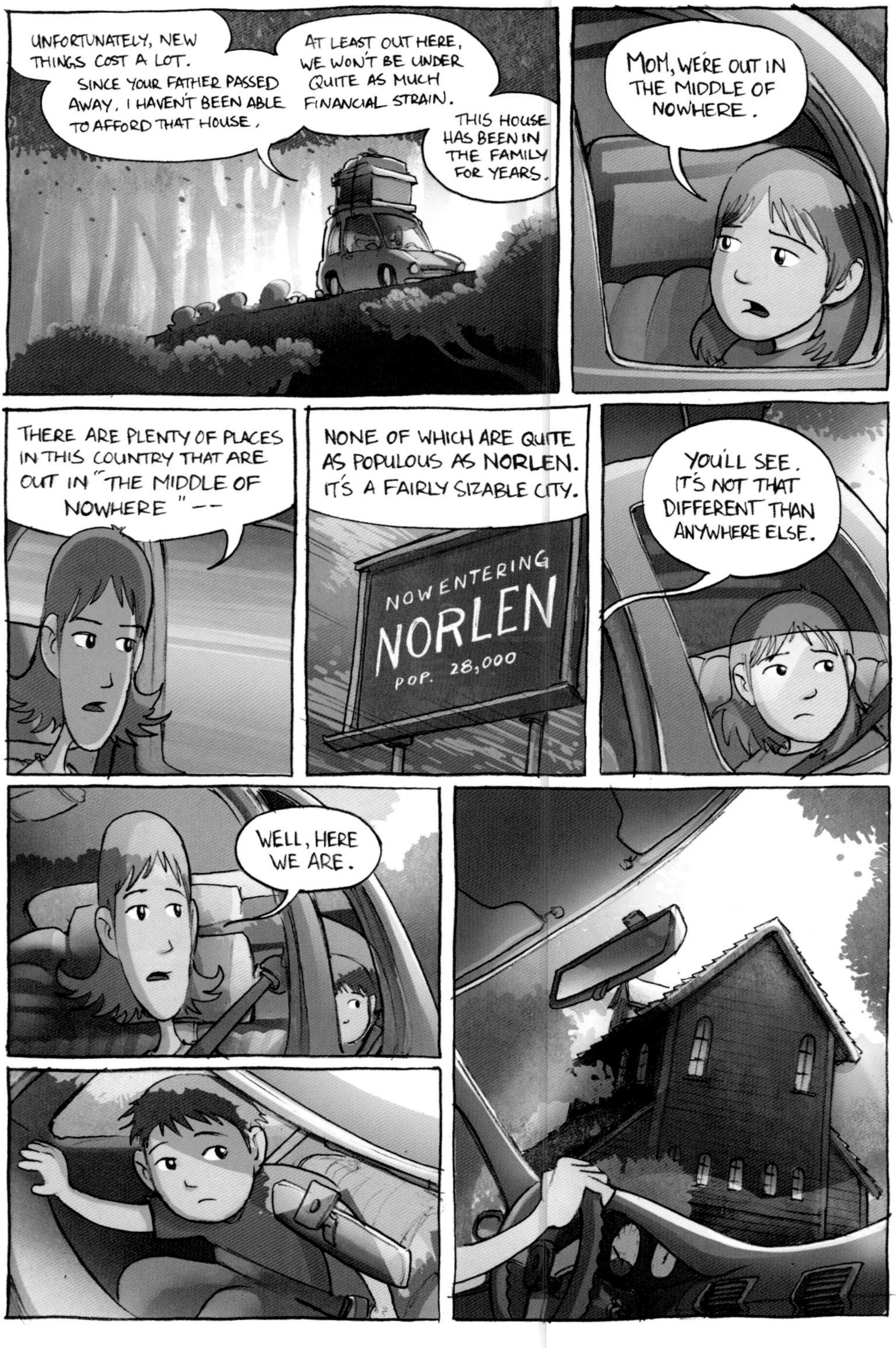
UNFORTUNATELY, NEW THINGS COST A LOT.
SINCE YOUR FATHER PASSED AWAY, I HAVEN'T BEEN ABLE TO AFFORD THAT HOUSE.
AT LEAST OUT HERE, WE WON'T BE UNDER QUITE AS MUCH FINANCIAL STRAIN.
THIS HOUSE HAS BEEN IN THE FAMILY FOR YEARS.
MOM, WE'RE OUT IN THE MIDDLE OF NOWHERE.
THERE ARE PLENTY OF PLACES IN THIS COUNTRY THAT ARE OUT IN "THE MIDDLE OF NOWHERE" --
NONE OF WHICH ARE QUITE AS POPULOUS AS NORLEN. IT'S A FAIRLY SIZABLE CITY.
NOW ENTERING NORLEN POP. 28,000
YOU'LL SEE. IT'S NOT THAT DIFFERENT THAN ANYWHERE ELSE.
WELL, HERE WE ARE.

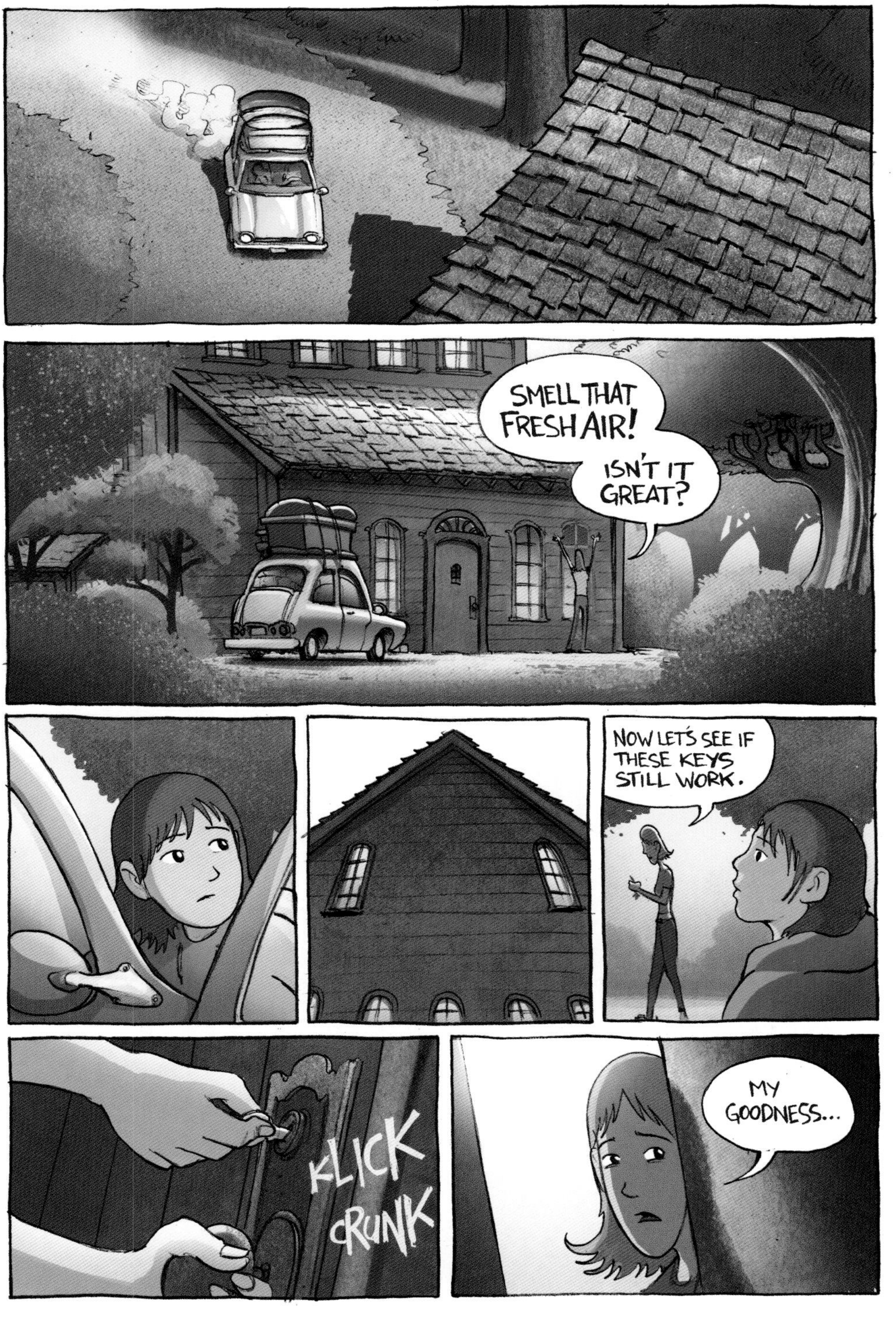
SMELL THAT FRESH AIR!
ISN'T IT GREAT?
NOW LET'S SEE IF THESE KEYS STILL WORK.
KLICK
CRUNK
MY GOODNESS...

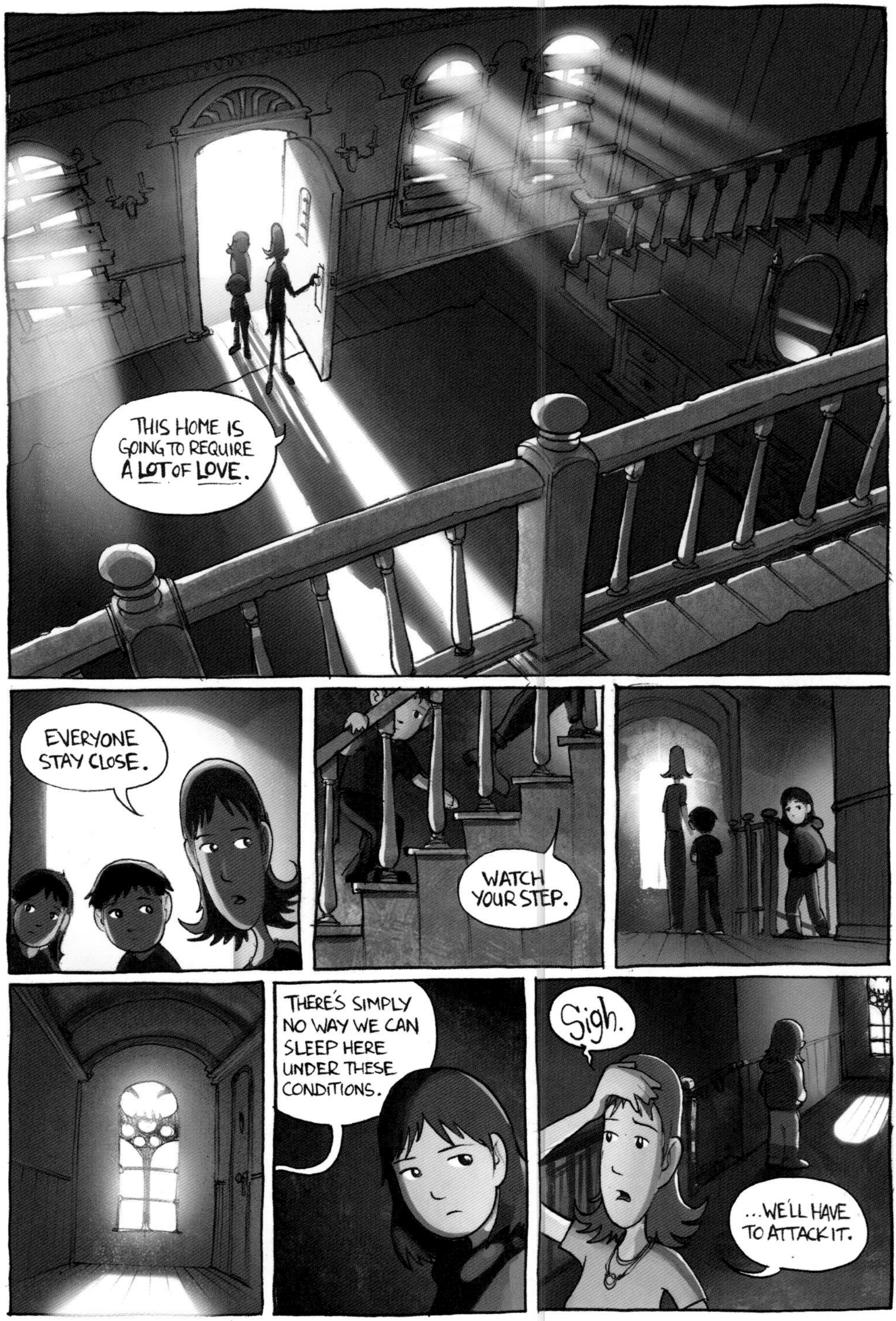
THIS HOME IS GOING TO REQUIRE A LOT OF LOVE.
EVERYONE STAY CLOSE.
WATCH YOUR STEP.
THERE'S SIMPLY NO WAY WE CAN SLEEP HERE UNDER THESE CONDITIONS.
Sigh.
...WE'LL HAVE TO ATTACK IT.

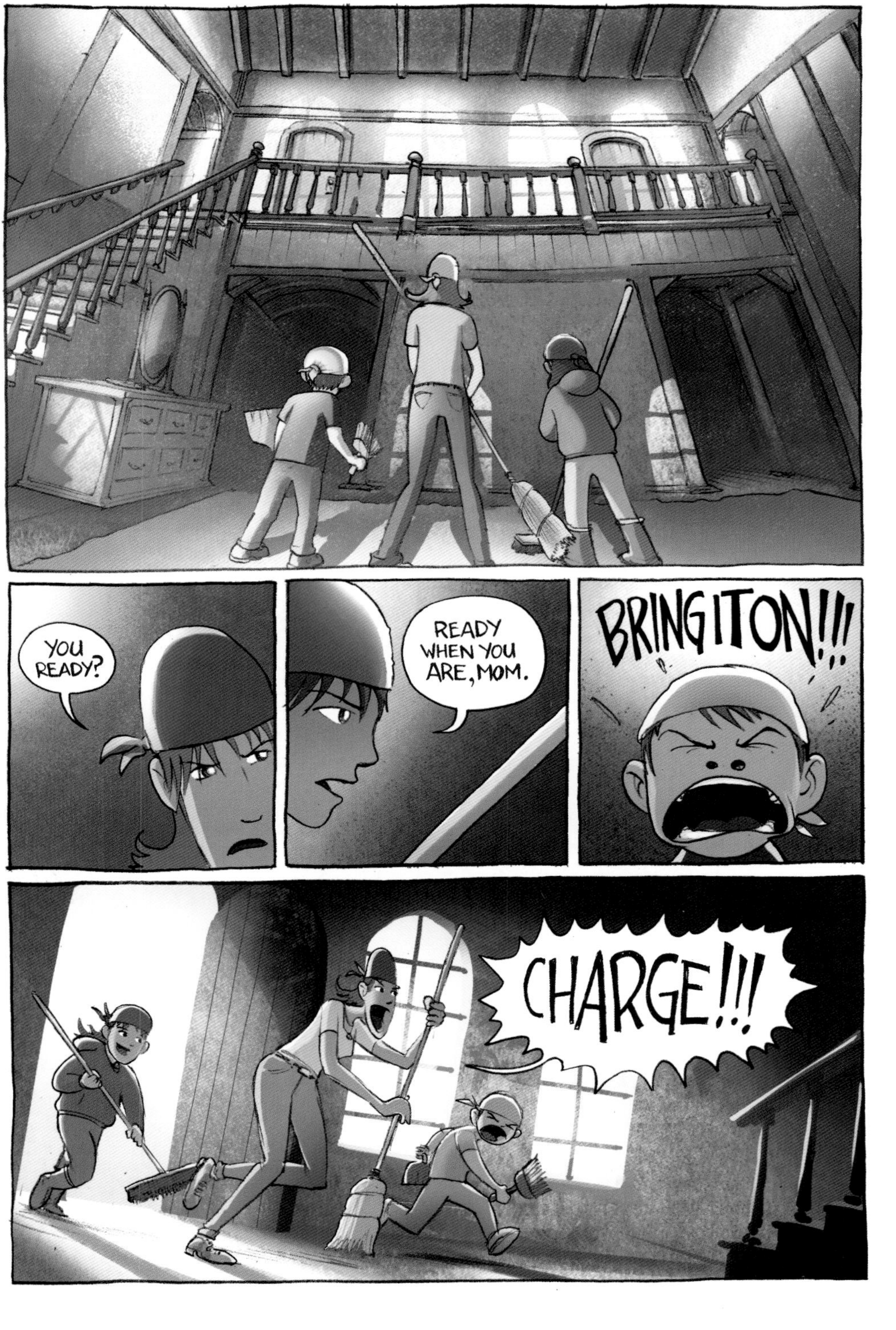
YOU READY?
READY WHEN YOU ARE, MOM.
BRING IT ON!!!
CHARGE!!!

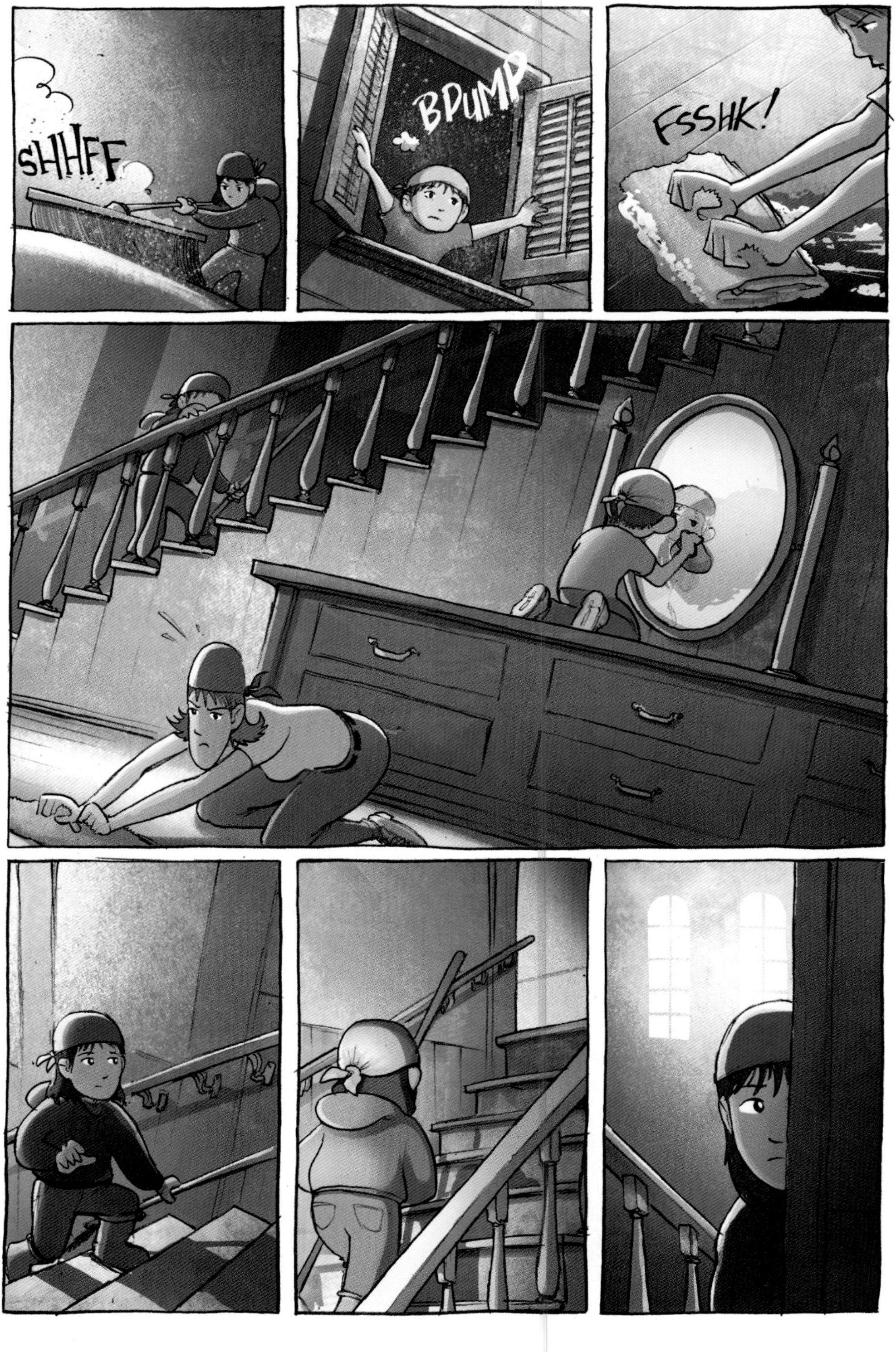
SHHFF
BPUMP
FSSHK!

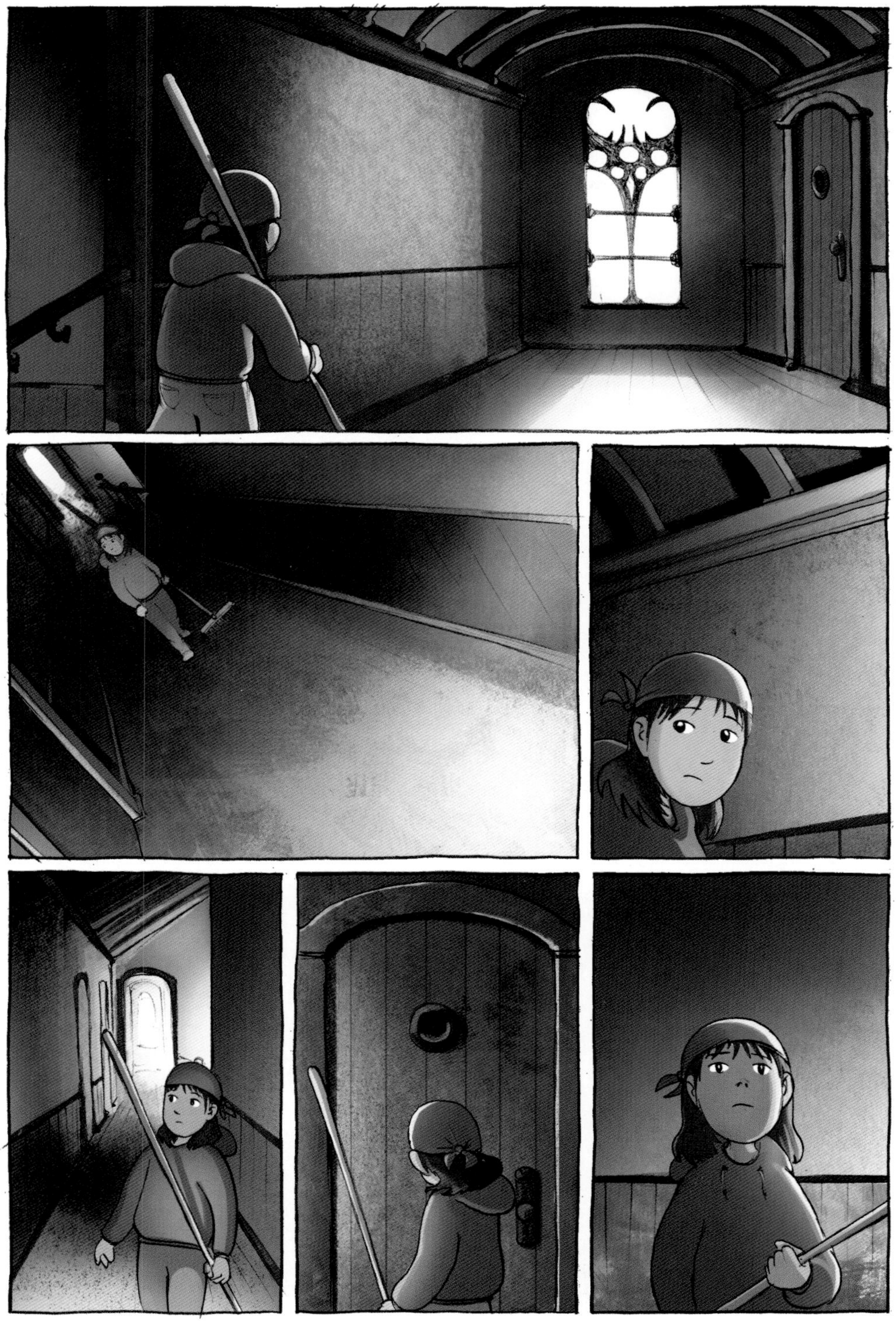

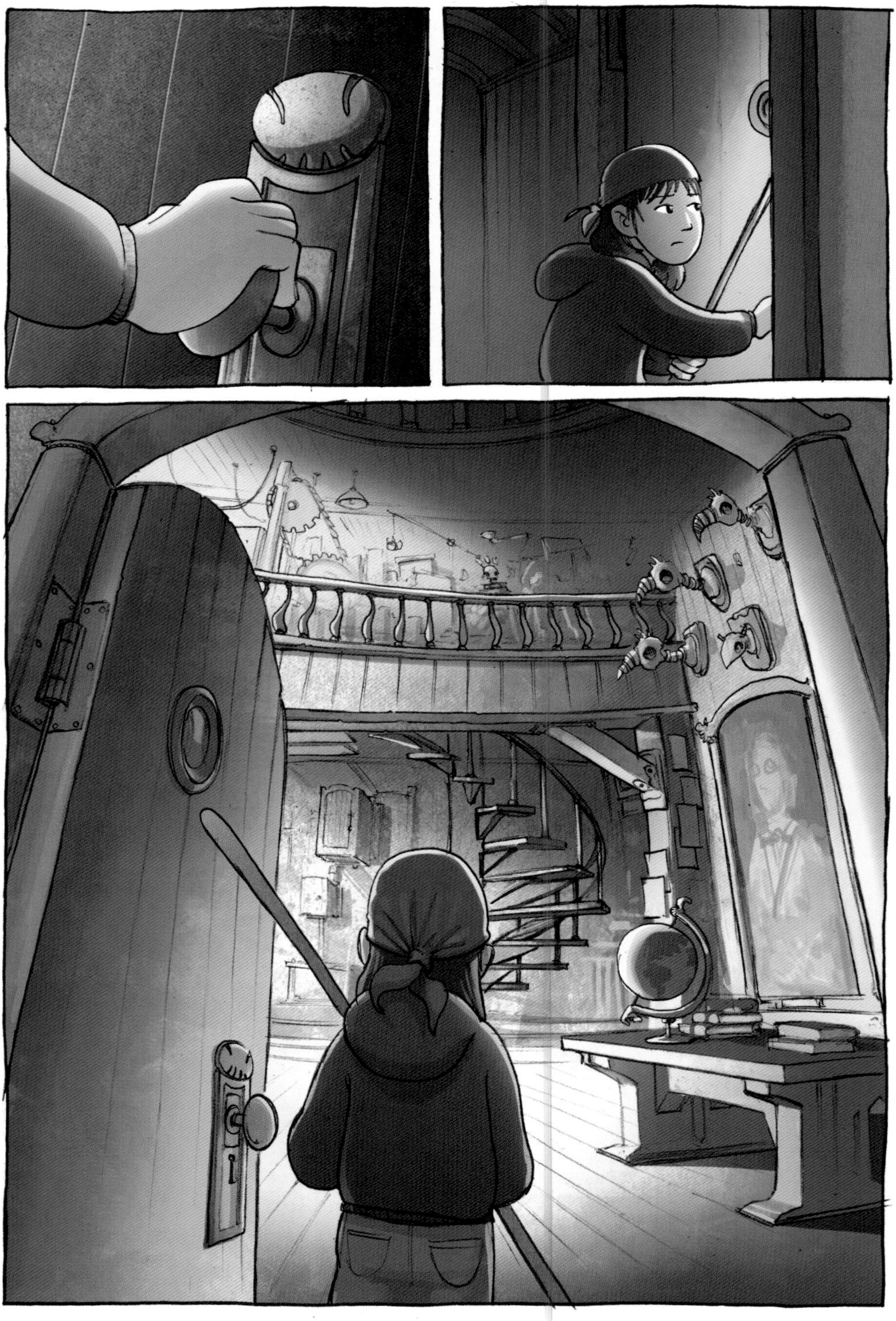

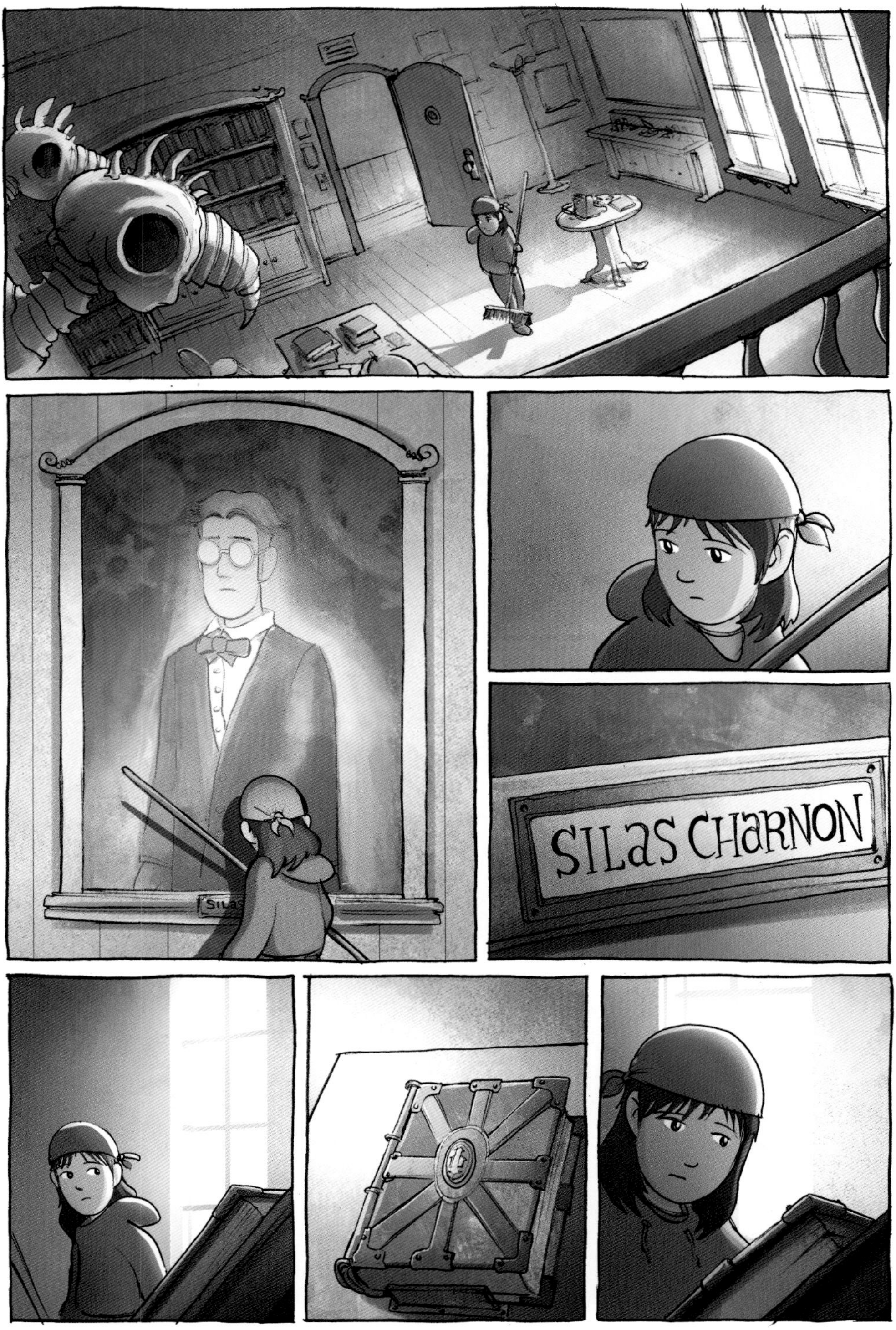
SILAS CHARNON

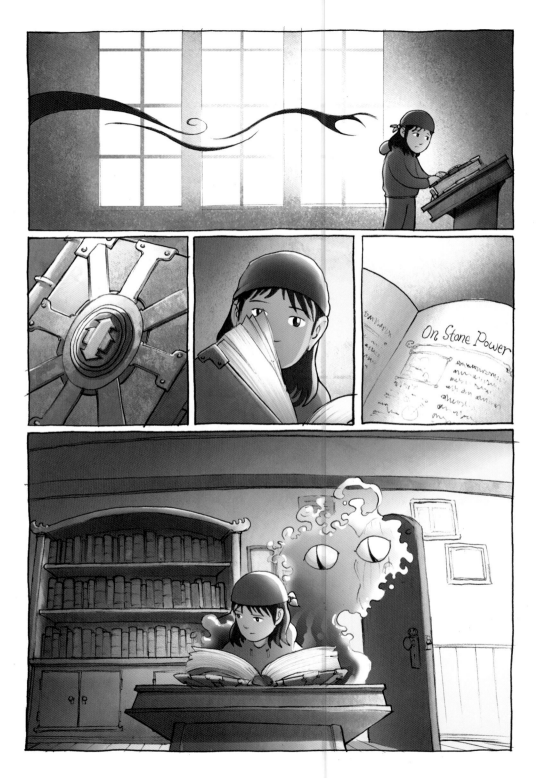

On Stone Power

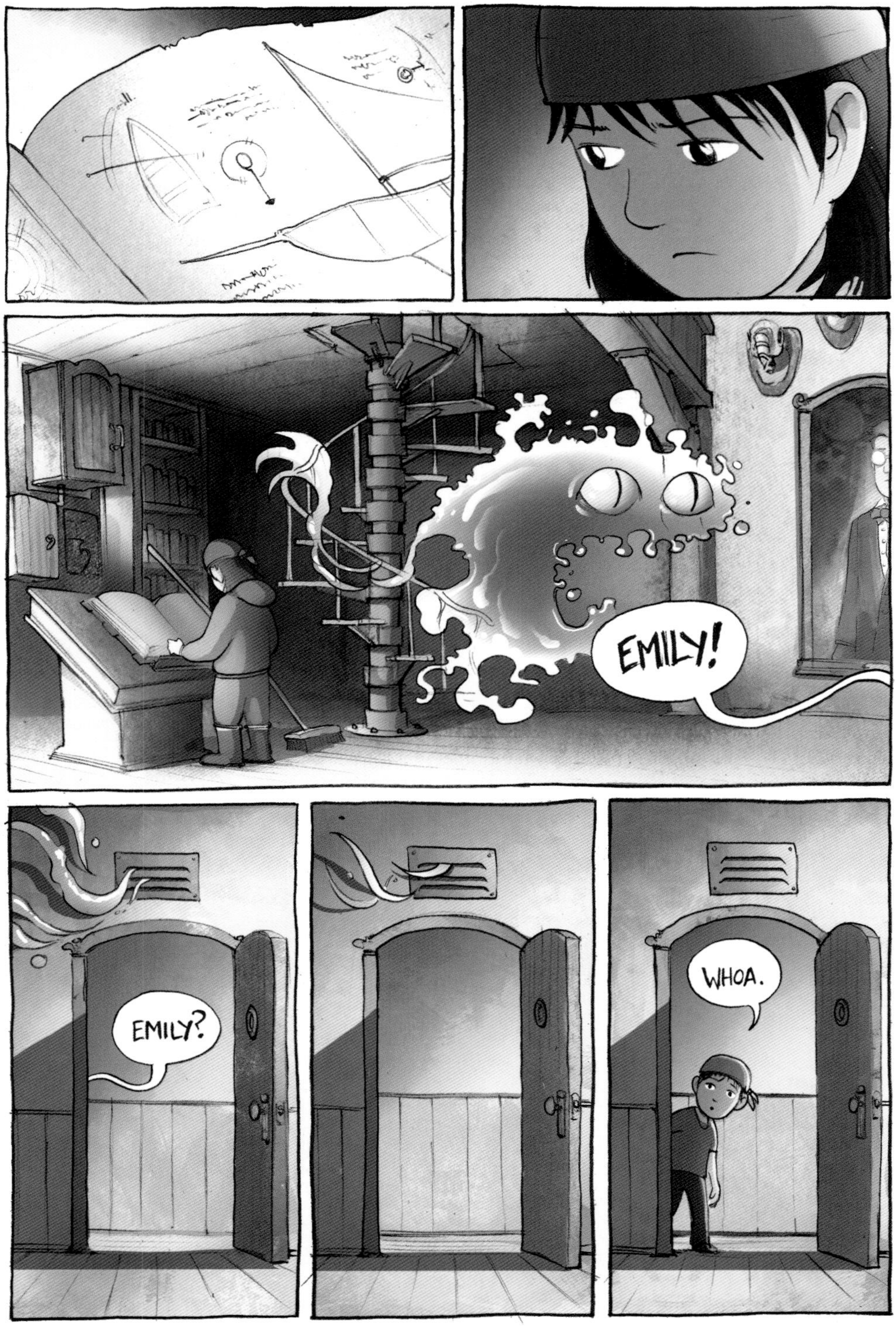
EMILY!
EMILY?
WHOA.

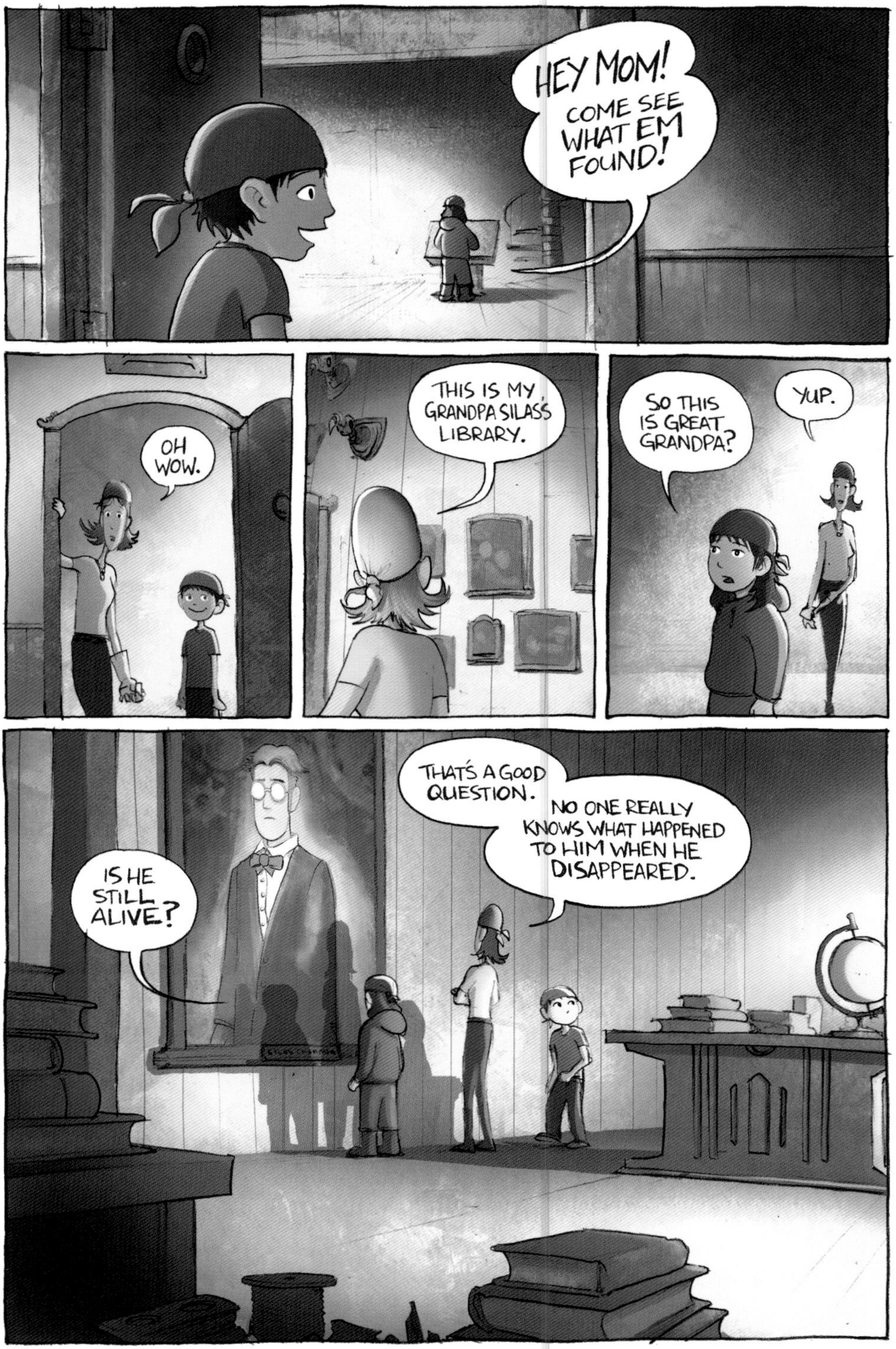
HEY MOM! COME SEE WHAT EM FOUND!
OH WOW.
THIS IS MY GRANDPA SILAS'S LIBRARY.
SO THIS IS GREAT GRANDPA?
YUP.
IS HE STILL ALIVE?
THAT'S A GOOD QUESTION.
NO ONE REALLY KNOWS WHAT HAPPENED TO HIM WHEN HE DISAPPEARED.

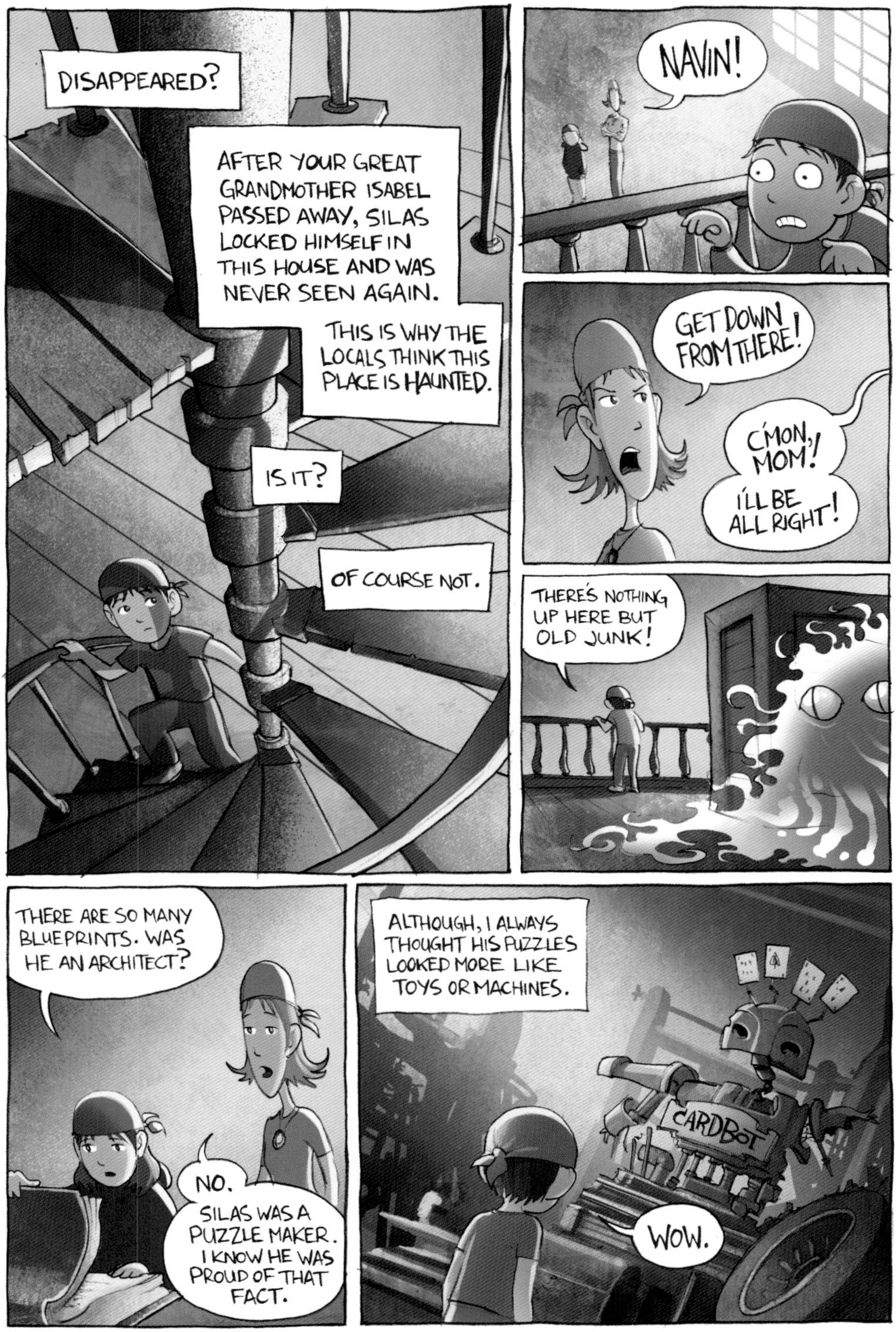
DISAPPEARED?
AFTER YOUR GREAT GRANDMOTHER ISABEL PASSED AWAY, SILAS LOCKED HIMSELF IN THIS HOUSE AND WAS NEVER SEEN AGAIN.
THIS IS WHY THE LOCALS THINK THIS PLACE IS HAUNTED.
IS IT?
OF COURSE NOT.
NAVIN!
GET DOWN FROM THERE!
C'MON, MOM!
I'LL BE ALL RIGHT!
THERE'S NOTHING UP HERE BUT OLD JUNK!
THERE ARE SO MANY BLUEPRINTS. WAS HE AN ARCHITECT?
NO.
SILAS WAS A PUZZLE MAKER. I KNOW HE WAS PROUD OF THAT FACT.
ALTHOUGH, I ALWAYS THOUGHT HIS PUZZLES LOOKED MORE LIKE TOYS OR MACHINES.
CARDBOT
WOW.

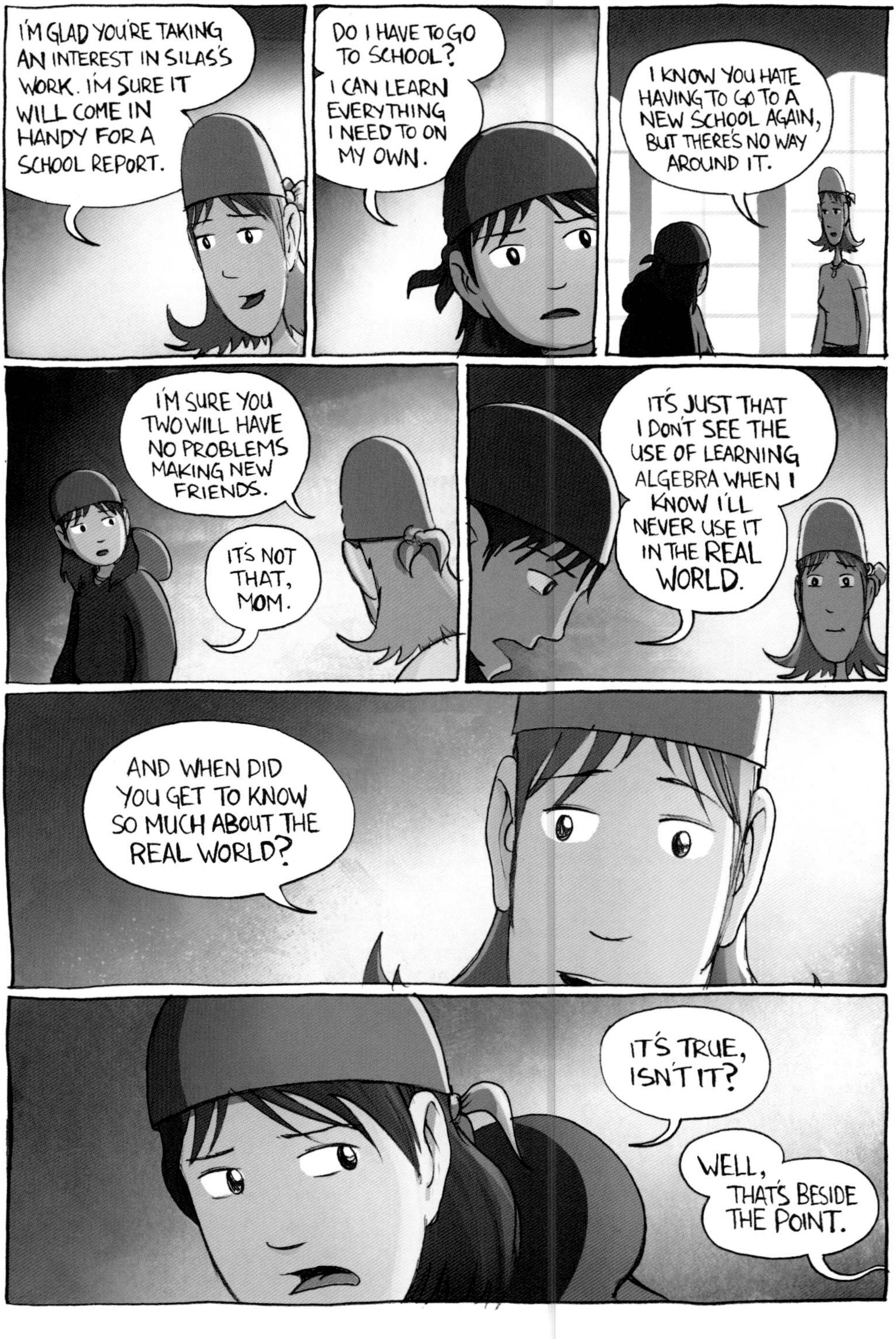
I'M GLAD YOU'RE TAKING AN INTEREST IN SILAS'S WORK. I'M SURE IT WILL COME IN HANDY FOR A SCHOOL REPORT.
DO I HAVE TO GO TO SCHOOL?
I CAN LEARN EVERYTHING I NEED TO ON MY OWN.
I KNOW YOU HATE HAVING TO GO TO A NEW SCHOOL AGAIN, BUT THERE'S NO WAY AROUND IT.
I'M SURE YOU TWO WILL HAVE NO PROBLEMS MAKING NEW FRIENDS.
IT'S NOT THAT, MOM.
IT'S JUST THAT I DON'T SEE THE USE OF LEARNING ALGEBRA WHEN I KNOW I'LL NEVER USE IT IN THE REAL WORLD.
AND WHEN DID YOU GET TO KNOW SO MUCH ABOUT THE REAL WORLD?
IT'S TRUE, ISN'T IT?
WELL, THAT'S BESIDE THE POINT.

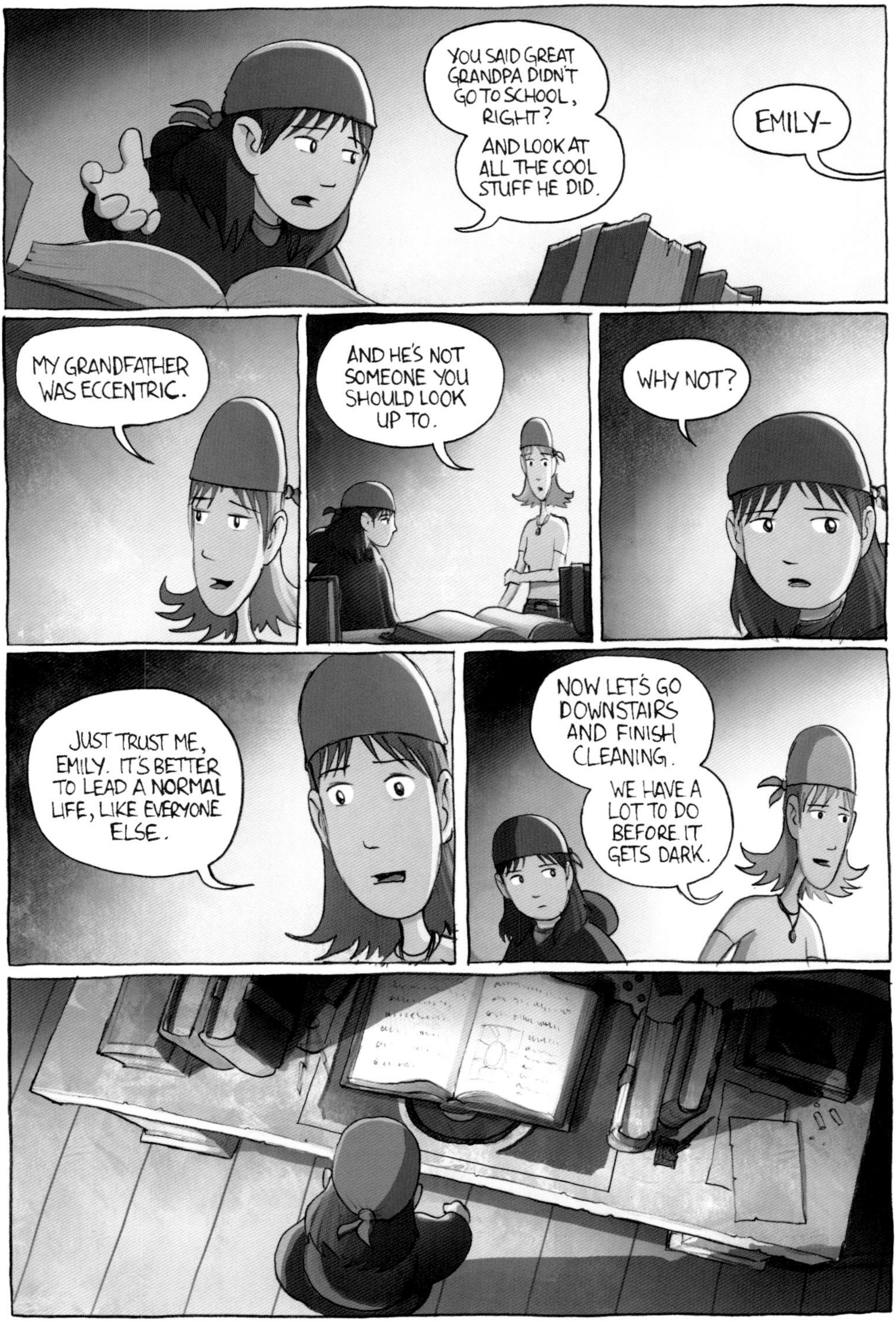
YOU SAID GREAT GRANDPA DIDN'T GO TO SCHOOL, RIGHT?
AND LOOK AT ALL THE COOL STUFF HE DID.
EMILY-
MY GRANDFATHER WAS ECCENTRIC.
AND HE'S NOT SOMEONE YOU SHOULD LOOK UP TO.
WHY NOT?
JUST TRUST ME, EMILY. IT'S BETTER TO LEAD A **NORMAL** LIFE, LIKE EVERYONE ELSE.
NOW LET'S GO DOWNSTAIRS AND FINISH CLEANING.
WE HAVE A LOT TO DO BEFORE IT GETS DARK.

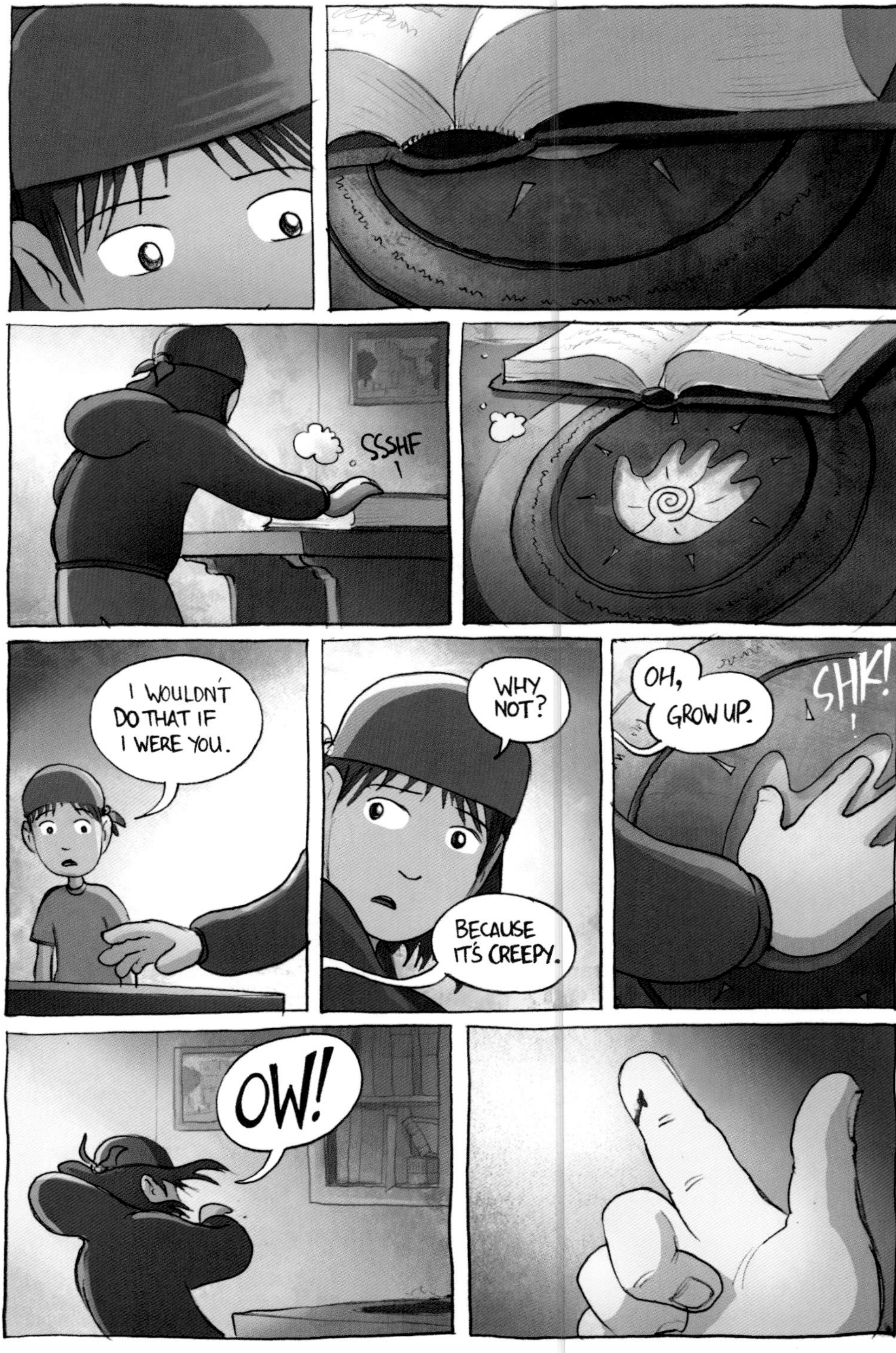
SSSHF
I WOULDN'T DO THAT IF I WERE YOU.
WHY NOT?
BECAUSE IT'S CREEPY.
OH, GROW UP.
SHK!
OW!

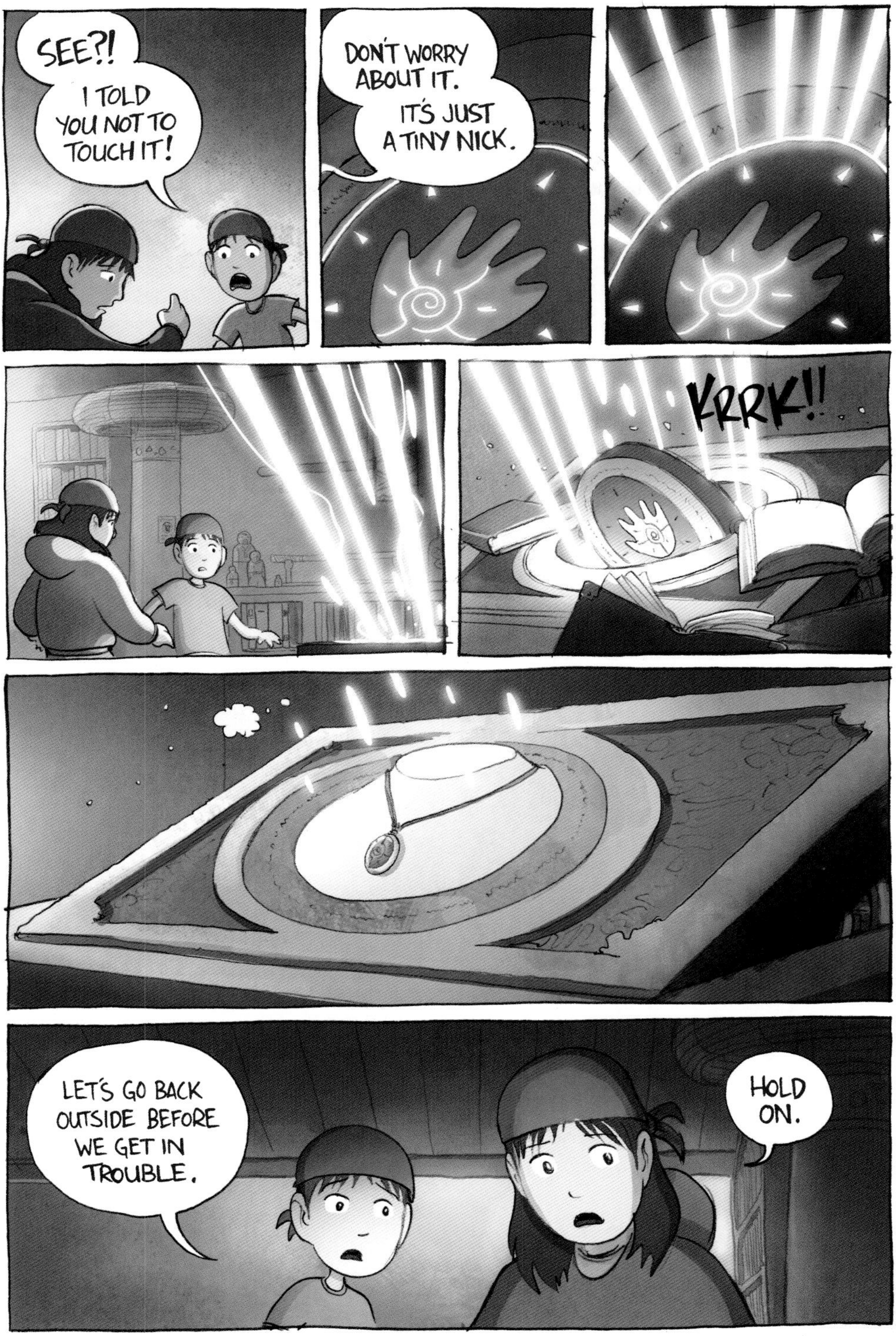
SEE?!
I TOLD YOU NOT TO TOUCH IT!
DON'T WORRY ABOUT IT.
IT'S JUST A TINY NICK.
KRRK!!
LET'S GO BACK OUTSIDE BEFORE WE GET IN TROUBLE.
HOLD ON.

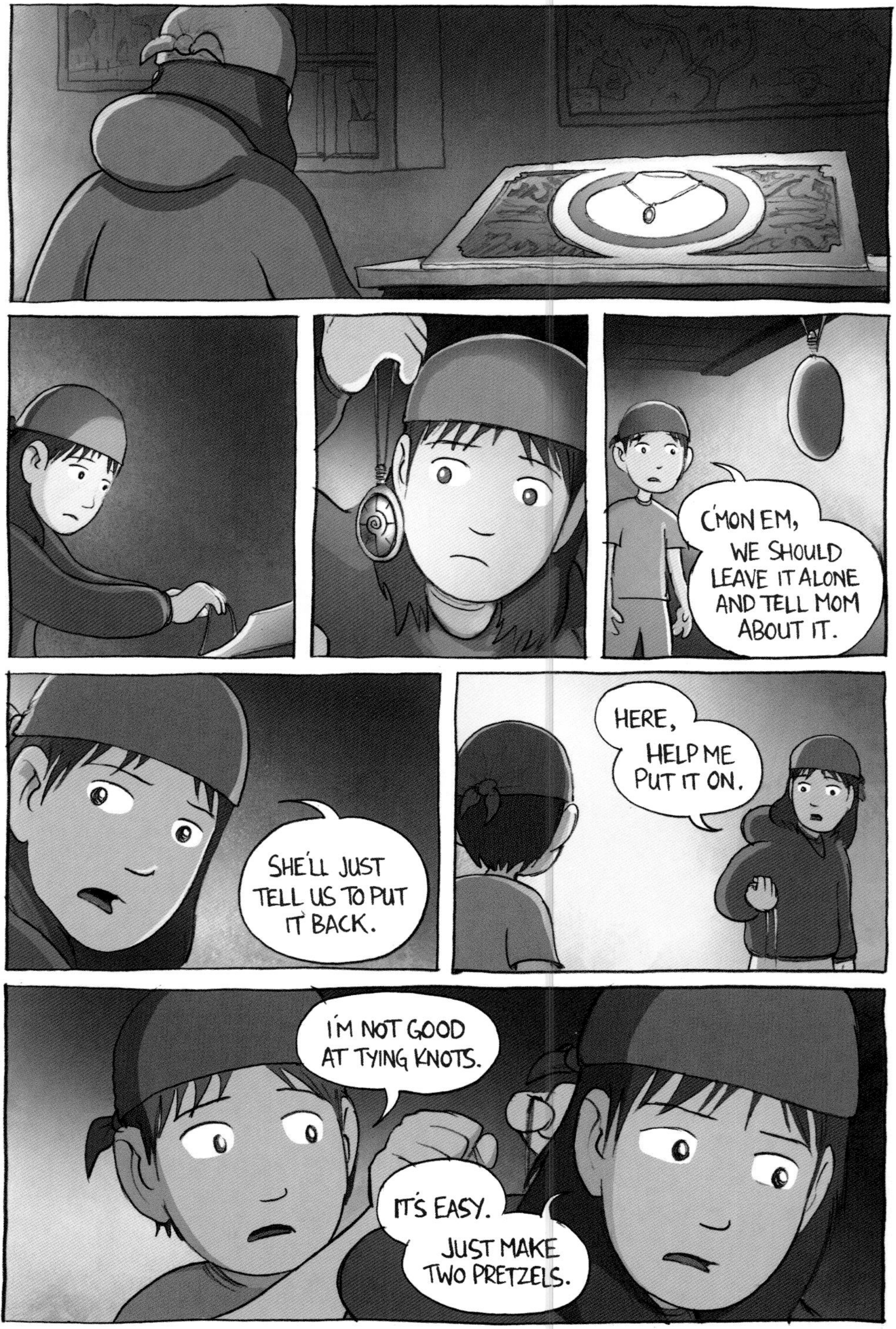
C'MON EM, WE SHOULD LEAVE IT ALONE AND TELL MOM ABOUT IT.
SHE'LL JUST TELL US TO PUT IT BACK.
HERE, HELP ME PUT IT ON.
I'M NOT GOOD AT TYING KNOTS.
IT'S EASY.
JUST MAKE TWO PRETZELS.

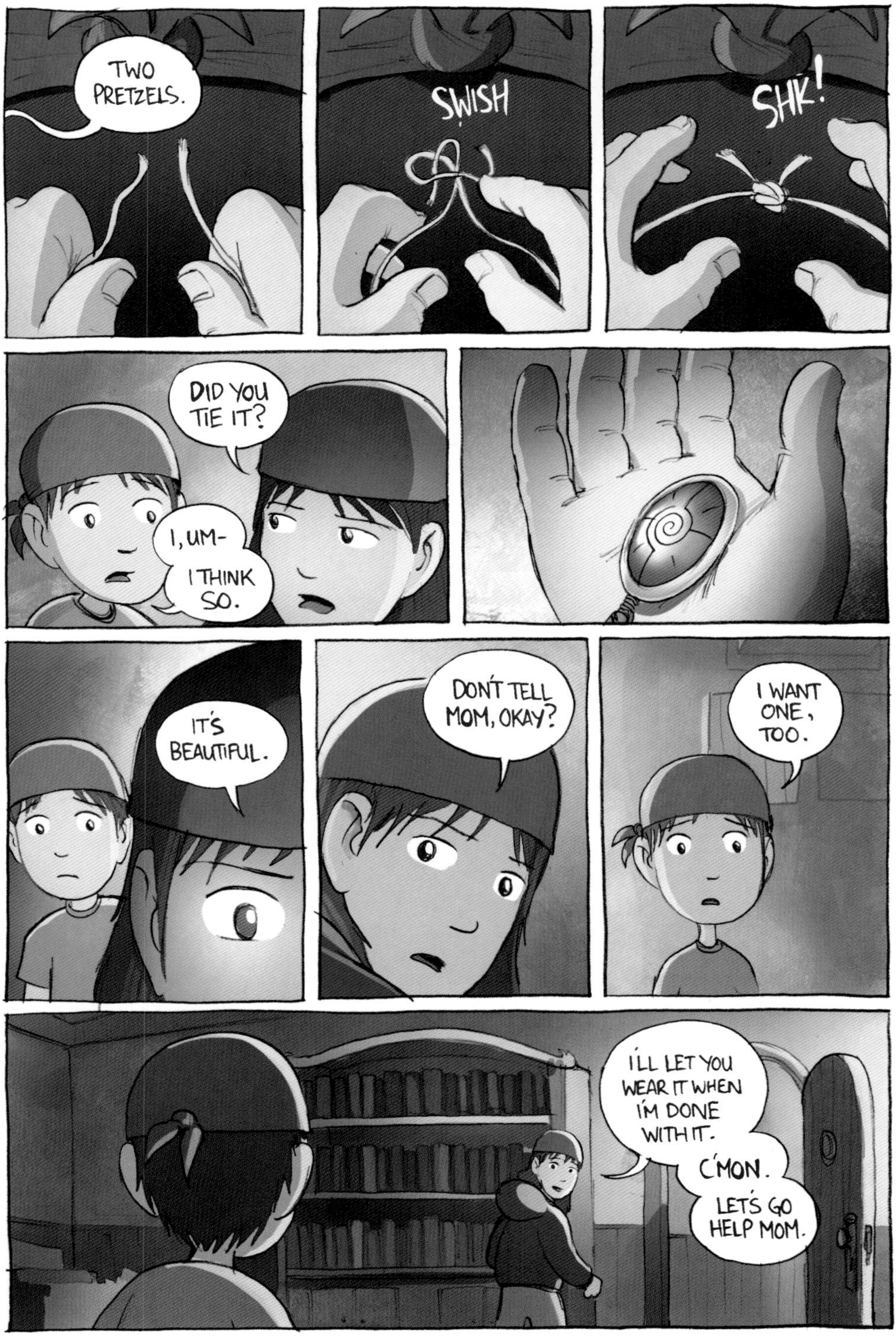
TWO PRETZELS.
SWISH
SHK!
DID YOU TIE IT?
I, UM-
I THINK SO.
IT'S BEAUTIFUL.
DON'T TELL MOM, OKAY?
I WANT ONE, TOO.
I'LL LET YOU WEAR IT WHEN I'M DONE WITH IT.
C'MON.
LET'S GO HELP MOM.

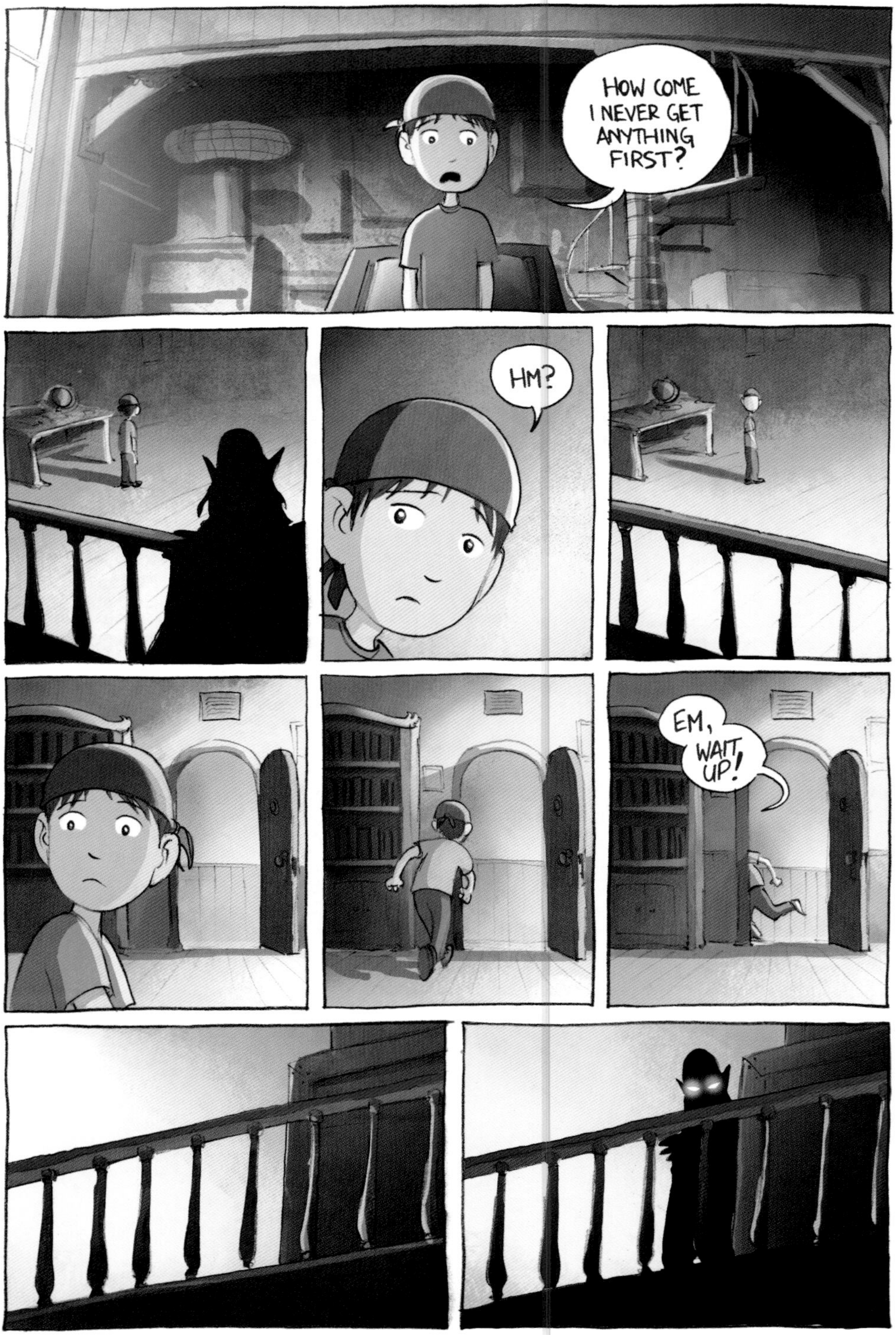
HOW COME I NEVER GET ANYTHING FIRST?
HM?
EM, WAIT UP!

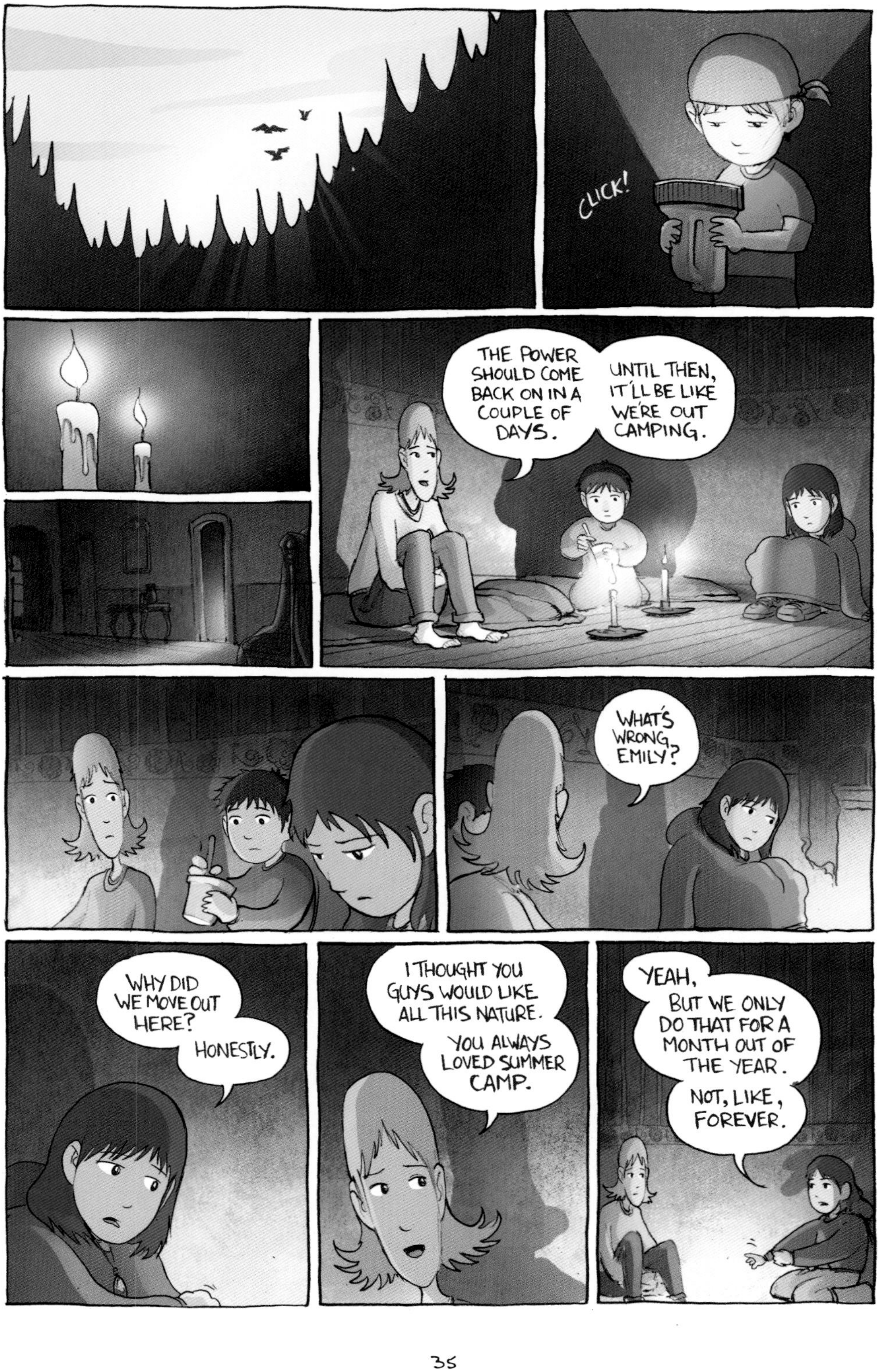
CLICK!
THE POWER SHOULD COME BACK ON IN A COUPLE OF DAYS.
UNTIL THEN, IT'LL BE LIKE WE'RE OUT CAMPING.
WHAT'S WRONG, EMILY?
WHY DID WE MOVE OUT HERE?
HONESTLY.
I THOUGHT YOU GUYS WOULD LIKE ALL THIS NATURE.
YOU ALWAYS LOVED SUMMER CAMP.
YEAH,
BUT WE ONLY DO THAT FOR A MONTH OUT OF THE YEAR.
NOT, LIKE, FOREVER.

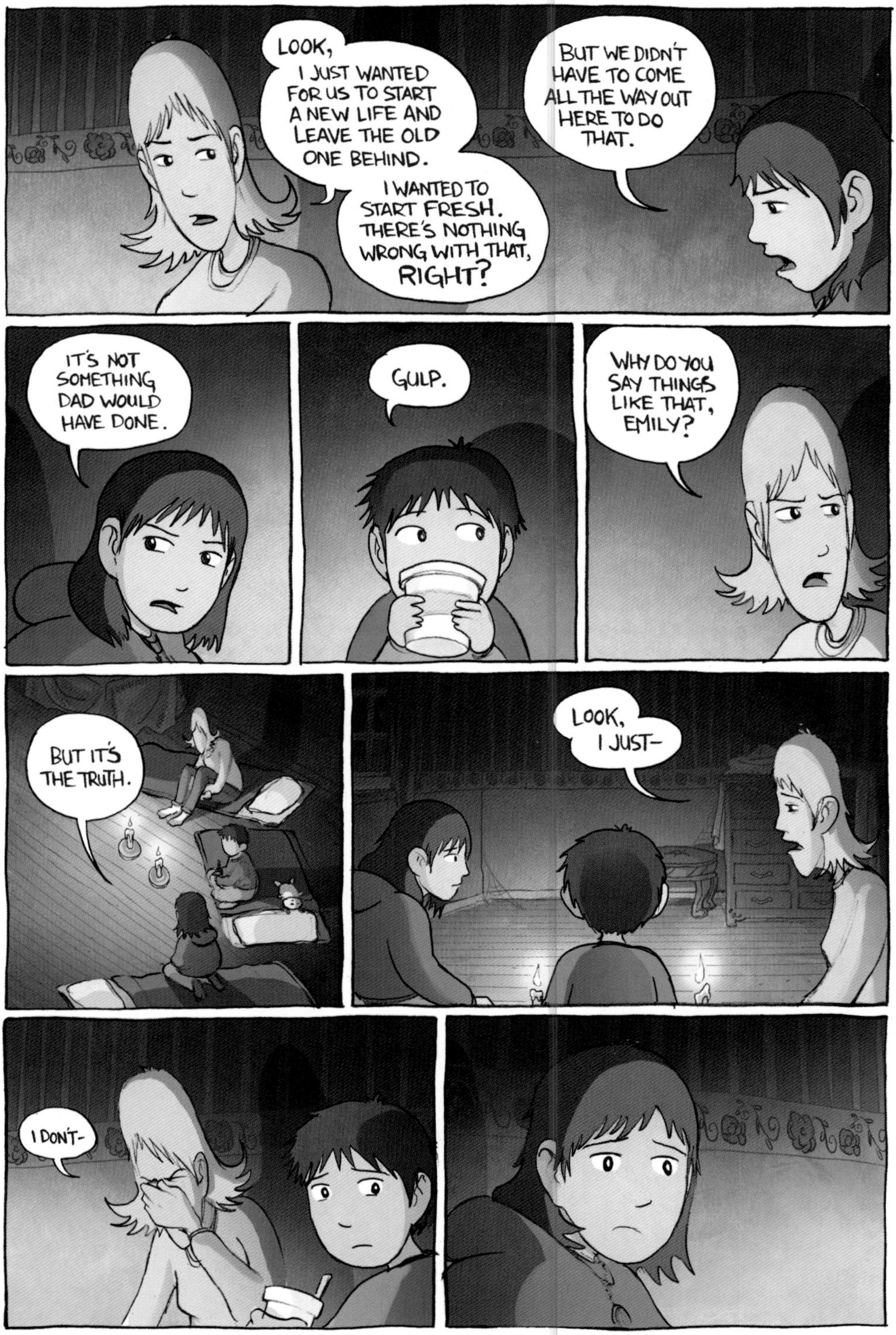
LOOK,
I JUST WANTED FOR US TO START A NEW LIFE AND LEAVE THE OLD ONE BEHIND.
I WANTED TO START FRESH. THERE'S NOTHING WRONG WITH THAT, RIGHT?
BUT WE DIDN'T HAVE TO COME ALL THE WAY OUT HERE TO DO THAT.
IT'S NOT SOMETHING DAD WOULD HAVE DONE.
GULP.
WHY DO YOU SAY THINGS LIKE THAT, EMILY?
BUT IT'S THE TRUTH.
LOOK, I JUST-
I DON'T-

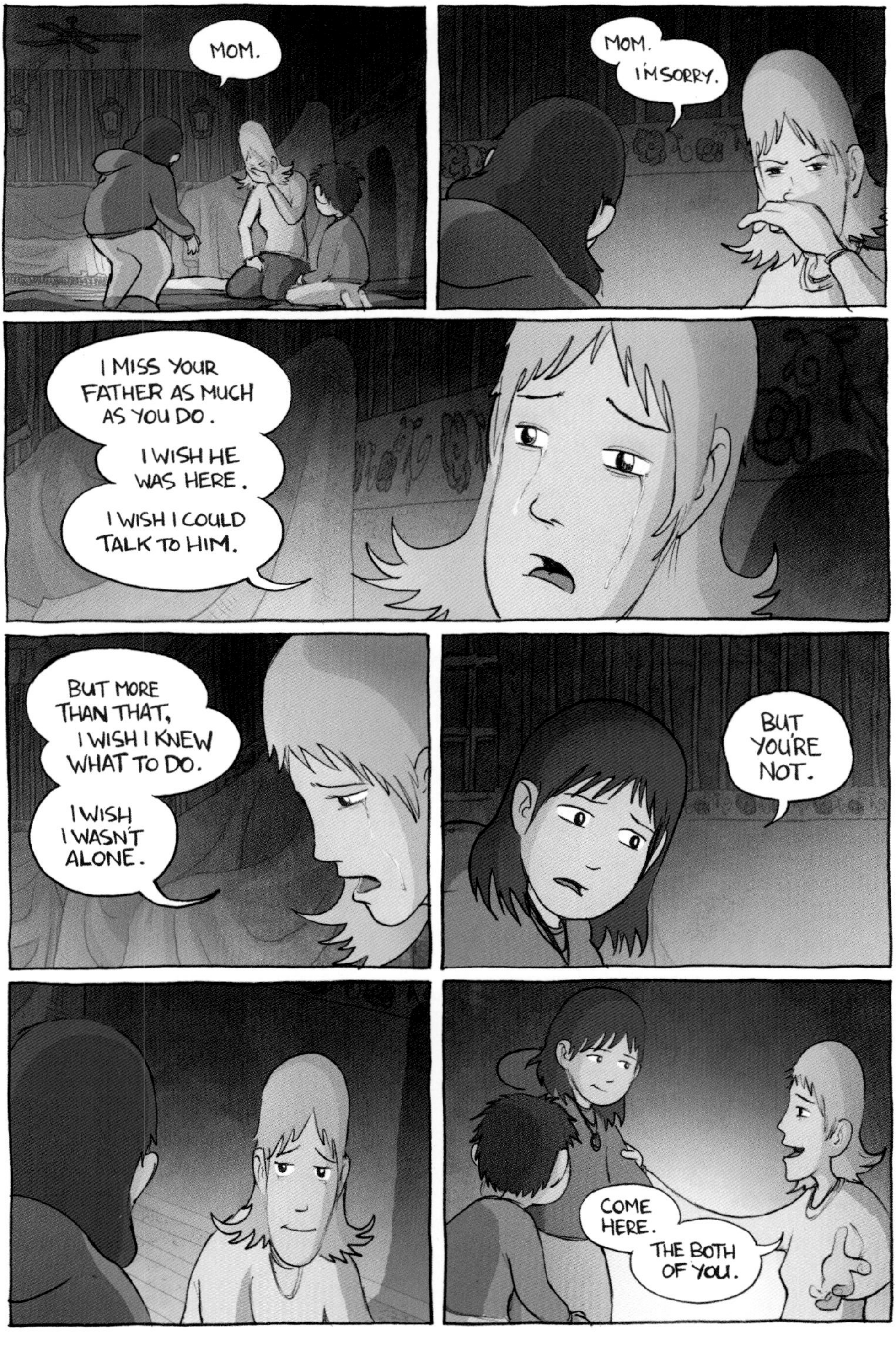
MOM.
MOM.
I'M SORRY.
I MISS YOUR FATHER AS MUCH AS YOU DO.
I WISH HE WAS HERE.
I WISH I COULD TALK TO HIM.
BUT MORE THAN THAT, I WISH I KNEW WHAT TO DO.
I WISH I WASN'T ALONE.
BUT YOU'RE NOT.
COME HERE.
THE BOTH OF YOU.

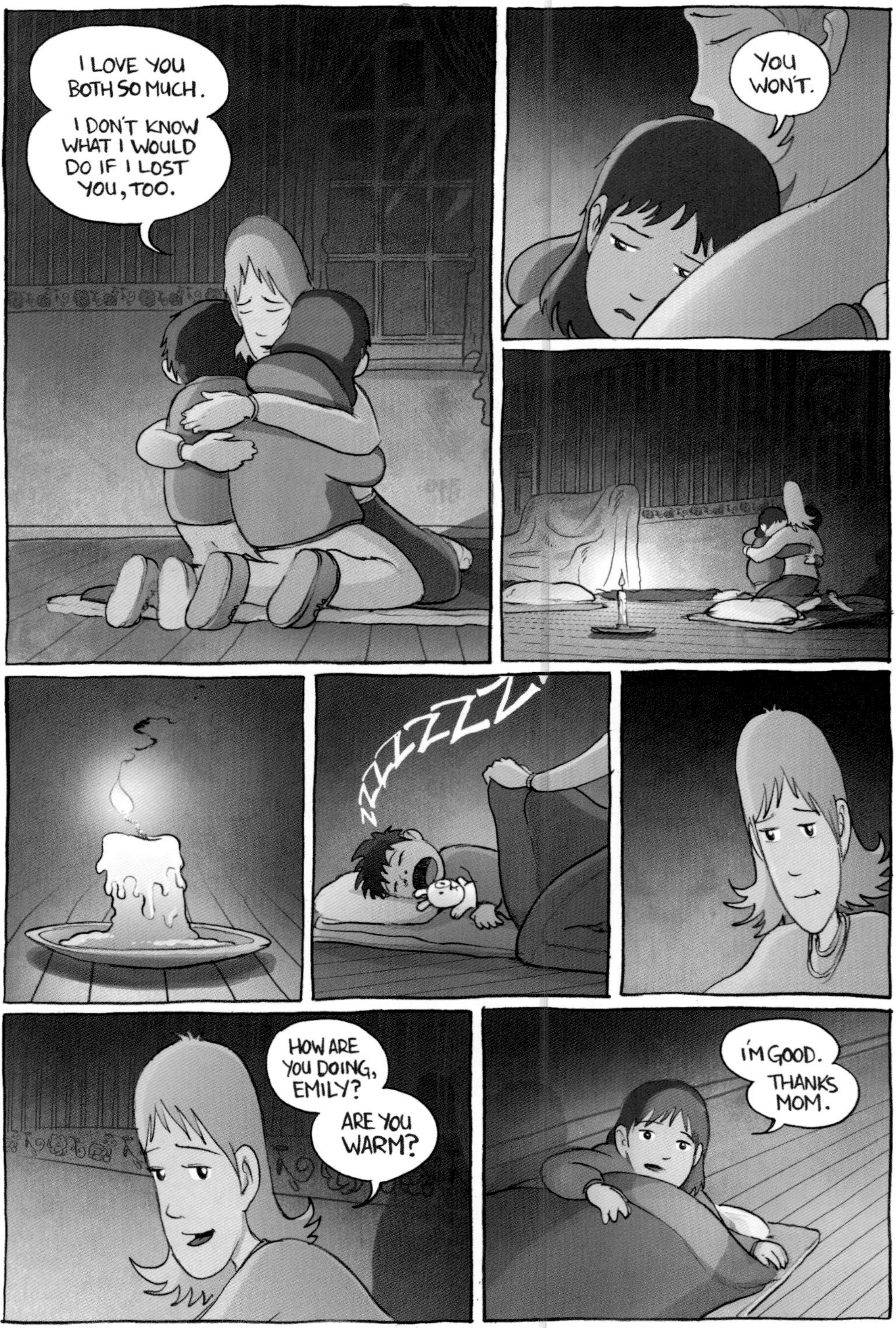
I LOVE YOU BOTH SO MUCH.
I DON'T KNOW WHAT I WOULD DO IF I LOST YOU, TOO.
YOU WON'T.
ZZZZZZZZZ
HOW ARE YOU DOING, EMILY?
ARE YOU WARM?
I'M GOOD.
THANKS MOM.

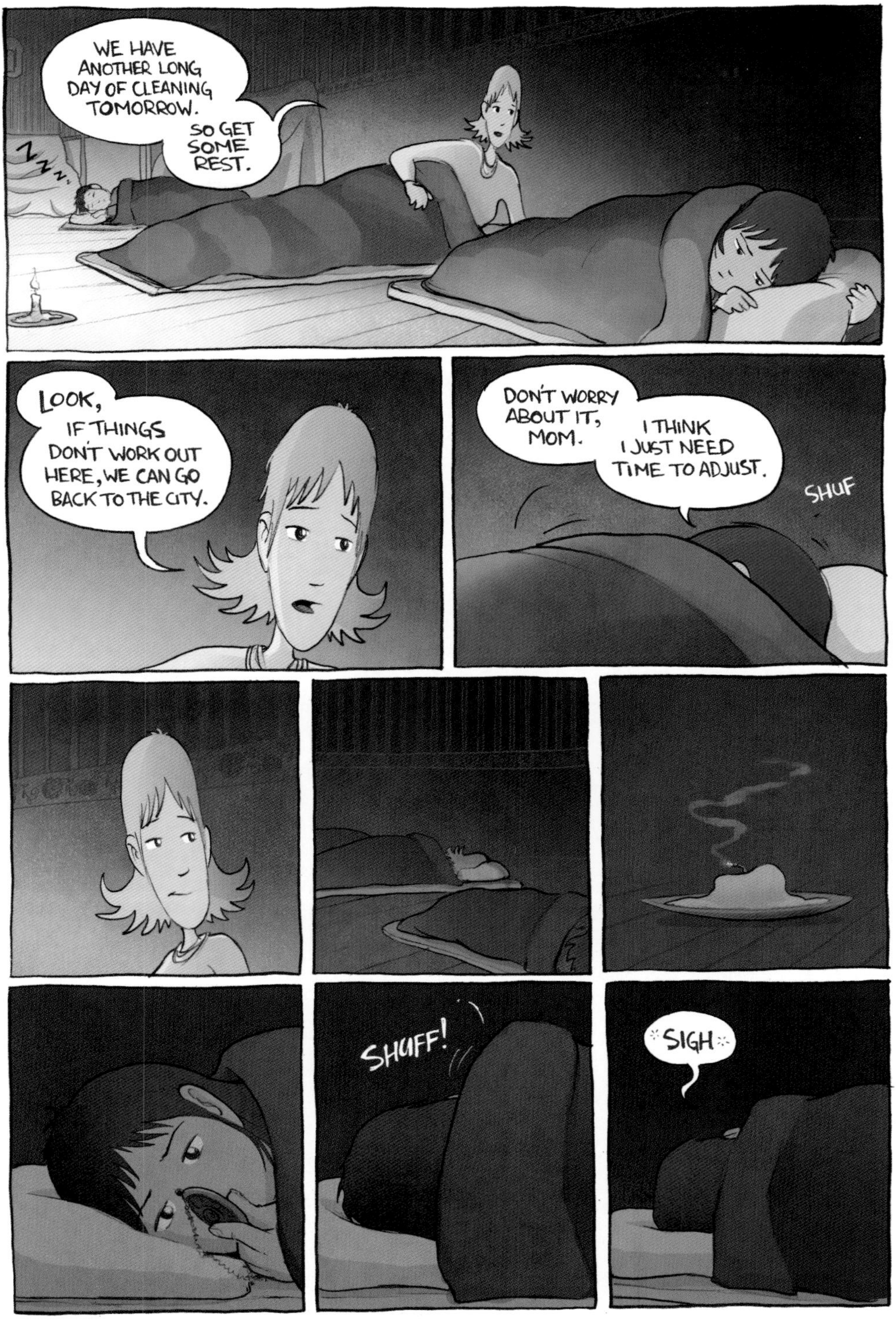
WE HAVE ANOTHER LONG DAY OF CLEANING TOMORROW.
SO GET SOME REST.
ZZZ
LOOK, IF THINGS DON'T WORK OUT HERE, WE CAN GO BACK TO THE CITY.
DON'T WORRY ABOUT IT, MOM.
I THINK I JUST NEED TIME TO ADJUST.
SHUF
SHUFF!
SIGH

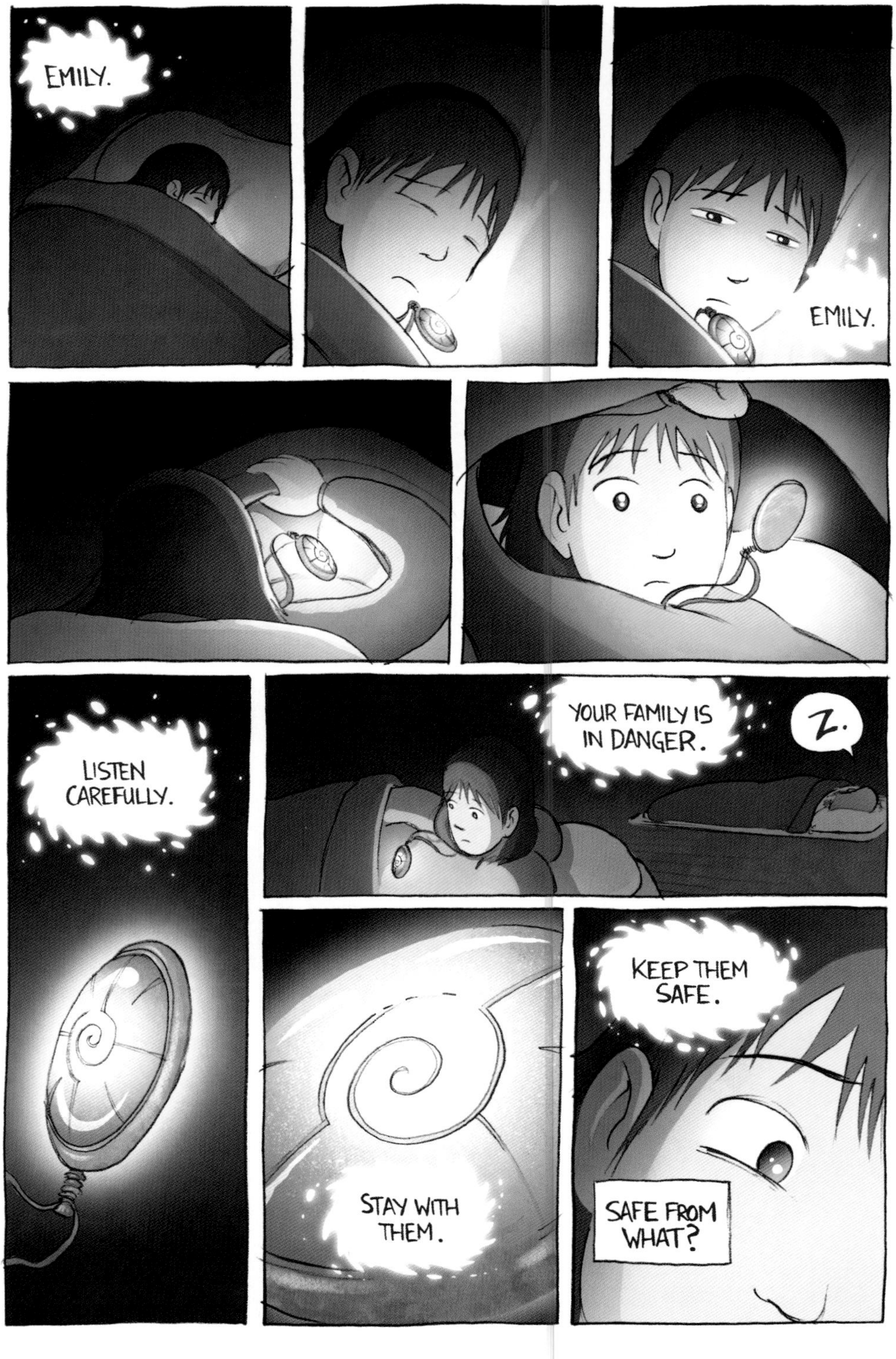
EMILY.
EMILY.
LISTEN CAREFULLY.
YOUR FAMILY IS IN DANGER.
Z.
STAY WITH THEM.
KEEP THEM SAFE.
SAFE FROM WHAT?

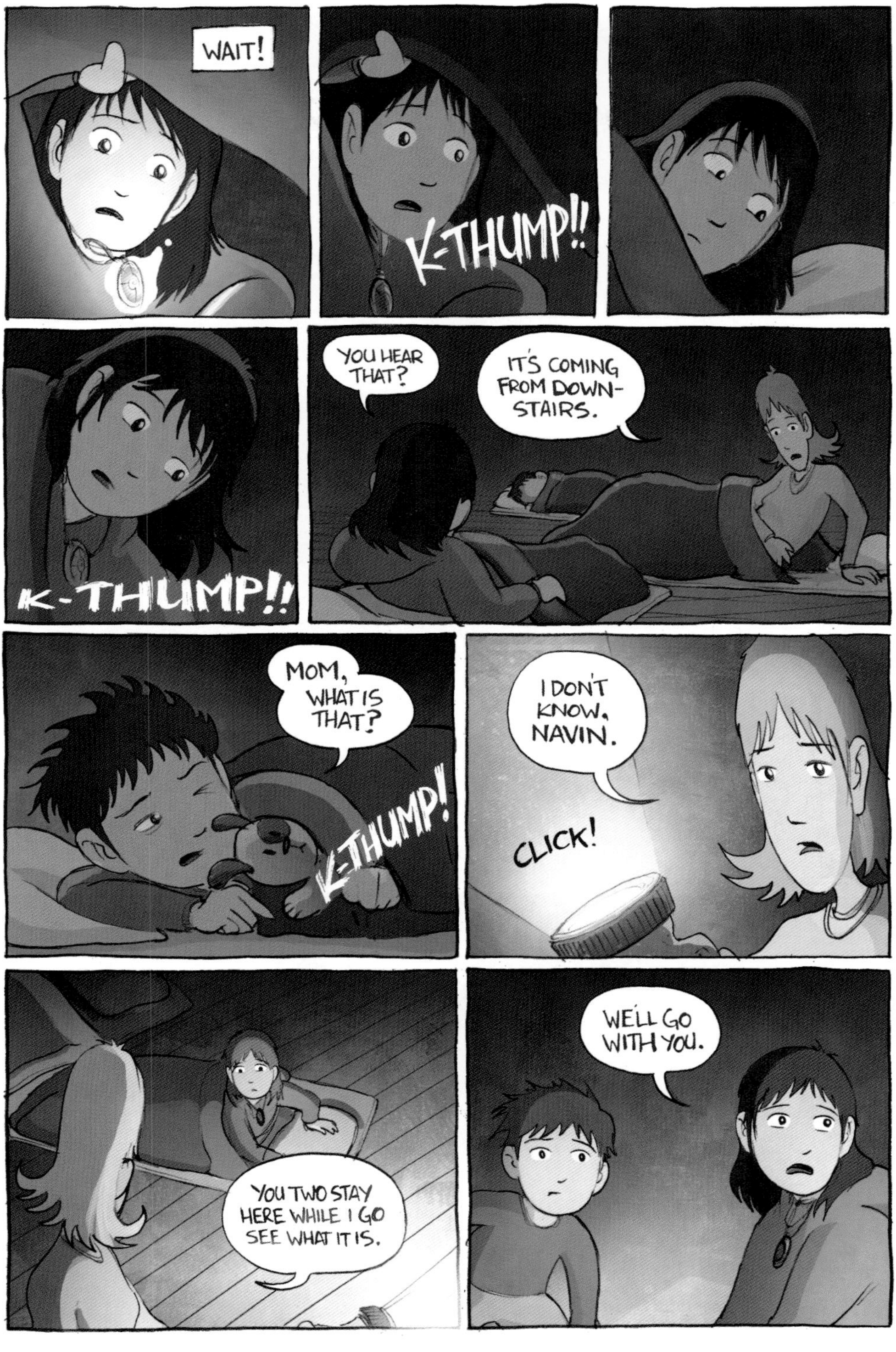
WAIT!
K-THUMP!!
K-THUMP!!
YOU HEAR THAT?
IT'S COMING FROM DOWN-STAIRS.
MOM, WHAT IS THAT?
K-THUMP!
I DON'T KNOW, NAVIN.
CLICK!
YOU TWO STAY HERE WHILE I GO SEE WHAT IT IS.
WE'LL GO WITH YOU.

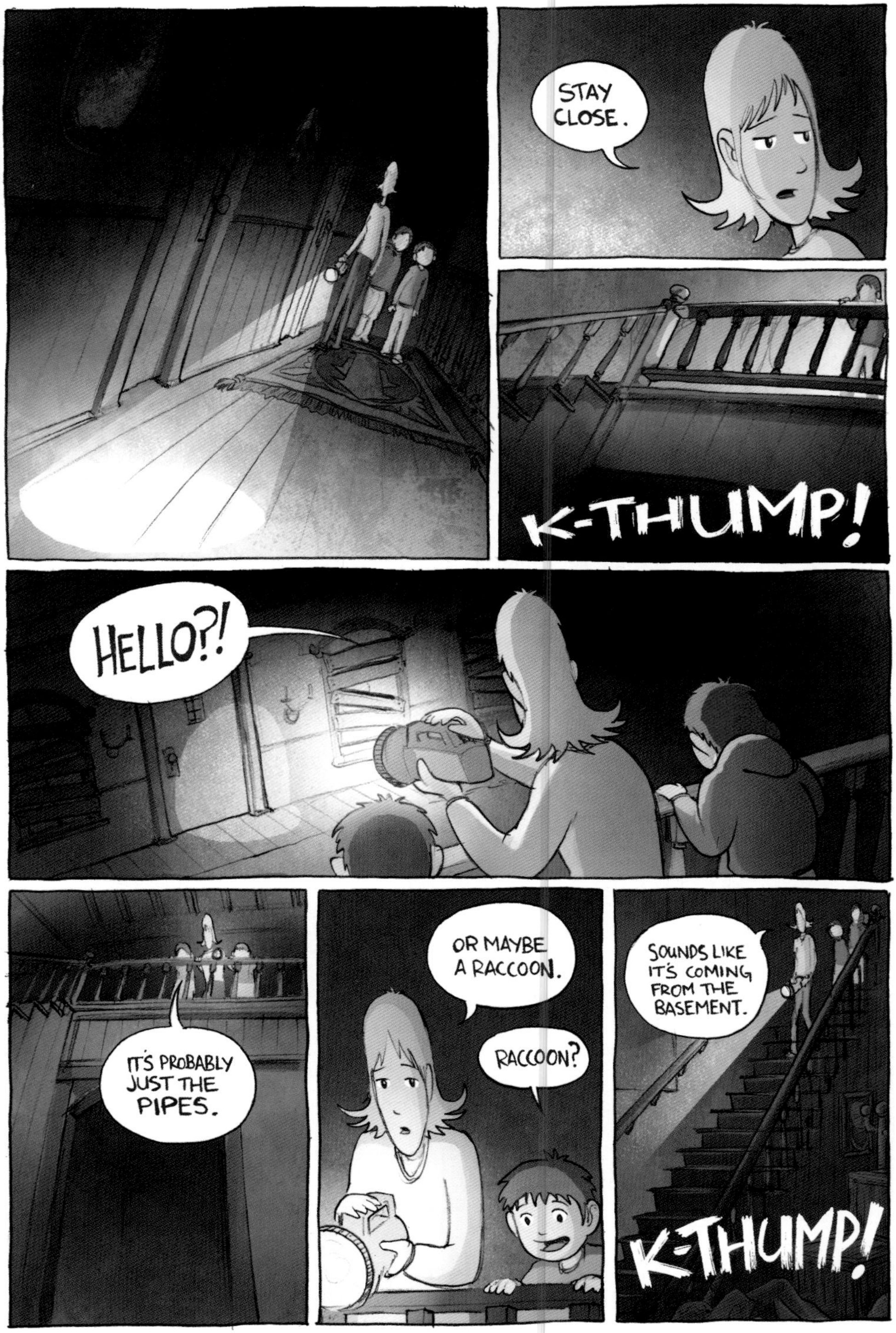
STAY CLOSE.
K-THUMP!
HELLO?!
IT'S PROBABLY JUST THE PIPES.
OR MAYBE A RACCOON.
RACCOON?
SOUNDS LIKE IT'S COMING FROM THE BASEMENT.
K-THUMP!

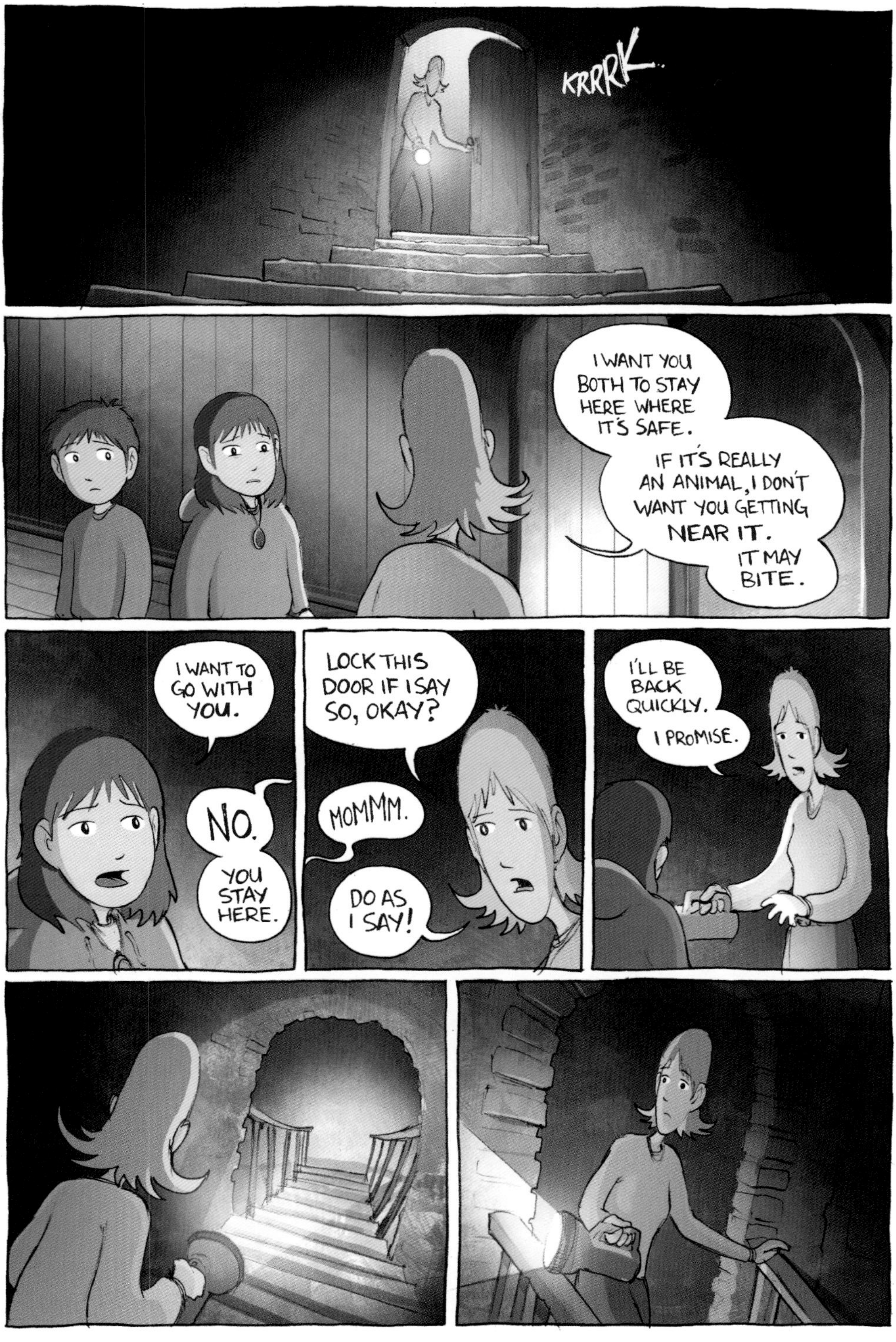
KRRRK...
I WANT YOU BOTH TO STAY HERE WHERE IT'S SAFE.
IF IT'S REALLY AN ANIMAL, I DON'T WANT YOU GETTING NEAR IT.
IT MAY BITE.
I WANT TO GO WITH YOU.
NO.
YOU STAY HERE.
LOCK THIS DOOR IF I SAY SO, OKAY?
MOMMM.
DO AS I SAY!
I'LL BE BACK QUICKLY.
I PROMISE.

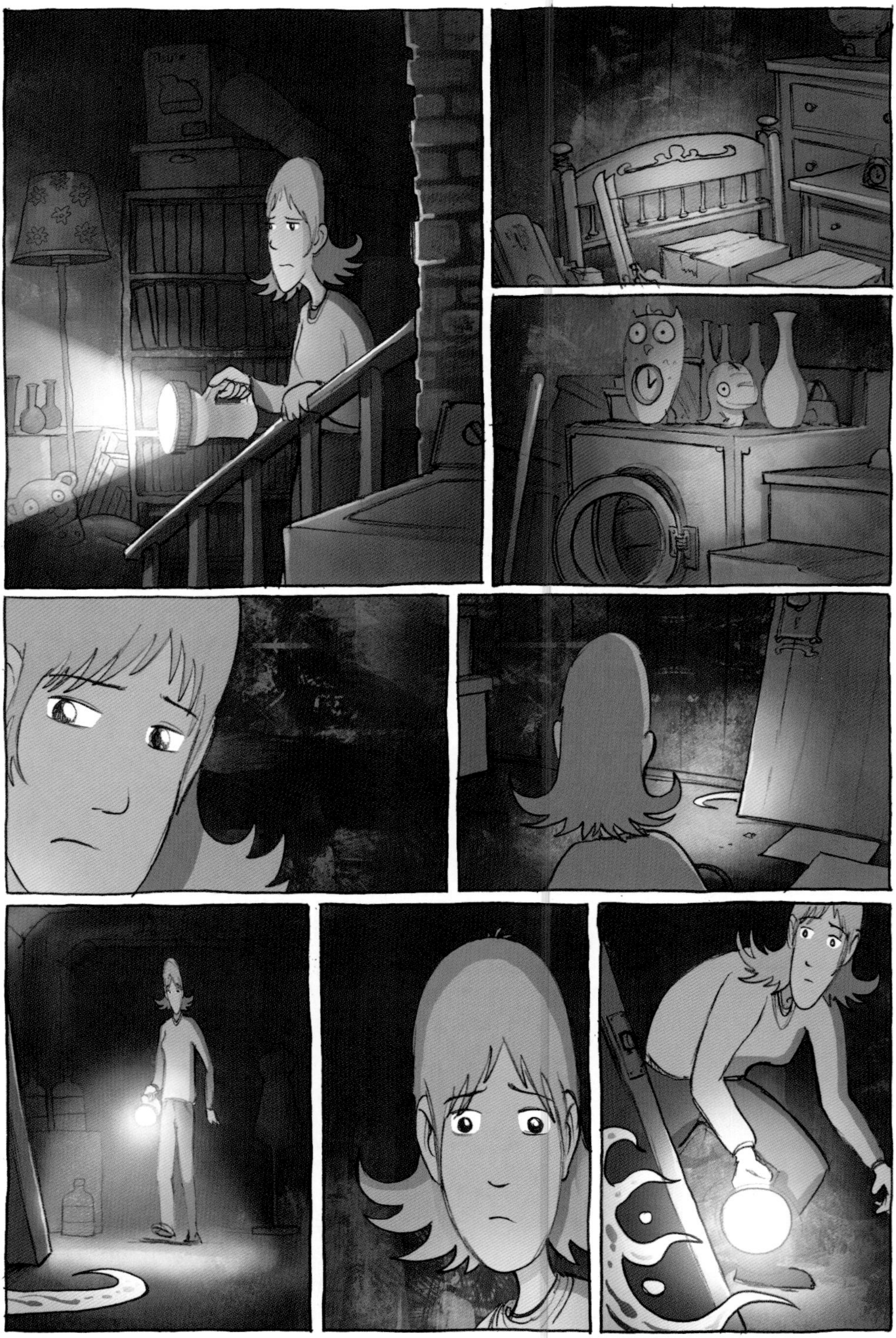

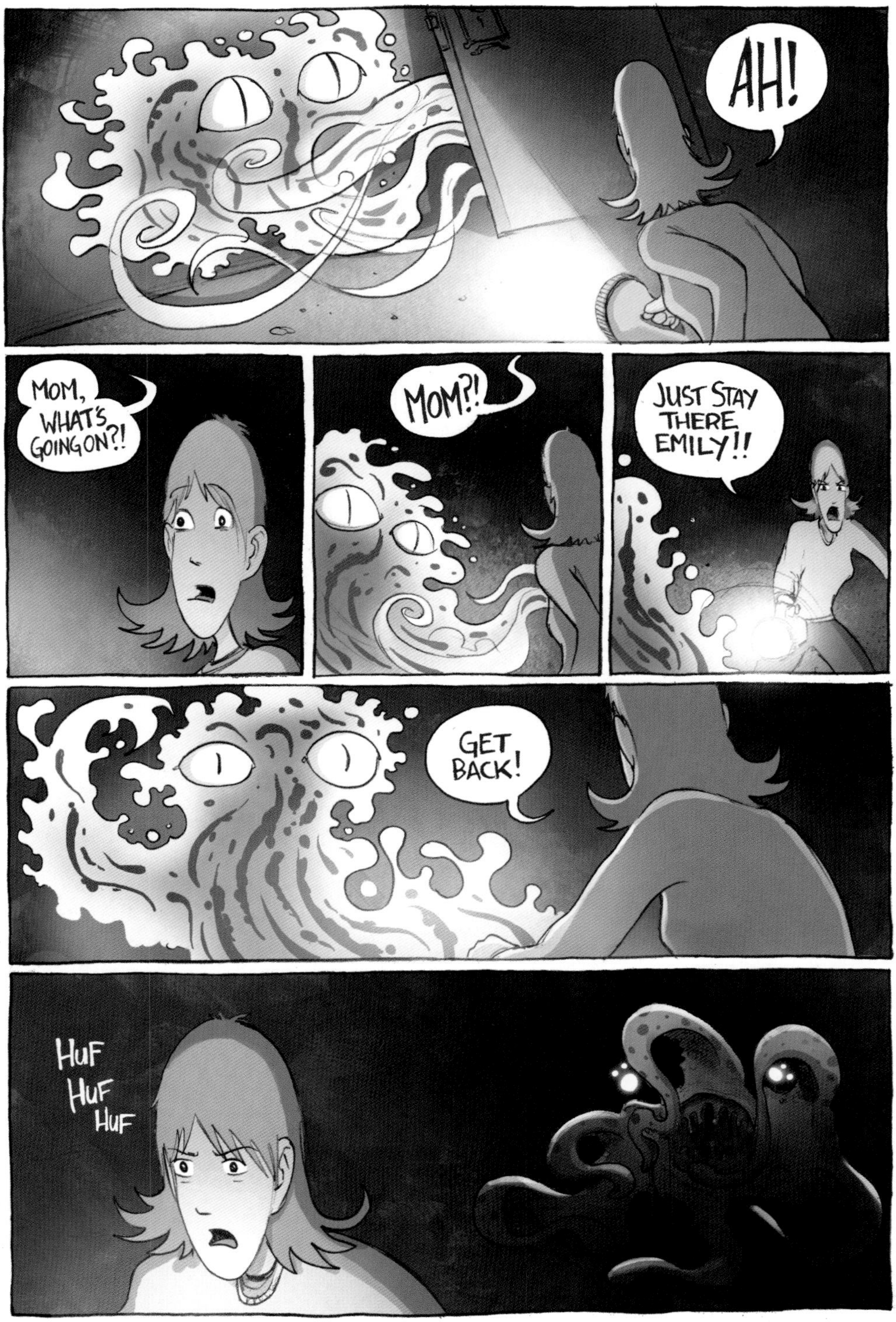
AH!
MOM, WHAT'S GOING ON?!
MOM?!
JUST STAY THERE EMILY!!
GET BACK!
HuF
HuF
HuF

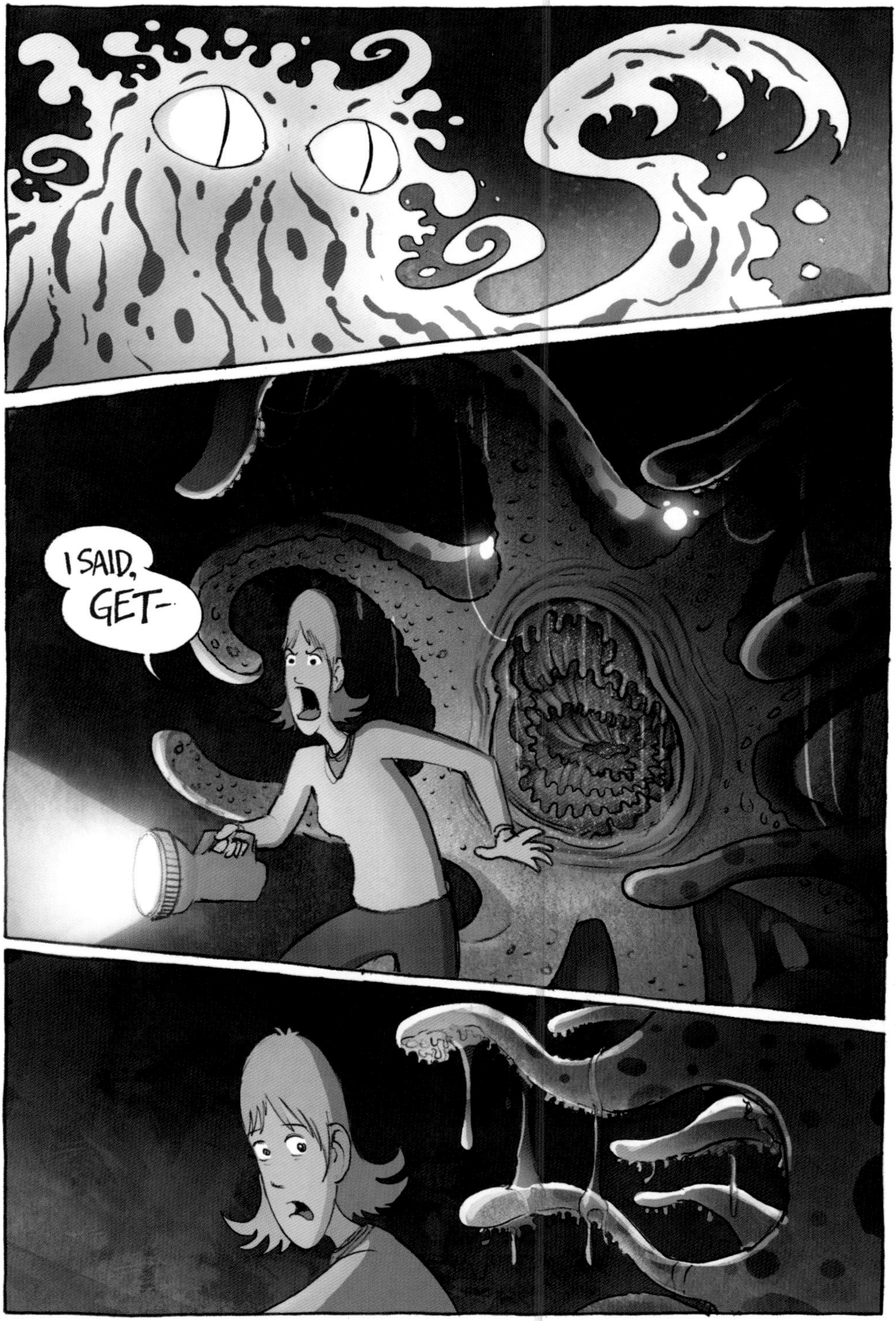
I SAID, GET-

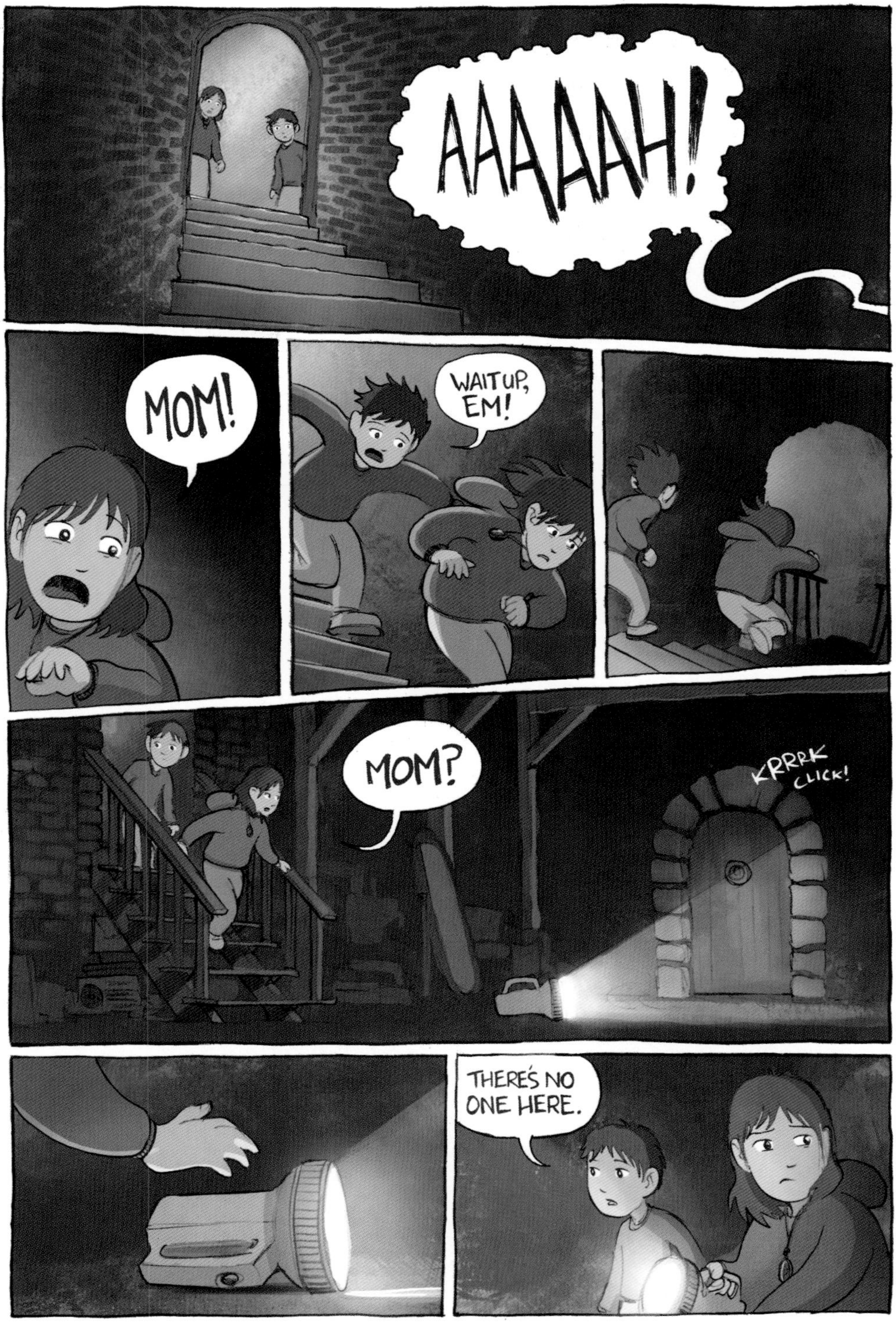
AAAAAH!
MOM!
WAIT UP, EM!
MOM?
KRRRK CLICK!
THERE'S NO ONE HERE.

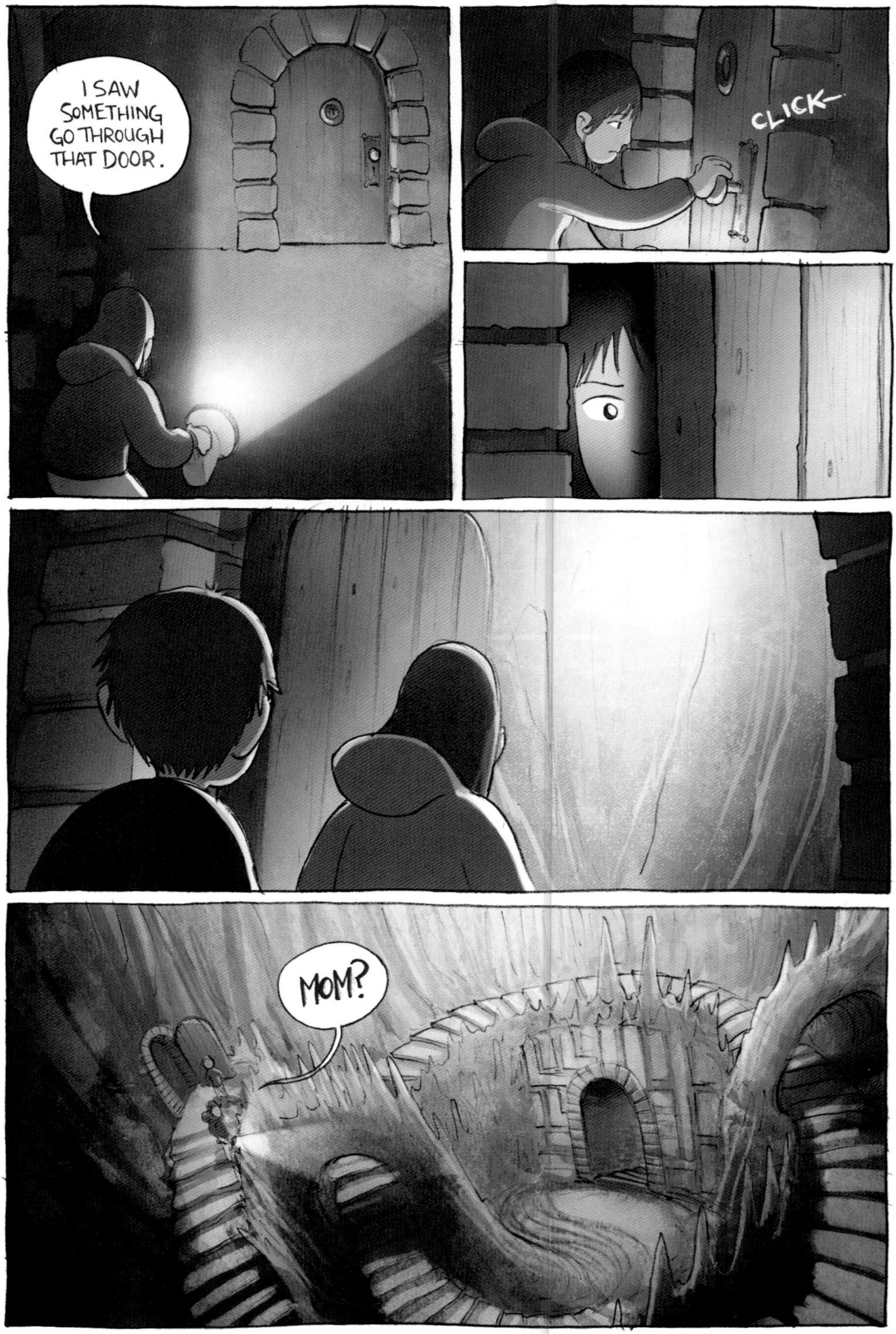
I SAW SOMETHING GO THROUGH THAT DOOR.
CLICK
MOM?

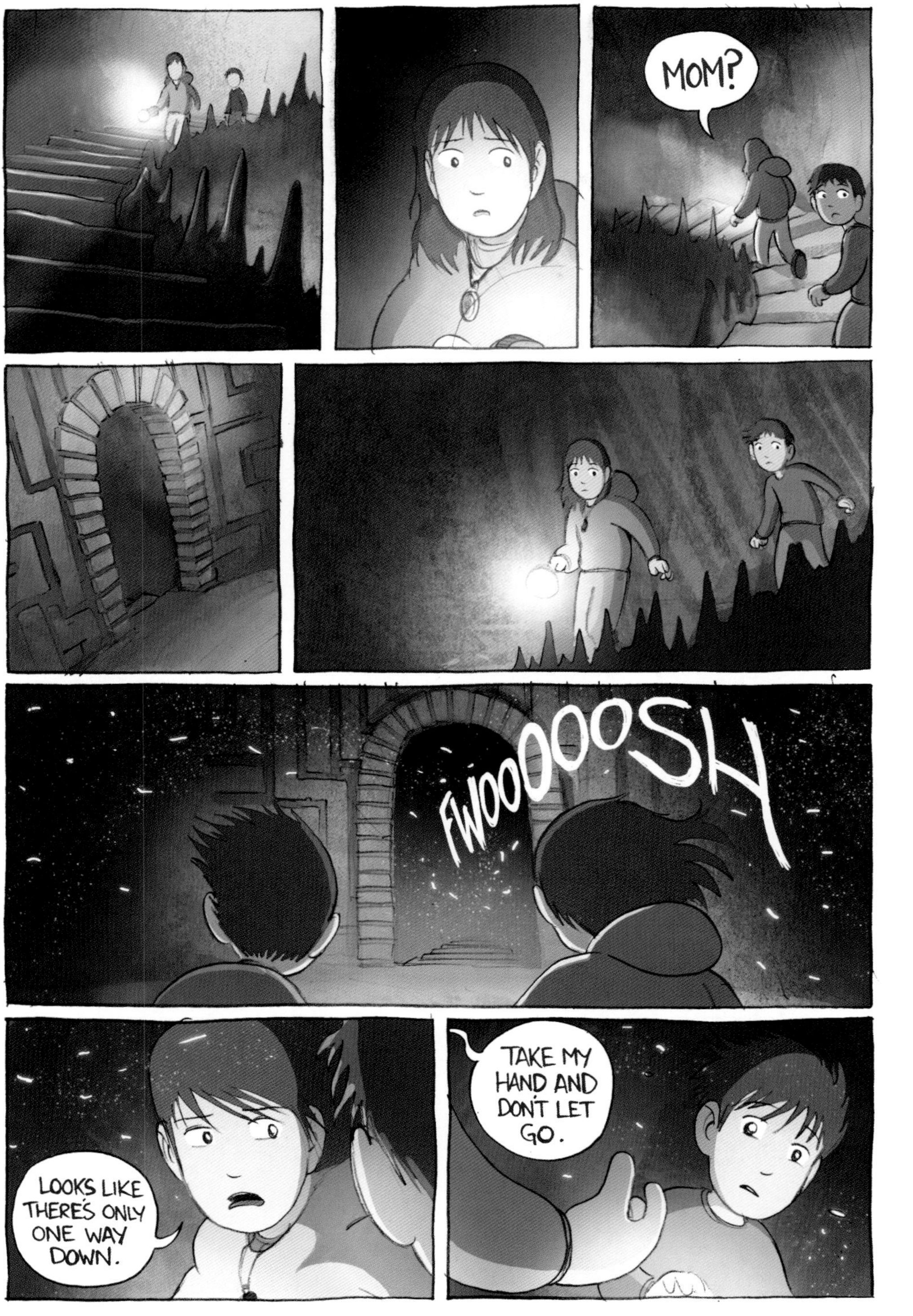
MOM?
FWOOOOOSH
LOOKS LIKE THERE'S ONLY ONE WAY DOWN.
TAKE MY HAND AND DON'T LET GO.

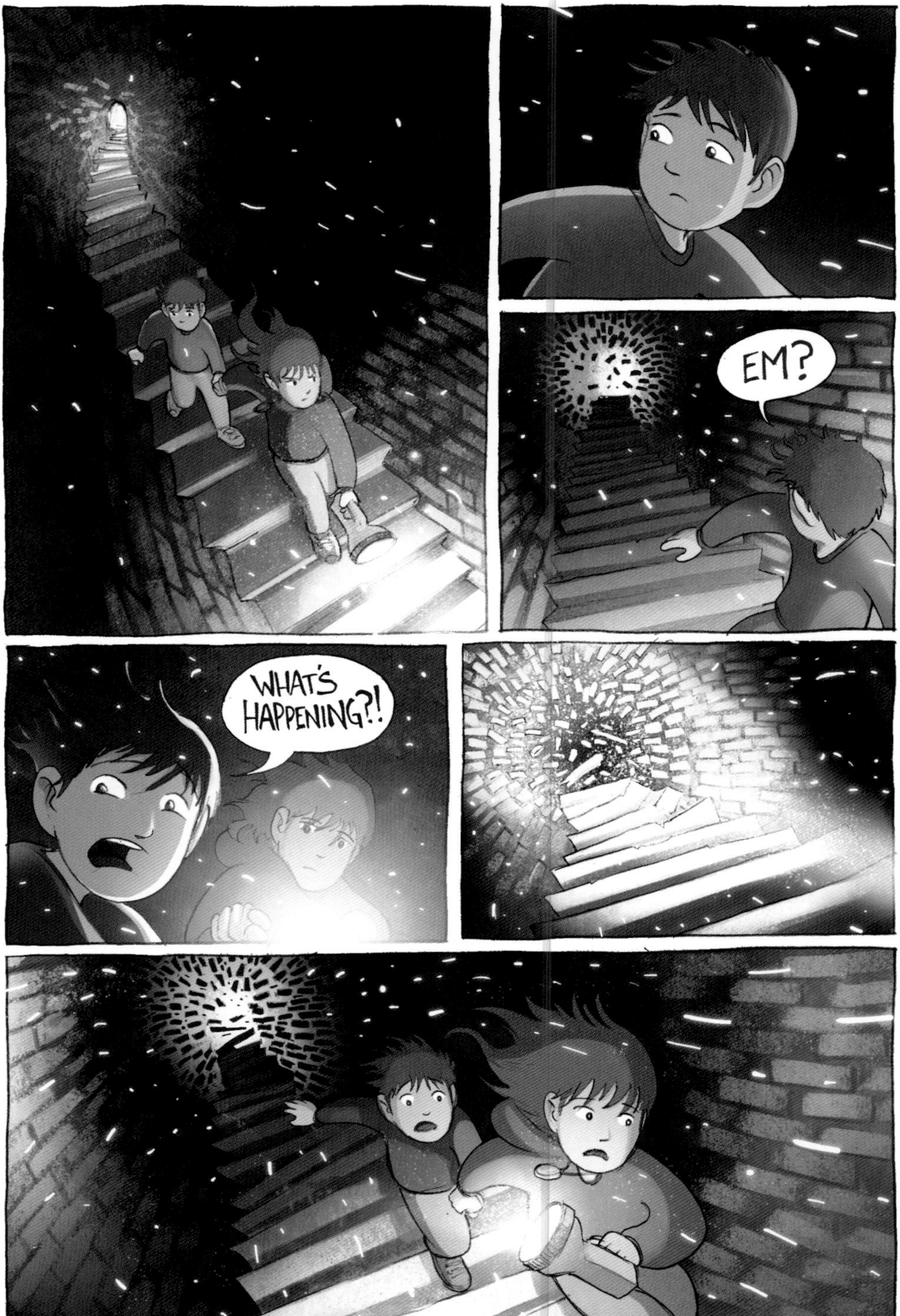
EM?
WHAT'S HAPPENING?!

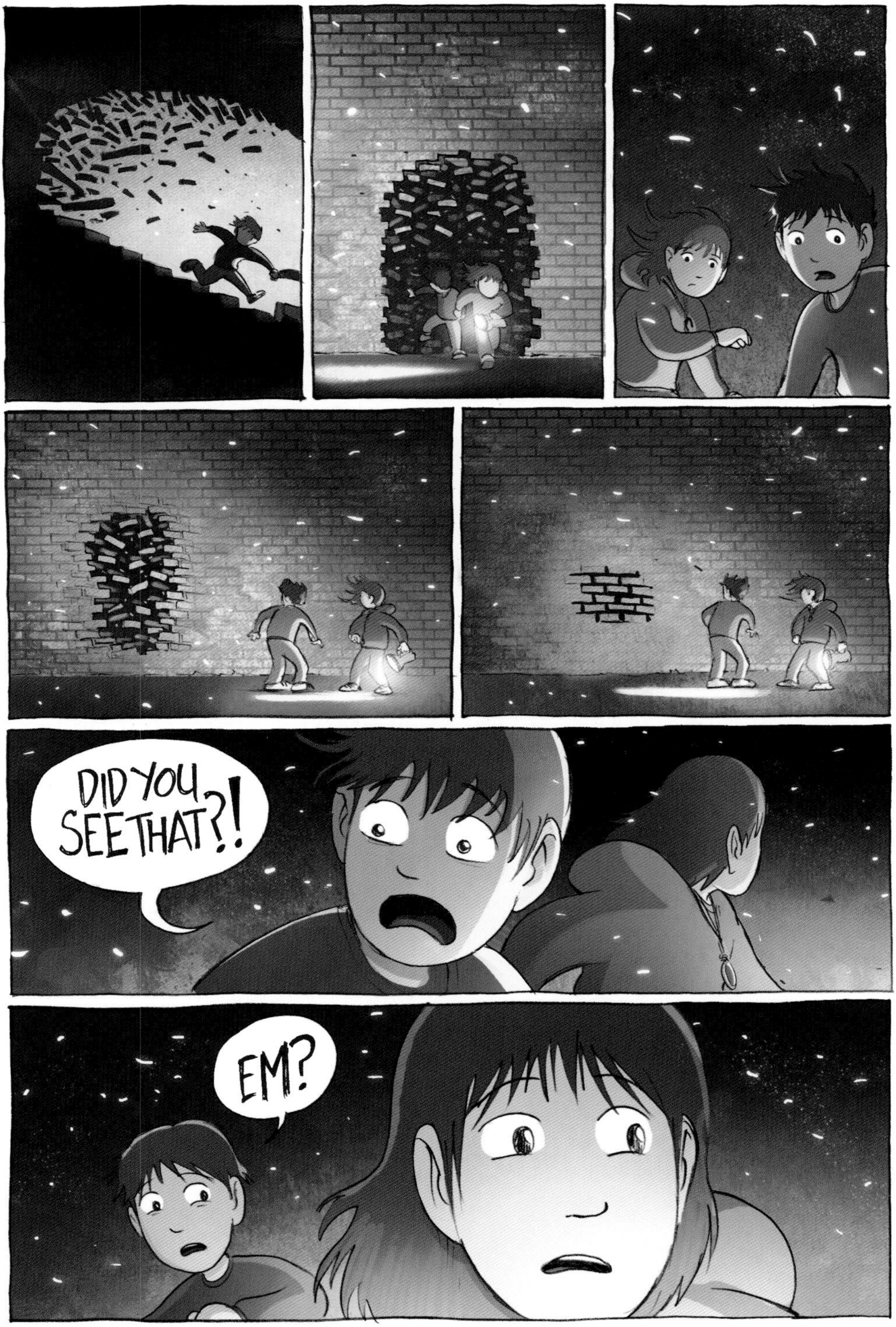
DID YOU SEE THAT?!
EM?

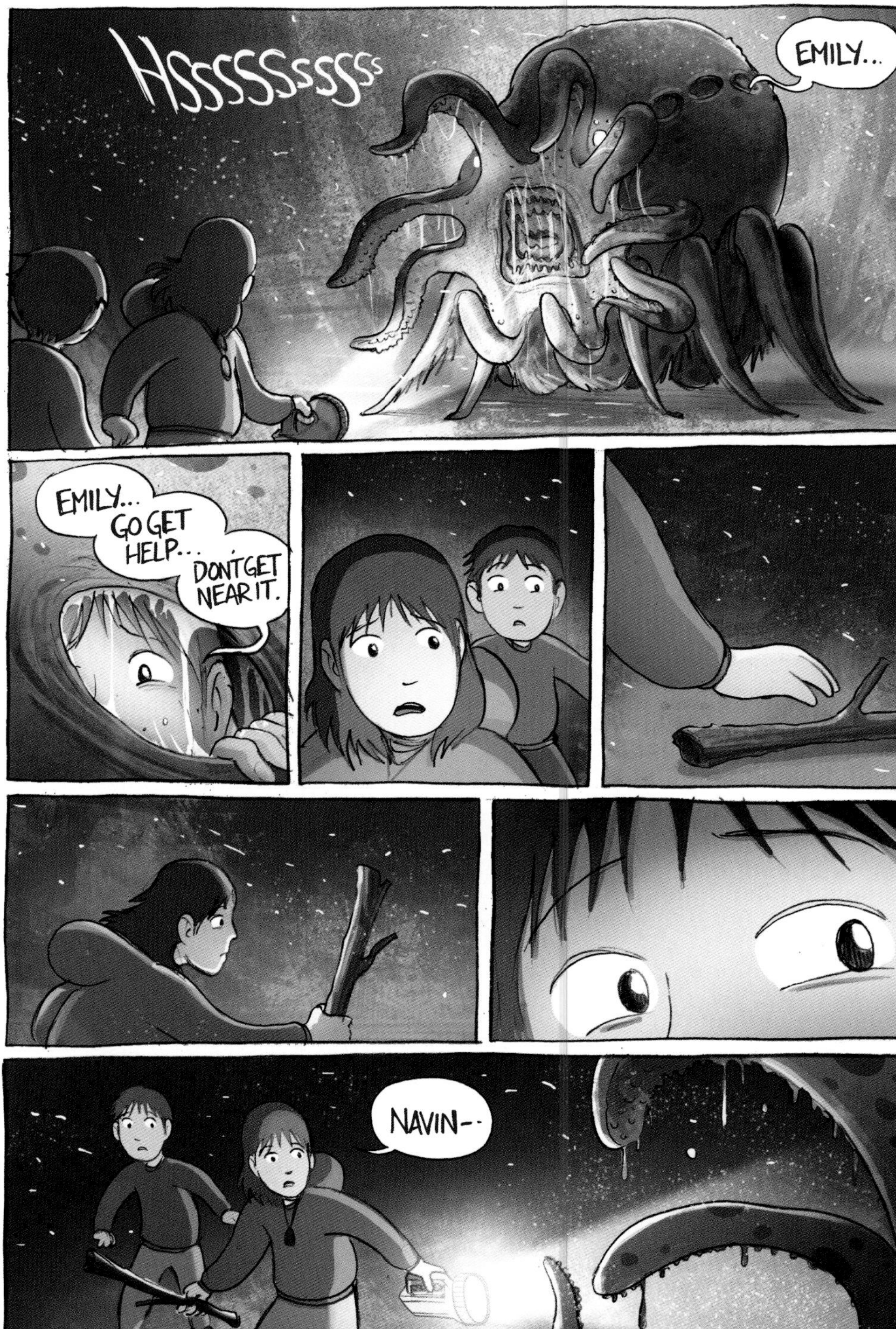
HSSSSSSSSSS
EMILY...
EMILY... GO GET HELP... DON'T GET NEAR IT.
NAVIN--

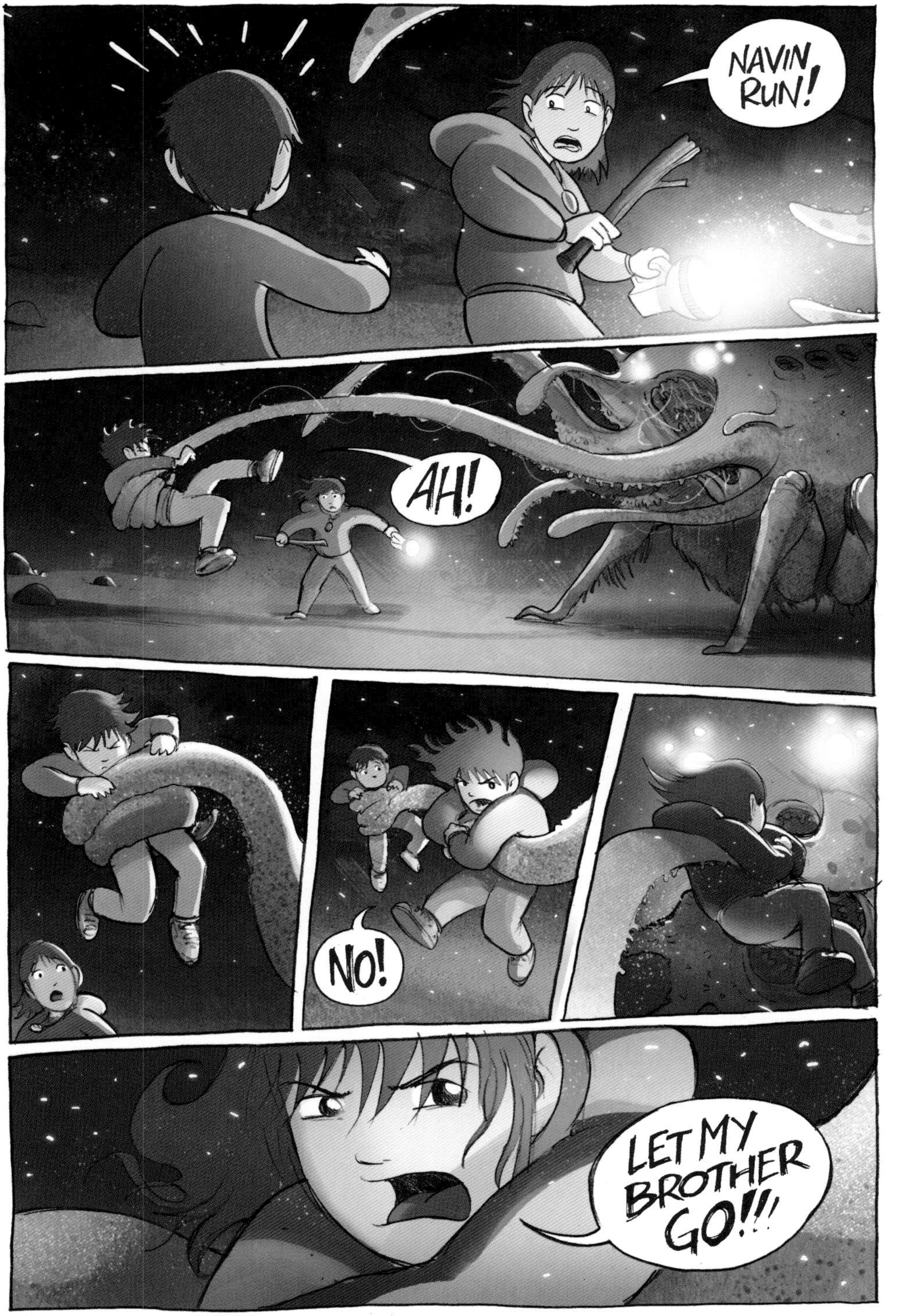
NAVIN RUN!
AH!
NO!
LET MY BROTHER GO!!!

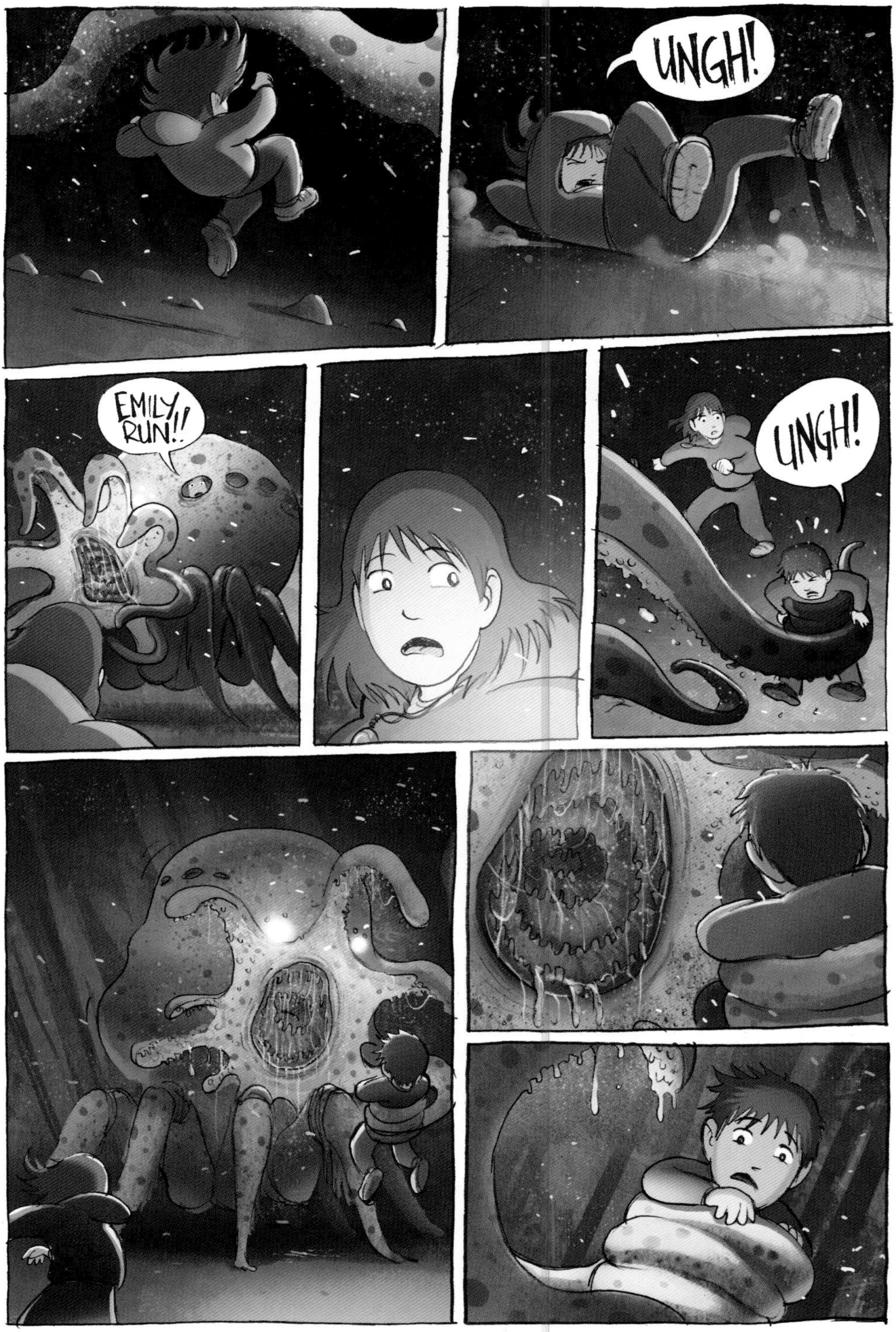
UNGH!
EMILY, RUN!!
UNGH!

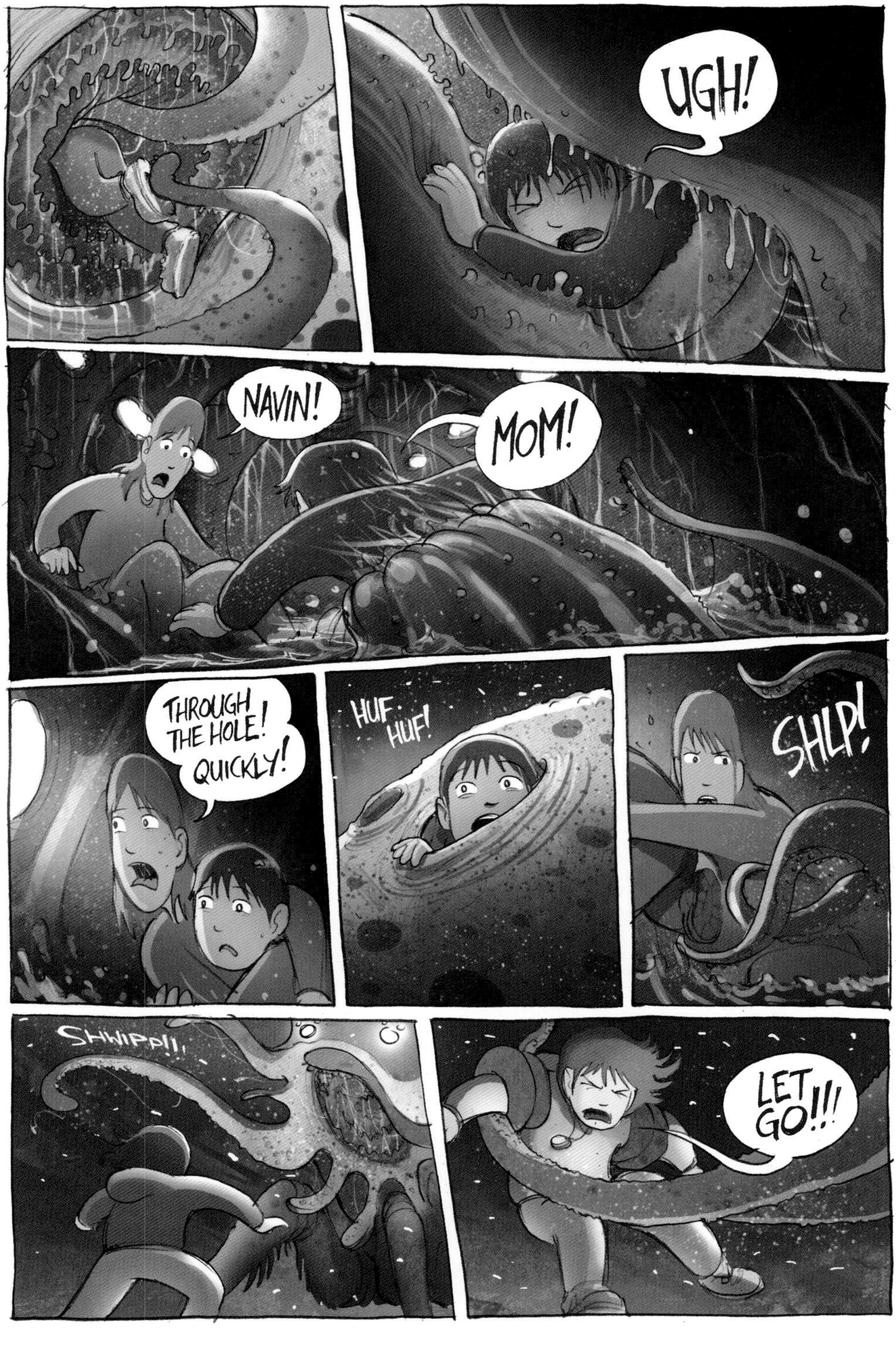
UGH!
NAVIN!
MOM!
THROUGH THE HOLE! QUICKLY!
HUF HUF!
SHLP!
SHWIPP!!
LET GO!!!

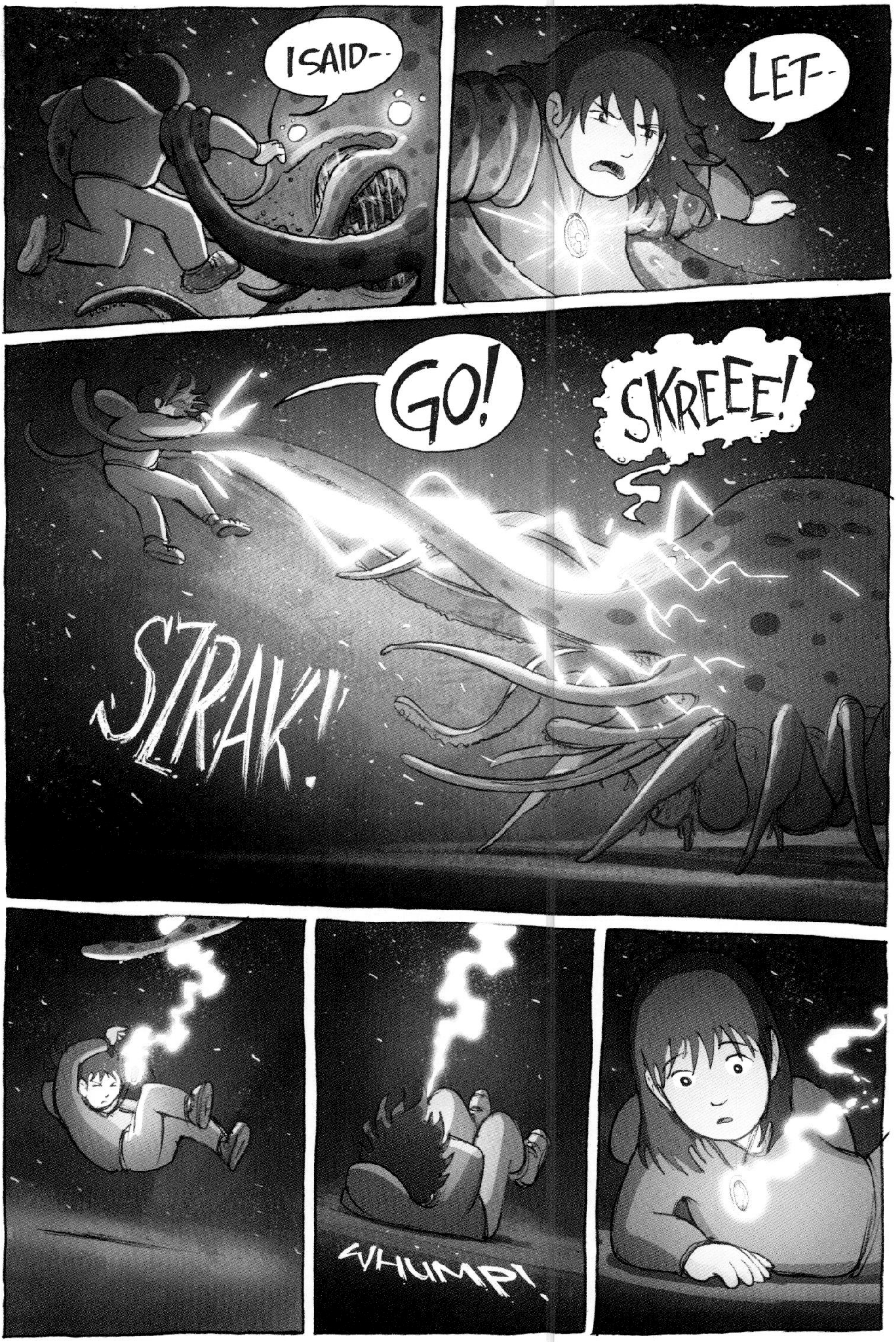
I SAID--
LET--
GO!
SKREEE!
STRAK!
WHUMP!

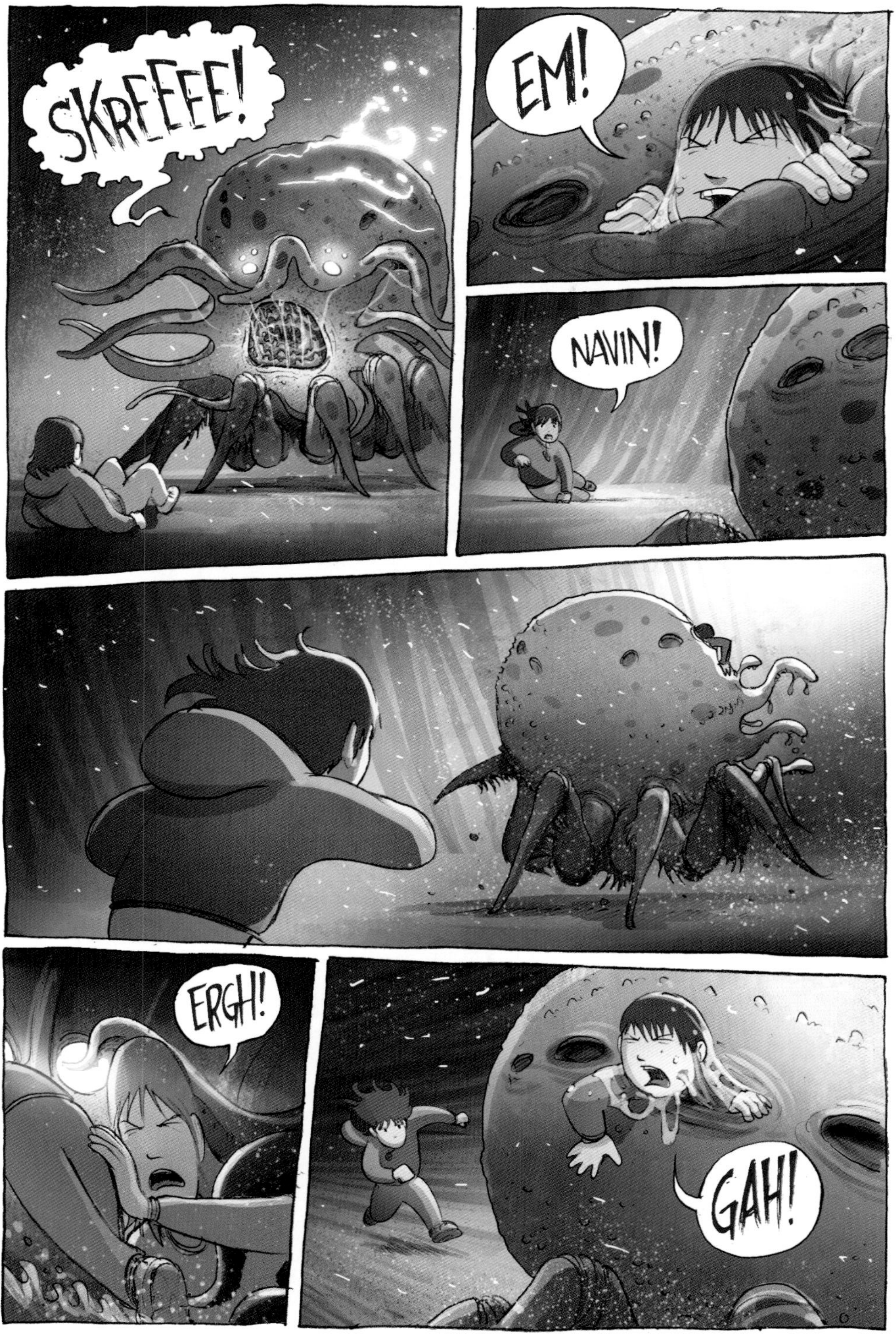
SKRFEEE!
EM!
NAVIN!
ERGH!
GAH!

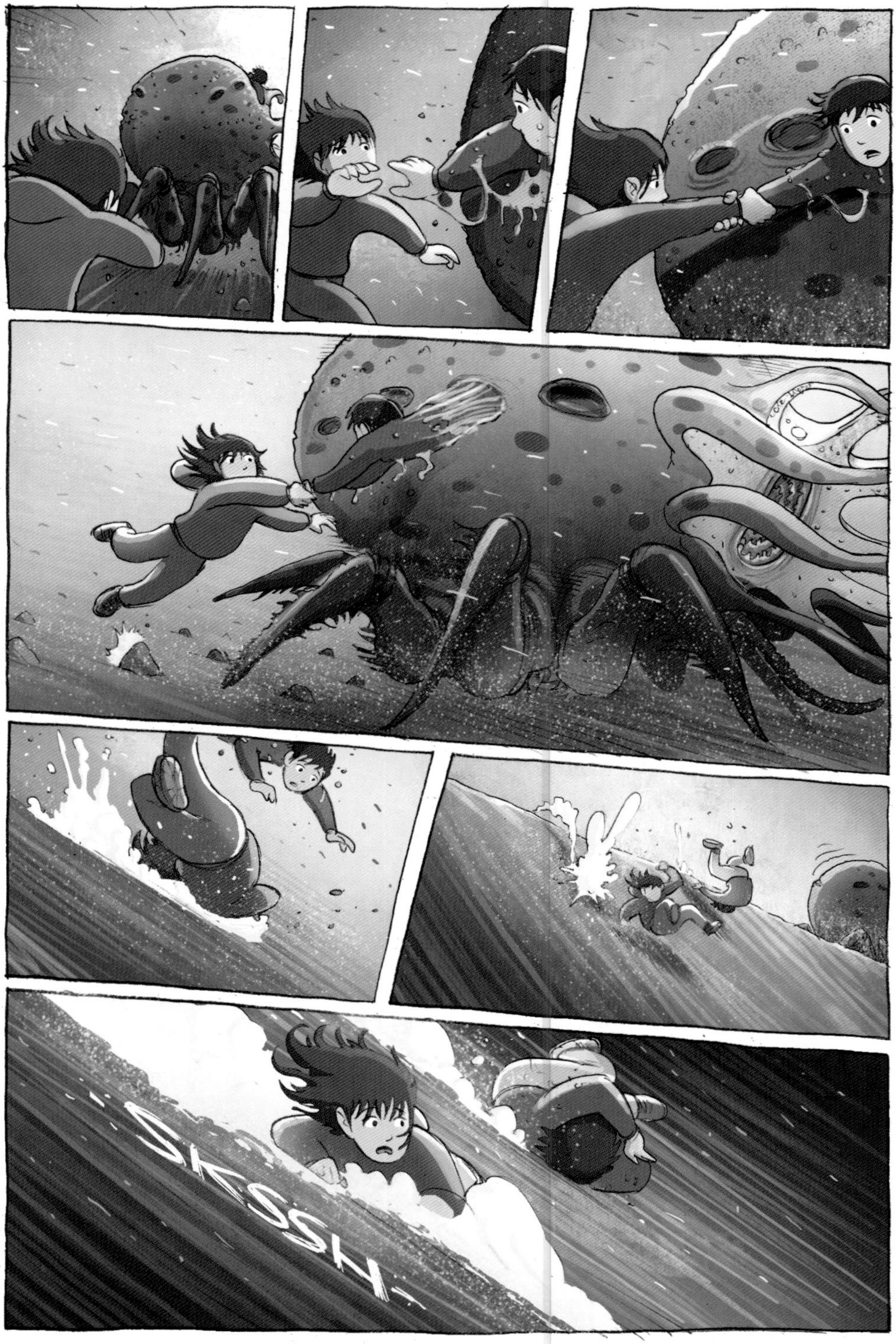
SKSSH

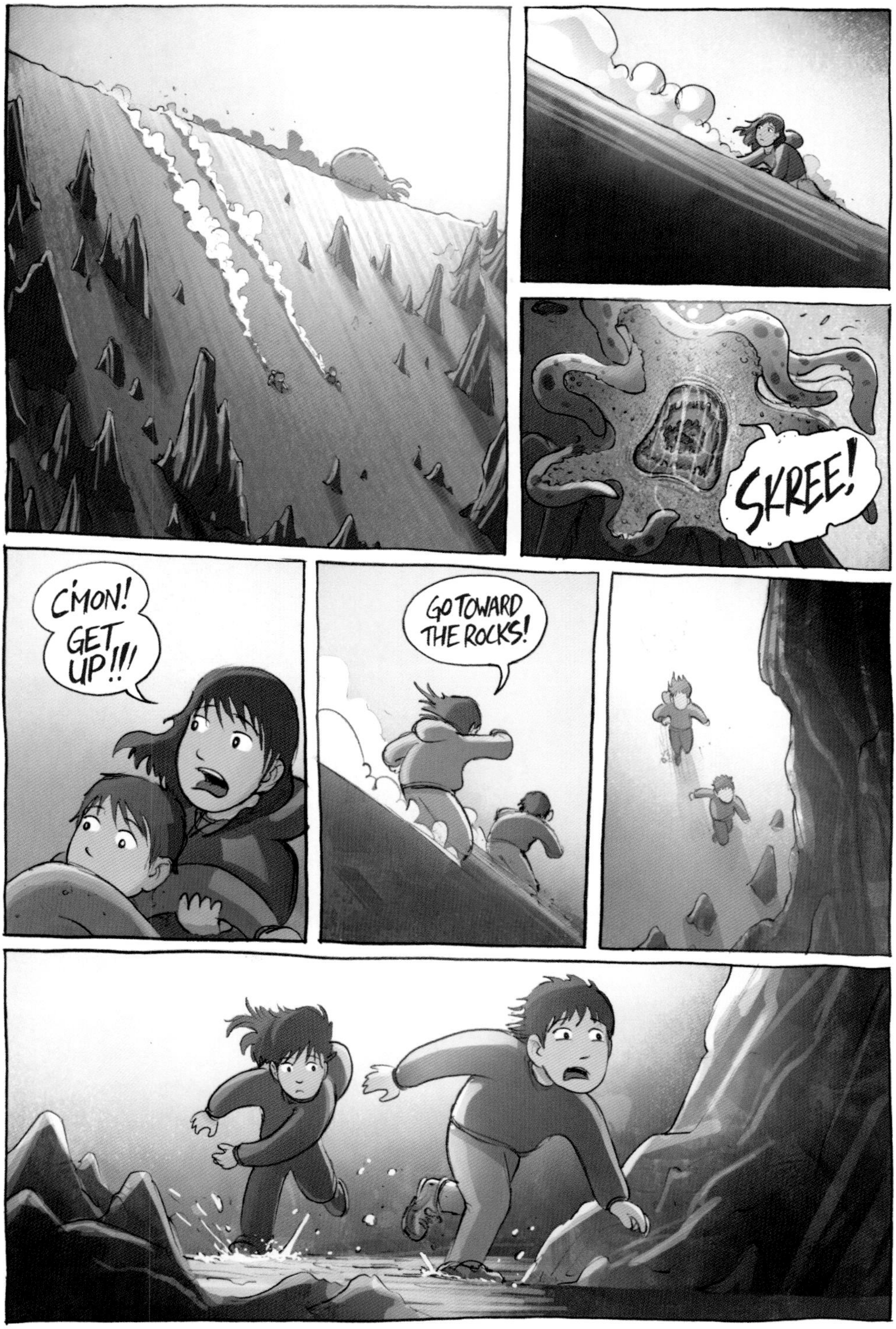
SKREE!
C'MON! GET UP!!!
GO TOWARD THE ROCKS!

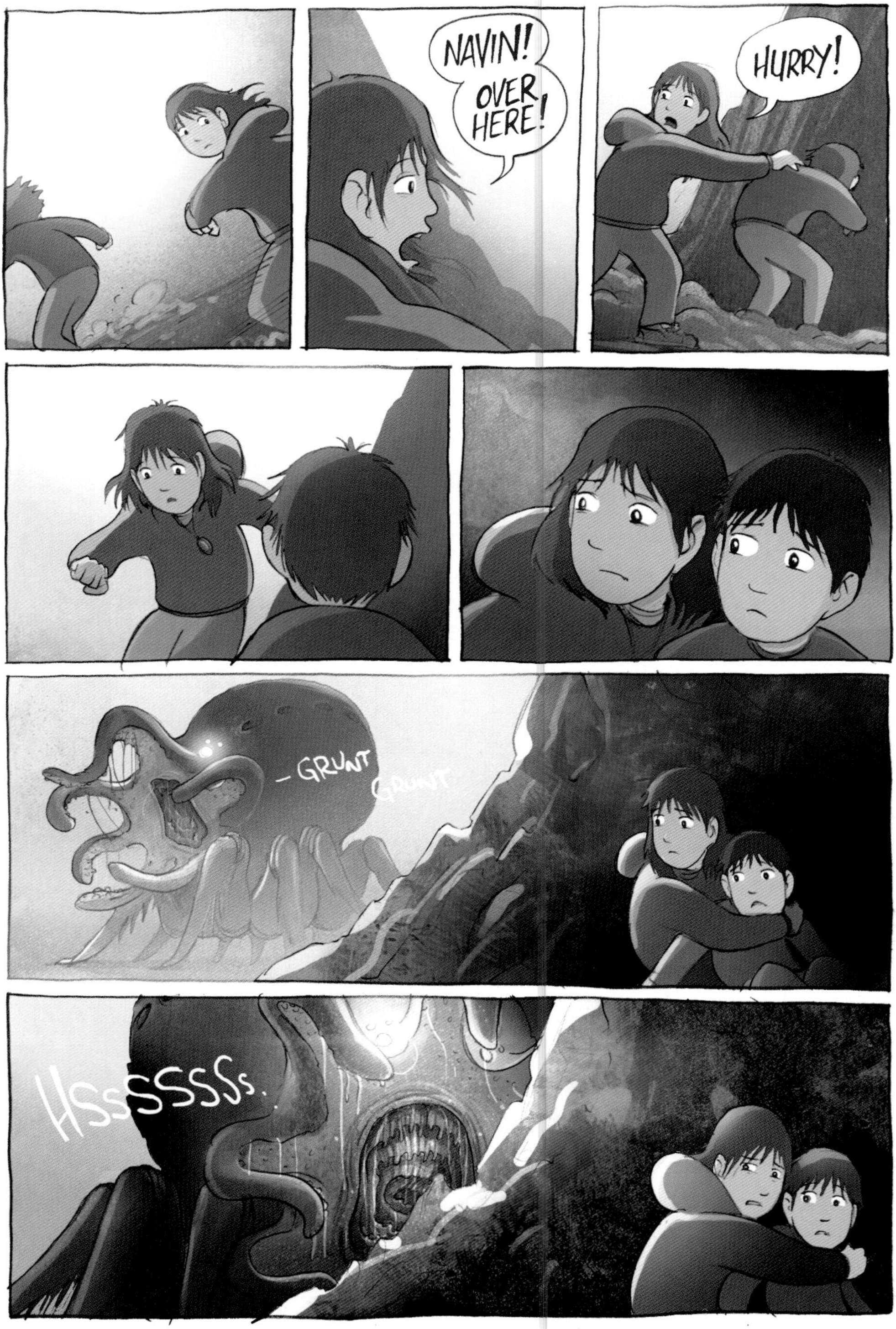
NAVIN!
OVER HERE!
HURRY!
GRUNT
GRUNT
HSSSSSSS.

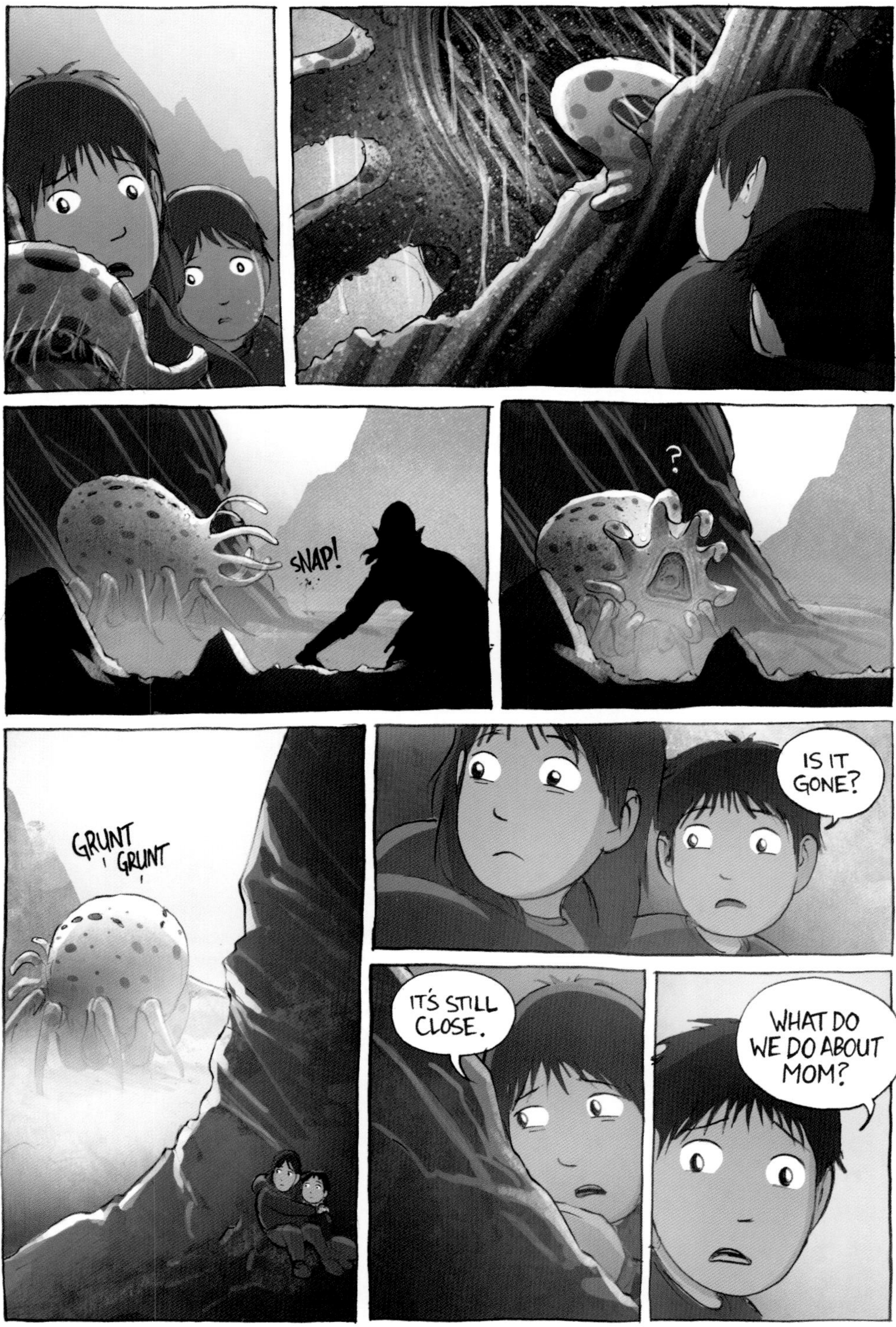
SNAP!
?
GRUNT
GRUNT
IS IT GONE?
IT'S STILL CLOSE.
WHAT DO WE DO ABOUT MOM?

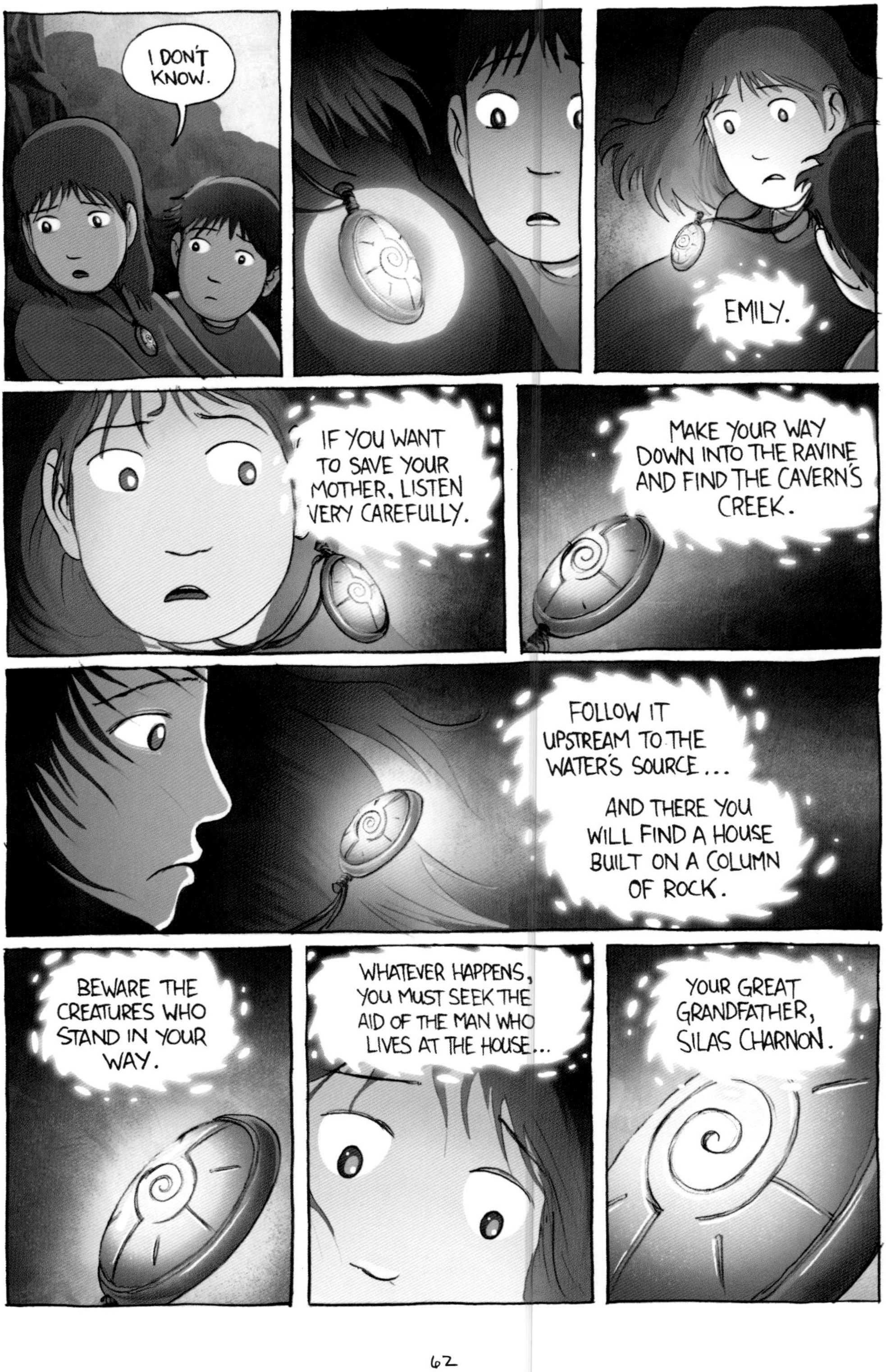
I DON'T KNOW.
EMILY.
IF YOU WANT TO SAVE YOUR MOTHER, LISTEN VERY CAREFULLY.
MAKE YOUR WAY DOWN INTO THE RAVINE AND FIND THE CAVERN'S CREEK.
FOLLOW IT UPSTREAM TO THE WATER'S SOURCE...
AND THERE YOU WILL FIND A HOUSE BUILT ON A COLUMN OF ROCK.
BEWARE THE CREATURES WHO STAND IN YOUR WAY.
WHATEVER HAPPENS, YOU MUST SEEK THE AID OF THE MAN WHO LIVES AT THE HOUSE...
YOUR GREAT GRANDFATHER, SILAS CHARNON.

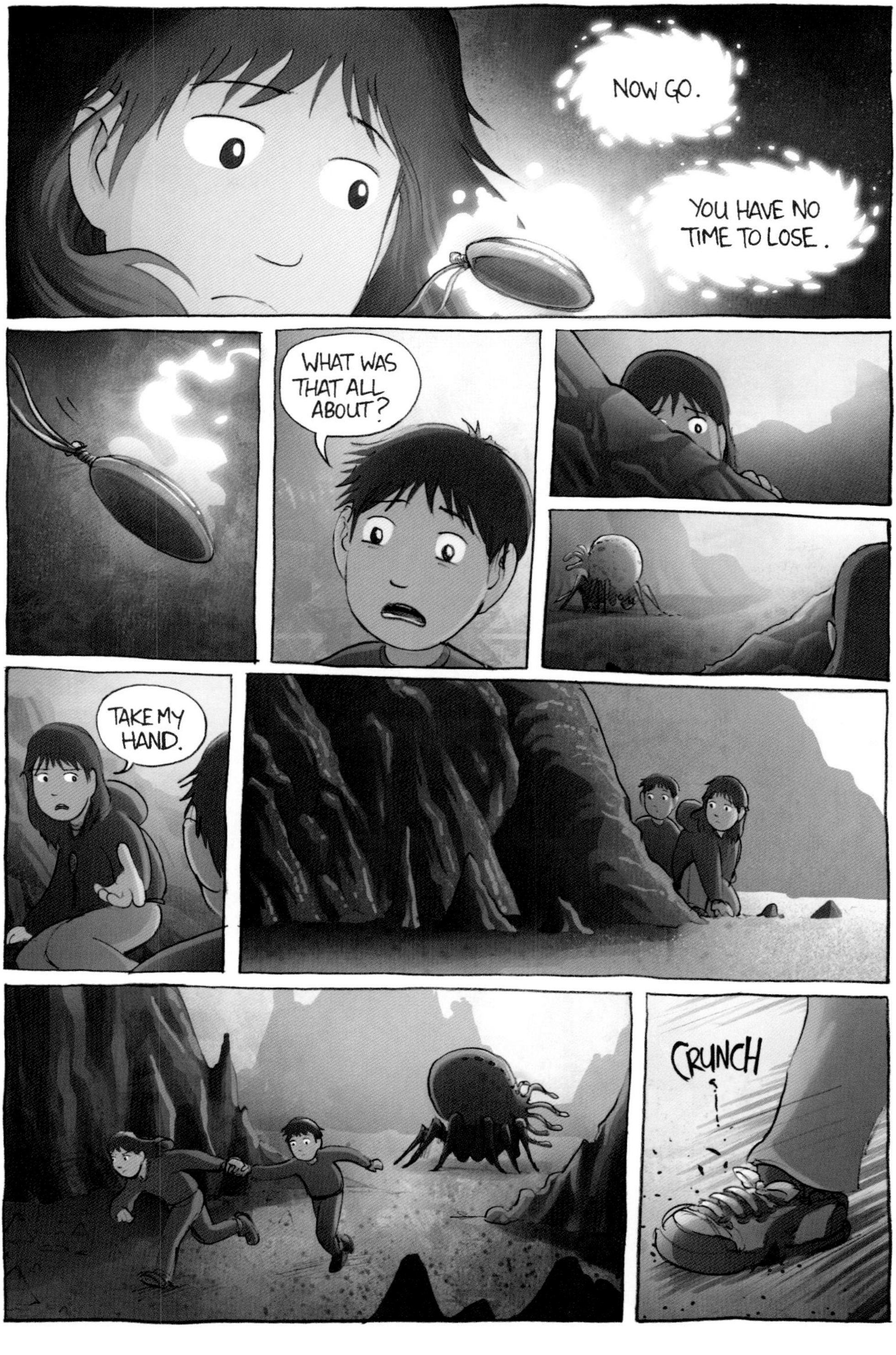
NOW GO.
YOU HAVE NO TIME TO LOSE.
WHAT WAS THAT ALL ABOUT?
TAKE MY HAND.
CRUNCH

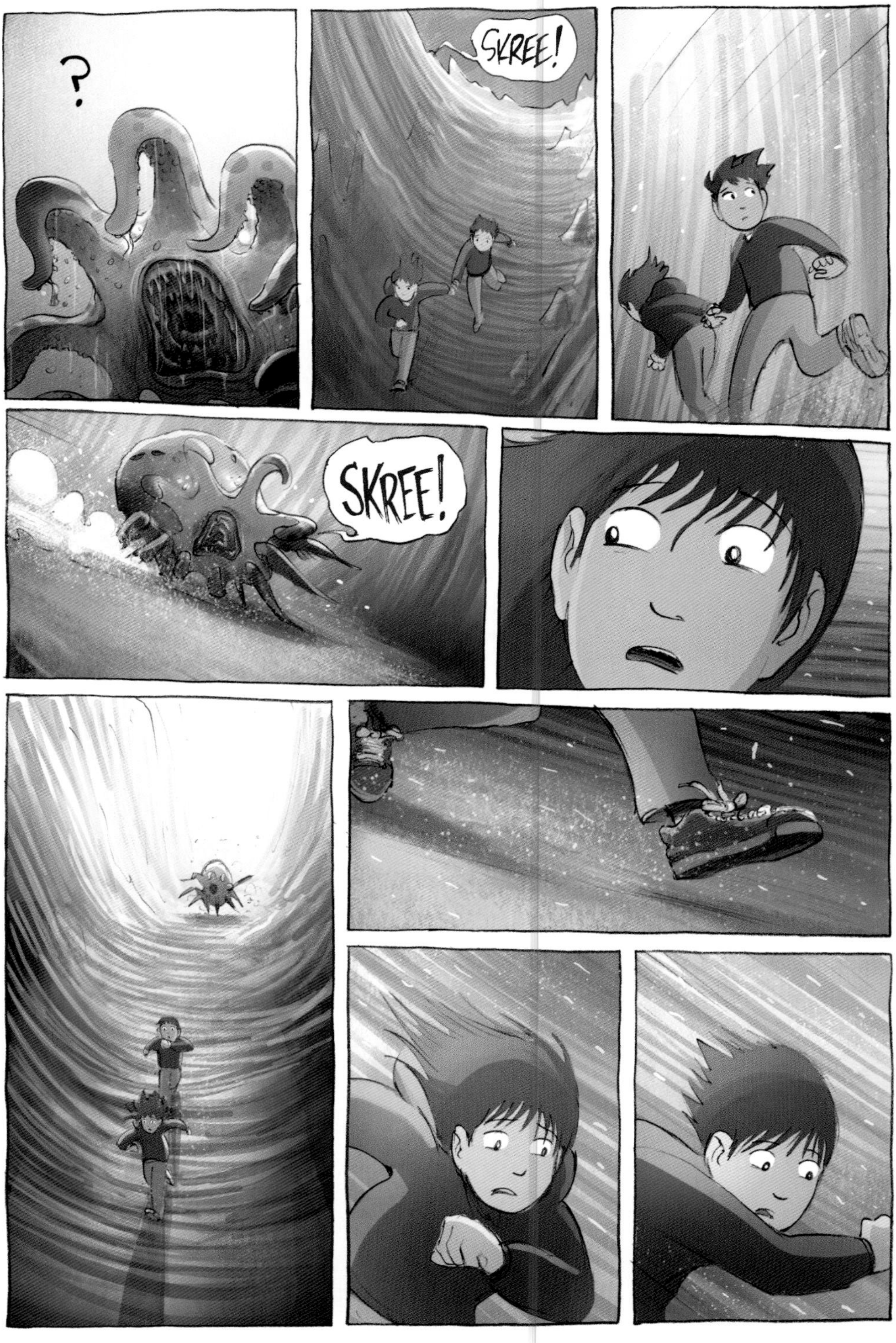
?
SKREE!
SKREE!

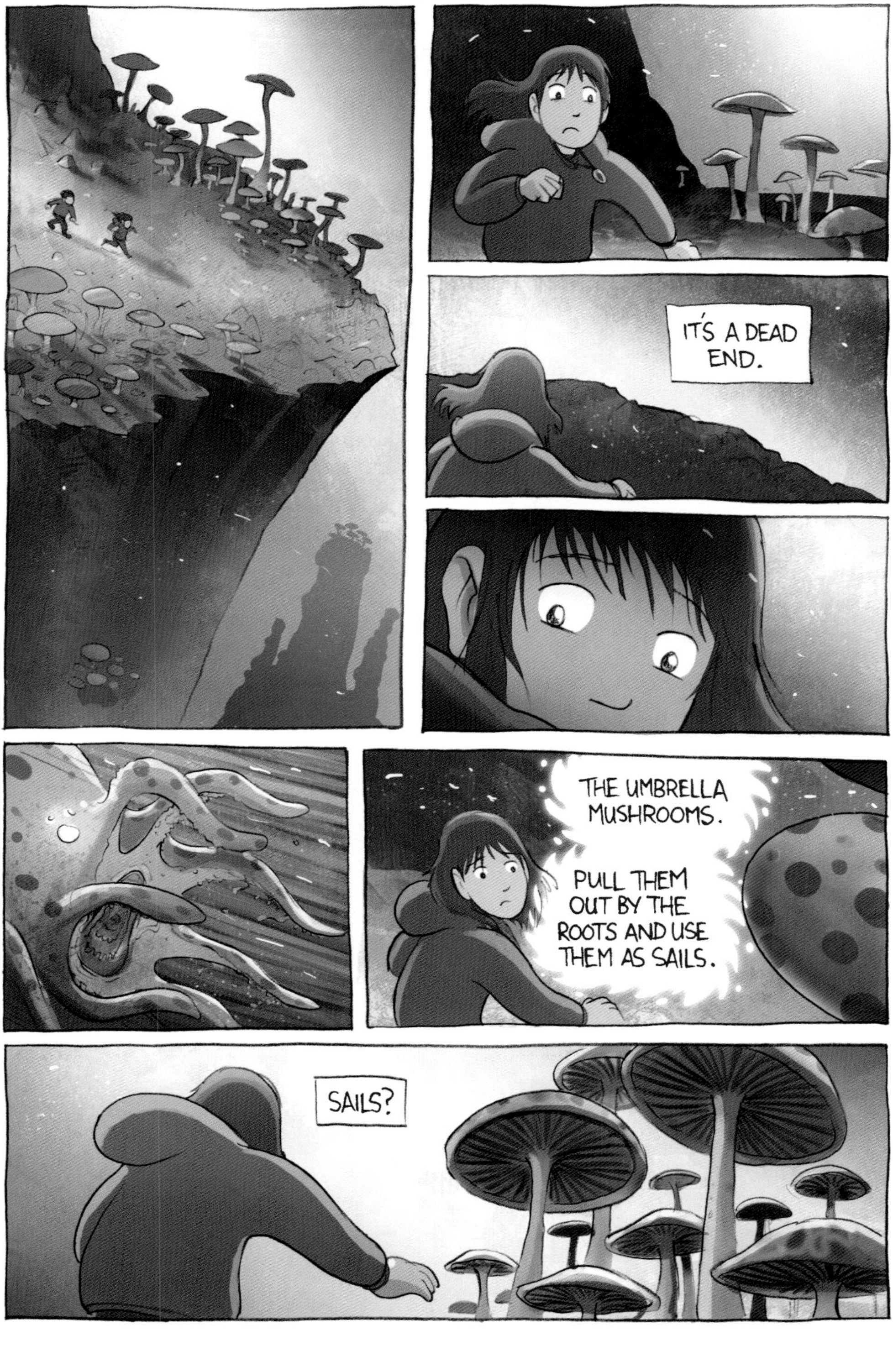
IT'S A DEAD END.
THE UMBRELLA MUSHROOMS.
PULL THEM OUT BY THE ROOTS AND USE THEM AS SAILS.
SAILS?

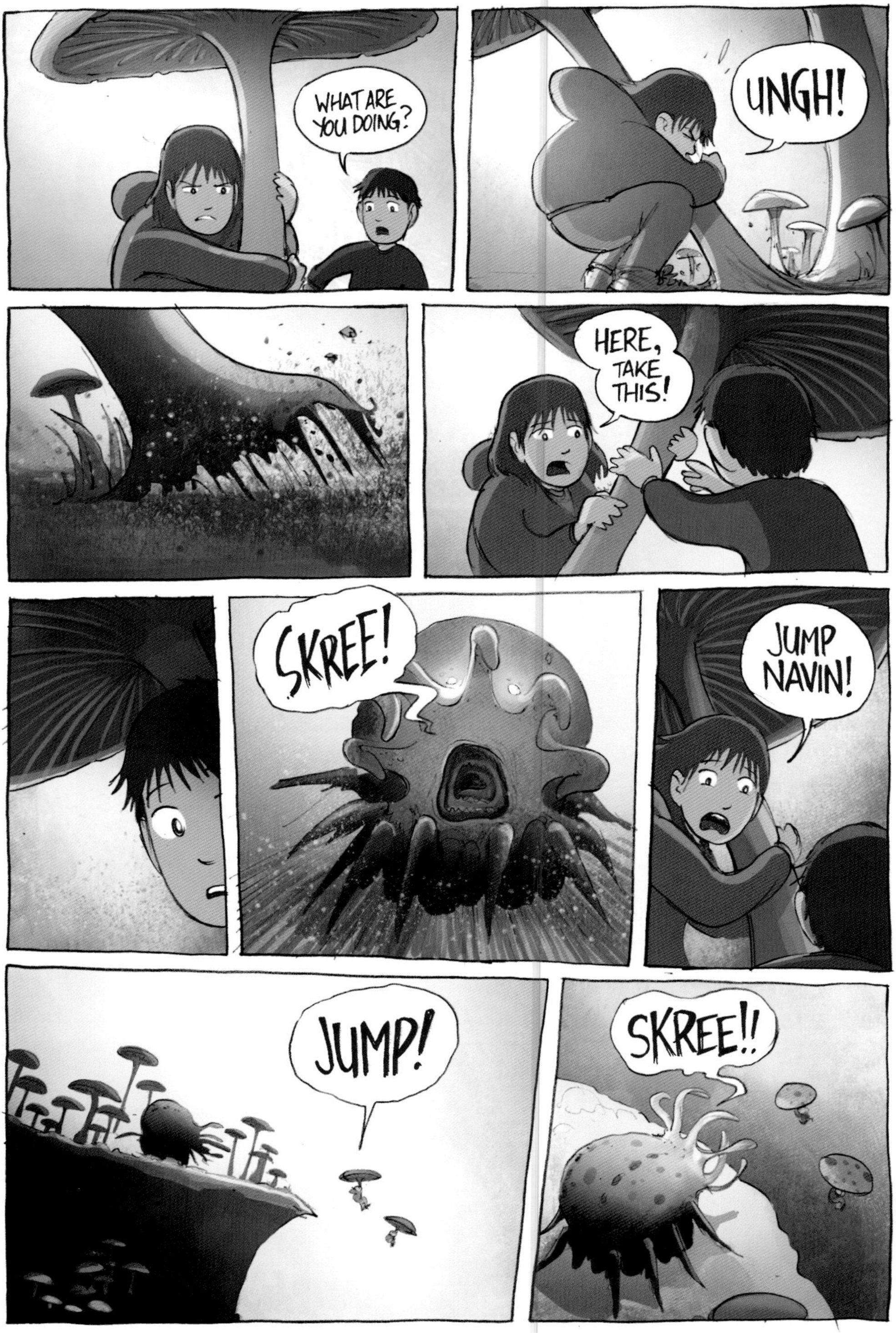
WHAT ARE YOU DOING?
UNGH!
HERE, TAKE THIS!
SKREE!
JUMP NAVIN!
JUMP!
SKREE!!

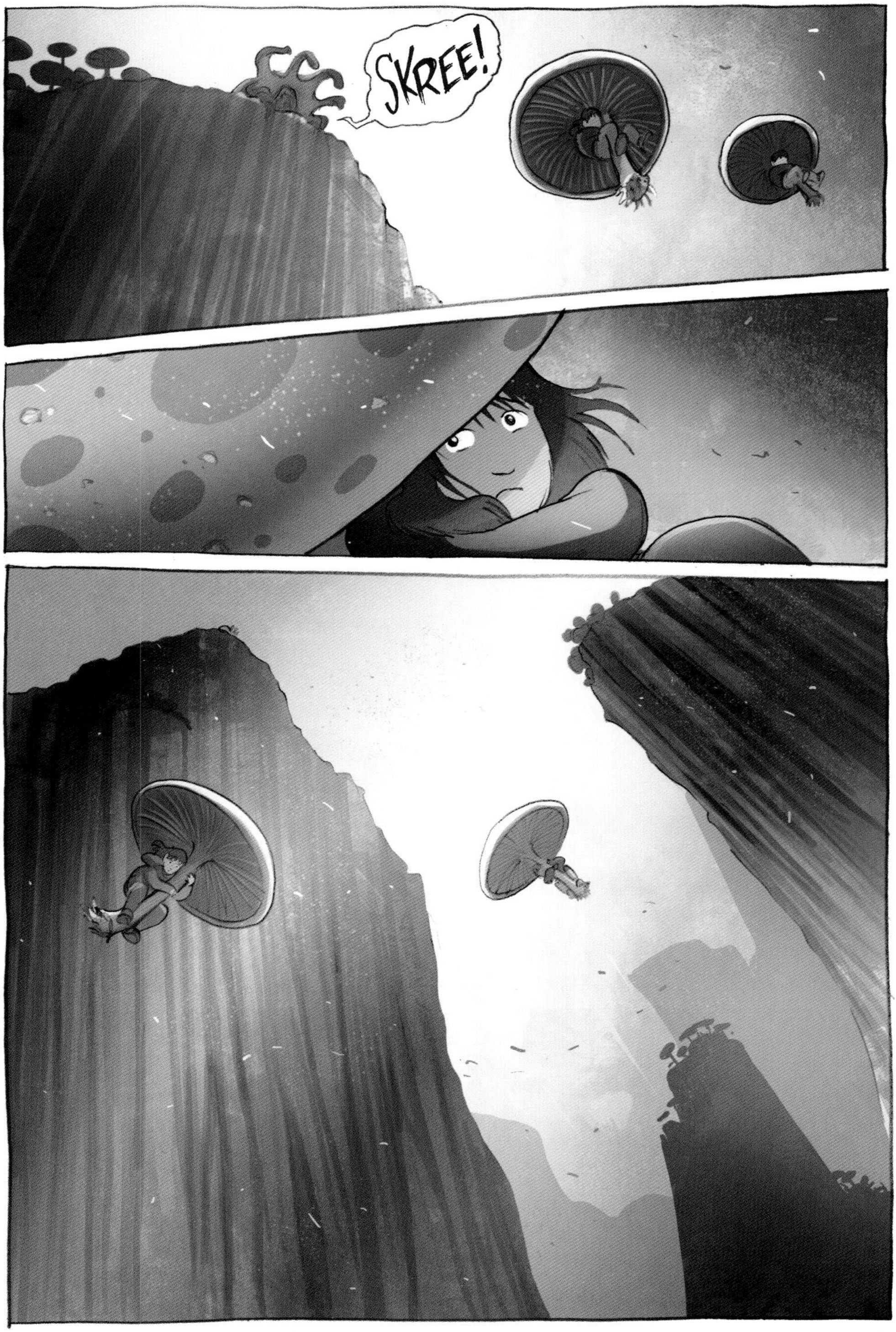
SKREE!

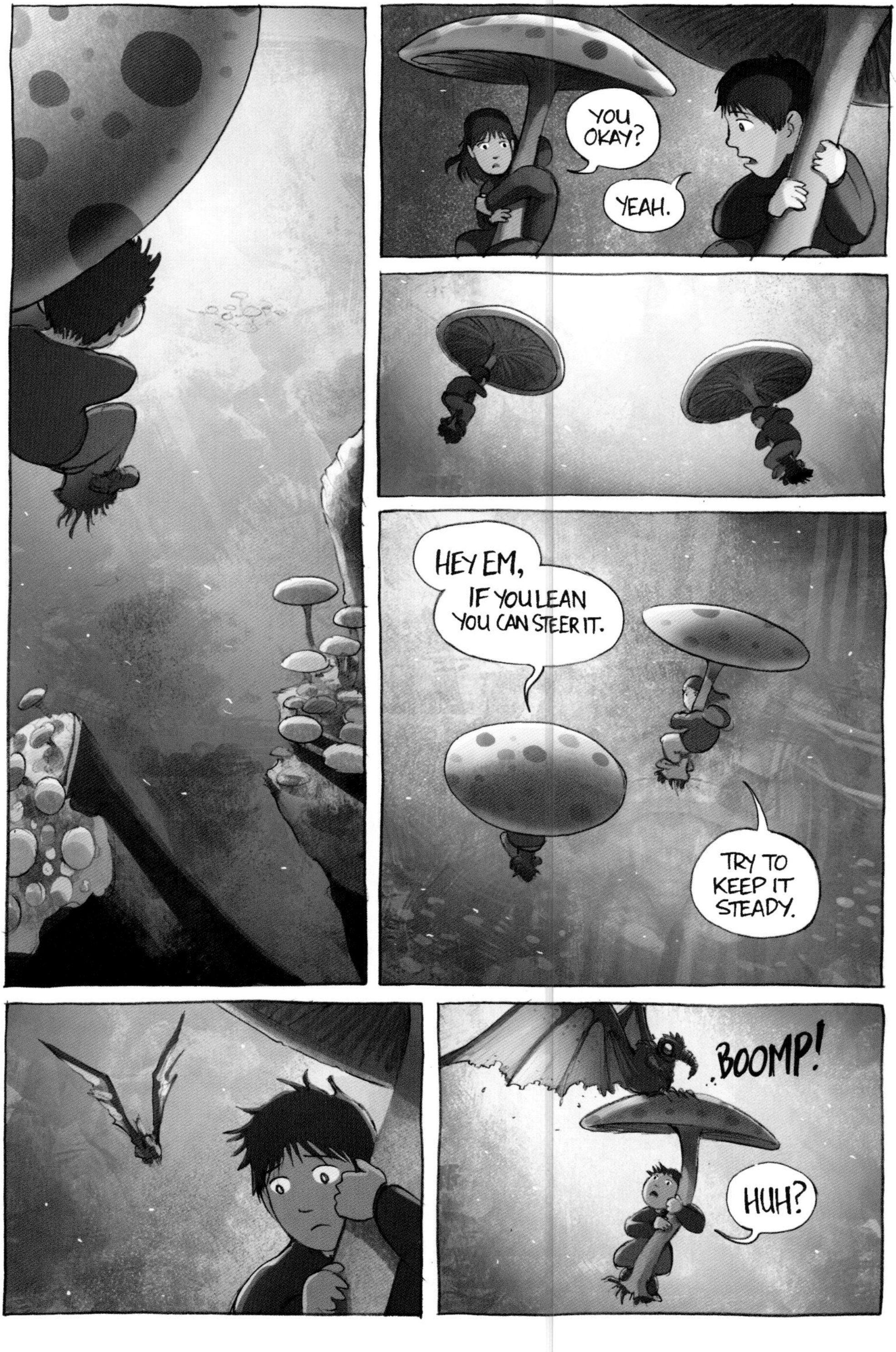

YOU OKAY?
YEAH.
HEY EM, IF YOU LEAN YOU CAN STEER IT.
TRY TO KEEP IT STEADY.
BOOMP!
HUH?

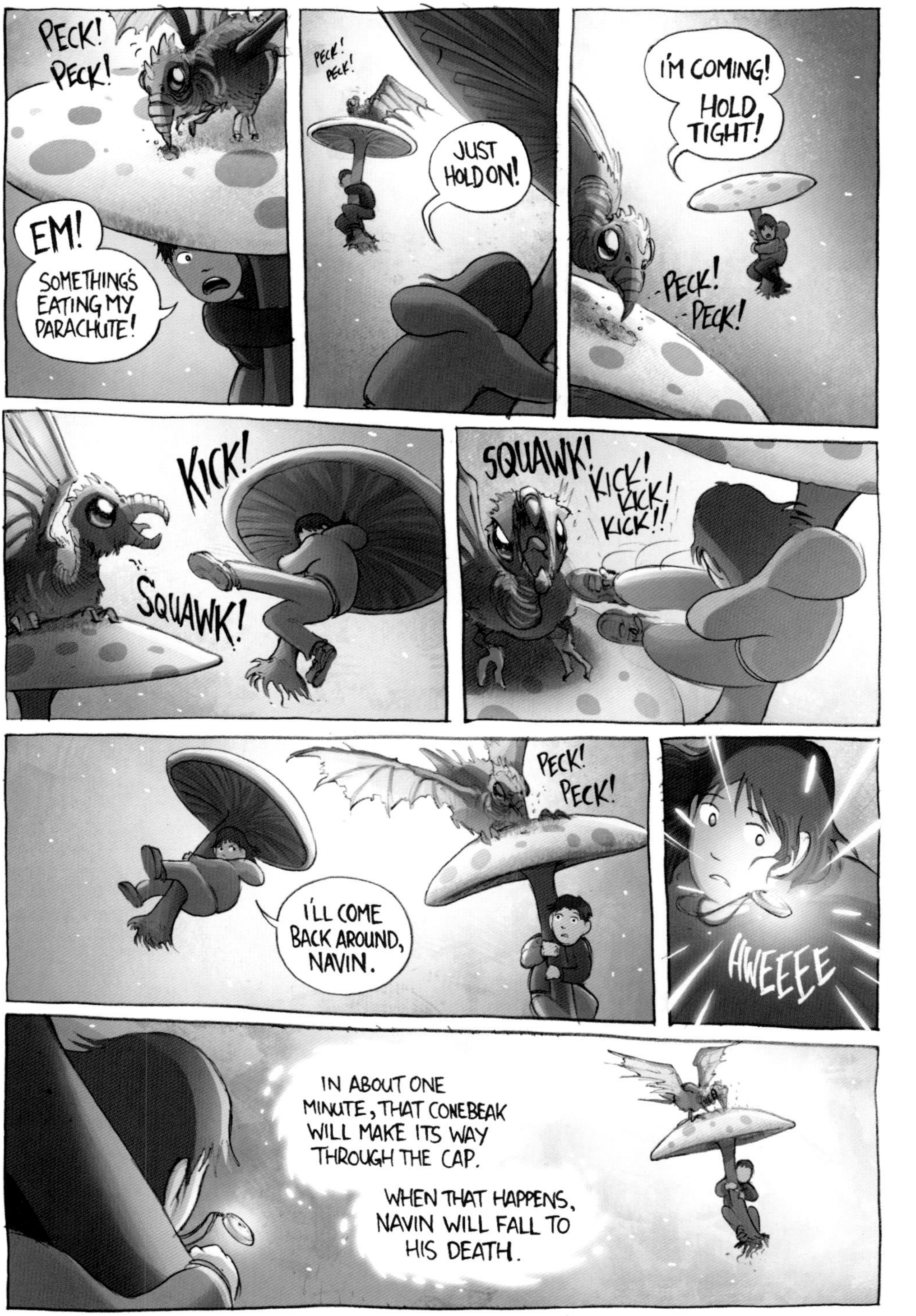
PECK! PECK!
EM!
SOMETHING'S EATING MY PARACHUTE!
PECK! PECK!
JUST HOLD ON!
I'M COMING! HOLD TIGHT!
PECK! PECK!
KICK!
SQUAWK!
SQUAWK!
KICK! KICK! KICK!!
PECK! PECK!
I'LL COME BACK AROUND, NAVIN.
HWEEEE
IN ABOUT ONE MINUTE, THAT CONEBEAK WILL MAKE ITS WAY THROUGH THE CAP.
WHEN THAT HAPPENS, NAVIN WILL FALL TO HIS DEATH.

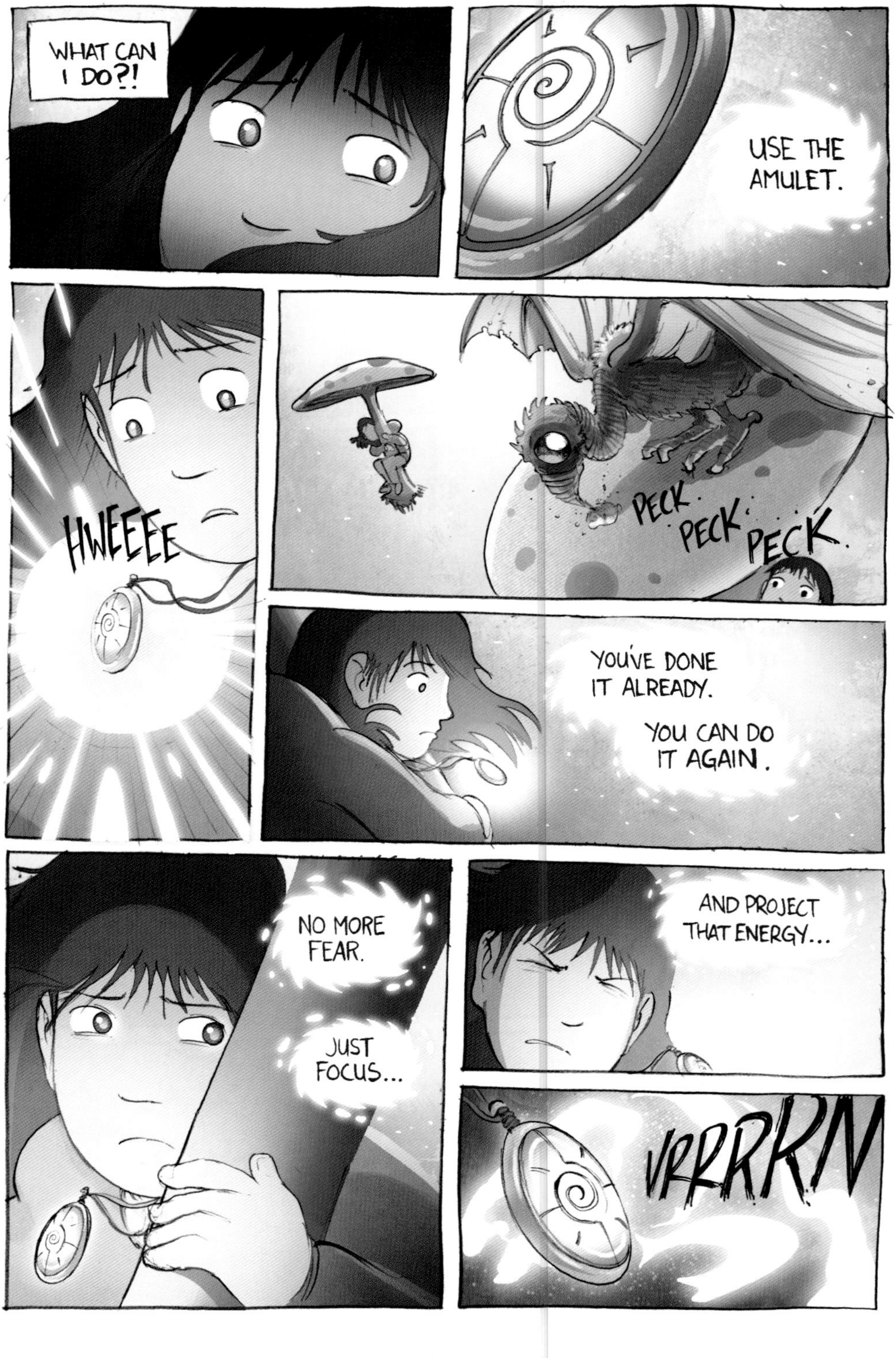
WHAT CAN I DO?!
USE THE AMULET.
HWEEEE
PECK. PECK. PECK.
YOU'VE DONE IT ALREADY.
YOU CAN DO IT AGAIN.
NO MORE FEAR.
JUST FOCUS...
AND PROJECT THAT ENERGY...
VRRRKN

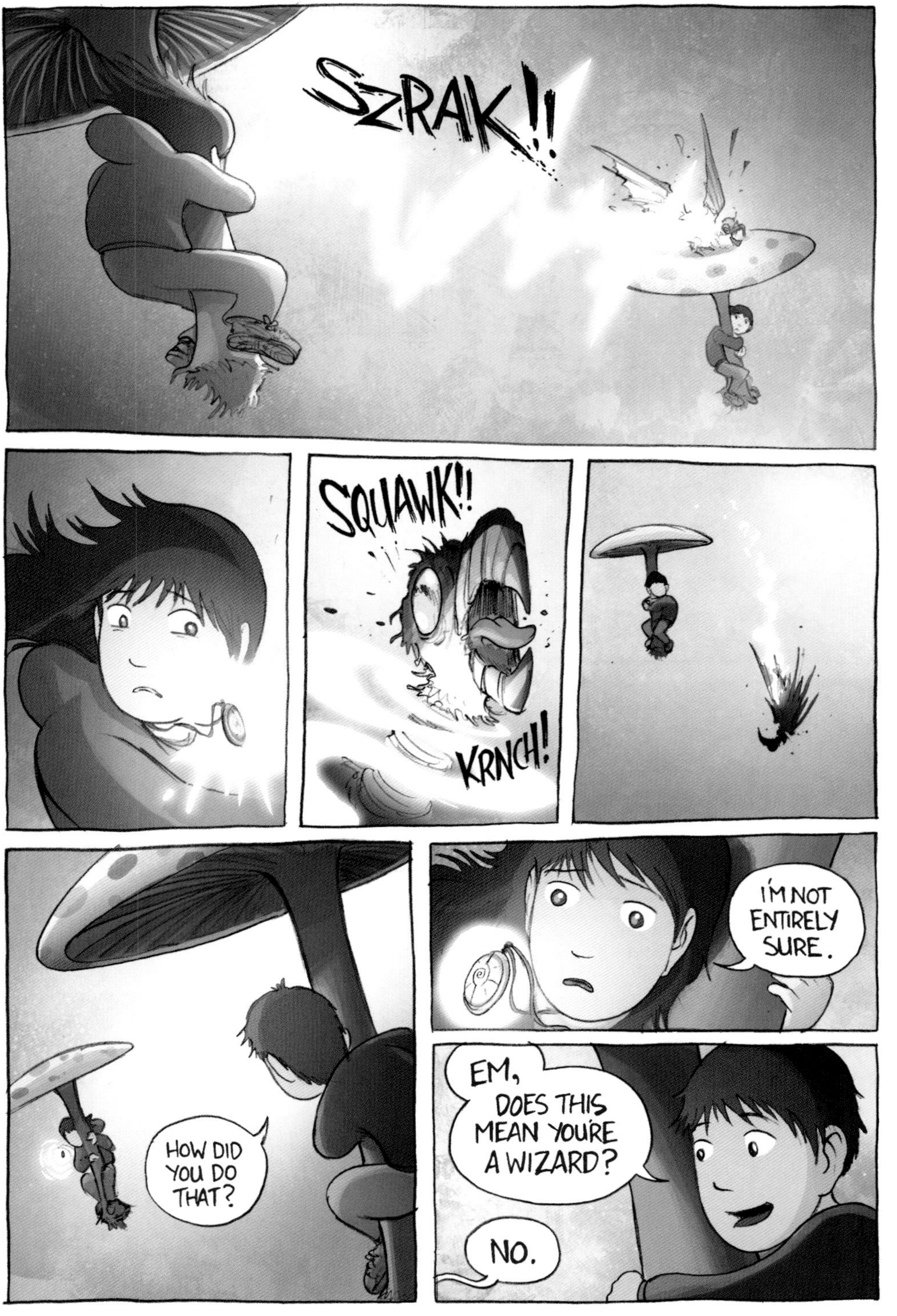
SZRAK!!
SQUAWK!!
KRNCH!
I'M NOT ENTIRELY SURE.
HOW DID YOU DO THAT?
EM, DOES THIS MEAN YOU'RE A WIZARD?
NO.

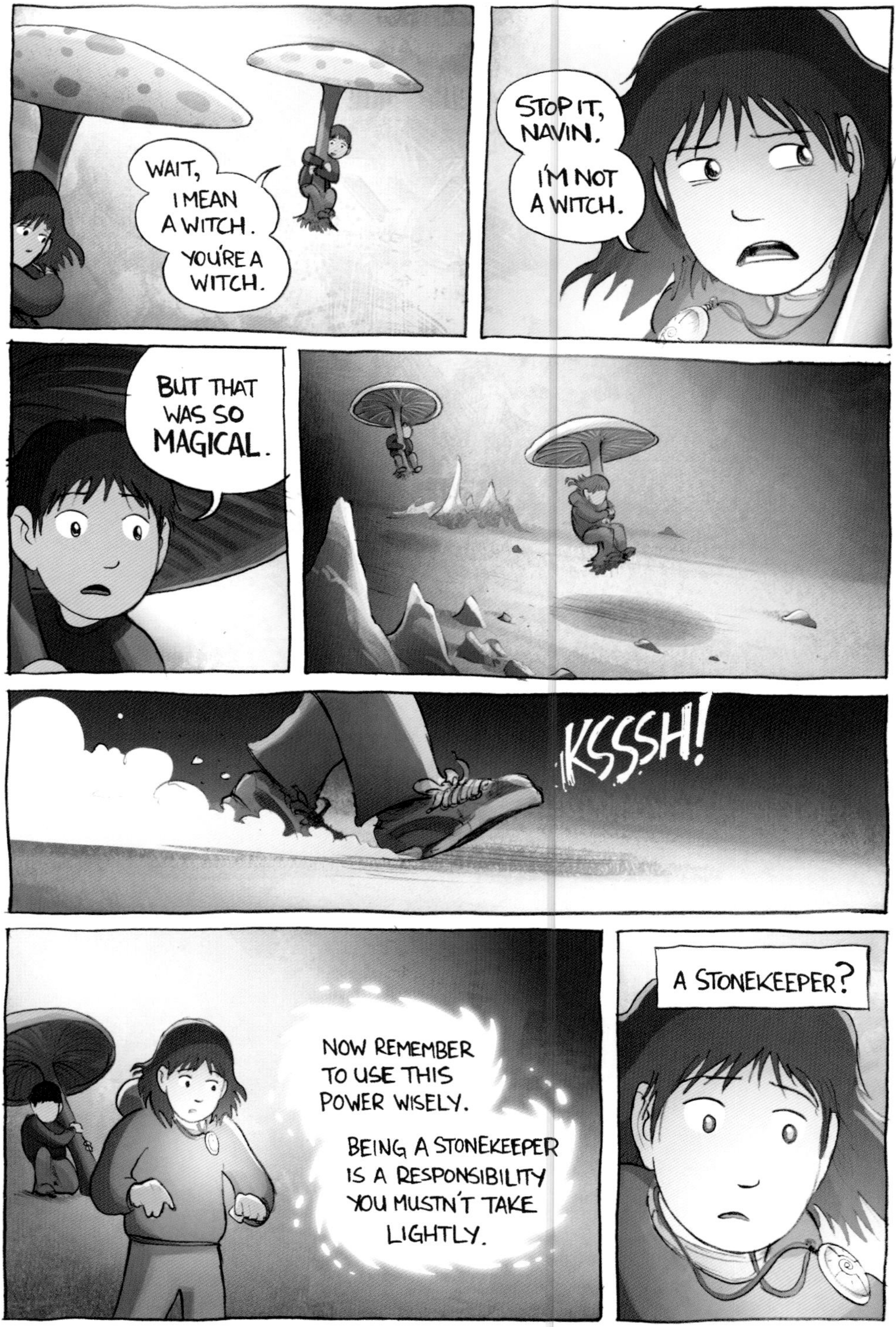
WAIT, I MEAN A WITCH. YOU'RE A WITCH.
STOP IT, NAVIN.
I'M NOT A WITCH.
BUT THAT WAS SO MAGICAL.
KSSSH!
NOW REMEMBER TO USE THIS POWER WISELY.
BEING A STONEKEEPER IS A RESPONSIBILITY YOU MUSTN'T TAKE LIGHTLY.
A STONEKEEPER?

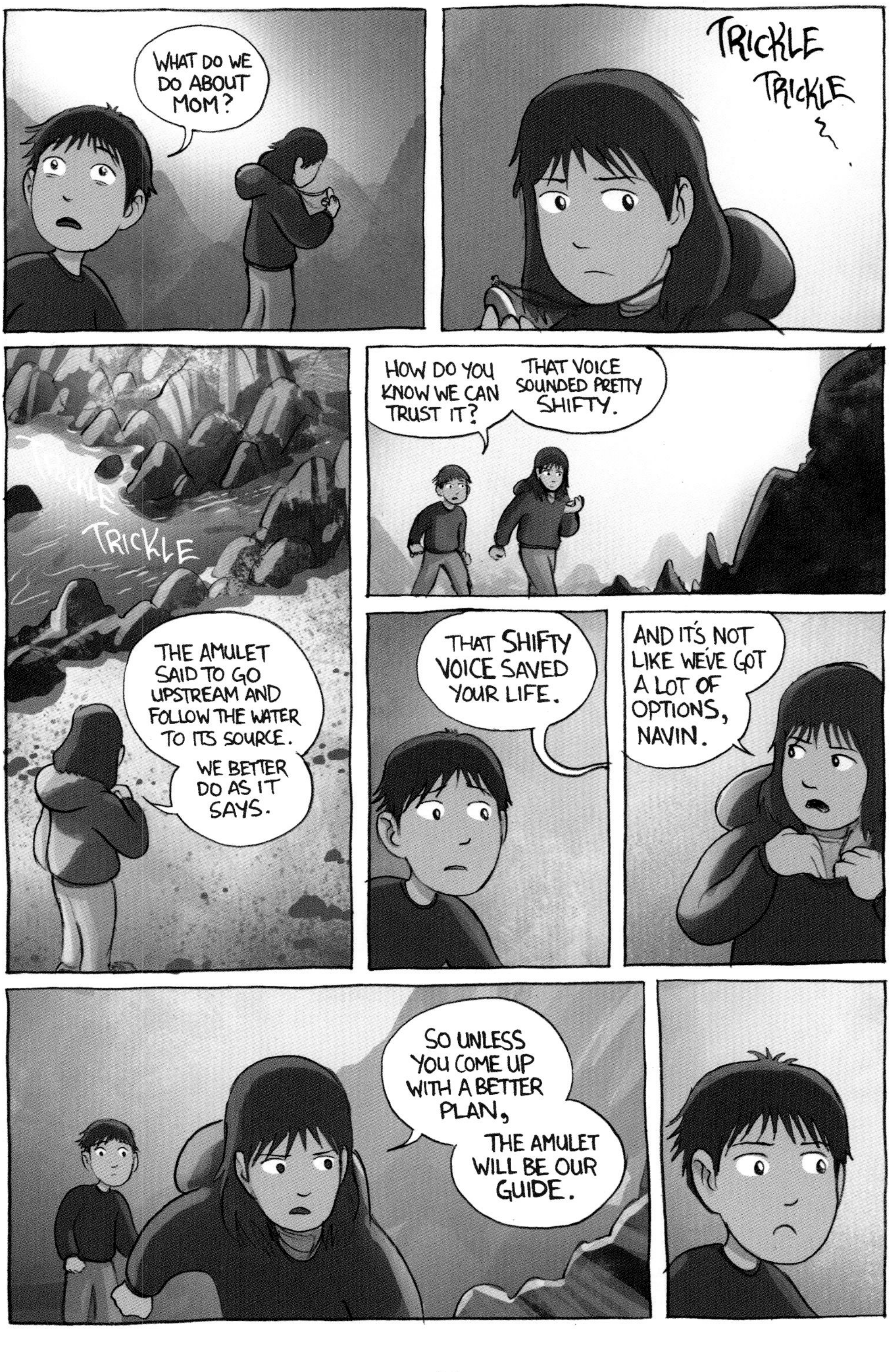
WHAT DO WE DO ABOUT MOM?
TRICKLE
TRICKLE
TRICKLE
TRICKLE
THE AMULET SAID TO GO UPSTREAM AND FOLLOW THE WATER TO ITS SOURCE.
WE BETTER DO AS IT SAYS.
HOW DO YOU KNOW WE CAN TRUST IT?
THAT VOICE SOUNDED PRETTY SHIFTY.
THAT SHIFTY VOICE SAVED YOUR LIFE.
AND IT'S NOT LIKE WE'VE GOT A LOT OF OPTIONS, NAVIN.
SO UNLESS YOU COME UP WITH A BETTER PLAN,
THE AMULET WILL BE OUR GUIDE.

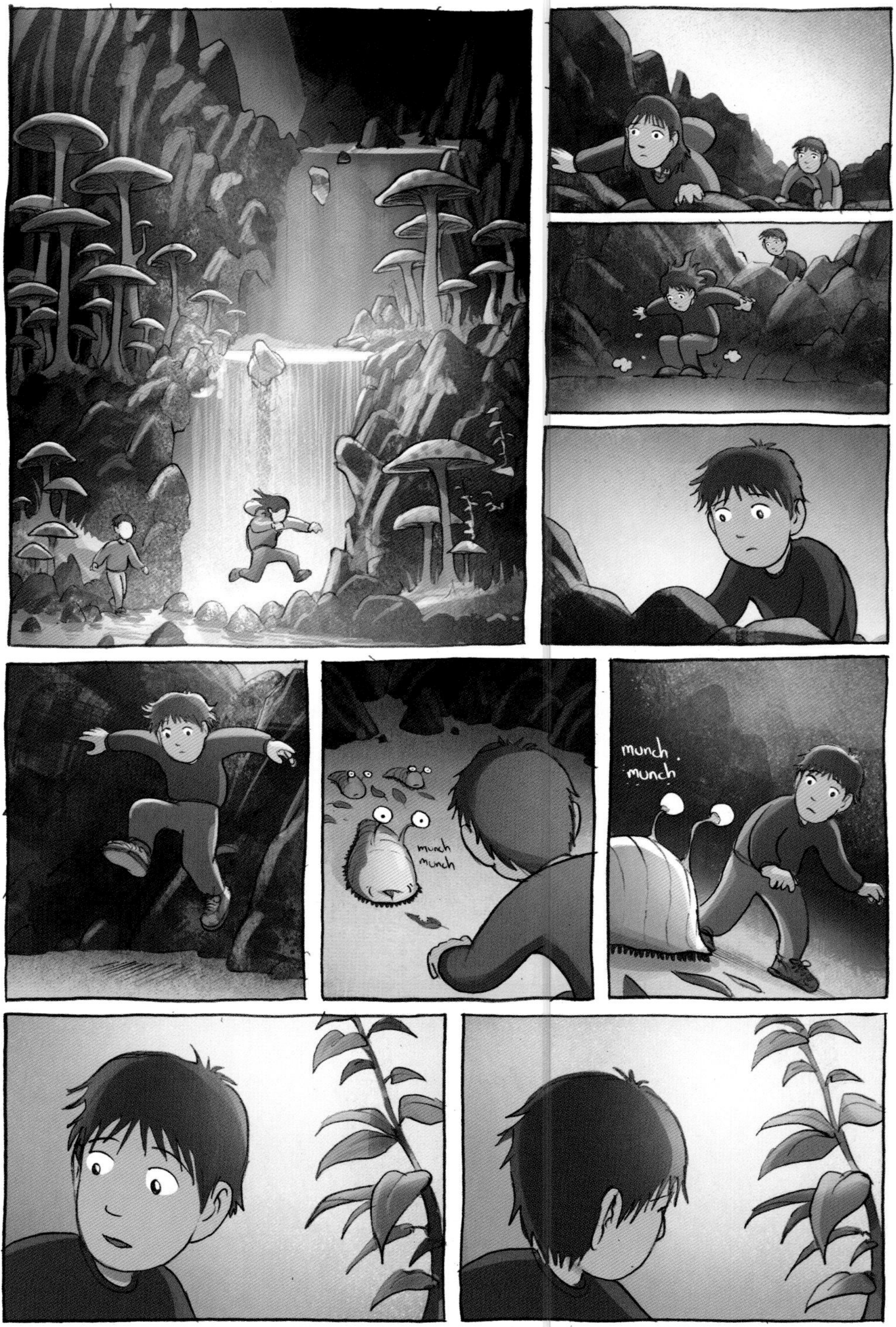
munch
munch
munch.
munch

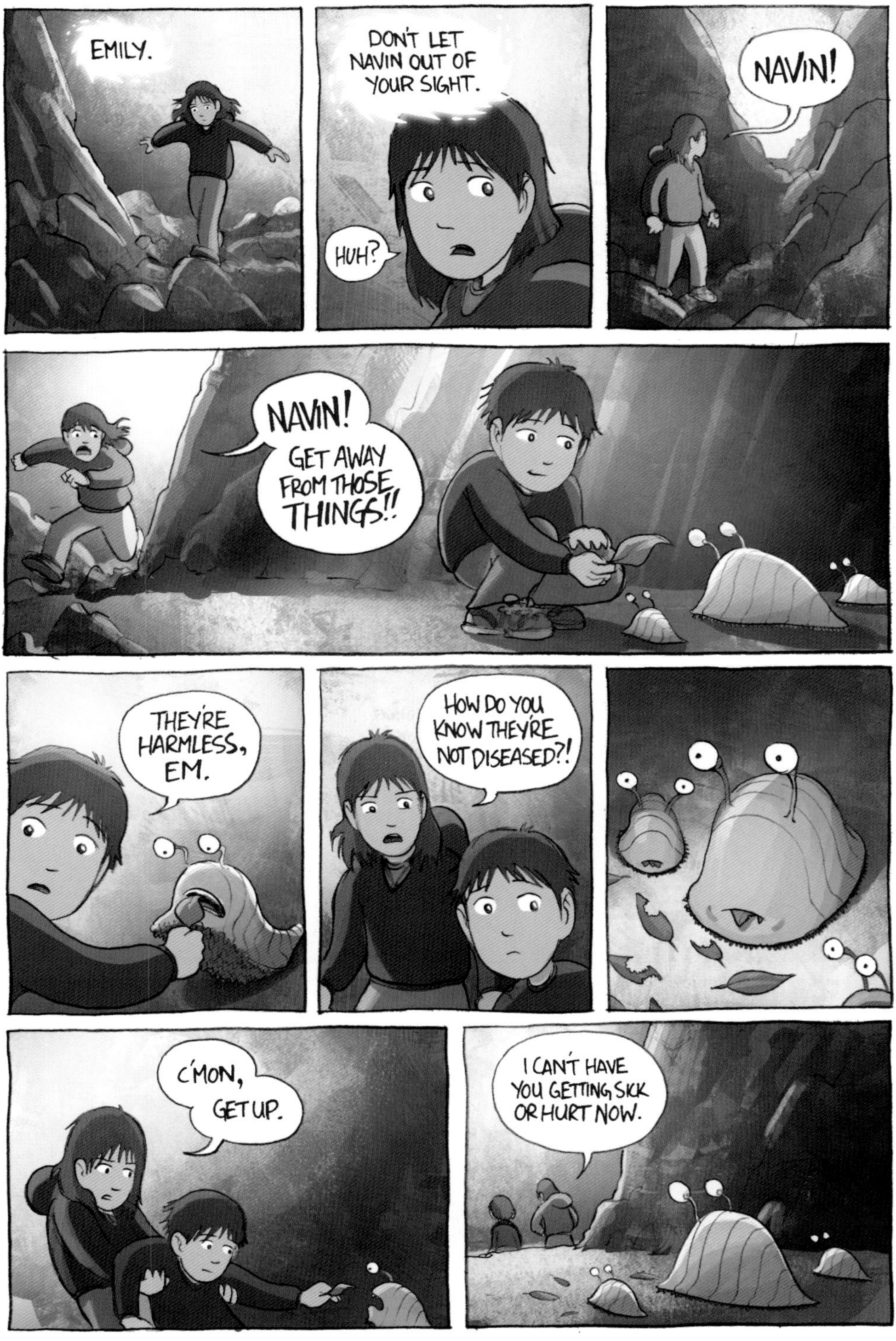
EMILY.
DON'T LET NAVIN OUT OF YOUR SIGHT.
HUH?
NAVIN!
NAVIN! GET AWAY FROM THOSE THINGS!!
THEY'RE HARMLESS, EM.
HOW DO YOU KNOW THEY'RE NOT DISEASED?!
C'MON, GET UP.
I CAN'T HAVE YOU GETTING SICK OR HURT NOW.

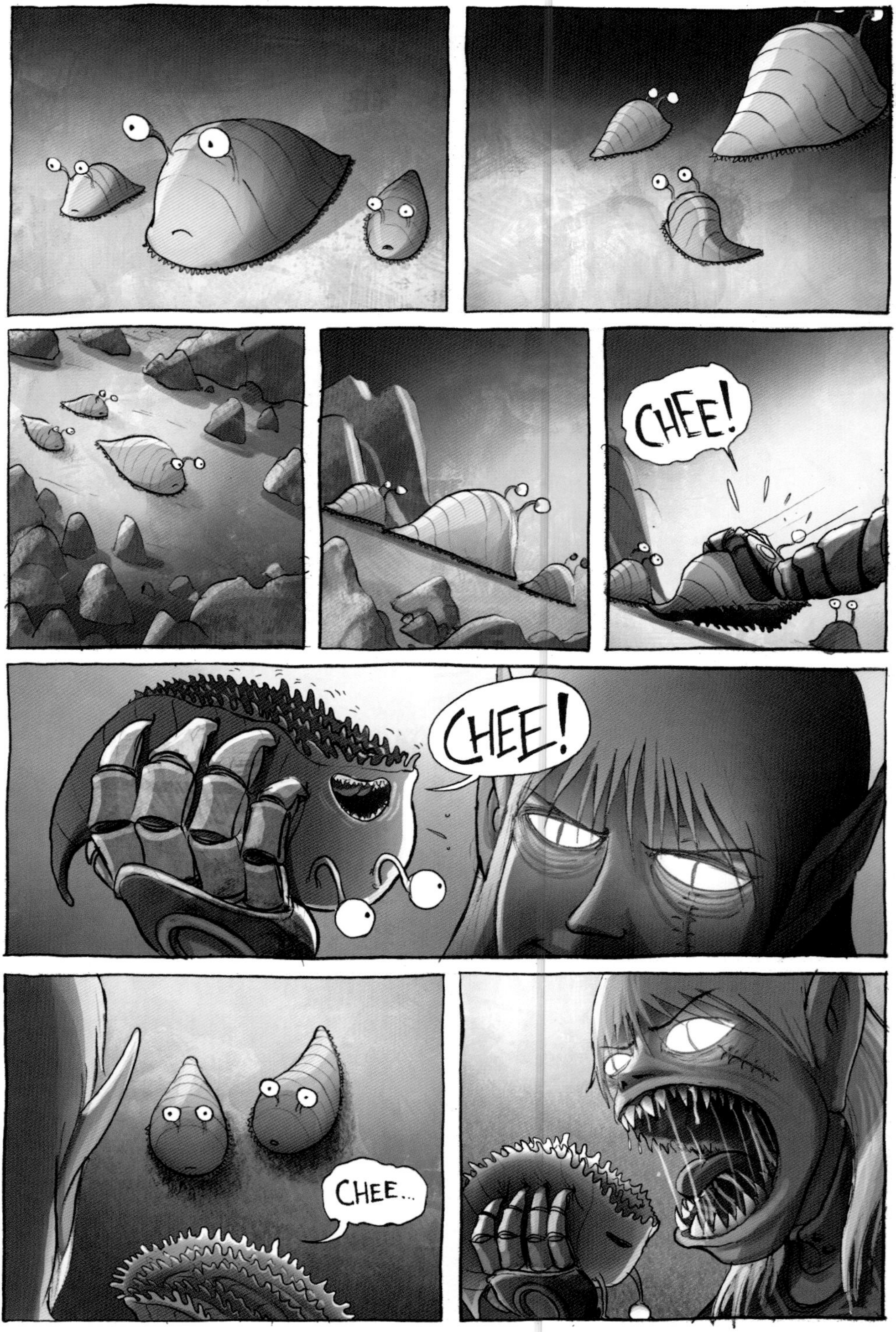
CHEE!
CHEE!
CHEE...

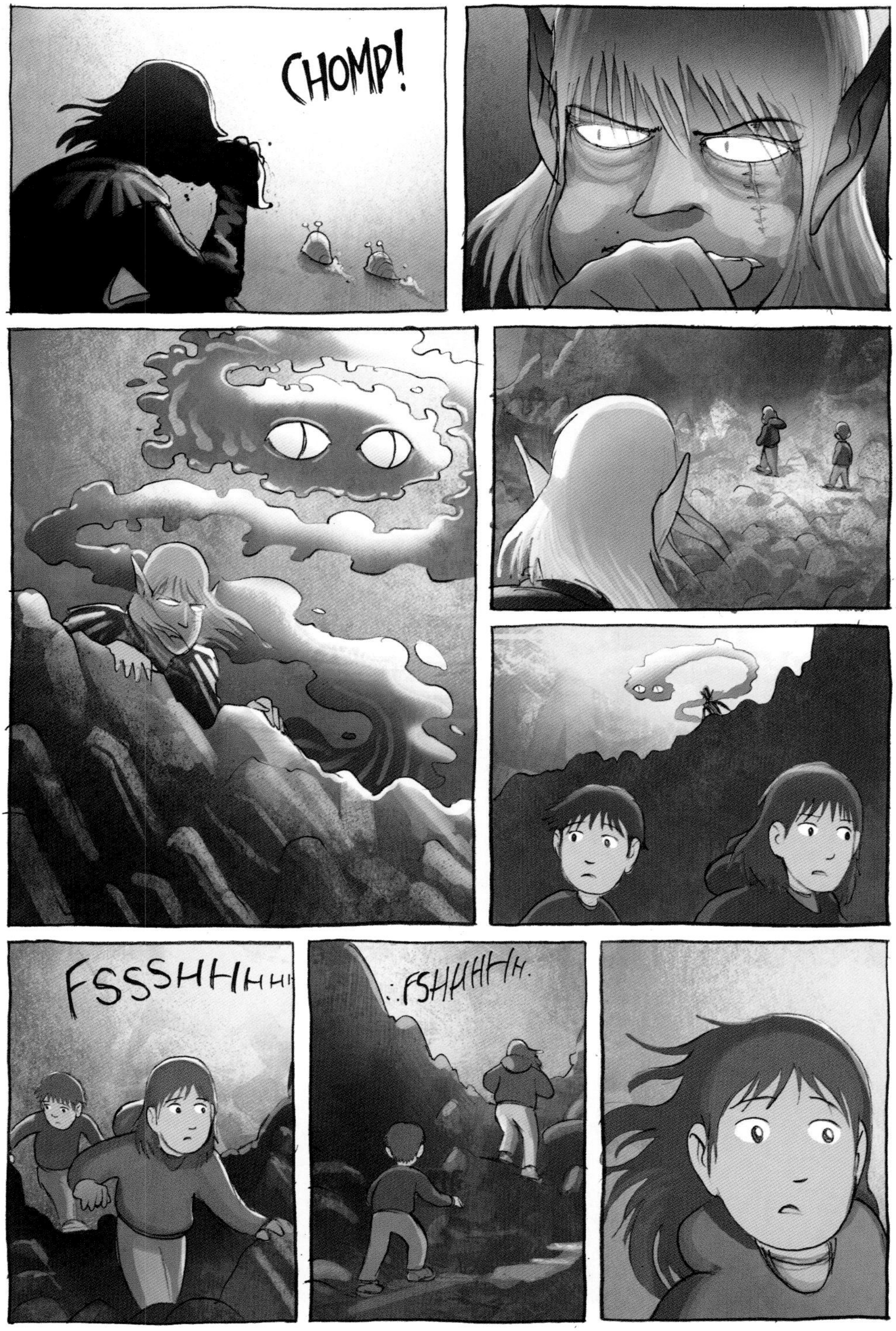

CHOMP!
FSSSHHhhh
.:.FSHHHHh.

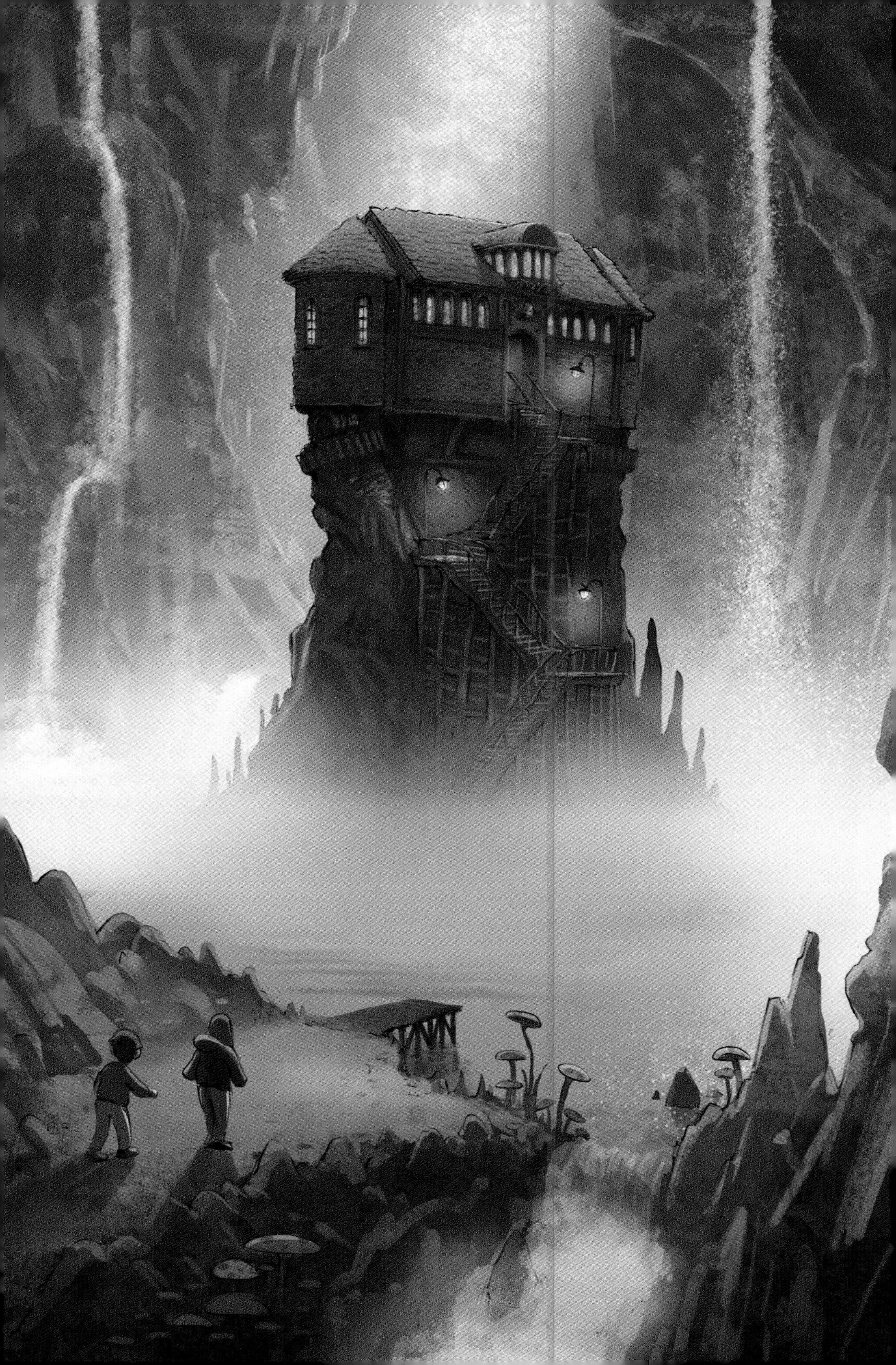

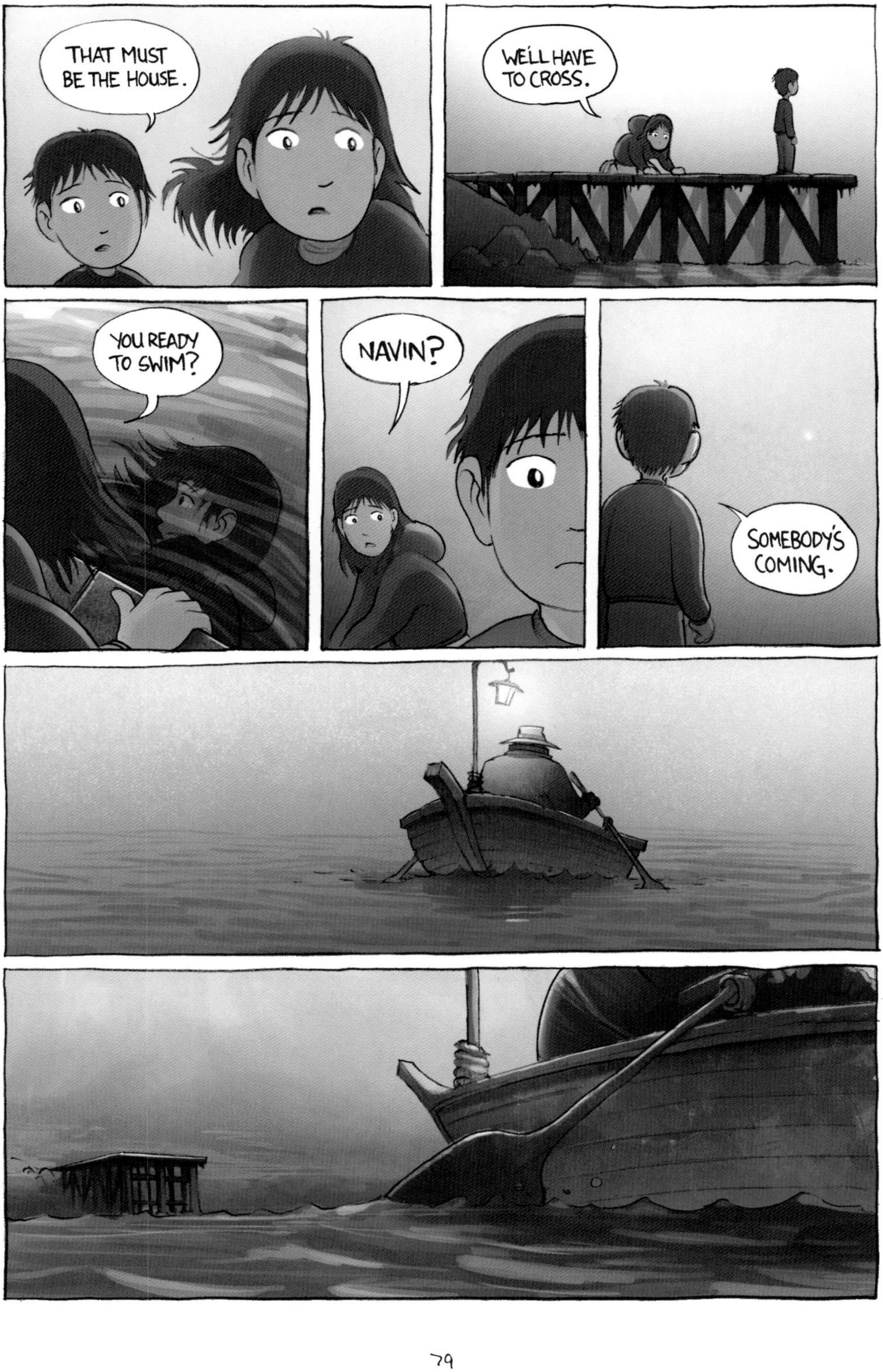
THAT MUST BE THE HOUSE.
WE'LL HAVE TO CROSS.
YOU READY TO SWIM?
NAVIN?
SOMEBODY'S COMING.

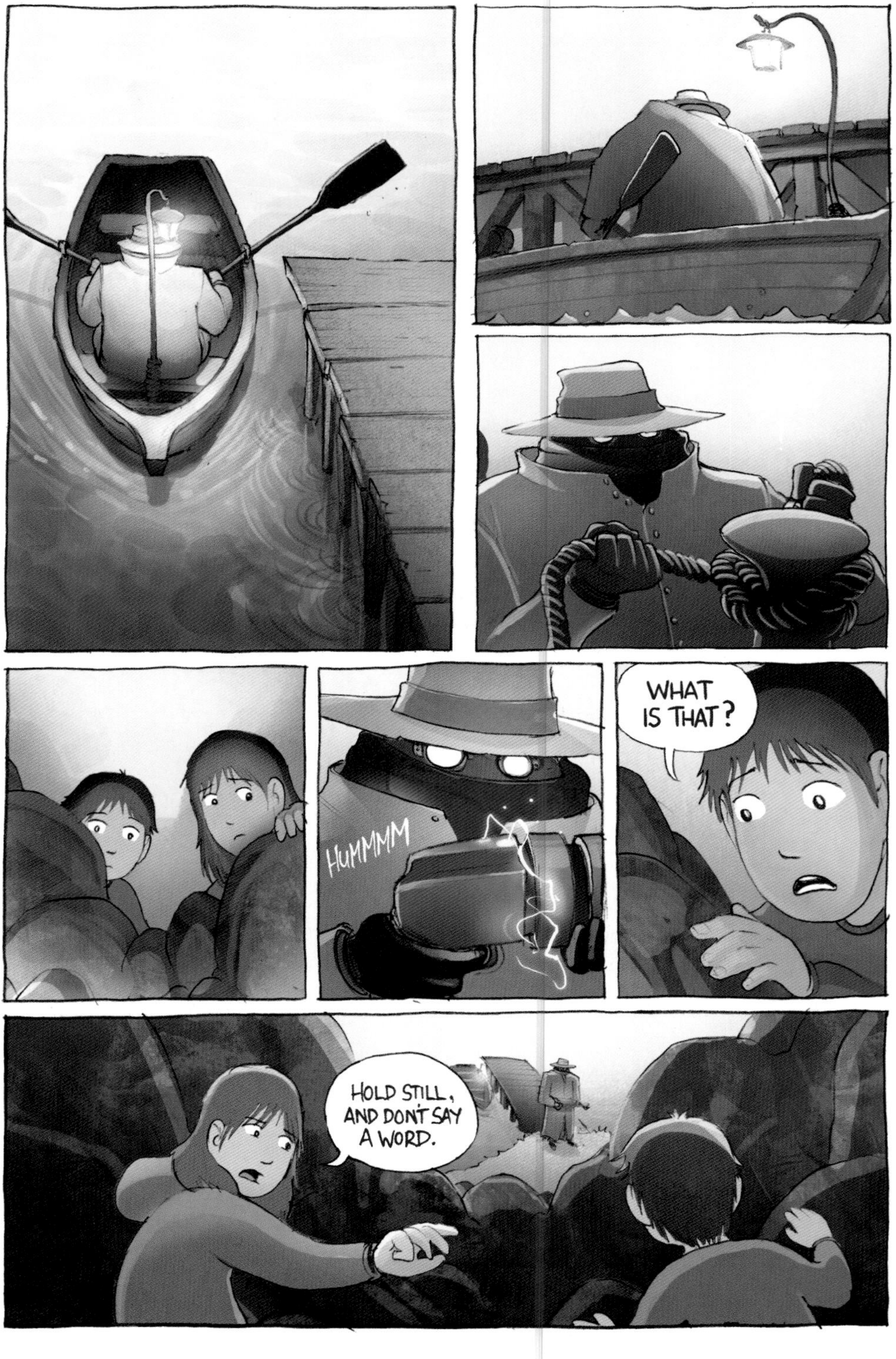
HUMMMM
WHAT IS THAT?
HOLD STILL, AND DON'T SAY A WORD.

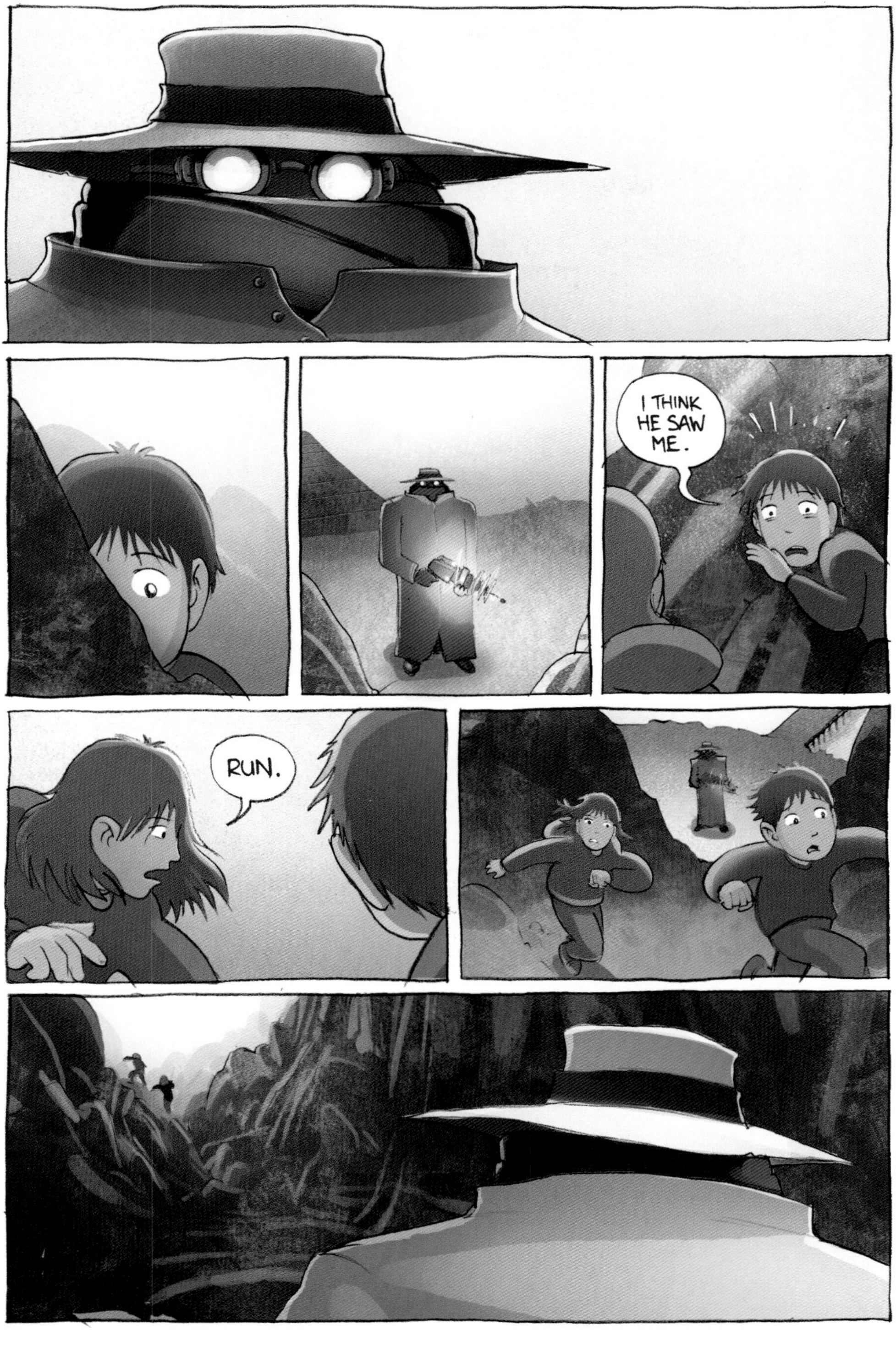
I THINK HE SAW ME.
RUN.

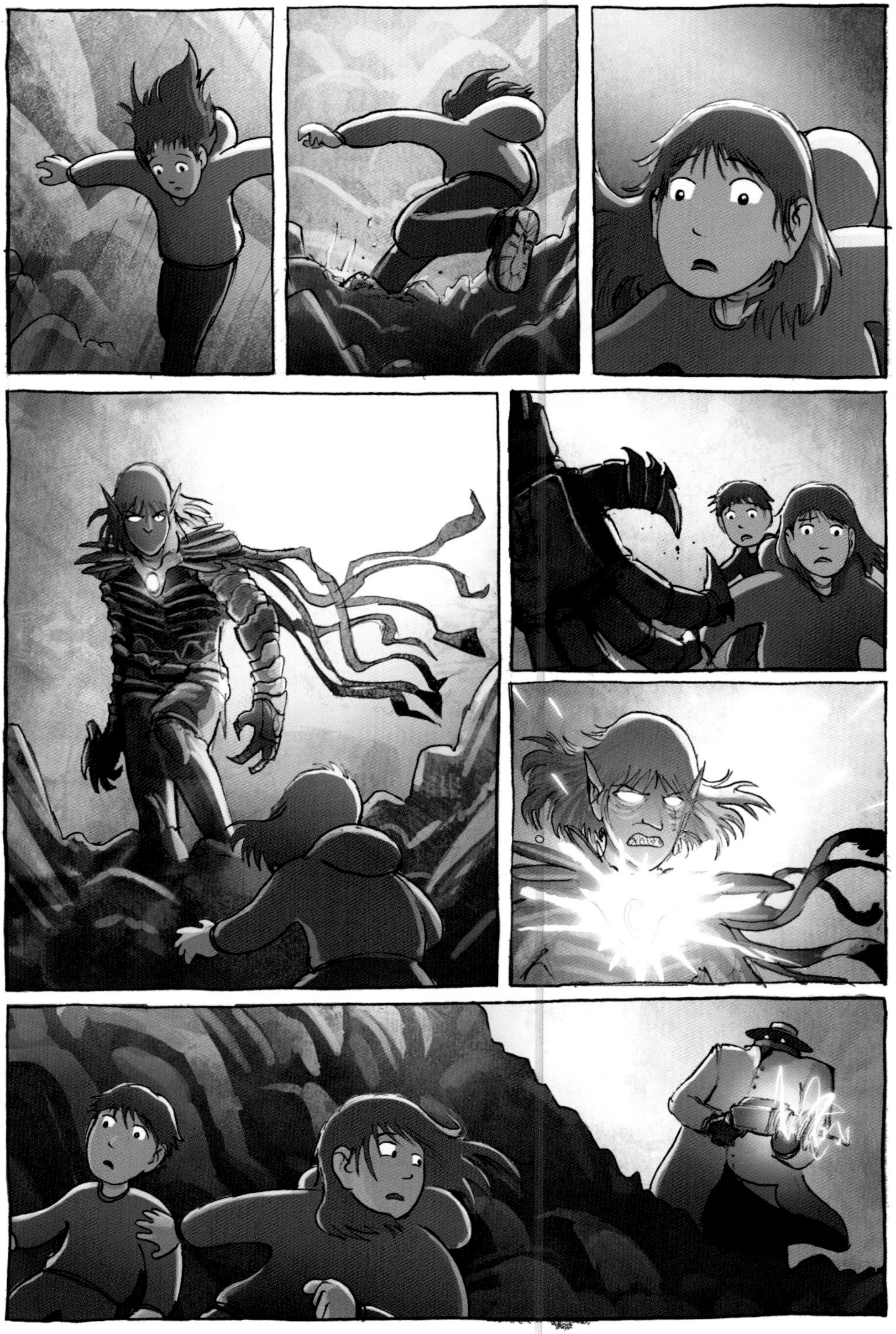

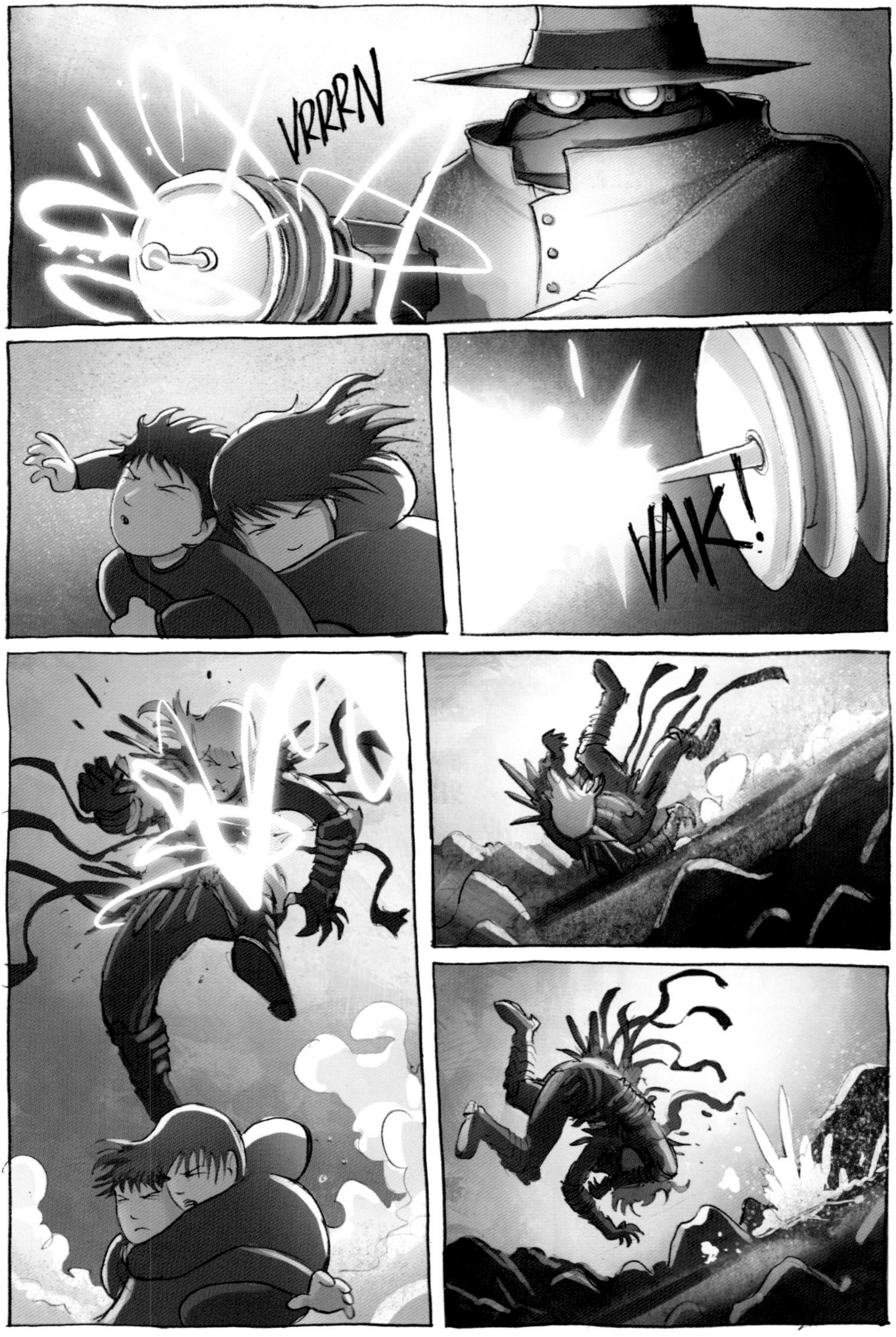
VRRRN
VAK!

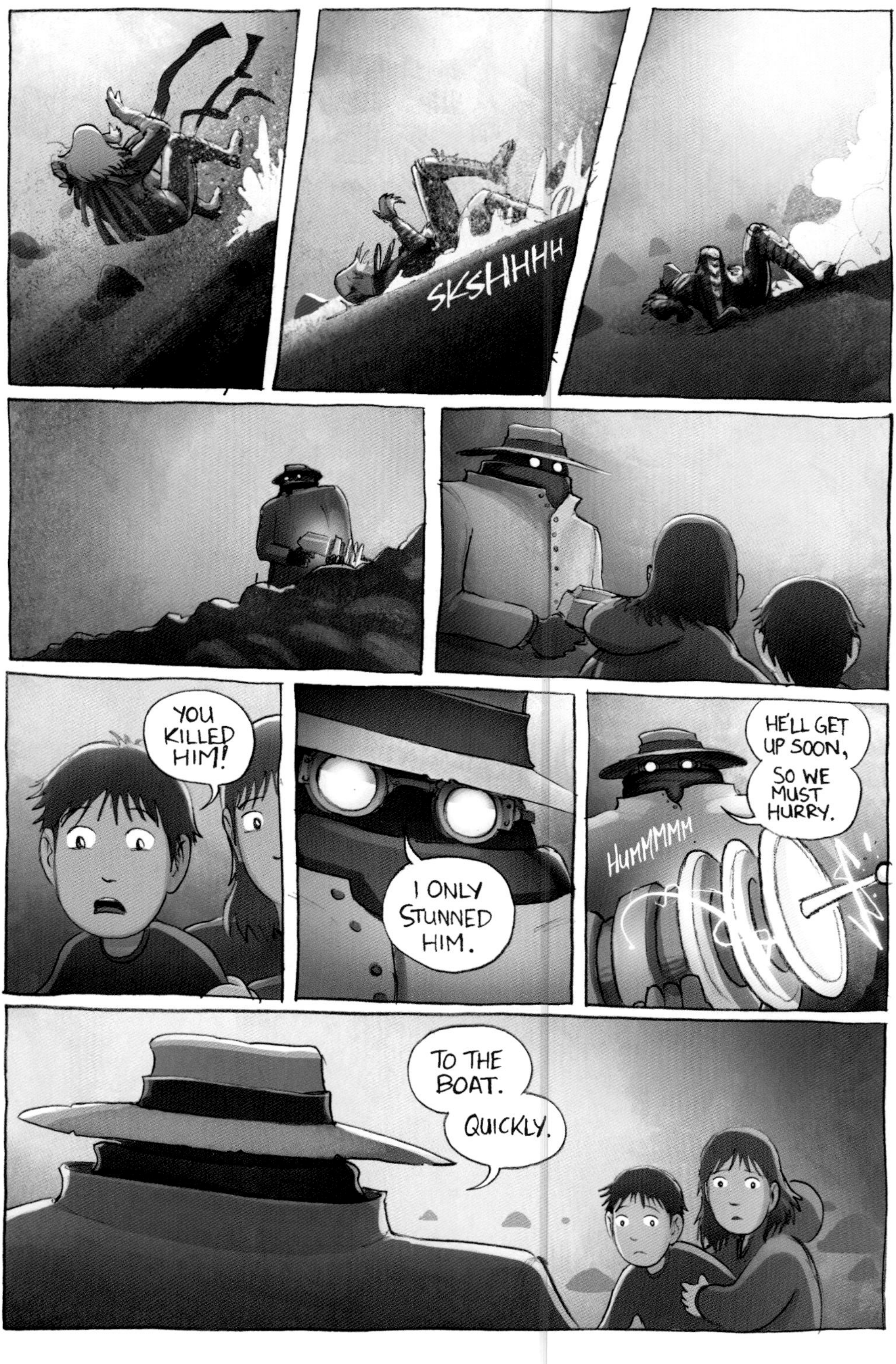
SKSHHHH
YOU KILLED HIM!
I ONLY STUNNED HIM.
HE'LL GET UP SOON, SO WE MUST HURRY.
HUMMMMM
TO THE BOAT. QUICKLY.

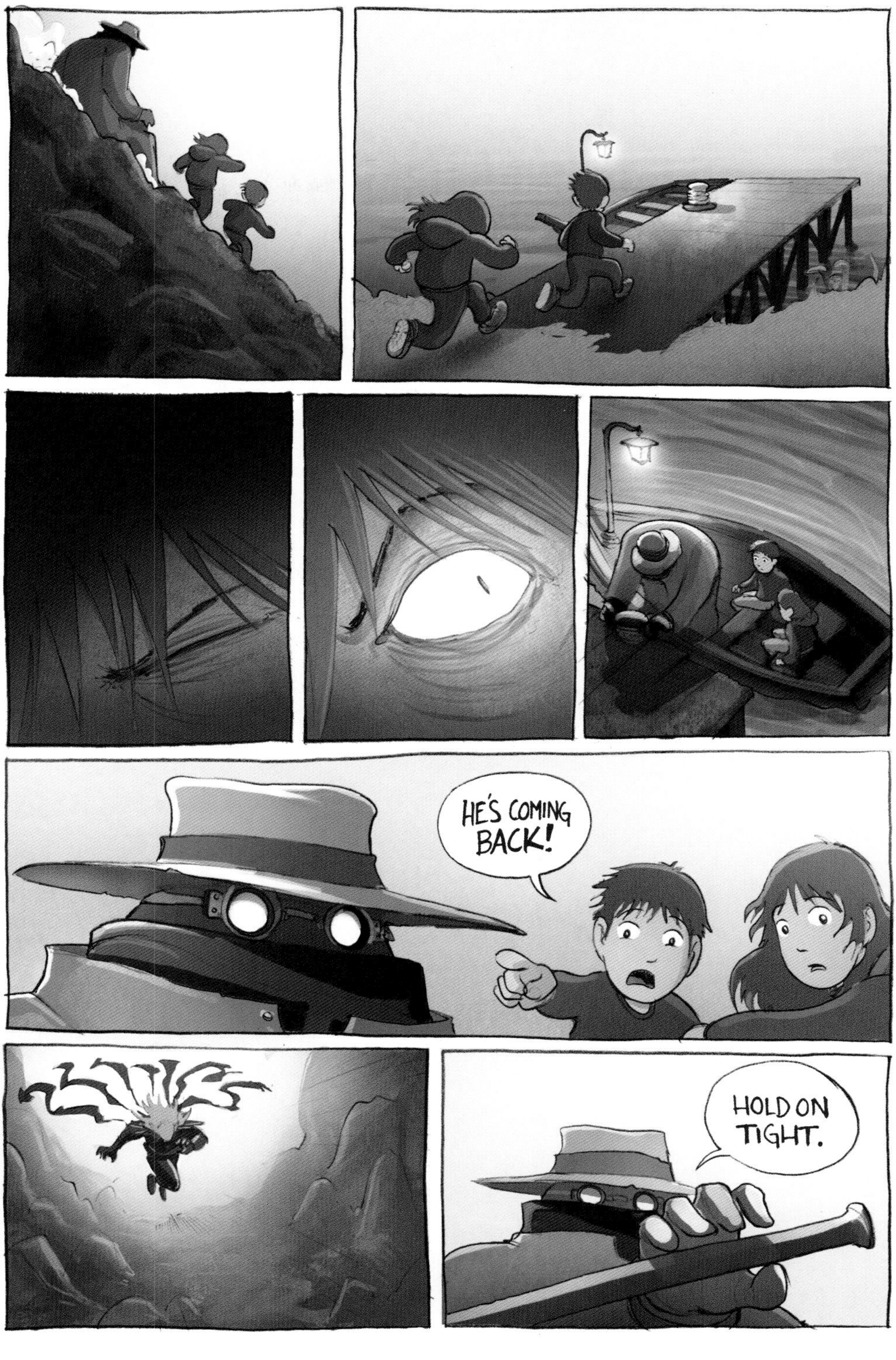
HE'S COMING BACK!
HOLD ON TIGHT.

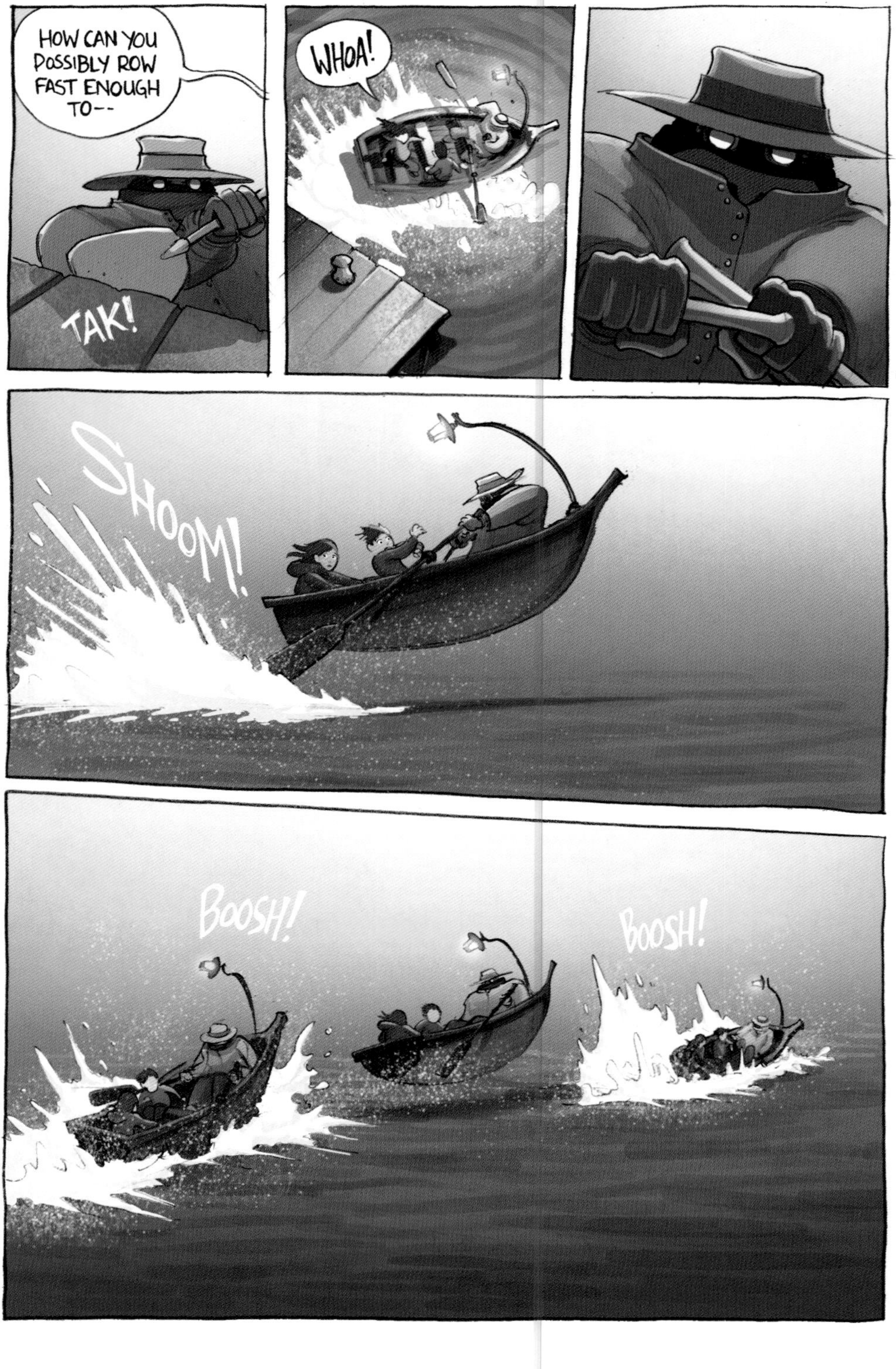
HOW CAN YOU POSSIBLY ROW FAST ENOUGH TO--
TAK!
WHOA!
SHOOM!
BOOSH!
BOOSH!

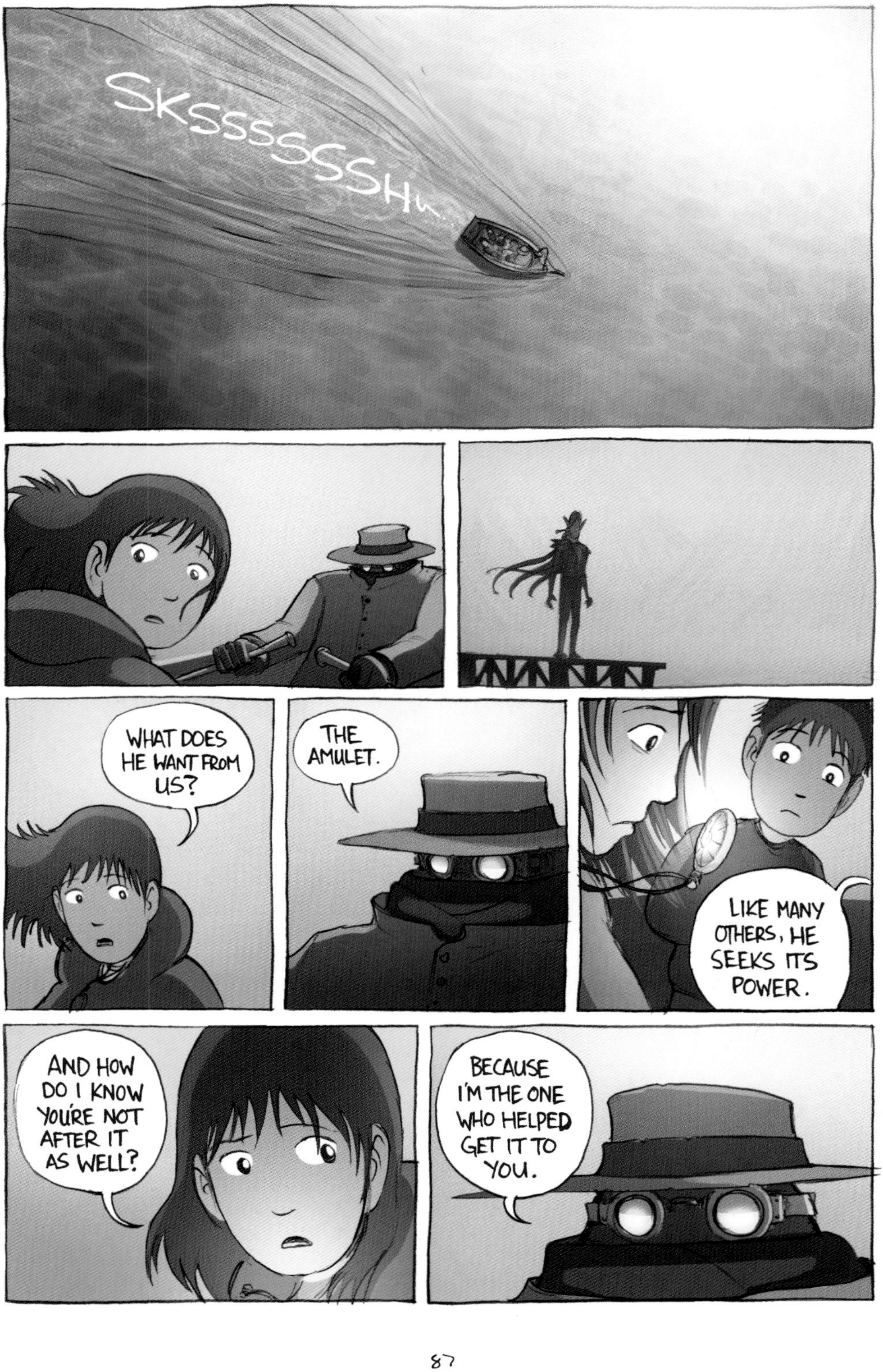
SKSSSSSSSHh...
WHAT DOES HE WANT FROM US?
THE AMULET.
LIKE MANY OTHERS, HE SEEKS ITS POWER.
AND HOW DO I KNOW YOU'RE NOT AFTER IT AS WELL?
BECAUSE I'M THE ONE WHO HELPED GET IT TO YOU.

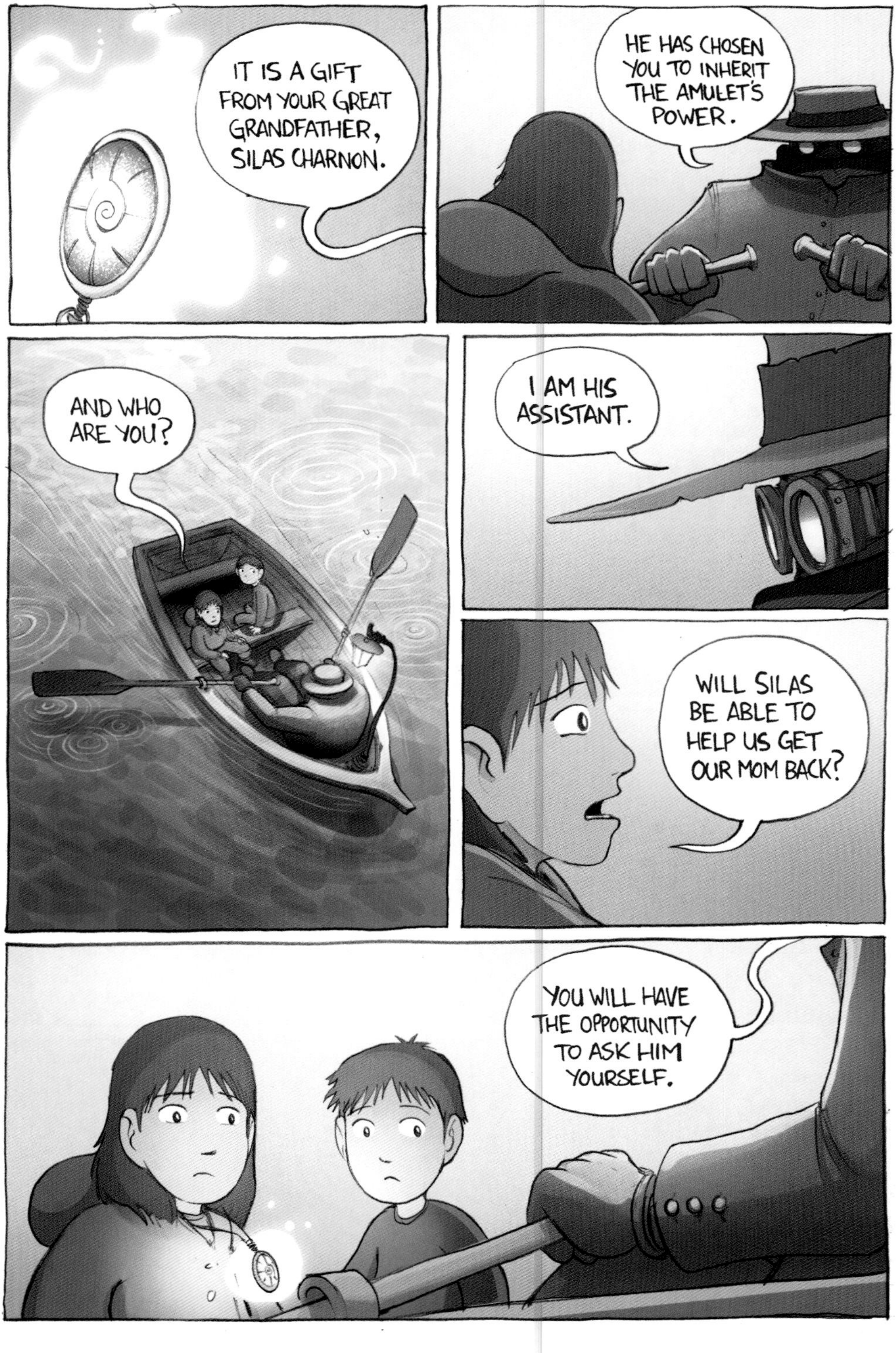
IT IS A GIFT FROM YOUR GREAT GRANDFATHER, SILAS CHARNON.
HE HAS CHOSEN YOU TO INHERIT THE AMULET'S POWER.
AND WHO ARE YOU?
I AM HIS ASSISTANT.
WILL SILAS BE ABLE TO HELP US GET OUR MOM BACK?
YOU WILL HAVE THE OPPORTUNITY TO ASK HIM YOURSELF.

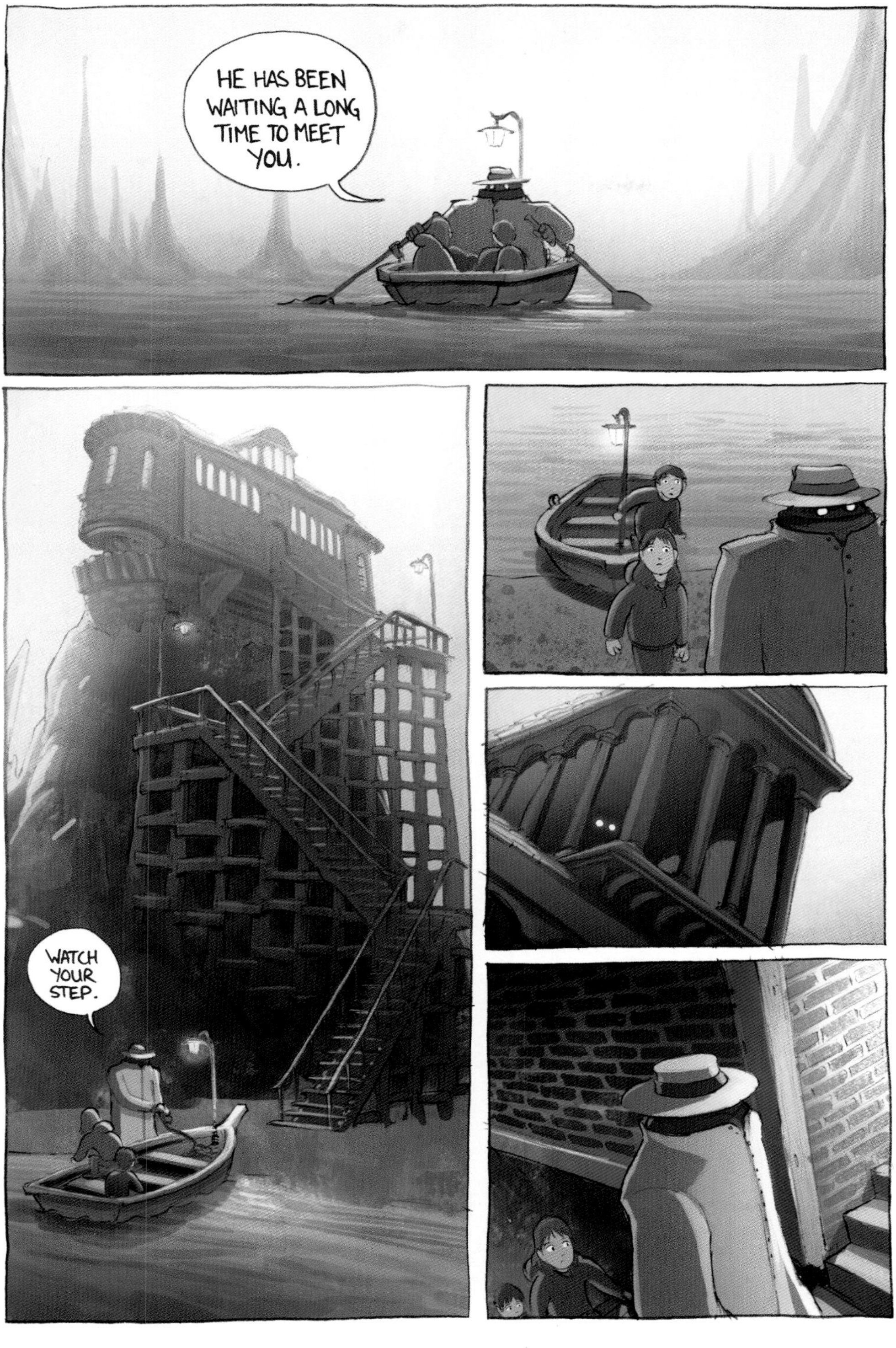
HE HAS BEEN WAITING A LONG TIME TO MEET YOU.
WATCH YOUR STEP.

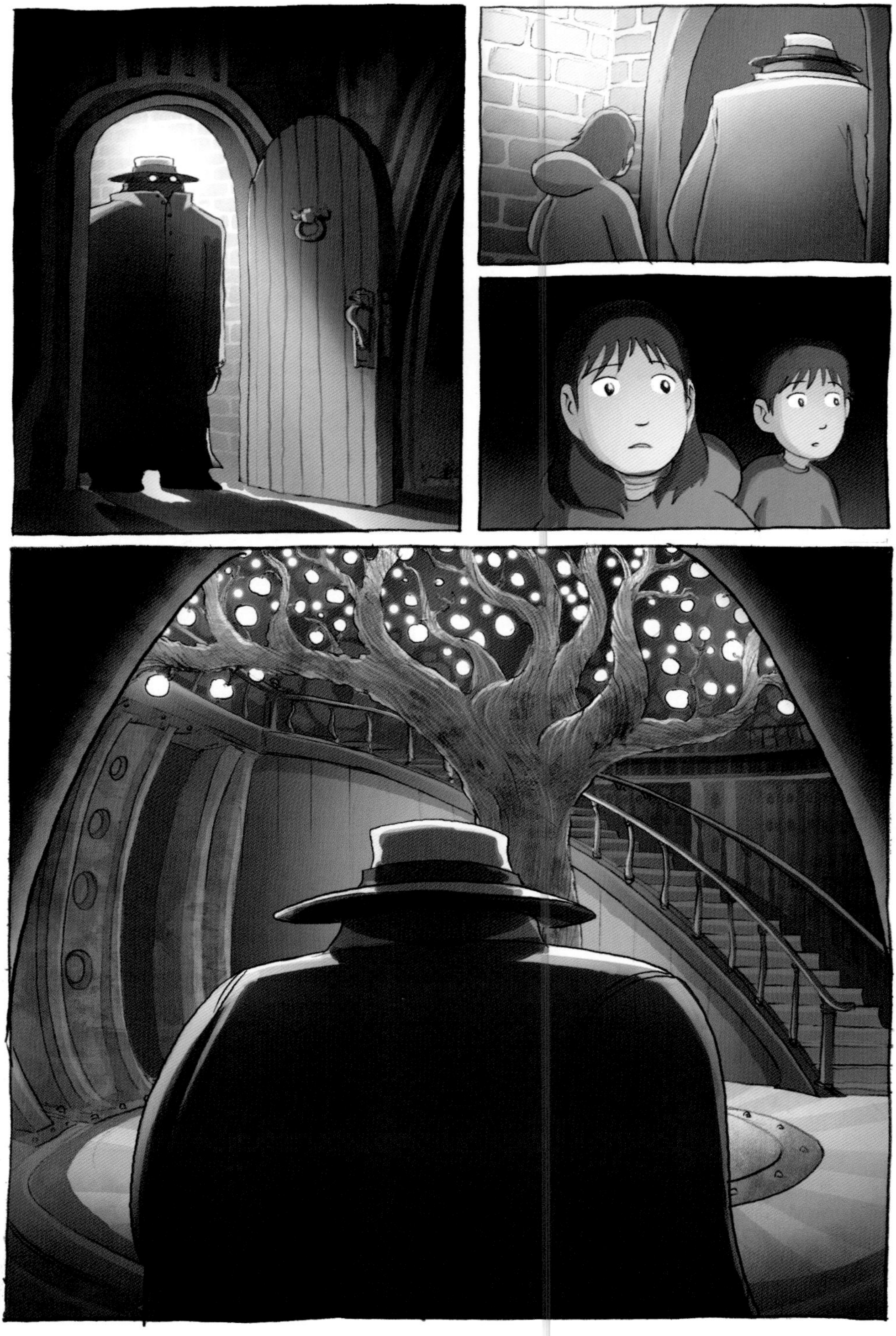

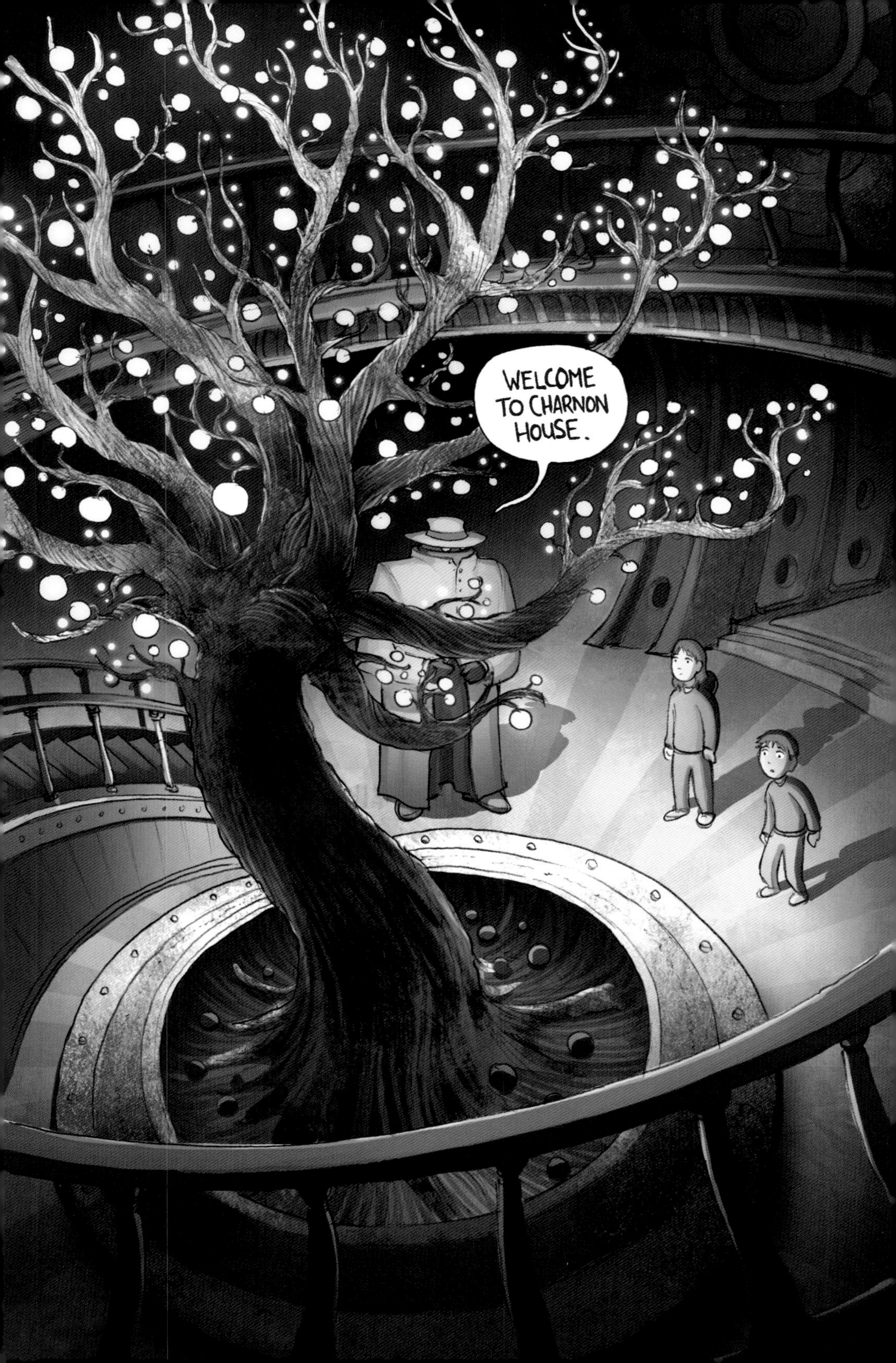
WELCOME TO CHARNON HOUSE.

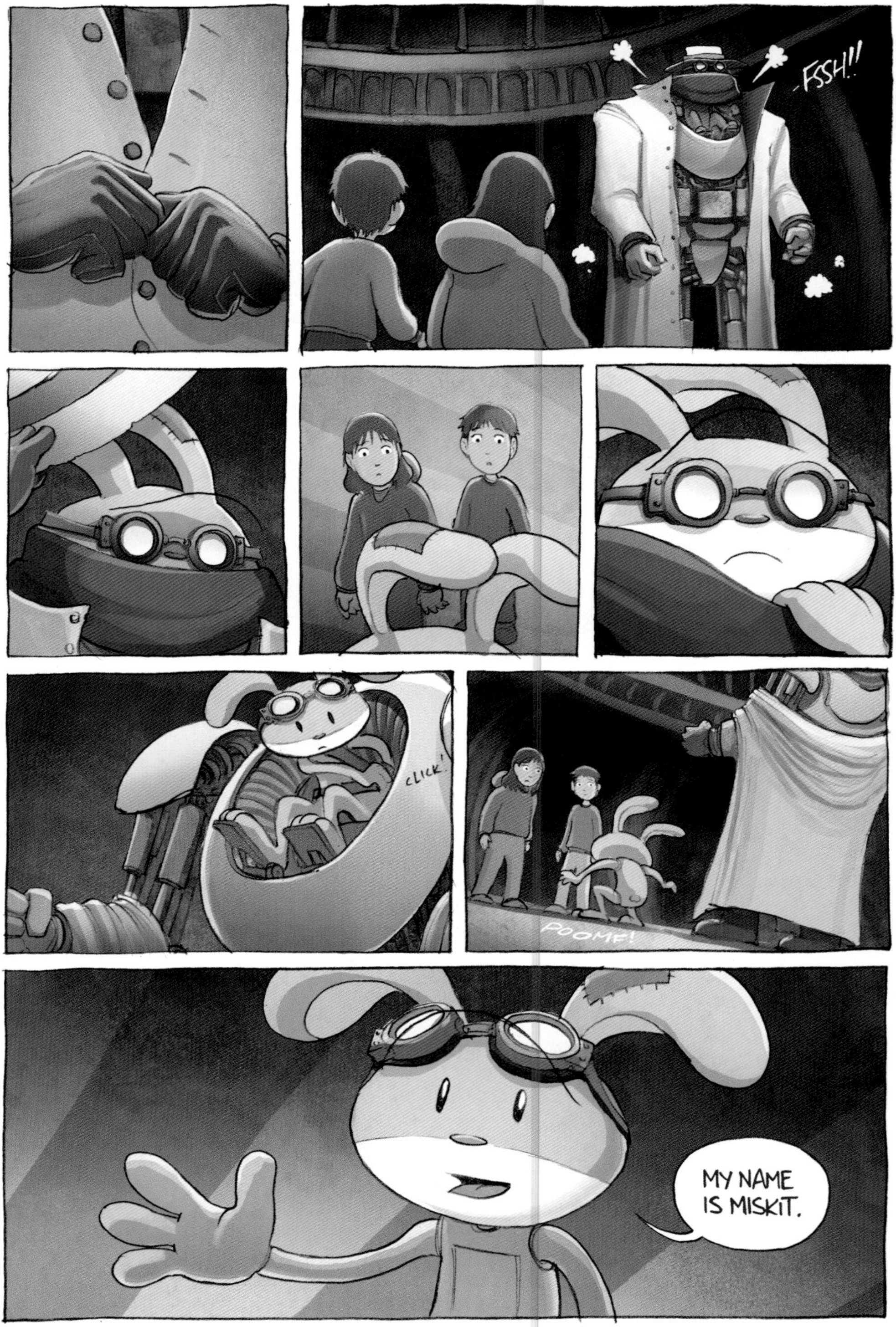
FSSH!!
CLICK!
POOMF!
MY NAME IS MISKIT.

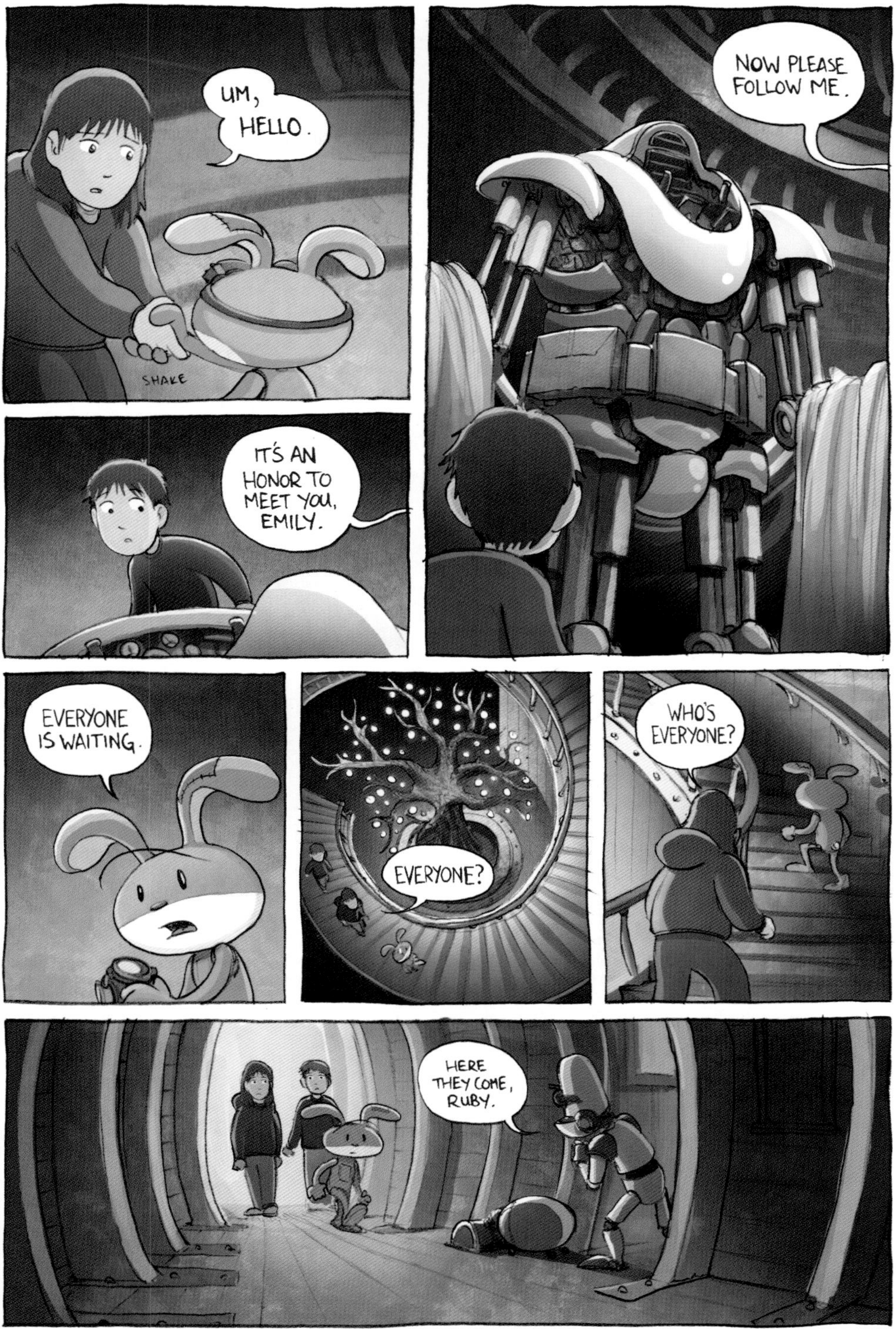
UM, HELLO.
SHAKE
NOW PLEASE FOLLOW ME.
IT'S AN HONOR TO MEET YOU, EMILY.
EVERYONE IS WAITING.
EVERYONE?
WHO'S EVERYONE?
HERE THEY COME, RUBY.

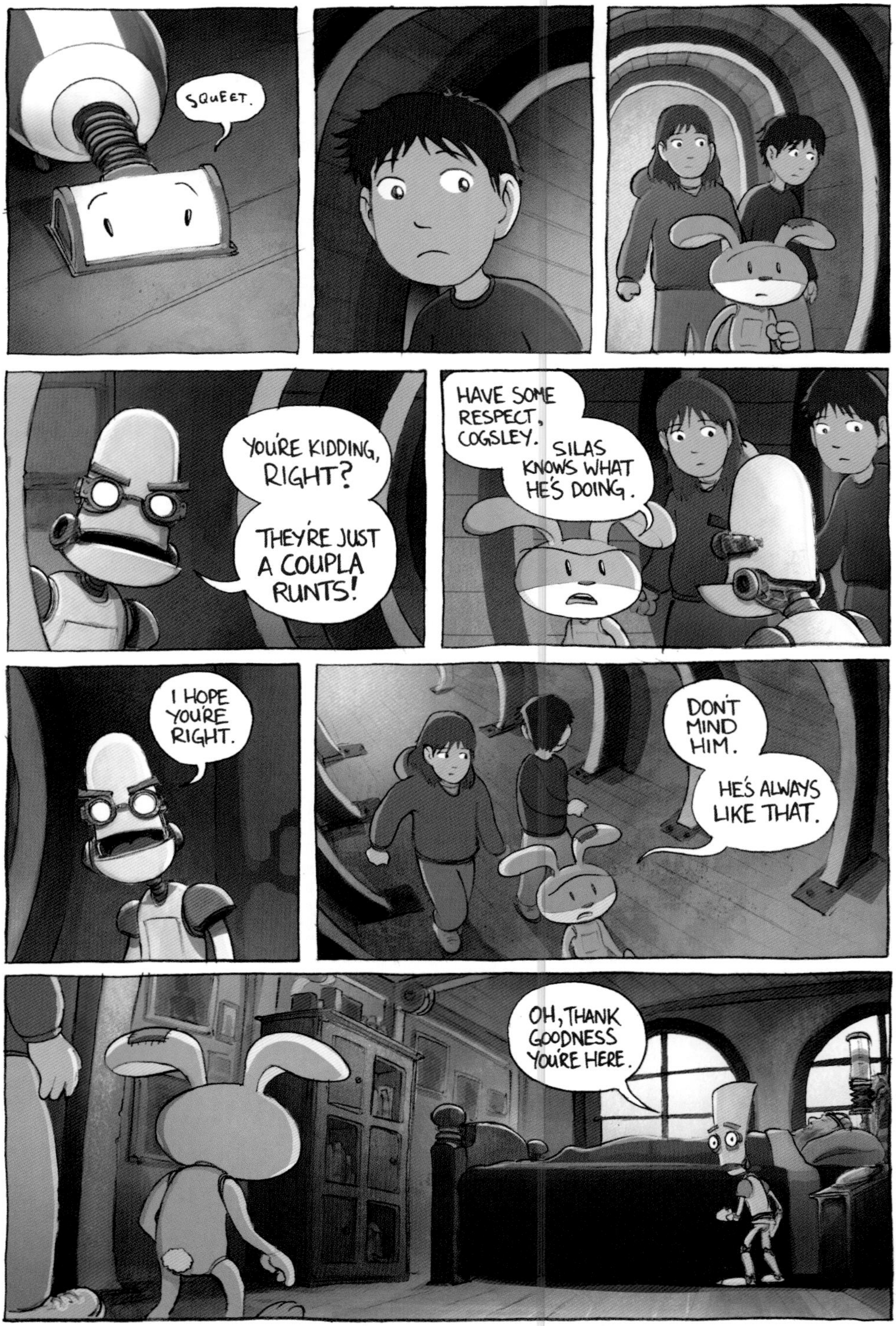
SQUEET.
YOU'RE KIDDING, RIGHT?
THEY'RE JUST A COUPLA RUNTS!
HAVE SOME RESPECT, COGSLEY.
SILAS KNOWS WHAT HE'S DOING.
I HOPE YOU'RE RIGHT.
DON'T MIND HIM.
HE'S ALWAYS LIKE THAT.
OH, THANK GOODNESS YOU'RE HERE.

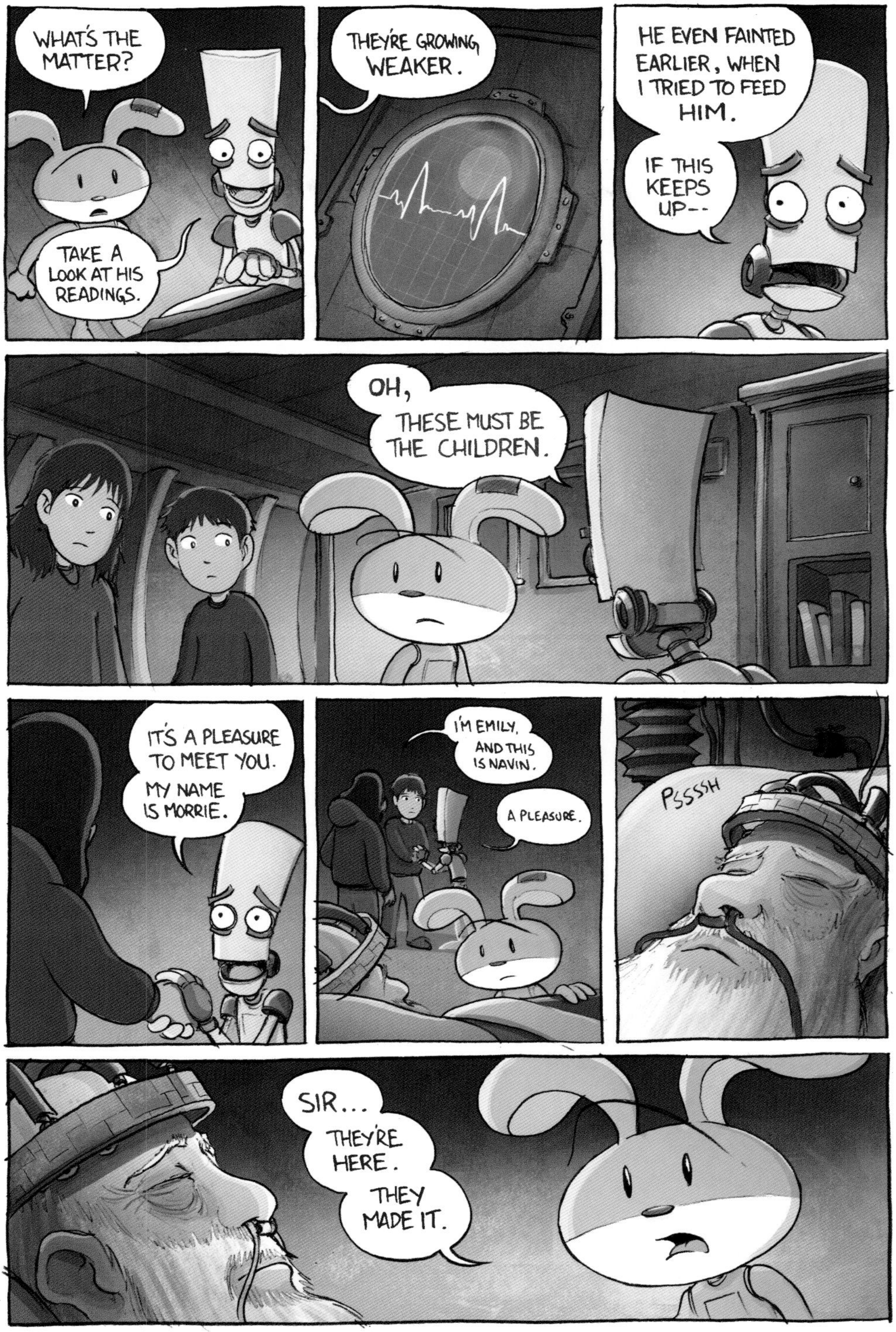
WHAT'S THE MATTER?
TAKE A LOOK AT HIS READINGS.
THEY'RE GROWING WEAKER.
HE EVEN FAINTED EARLIER, WHEN I TRIED TO FEED HIM.
IF THIS KEEPS UP--
OH,
THESE MUST BE THE CHILDREN.
IT'S A PLEASURE TO MEET YOU.
MY NAME IS MORRIE.
I'M EMILY.
AND THIS IS NAVIN.
A PLEASURE.
PSSSSH
SIR...
THEY'RE HERE.
THEY MADE IT.

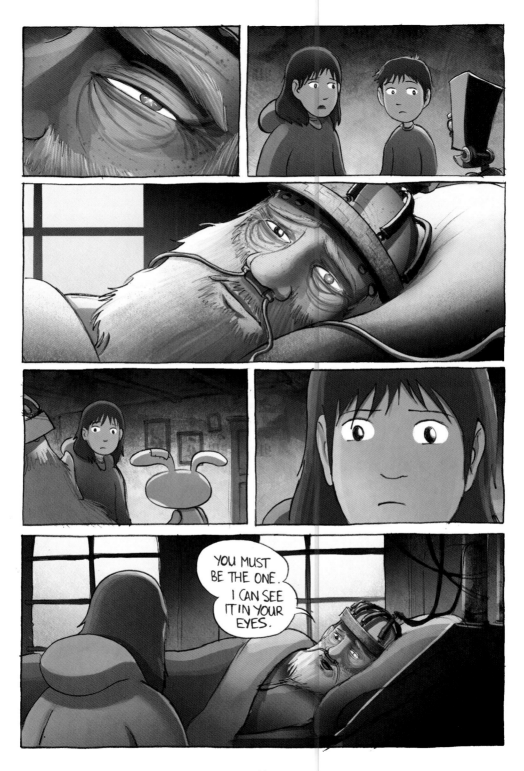

YOU MUST BE THE ONE. I CAN SEE IT IN YOUR EYES.

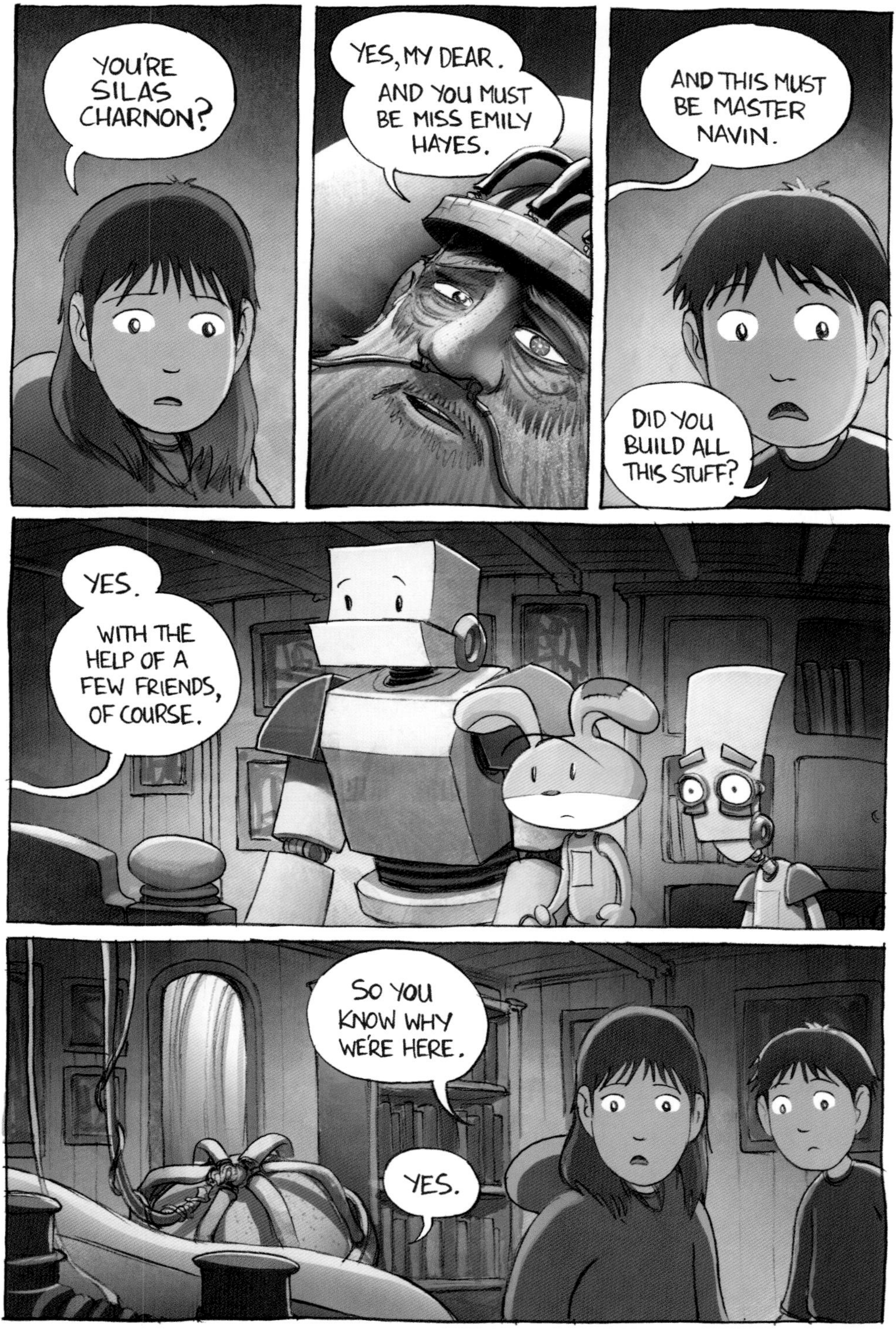
YOU'RE SILAS CHARNON?
YES, MY DEAR.
AND YOU MUST BE MISS EMILY HAYES.
AND THIS MUST BE MASTER NAVIN.
DID YOU BUILD ALL THIS STUFF?
YES.
WITH THE HELP OF A FEW FRIENDS, OF COURSE.
SO YOU KNOW WHY WE'RE HERE.
YES.

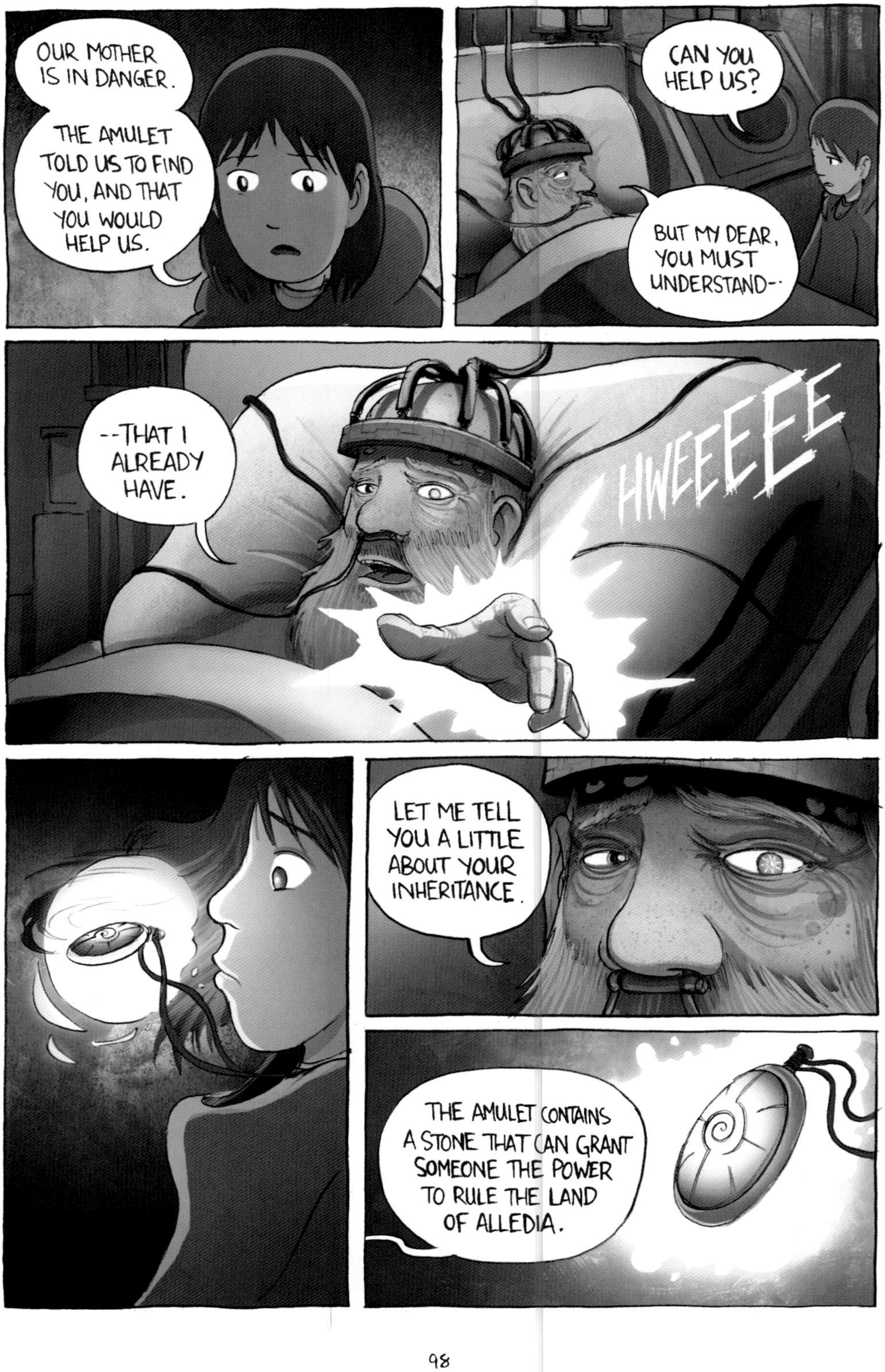
OUR MOTHER IS IN DANGER.
THE AMULET TOLD US TO FIND YOU, AND THAT YOU WOULD HELP US.
CAN YOU HELP US?
BUT MY DEAR, YOU MUST UNDERSTAND--
--THAT I ALREADY HAVE.
HWEEEEE
LET ME TELL YOU A LITTLE ABOUT YOUR INHERITANCE.
THE AMULET CONTAINS A STONE THAT CAN GRANT SOMEONE THE POWER TO RULE THE LAND OF ALLEDIA.

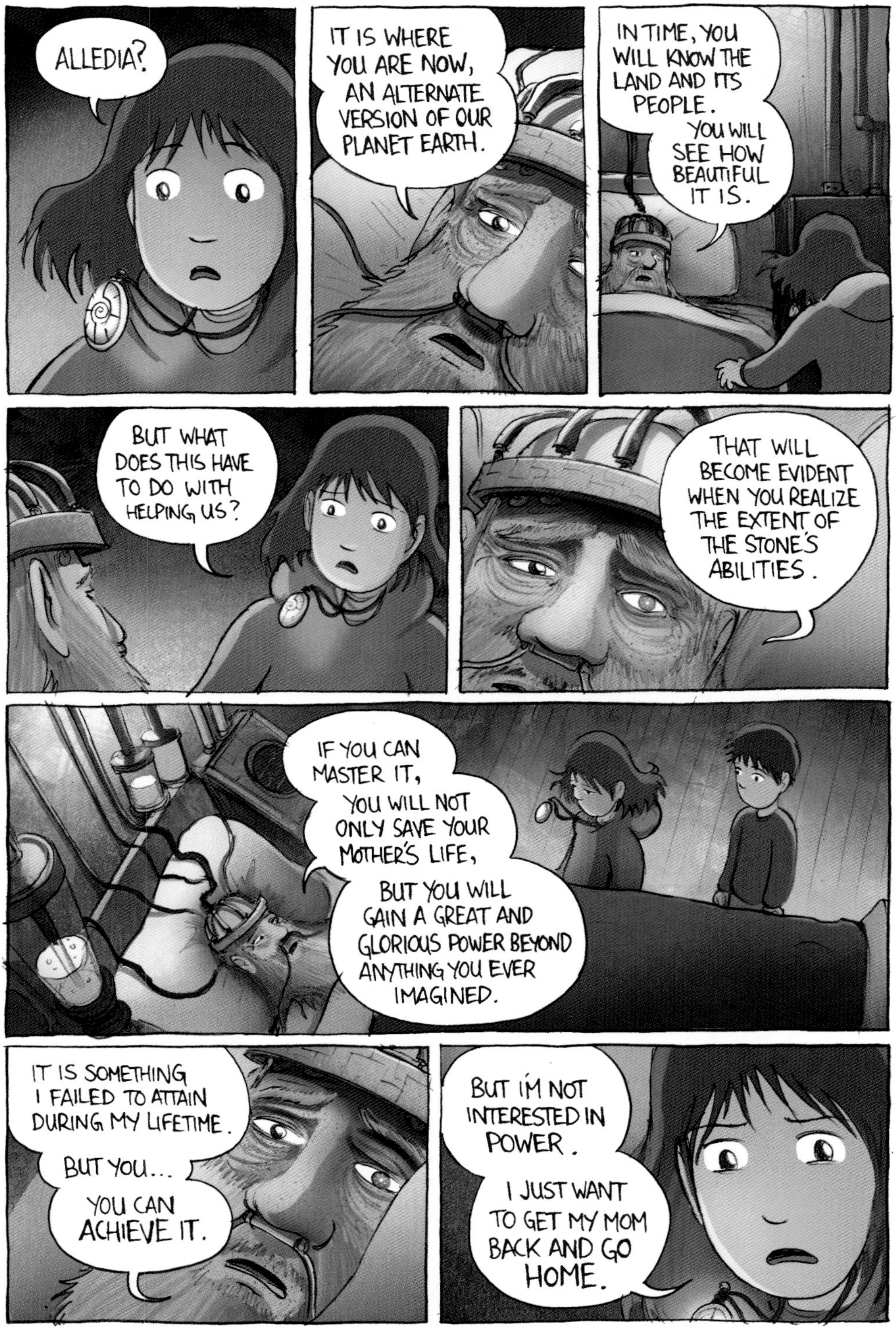
ALLEDIA?
IT IS WHERE YOU ARE NOW, AN ALTERNATE VERSION OF OUR PLANET EARTH.
IN TIME, YOU WILL KNOW THE LAND AND ITS PEOPLE.
YOU WILL SEE HOW BEAUTIFUL IT IS.
BUT WHAT DOES THIS HAVE TO DO WITH HELPING US?
THAT WILL BECOME EVIDENT WHEN YOU REALIZE THE EXTENT OF THE STONE'S ABILITIES.
IF YOU CAN MASTER IT,
YOU WILL NOT ONLY SAVE YOUR MOTHER'S LIFE,
BUT YOU WILL GAIN A GREAT AND GLORIOUS POWER BEYOND ANYTHING YOU EVER IMAGINED.
IT IS SOMETHING I FAILED TO ATTAIN DURING MY LIFETIME.
BUT YOU...
YOU CAN ACHIEVE IT.
BUT I'M NOT INTERESTED IN POWER.
I JUST WANT TO GET MY MOM BACK AND GO HOME.

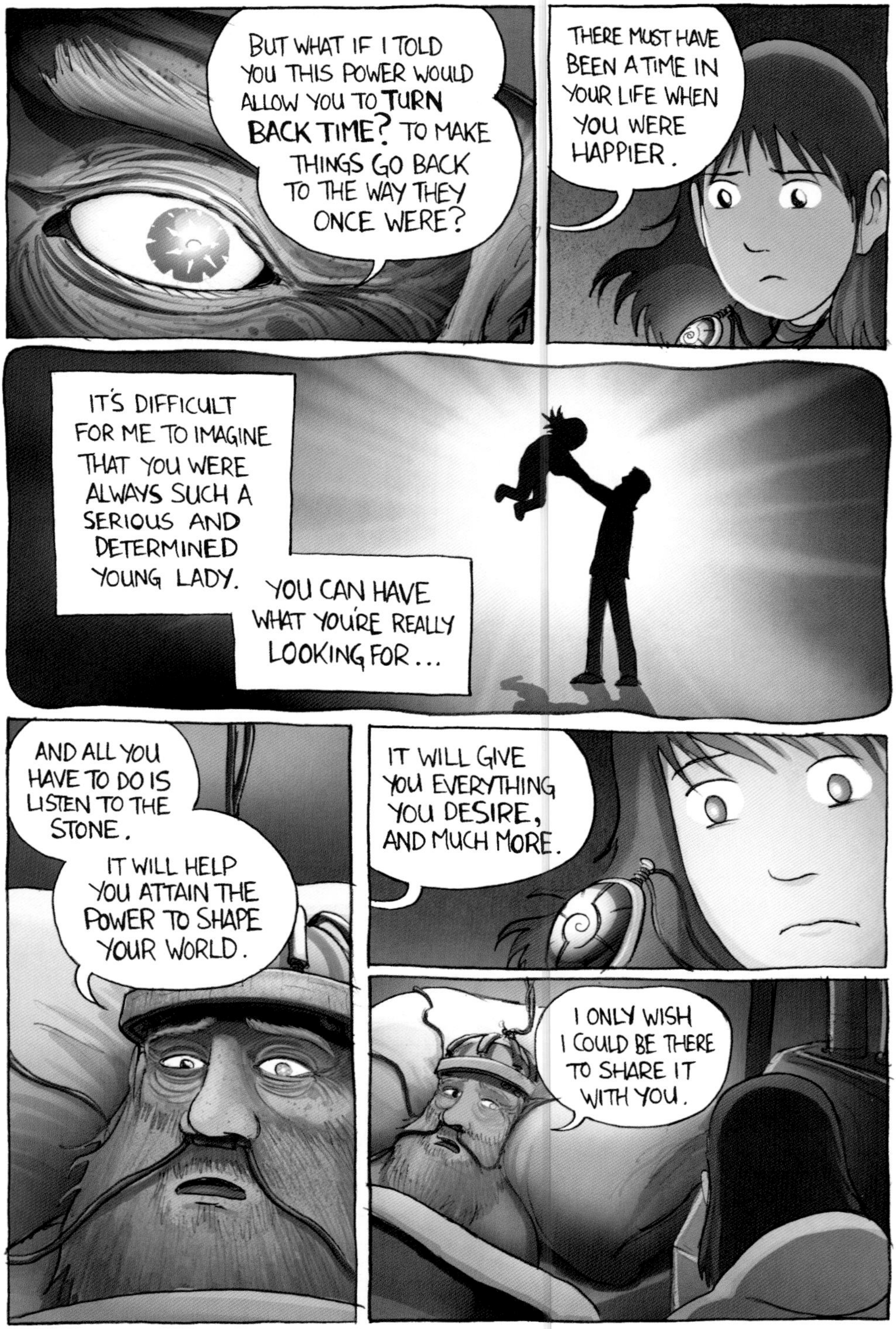
BUT WHAT IF I TOLD YOU THIS POWER WOULD ALLOW YOU TO TURN BACK TIME? TO MAKE THINGS GO BACK TO THE WAY THEY ONCE WERE?
THERE MUST HAVE BEEN A TIME IN YOUR LIFE WHEN YOU WERE HAPPIER.
IT'S DIFFICULT FOR ME TO IMAGINE THAT YOU WERE ALWAYS SUCH A SERIOUS AND DETERMINED YOUNG LADY.
YOU CAN HAVE WHAT YOU'RE REALLY LOOKING FOR...
AND ALL YOU HAVE TO DO IS LISTEN TO THE STONE.
IT WILL HELP YOU ATTAIN THE POWER TO SHAPE YOUR WORLD.
IT WILL GIVE YOU EVERYTHING YOU DESIRE, AND MUCH MORE.
I ONLY WISH I COULD BE THERE TO SHARE IT WITH YOU.

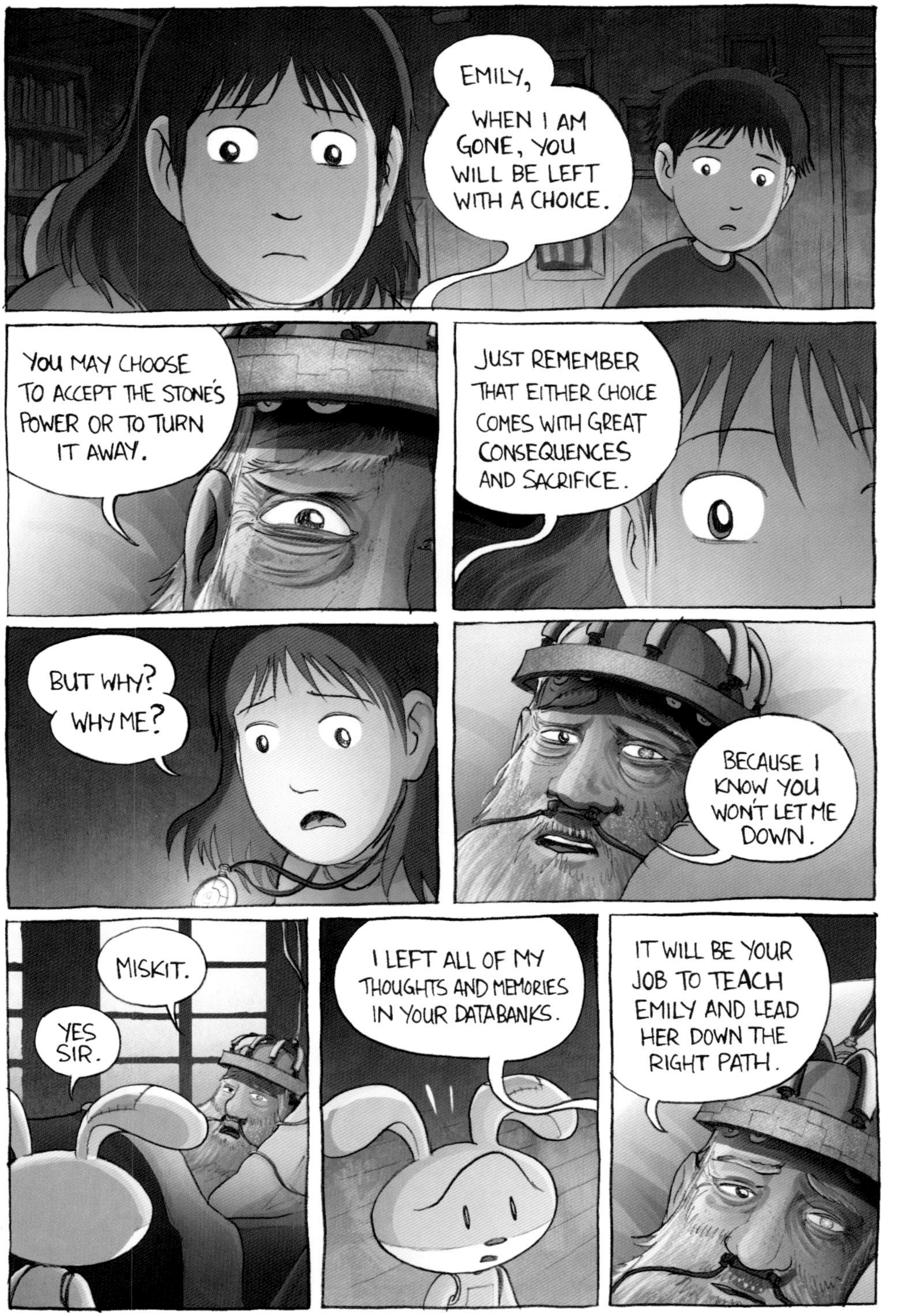
EMILY,
WHEN I AM GONE, YOU WILL BE LEFT WITH A CHOICE.
YOU MAY CHOOSE TO ACCEPT THE STONE'S POWER OR TO TURN IT AWAY.
JUST REMEMBER THAT EITHER CHOICE COMES WITH GREAT CONSEQUENCES AND SACRIFICE.
BUT WHY?
WHY ME?
BECAUSE I KNOW YOU WON'T LET ME DOWN.
MISKIT.
YES SIR.
I LEFT ALL OF MY THOUGHTS AND MEMORIES IN YOUR DATABANKS.
IT WILL BE YOUR JOB TO TEACH EMILY AND LEAD HER DOWN THE RIGHT PATH.

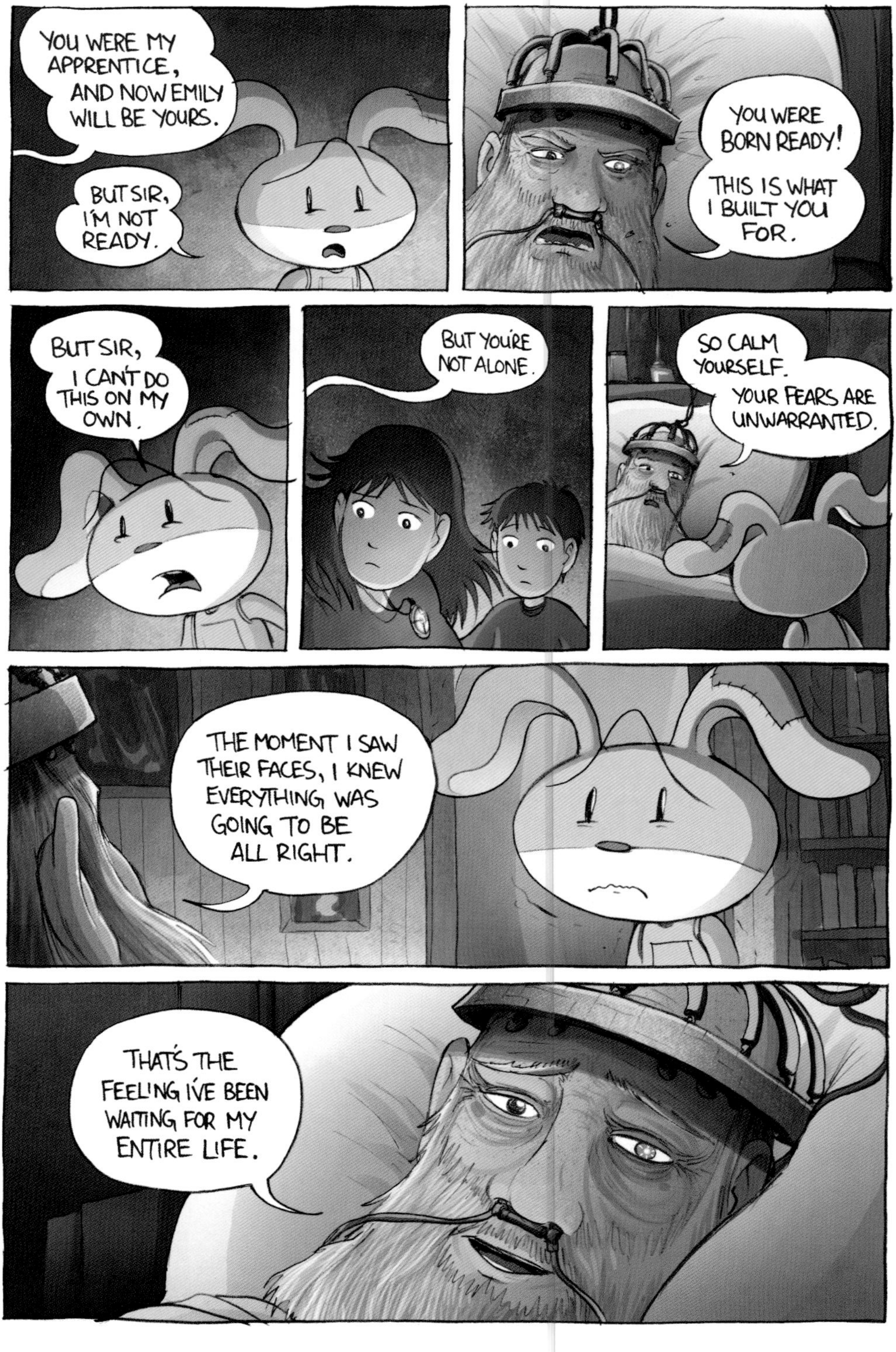
YOU WERE MY APPRENTICE, AND NOW EMILY WILL BE YOURS.
BUT SIR, I'M NOT READY.
YOU WERE BORN READY!
THIS IS WHAT I BUILT YOU FOR.
BUT SIR, I CAN'T DO THIS ON MY OWN.
BUT YOU'RE NOT ALONE.
SO CALM YOURSELF.
YOUR FEARS ARE UNWARRANTED.
THE MOMENT I SAW THEIR FACES, I KNEW EVERYTHING WAS GOING TO BE ALL RIGHT.
THAT'S THE FEELING I'VE BEEN WAITING FOR MY ENTIRE LIFE.

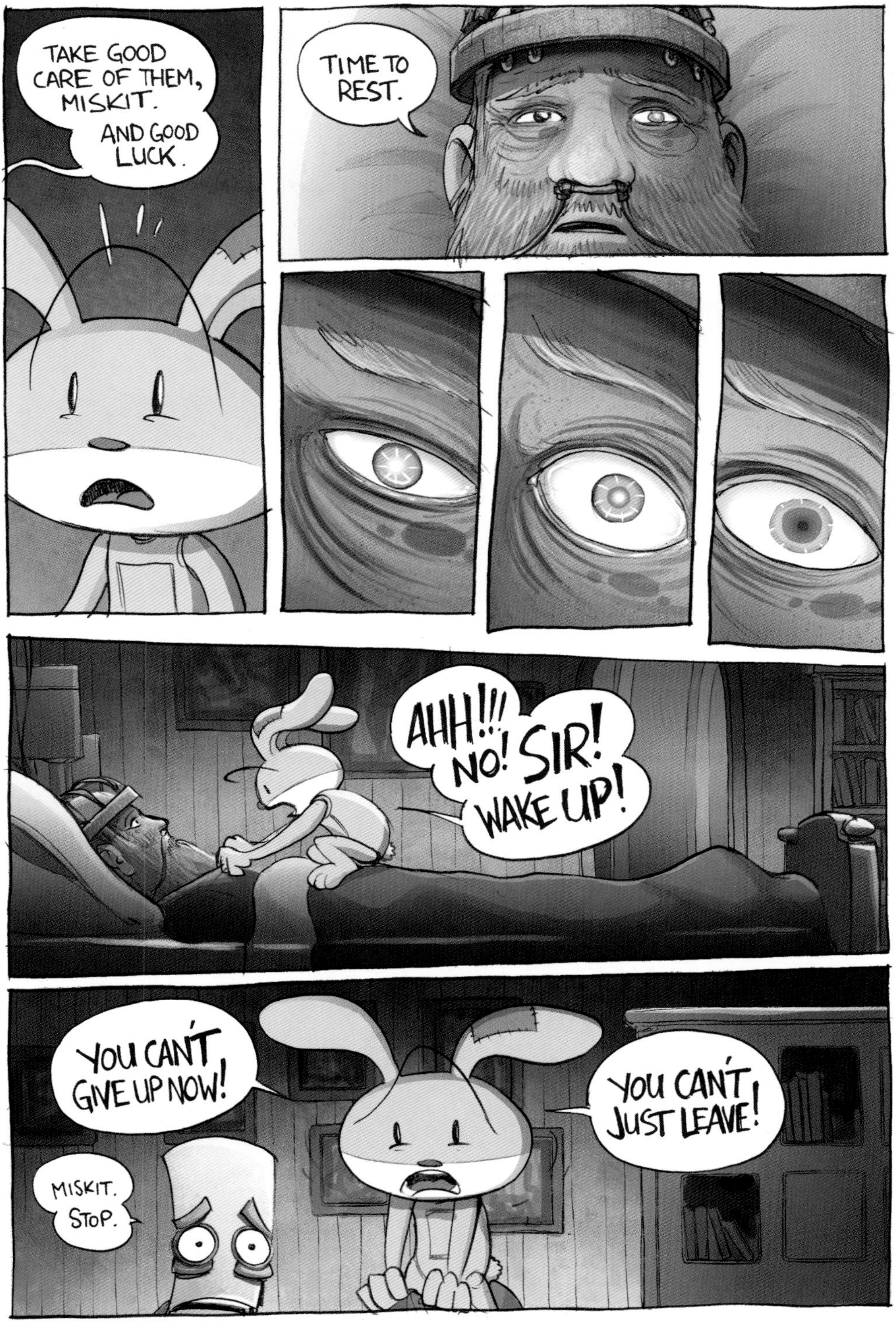
TAKE GOOD CARE OF THEM, MISKIT.
AND GOOD LUCK.
TIME TO REST.
AHH!!! NO! SIR! WAKE UP!
YOU CAN'T GIVE UP NOW!
YOU CAN'T JUST LEAVE!
MISKIT. STOP.

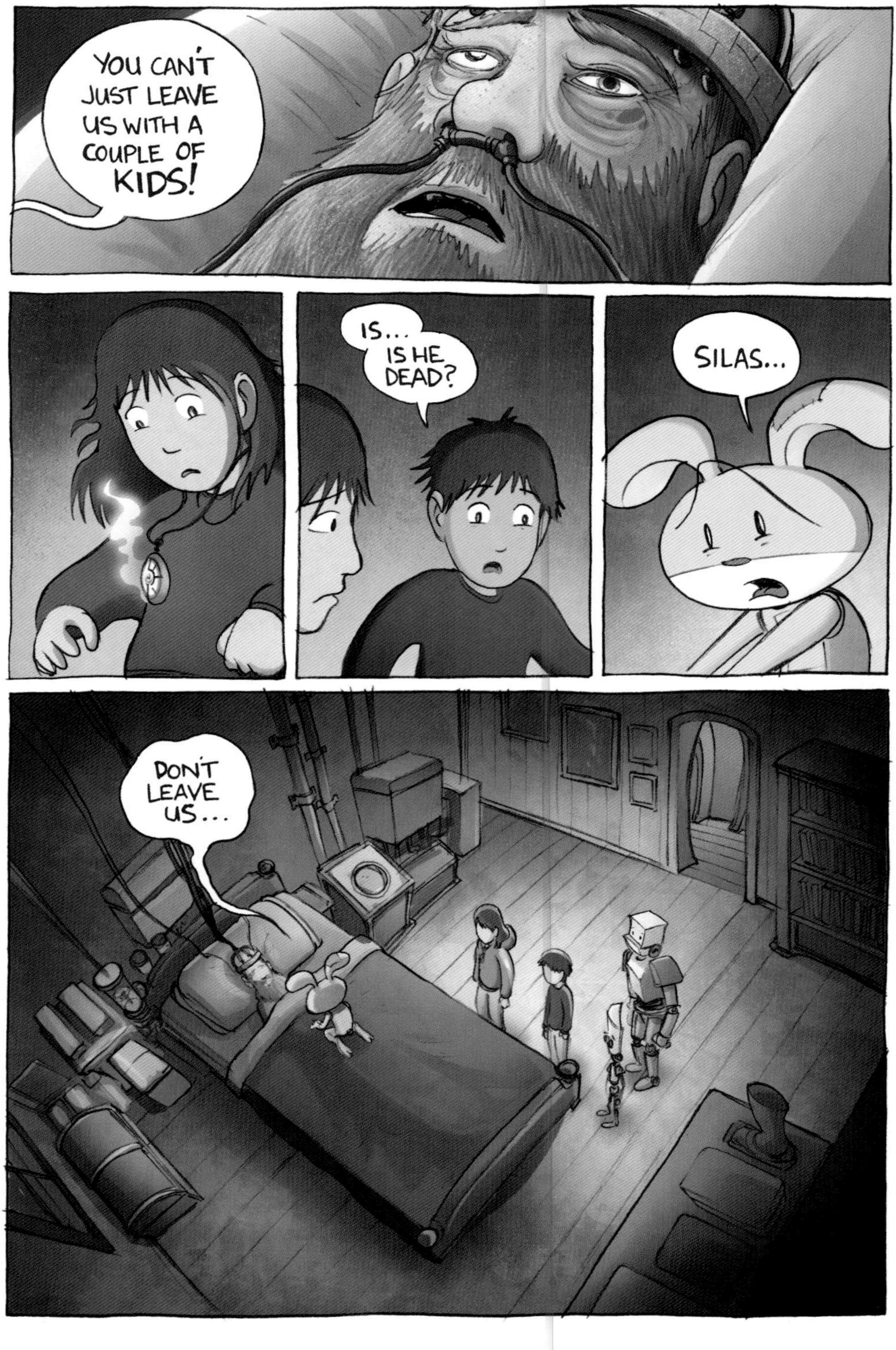
YOU CAN'T JUST LEAVE US WITH A COUPLE OF KIDS!
IS... IS HE DEAD?
SILAS...
DON'T LEAVE US...

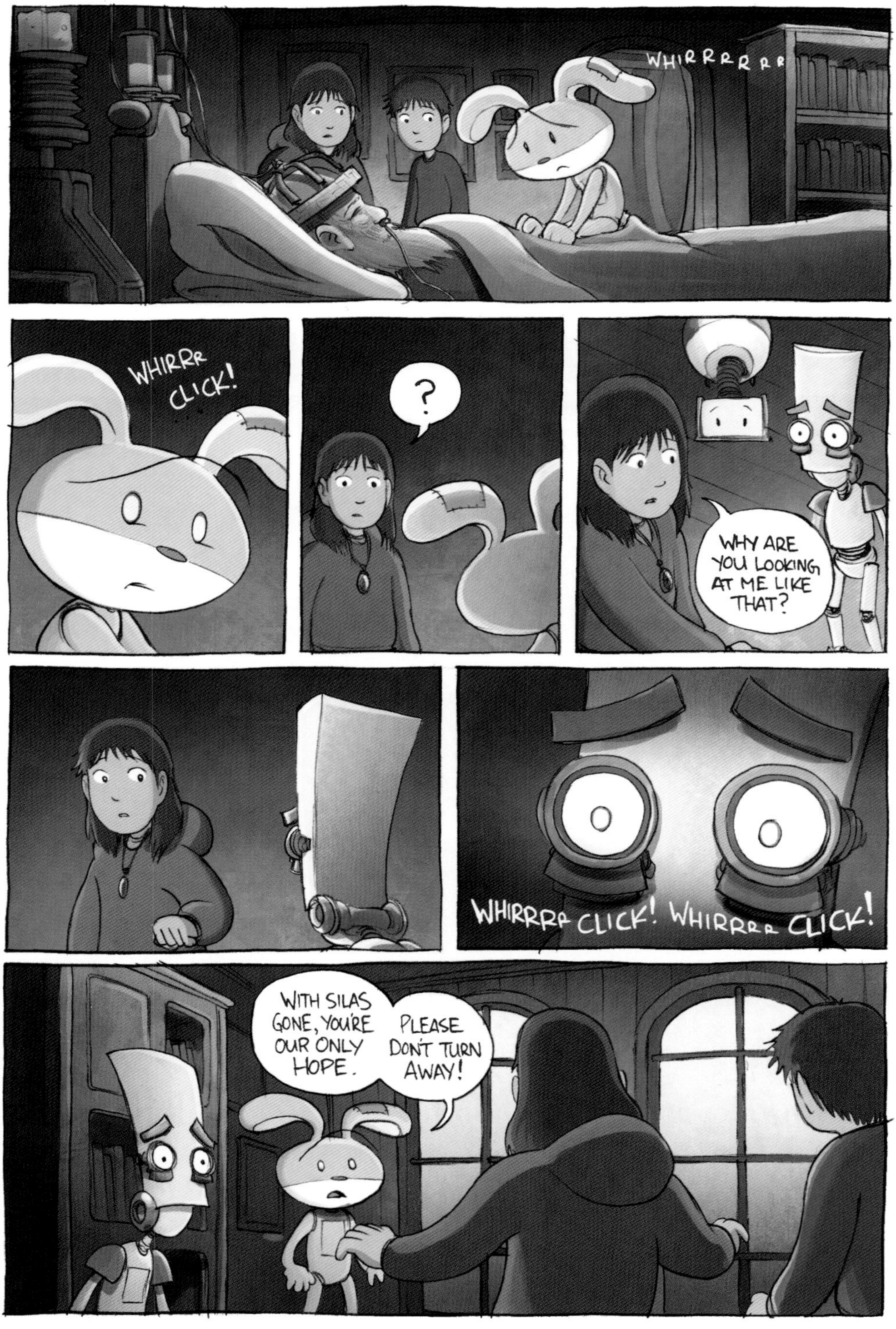
WHIRRRRRRR
WHIRRR CLICK!
?
WHY ARE YOU LOOKING AT ME LIKE THAT?
WHIRRRR CLICK! WHIRRRR CLICK!
WITH SILAS GONE, YOU'RE OUR ONLY HOPE.
PLEASE DON'T TURN AWAY!

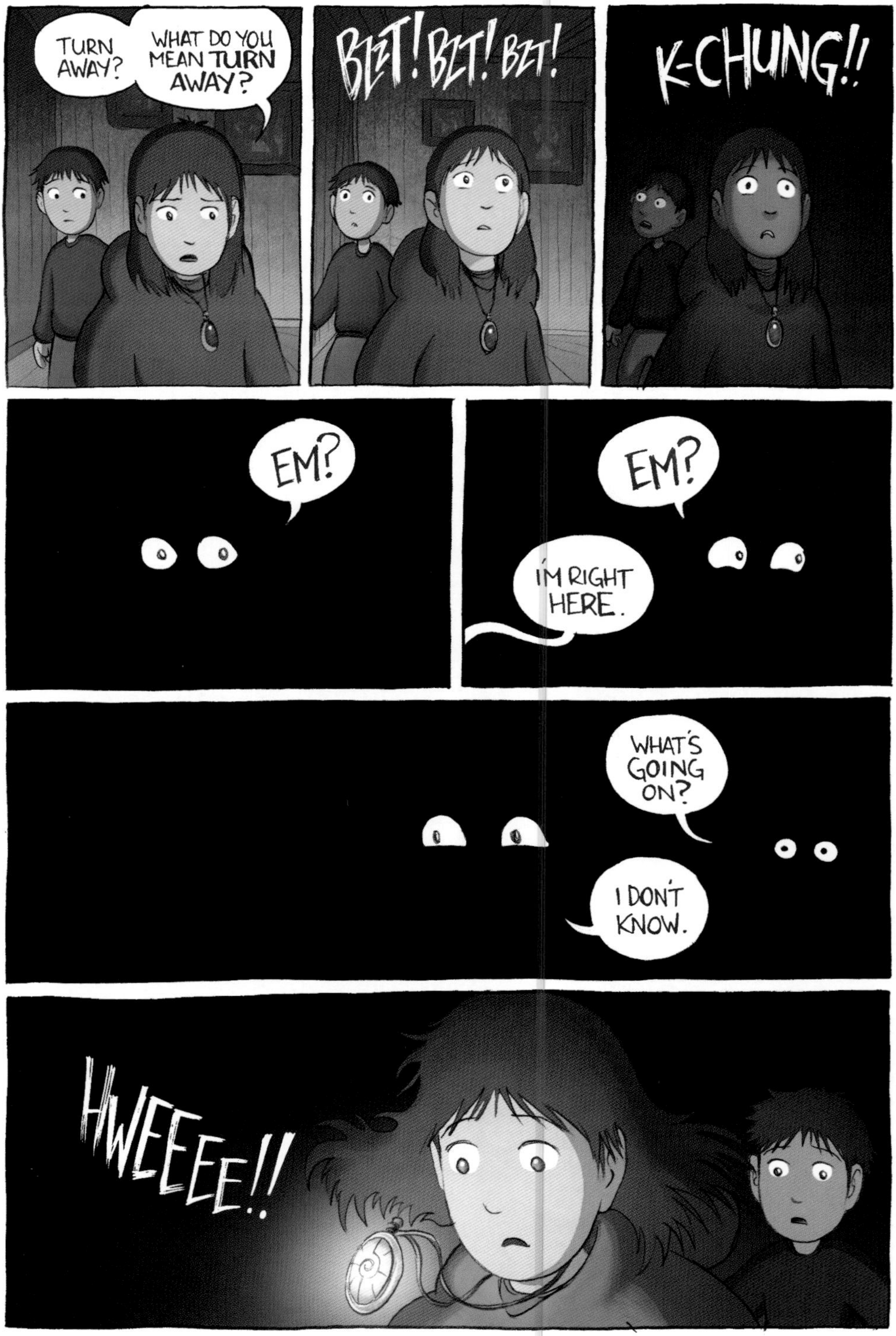
TURN AWAY?
WHAT DO YOU MEAN TURN AWAY?
BZZT! BZT! BZT!
K-CHUNG!!
EM?
EM?
I'M RIGHT HERE.
WHAT'S GOING ON?
I DON'T KNOW.
HWEEEEE!!

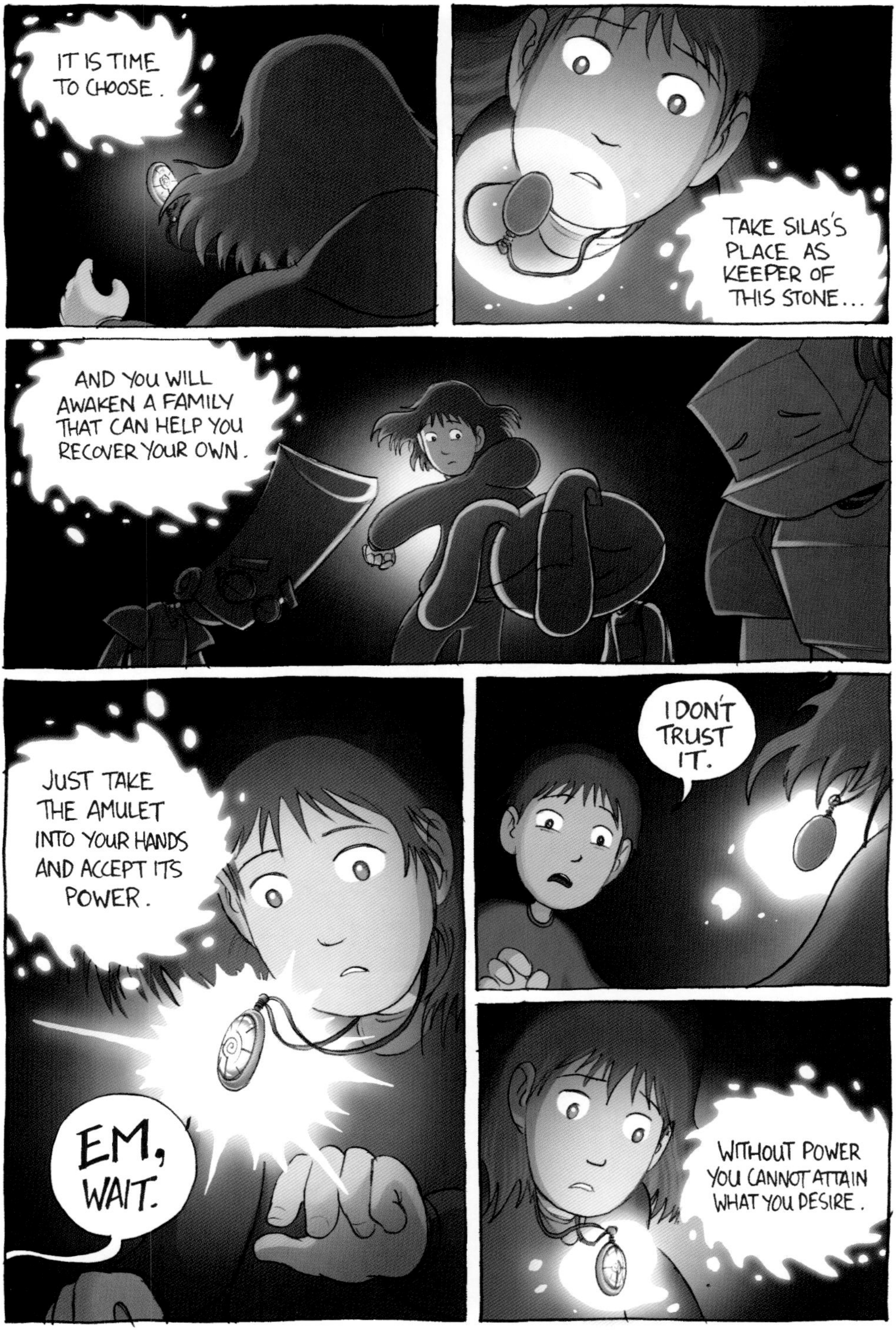
IT IS TIME TO CHOOSE.
TAKE SILAS'S PLACE AS KEEPER OF THIS STONE...
AND YOU WILL AWAKEN A FAMILY THAT CAN HELP YOU RECOVER YOUR OWN.
JUST TAKE THE AMULET INTO YOUR HANDS AND ACCEPT ITS POWER.
EM, WAIT.
I DON'T TRUST IT.
WITHOUT POWER YOU CANNOT ATTAIN WHAT YOU DESIRE.

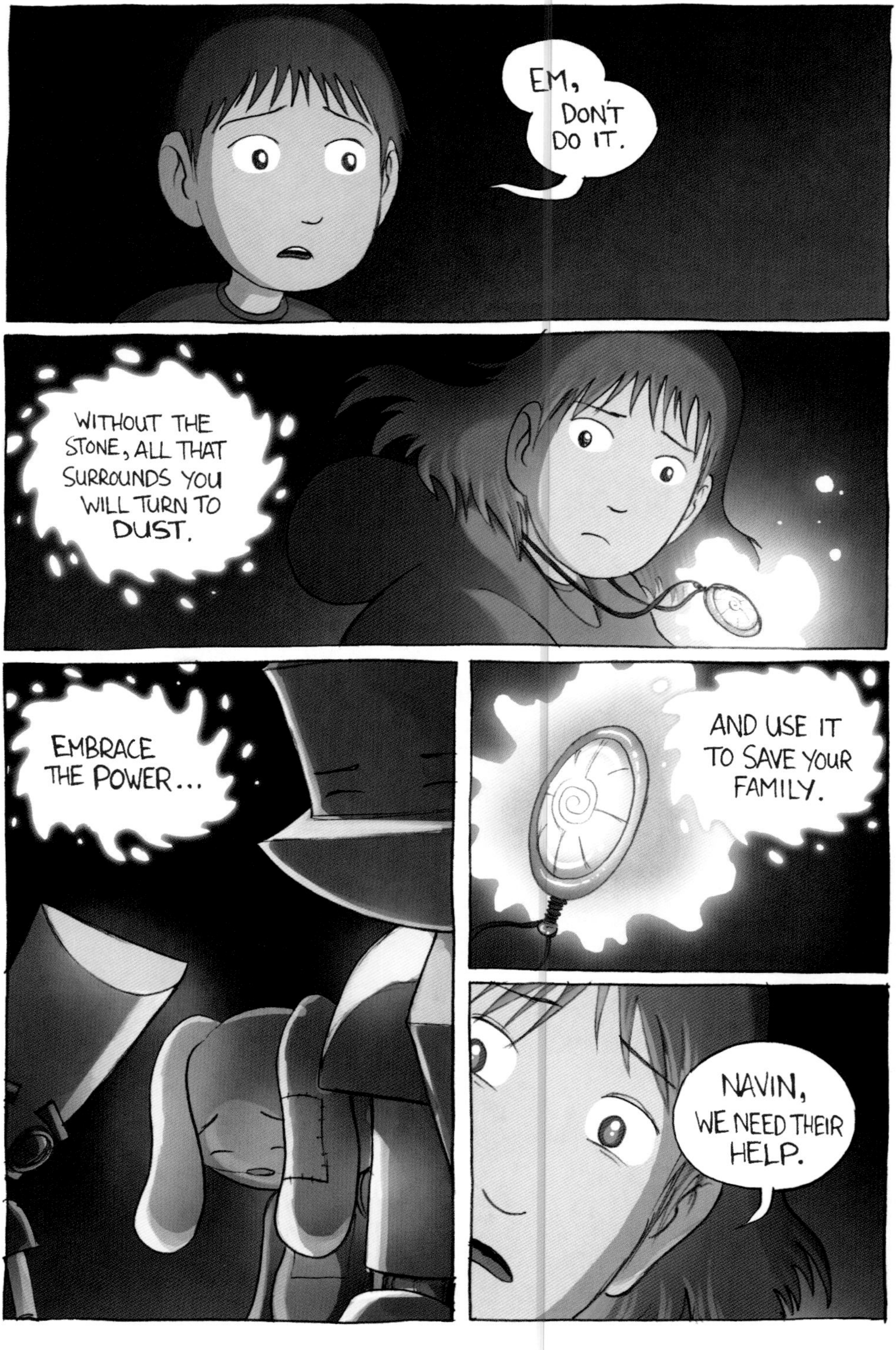
EM, DON'T DO IT.
WITHOUT THE STONE, ALL THAT SURROUNDS YOU WILL TURN TO DUST.
EMBRACE THE POWER...
AND USE IT TO SAVE YOUR FAMILY.
NAVIN, WE NEED THEIR HELP.

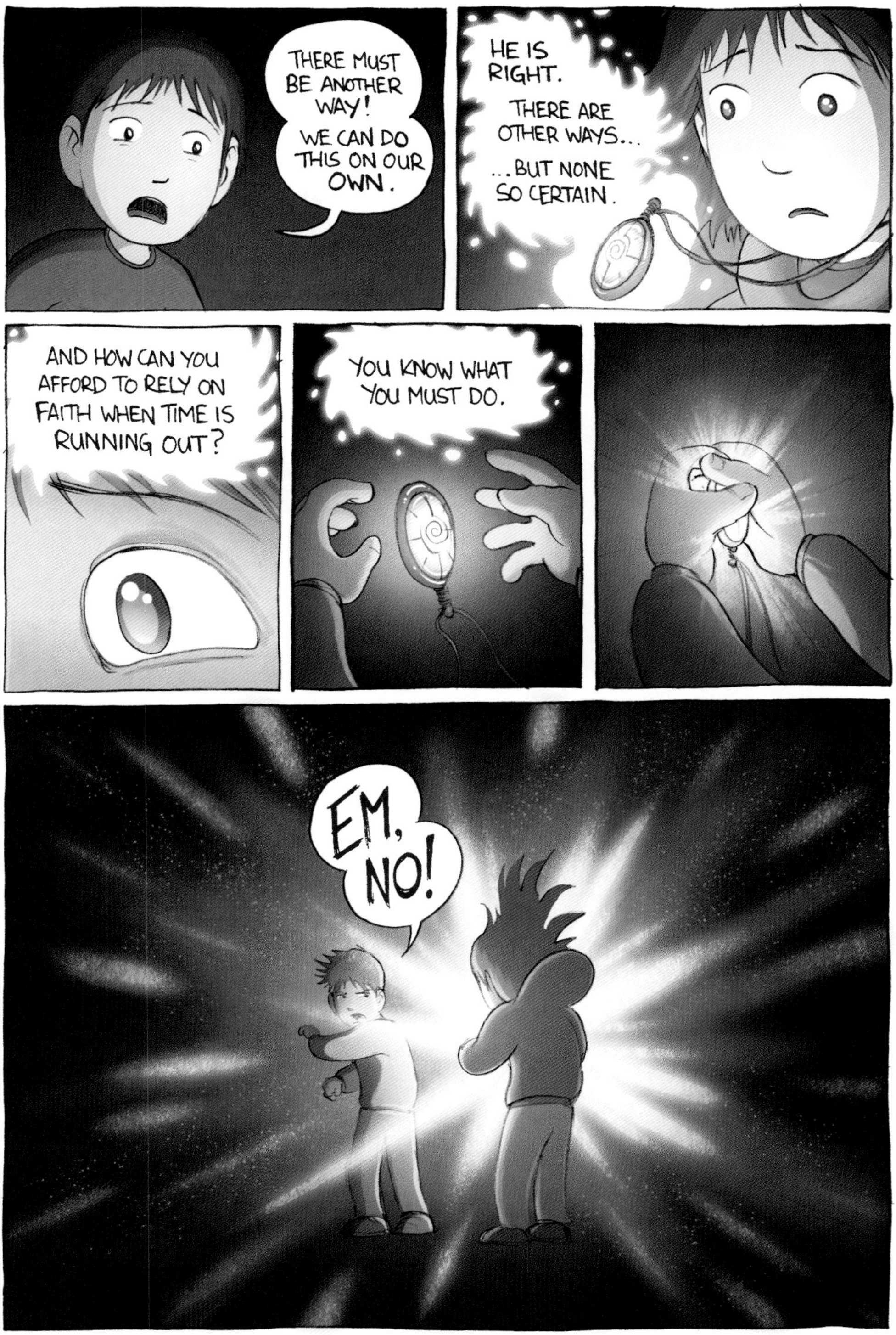
THERE MUST BE ANOTHER WAY! WE CAN DO THIS ON OUR OWN.
HE IS RIGHT.
THERE ARE OTHER WAYS...
...BUT NONE SO CERTAIN.
AND HOW CAN YOU AFFORD TO RELY ON FAITH WHEN TIME IS RUNNING OUT?
YOU KNOW WHAT YOU MUST DO.
EM, NO!

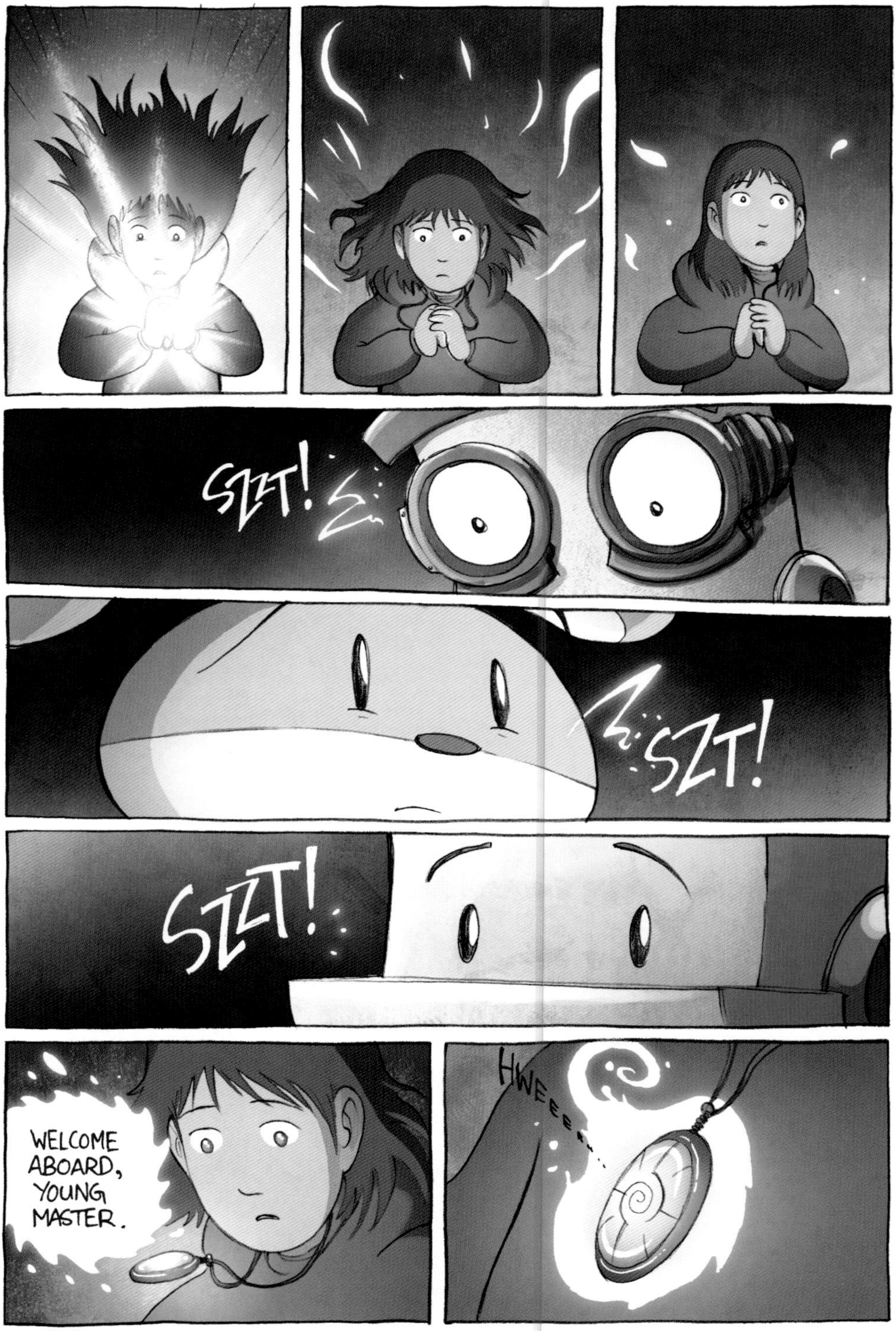
SZZT!
SZT!
SZZT!
WELCOME ABOARD, YOUNG MASTER.
HWEEE...

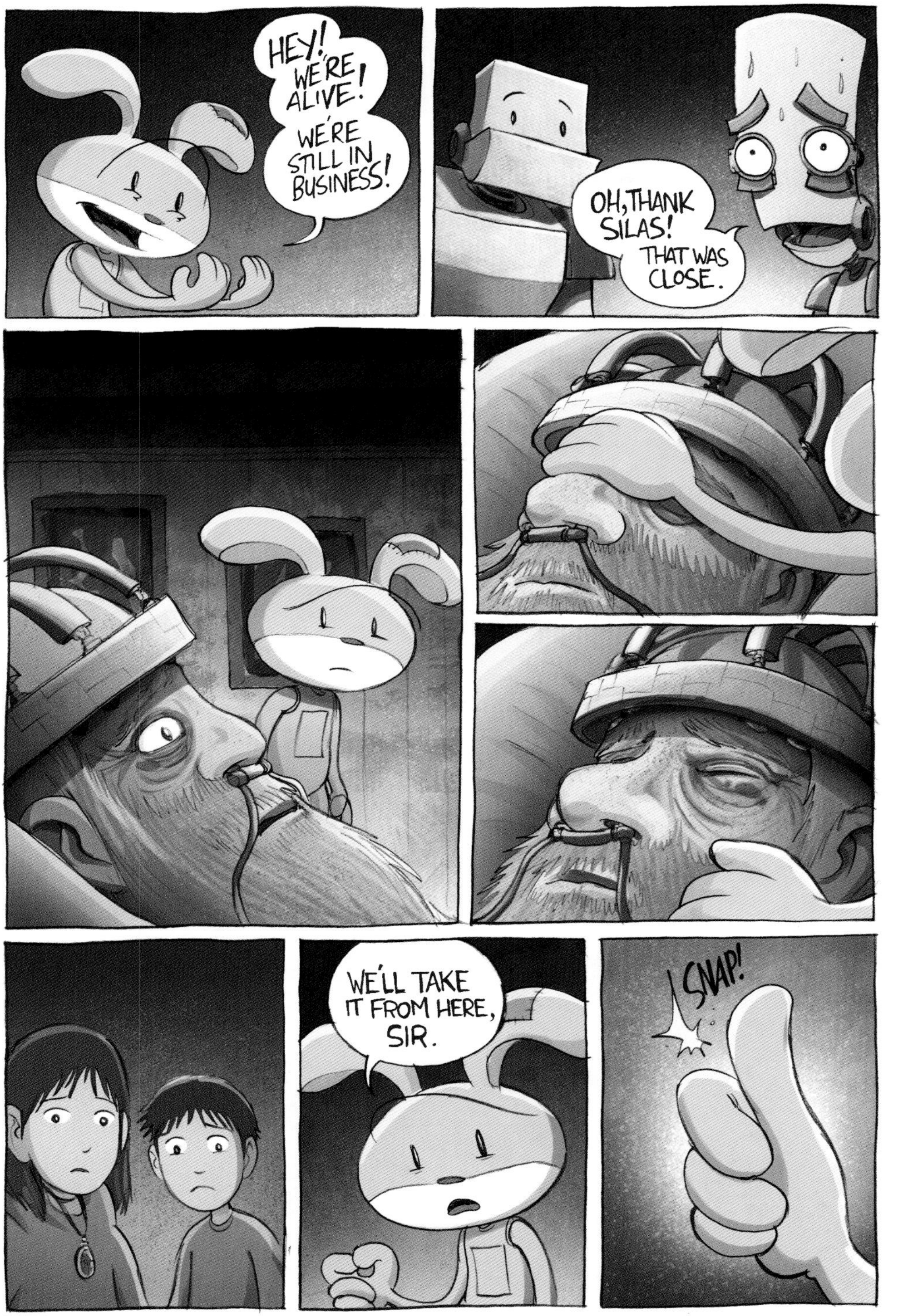
HEY! WE'RE ALIVE! WE'RE STILL IN BUSINESS!
OH, THANK SILAS! THAT WAS CLOSE.
WE'LL TAKE IT FROM HERE, SIR.
SNAP!

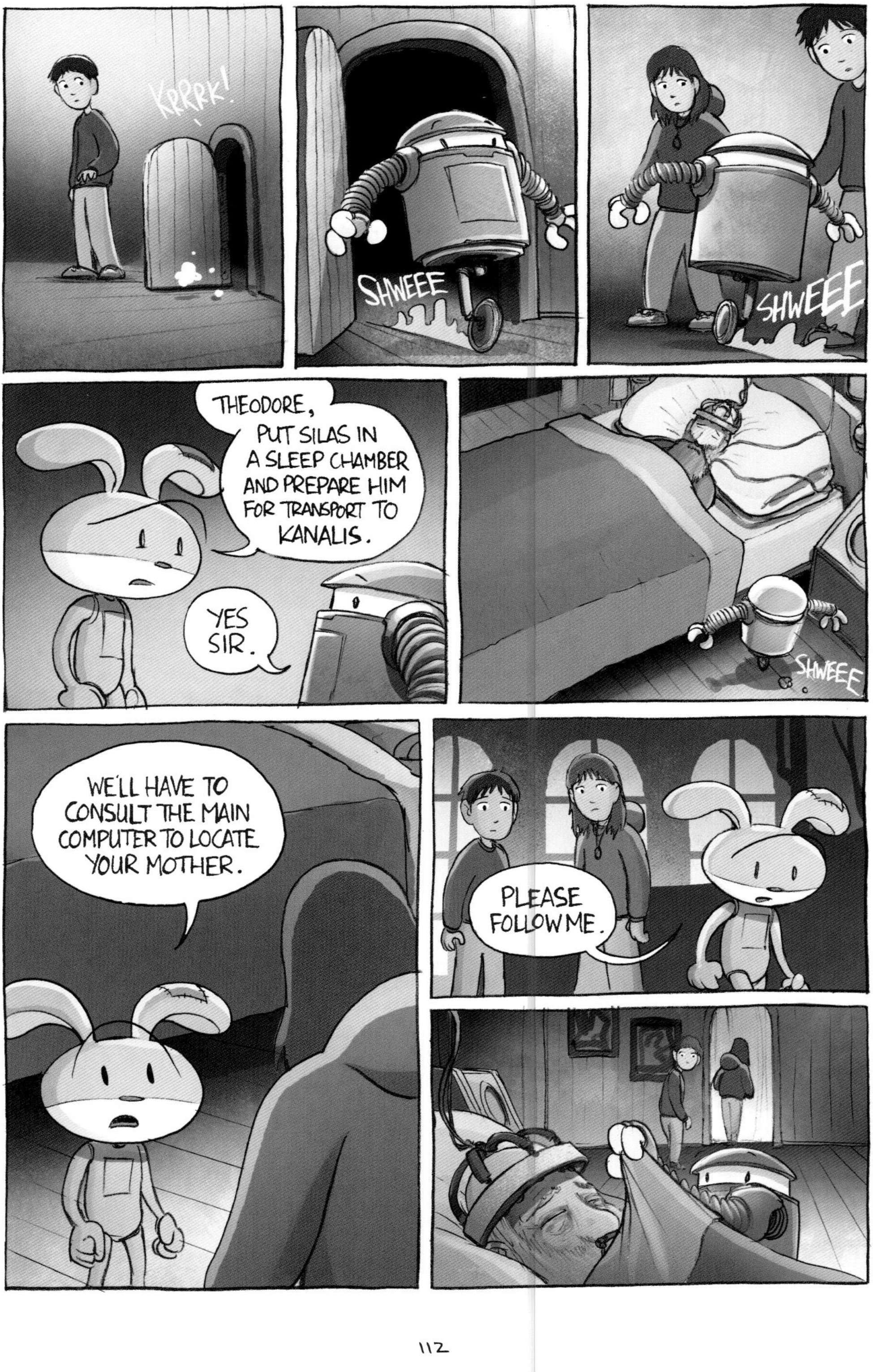
KRRRK!
SHWEEE
SHWEEE
THEODORE, PUT SILAS IN A SLEEP CHAMBER AND PREPARE HIM FOR TRANSPORT TO KANALIS.
YES SIR.
SHWEEE
WE'LL HAVE TO CONSULT THE MAIN COMPUTER TO LOCATE YOUR MOTHER.
PLEASE FOLLOW ME.

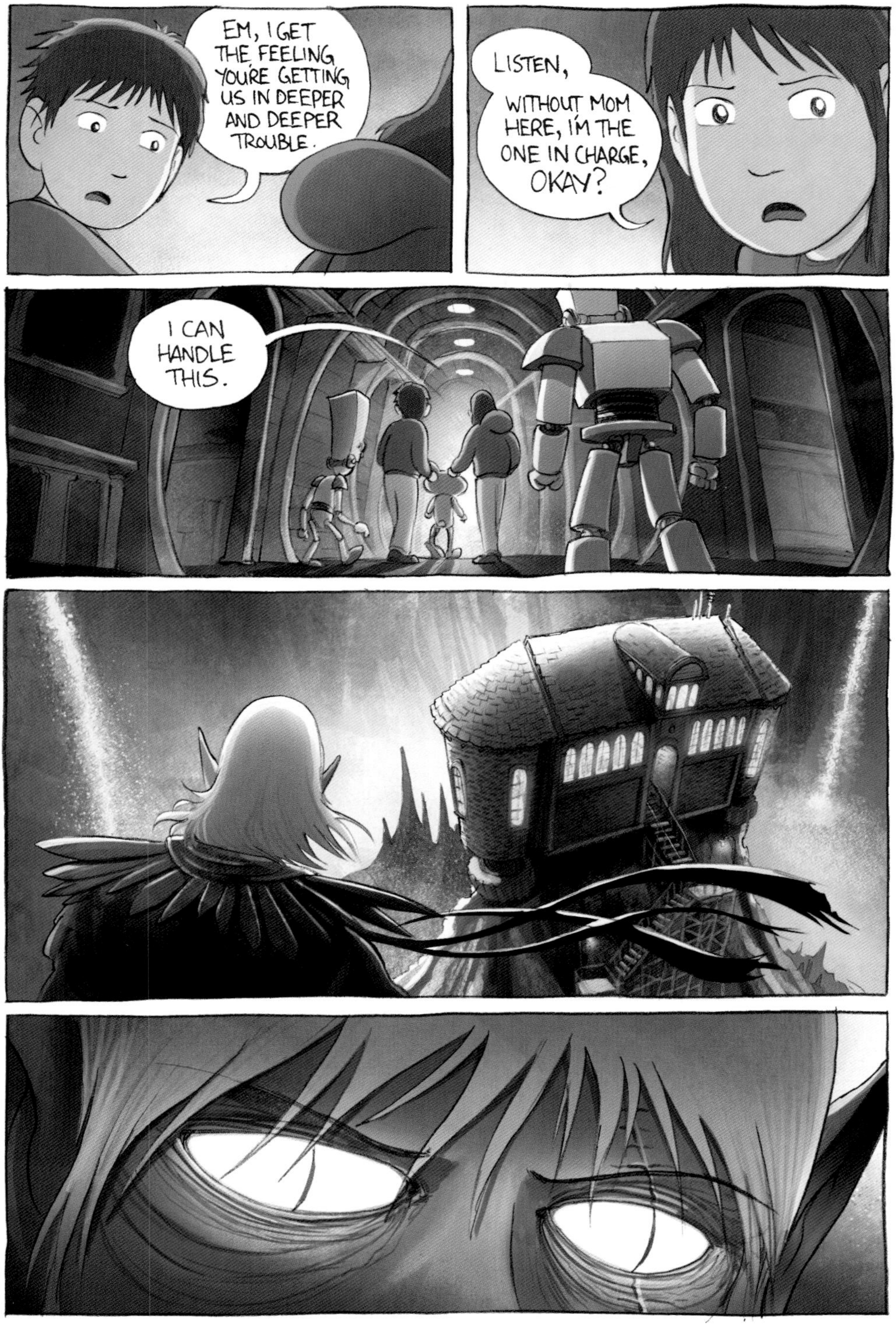

EM, I GET THE FEELING YOU'RE GETTING US IN DEEPER AND DEEPER TROUBLE.
LISTEN,
WITHOUT MOM HERE, I'M THE ONE IN CHARGE, OKAY?
I CAN HANDLE THIS.

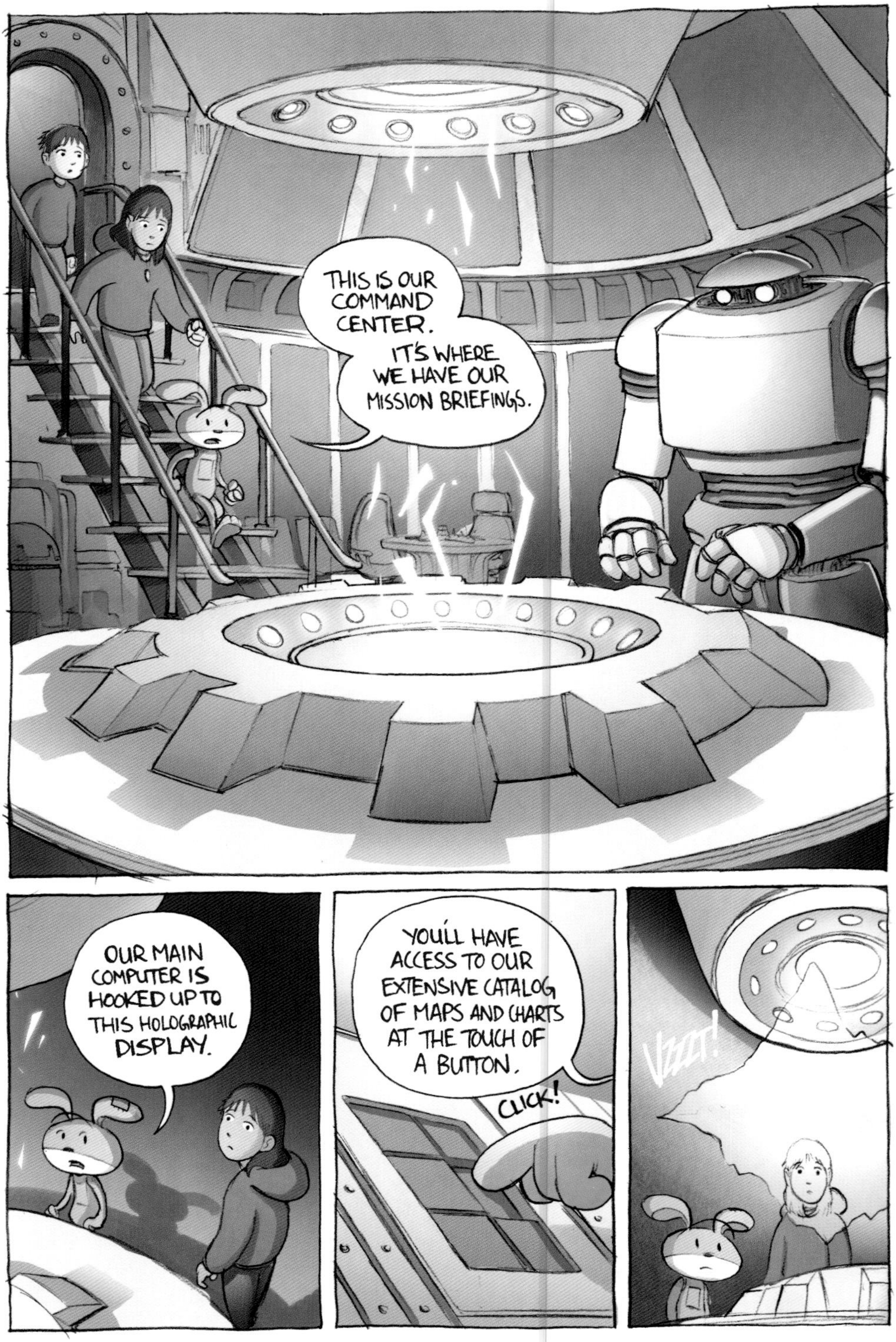

THIS IS OUR COMMAND CENTER.
IT'S WHERE WE HAVE OUR MISSION BRIEFINGS.
OUR MAIN COMPUTER IS HOOKED UP TO THIS HOLOGRAPHIC DISPLAY.
YOU'LL HAVE ACCESS TO OUR EXTENSIVE CATALOG OF MAPS AND CHARTS AT THE TOUCH OF A BUTTON.
CLICK!
VZZZT!

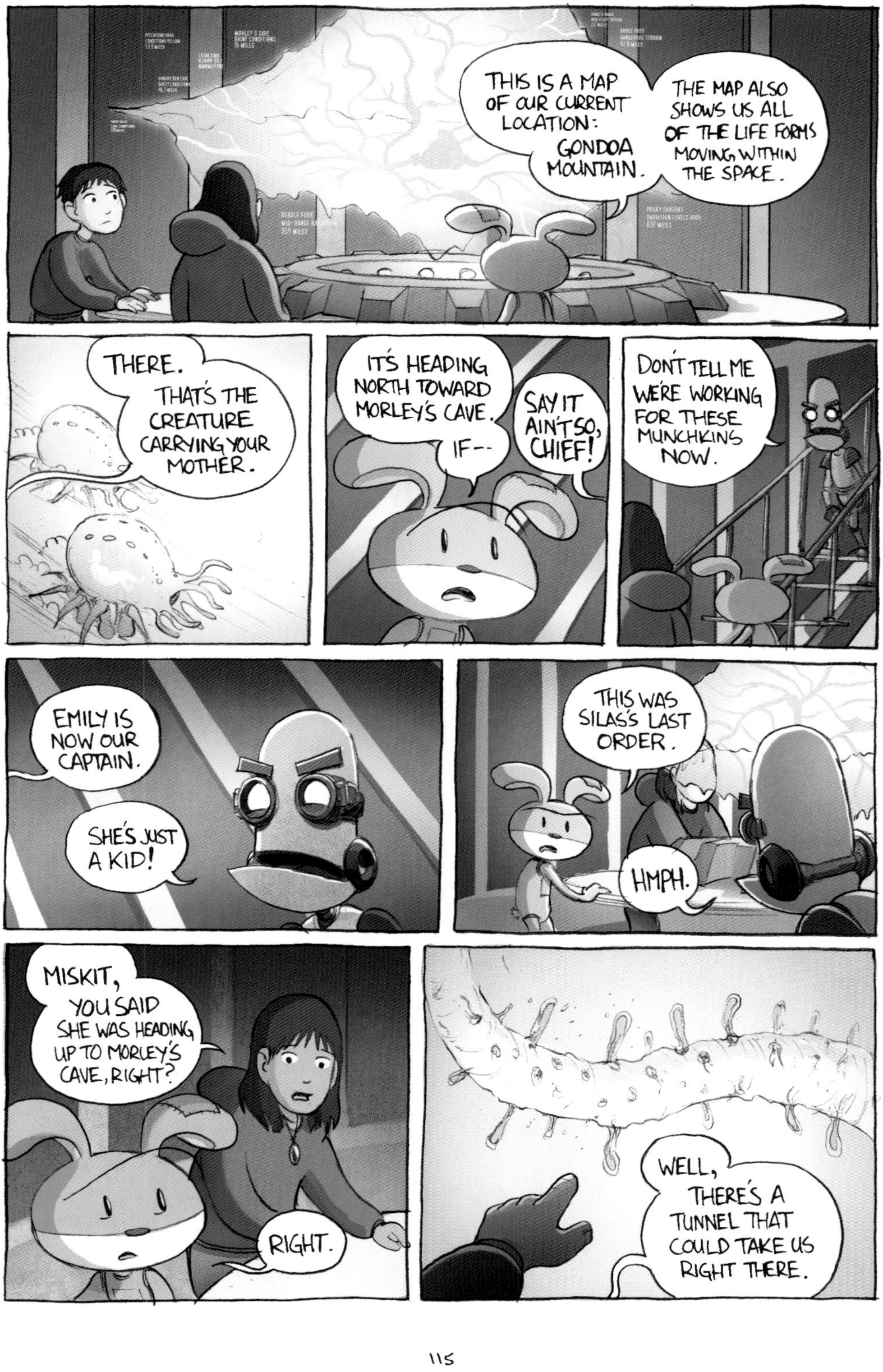
THIS IS A MAP OF OUR CURRENT LOCATION: GONDOA MOUNTAIN.
THE MAP ALSO SHOWS US ALL OF THE LIFE FORMS MOVING WITHIN THE SPACE.
THERE. THAT'S THE CREATURE CARRYING YOUR MOTHER.
IT'S HEADING NORTH TOWARD MORLEY'S CAVE.
IF--
SAY IT AIN'T SO, CHIEF!
DON'T TELL ME WE'RE WORKING FOR THESE MUNCHKINS NOW.
EMILY IS NOW OUR CAPTAIN.
SHE'S JUST A KID!
THIS WAS SILAS'S LAST ORDER.
HMPH.
MISKIT, YOU SAID SHE WAS HEADING UP TO MORLEY'S CAVE, RIGHT?
RIGHT.
WELL, THERE'S A TUNNEL THAT COULD TAKE US RIGHT THERE.

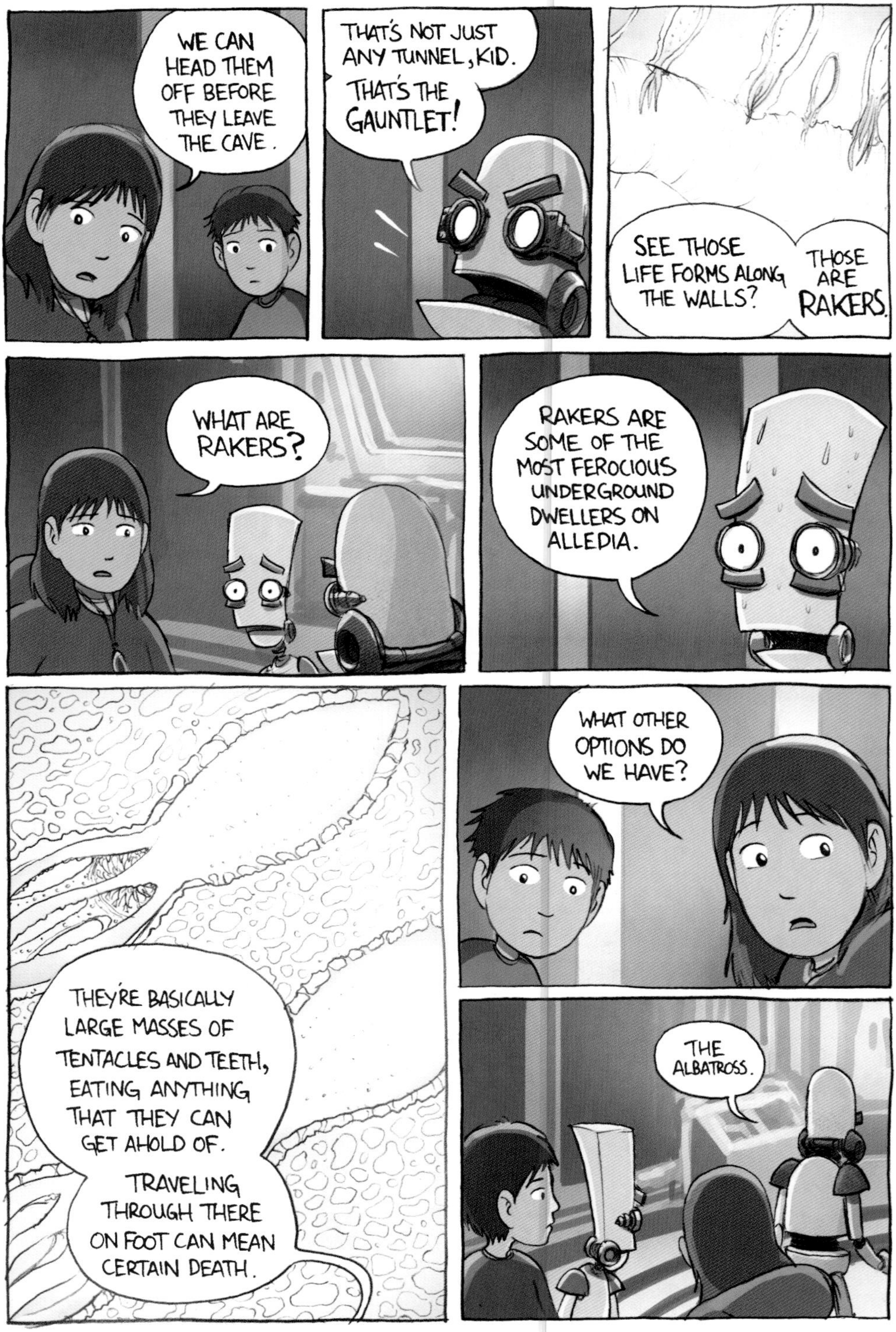
WE CAN HEAD THEM OFF BEFORE THEY LEAVE THE CAVE.
THAT'S NOT JUST ANY TUNNEL, KID.
THAT'S THE GAUNTLET!
SEE THOSE LIFE FORMS ALONG THE WALLS?
THOSE ARE RAKERS.
WHAT ARE RAKERS?
RAKERS ARE SOME OF THE MOST FEROCIOUS UNDERGROUND DWELLERS ON ALLEDIA.
THEY'RE BASICALLY LARGE MASSES OF TENTACLES AND TEETH, EATING ANYTHING THAT THEY CAN GET AHOLD OF.
TRAVELING THROUGH THERE ON FOOT CAN MEAN CERTAIN DEATH.
WHAT OTHER OPTIONS DO WE HAVE?
THE ALBATROSS.

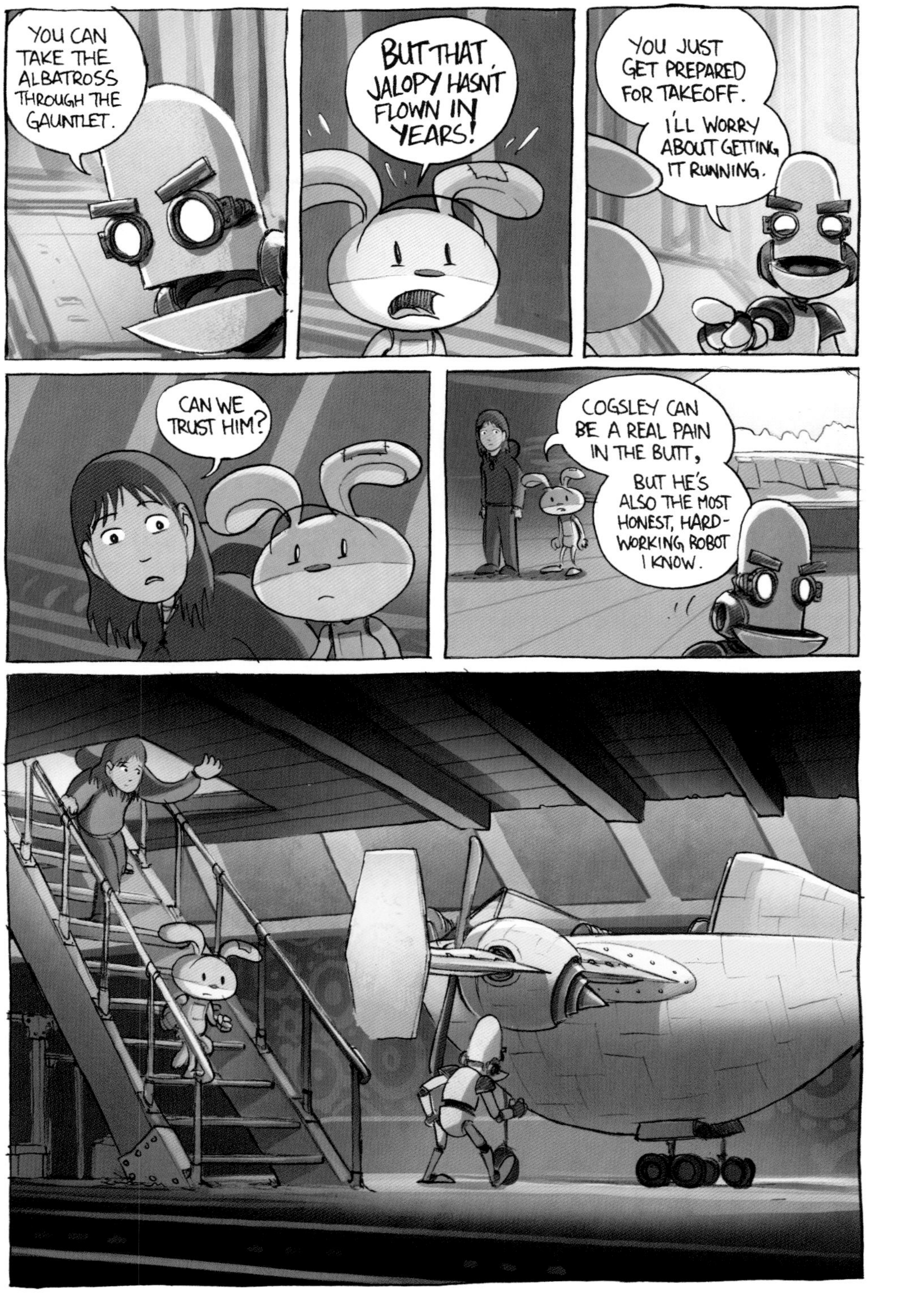
YOU CAN TAKE THE ALBATROSS THROUGH THE GAUNTLET.
BUT THAT JALOPY HASN'T FLOWN IN YEARS!
YOU JUST GET PREPARED FOR TAKEOFF.
I'LL WORRY ABOUT GETTING IT RUNNING.
CAN WE TRUST HIM?
COGSLEY CAN BE A REAL PAIN IN THE BUTT,
BUT HE'S ALSO THE MOST HONEST, HARD-WORKING ROBOT I KNOW.

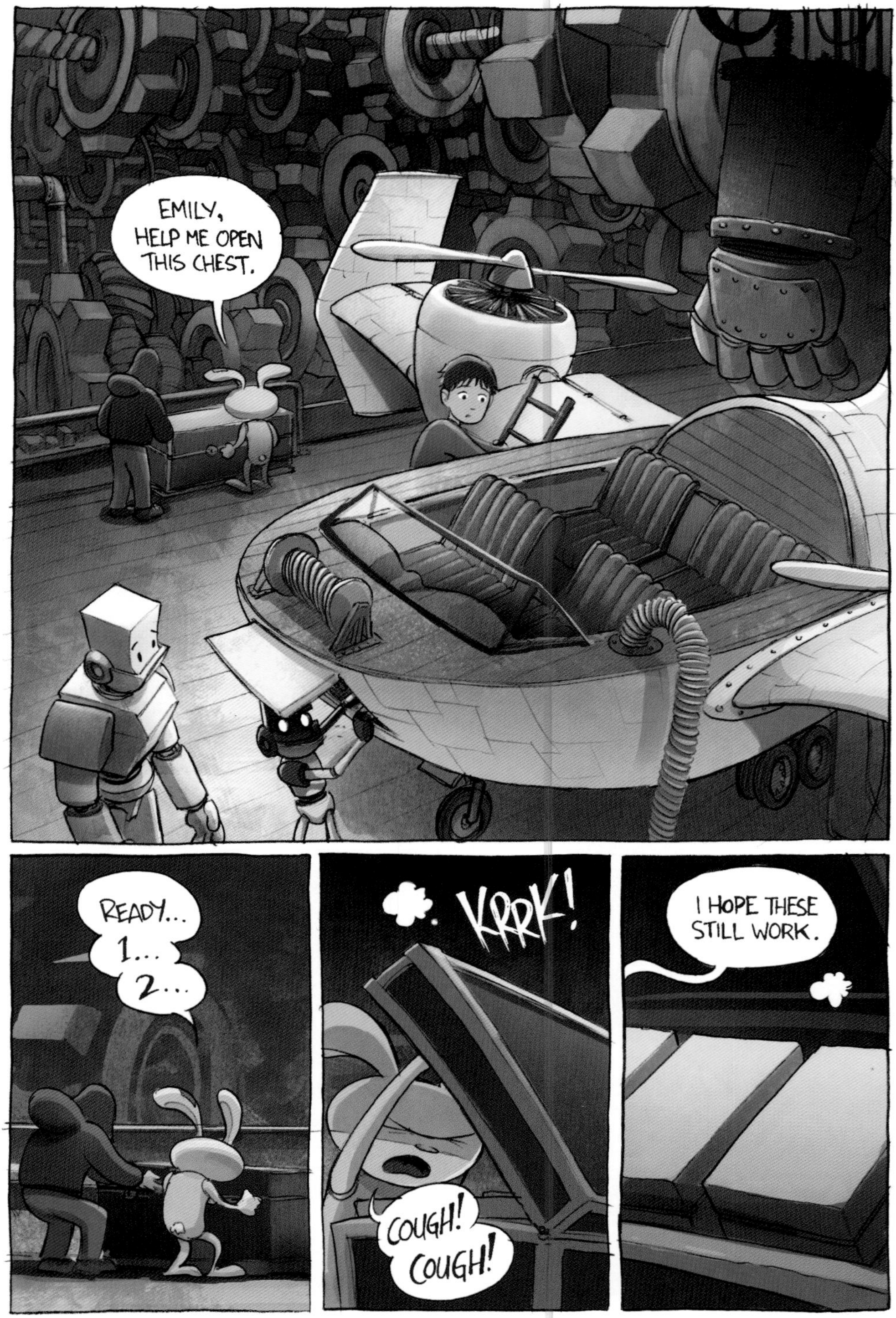
EMILY, HELP ME OPEN THIS CHEST.
READY... 1... 2...
KRRK!
COUGH! COUGH!
I HOPE THESE STILL WORK.

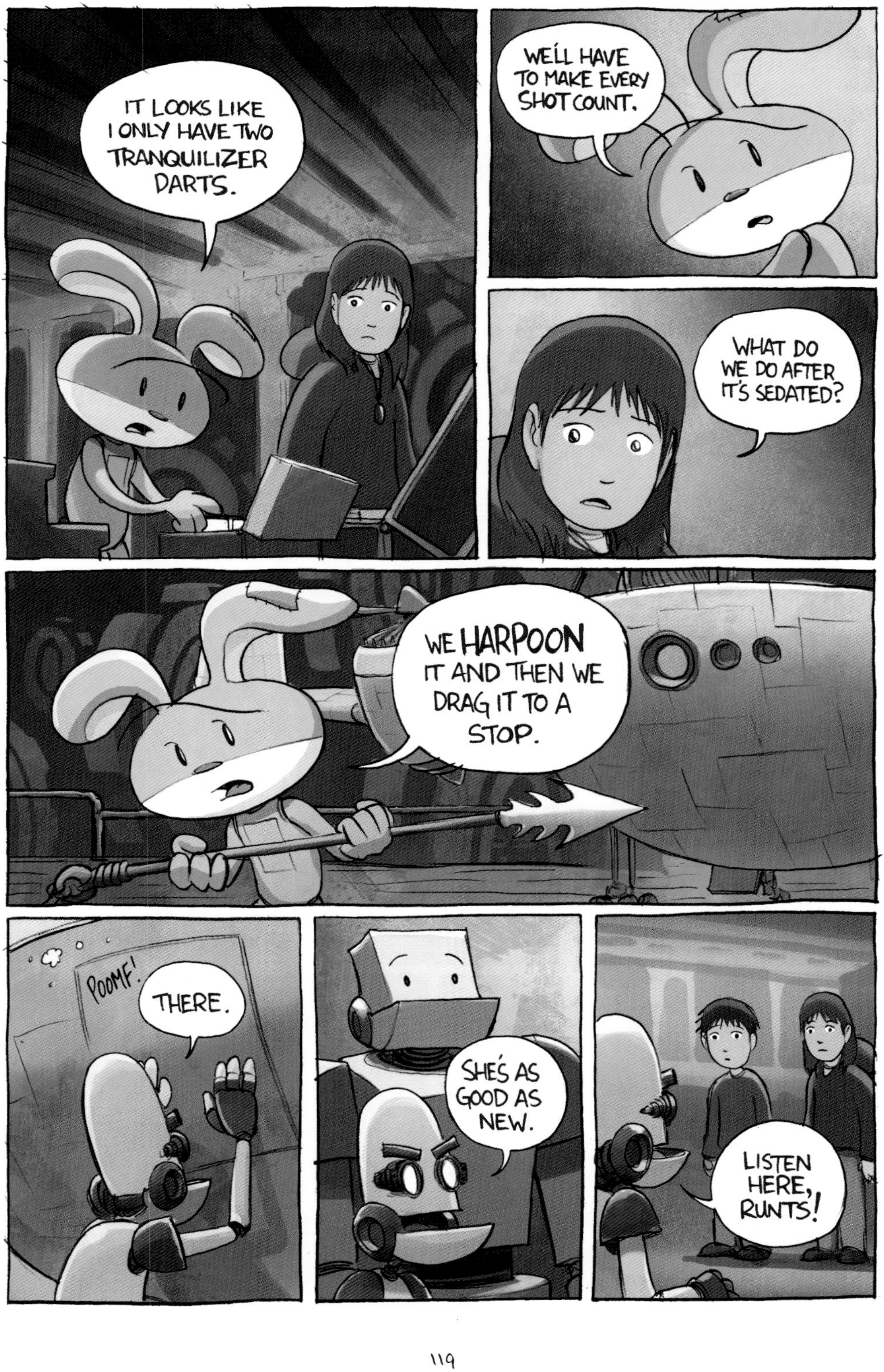
IT LOOKS LIKE I ONLY HAVE TWO TRANQUILIZER DARTS.
WE'LL HAVE TO MAKE EVERY SHOT COUNT.
WHAT DO WE DO AFTER IT'S SEDATED?
WE HARPOON IT AND THEN WE DRAG IT TO A STOP.
POOMF!
THERE.
SHE'S AS GOOD AS NEW.
LISTEN HERE, RUNTS!

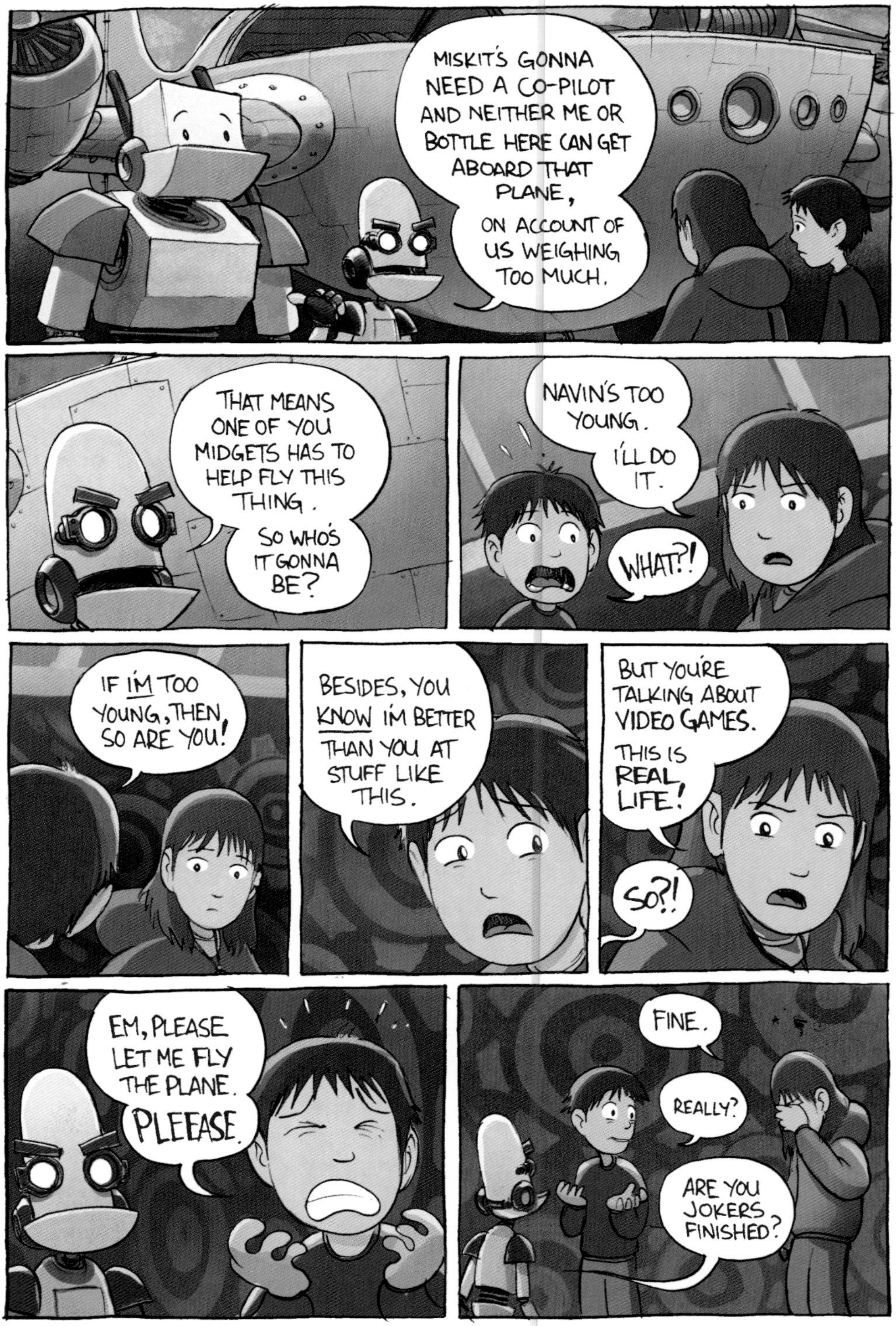
MISKIT'S GONNA NEED A CO-PILOT AND NEITHER ME OR BOTTLE HERE CAN GET ABOARD THAT PLANE,
ON ACCOUNT OF US WEIGHING TOO MUCH.
THAT MEANS ONE OF YOU MIDGETS HAS TO HELP FLY THIS THING.
SO WHO'S IT GONNA BE?
NAVIN'S TOO YOUNG.
I'LL DO IT.
WHAT?!
IF I'M TOO YOUNG, THEN, SO ARE YOU!
BESIDES, YOU KNOW I'M BETTER THAN YOU AT STUFF LIKE THIS.
BUT YOU'RE TALKING ABOUT VIDEO GAMES.
THIS IS REAL LIFE!
SO?!
EM, PLEASE LET ME FLY THE PLANE.
PLEEASE.
FINE.
REALLY?
ARE YOU JOKERS FINISHED?

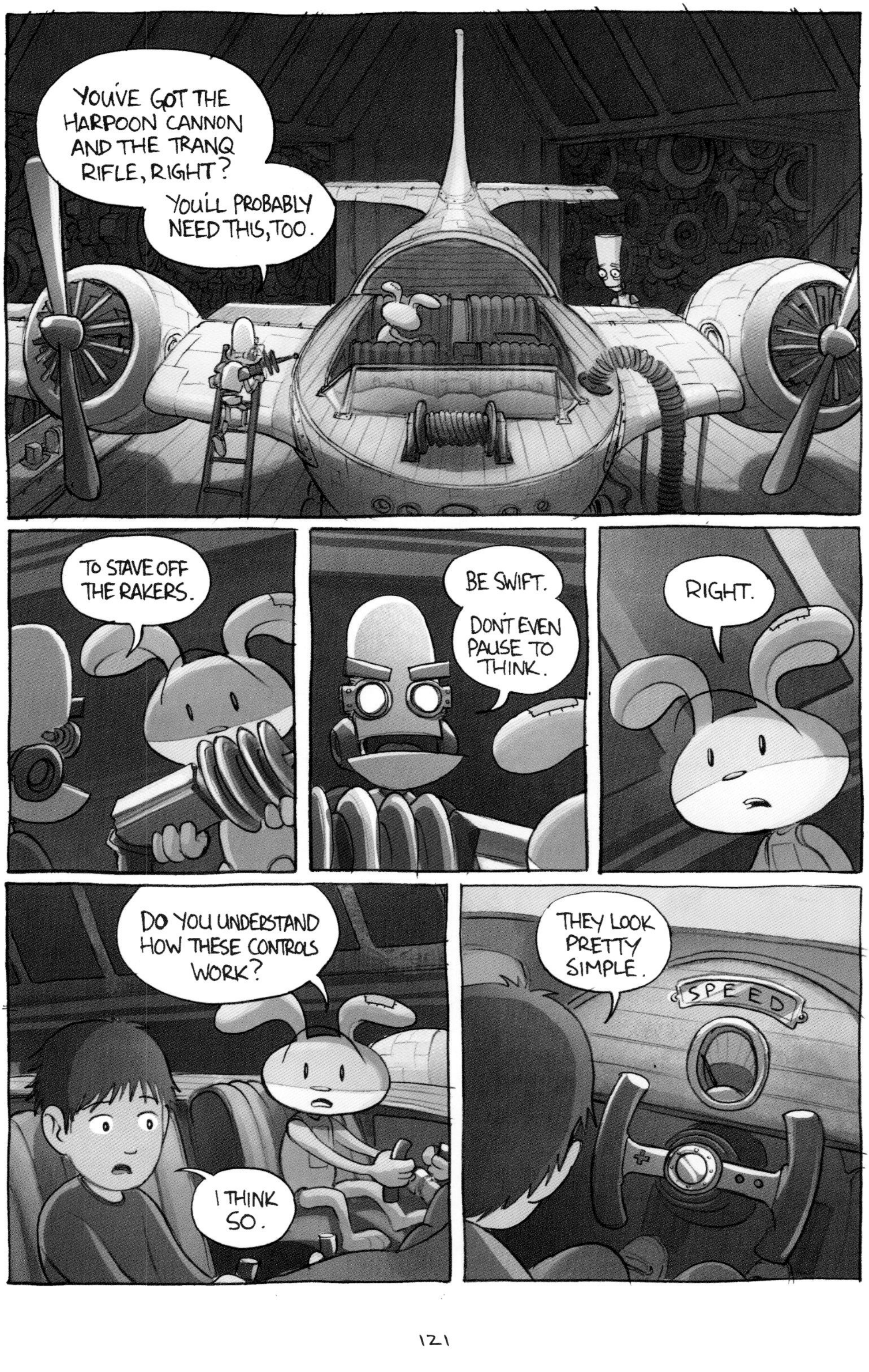
YOU'VE GOT THE HARPOON CANNON AND THE TRANQ RIFLE, RIGHT?
YOU'LL PROBABLY NEED THIS, TOO.
TO STAVE OFF THE RAKERS.
BE SWIFT.
DON'T EVEN PAUSE TO THINK.
RIGHT.
DO YOU UNDERSTAND HOW THESE CONTROLS WORK?
I THINK SO.
THEY LOOK PRETTY SIMPLE.
SPEED

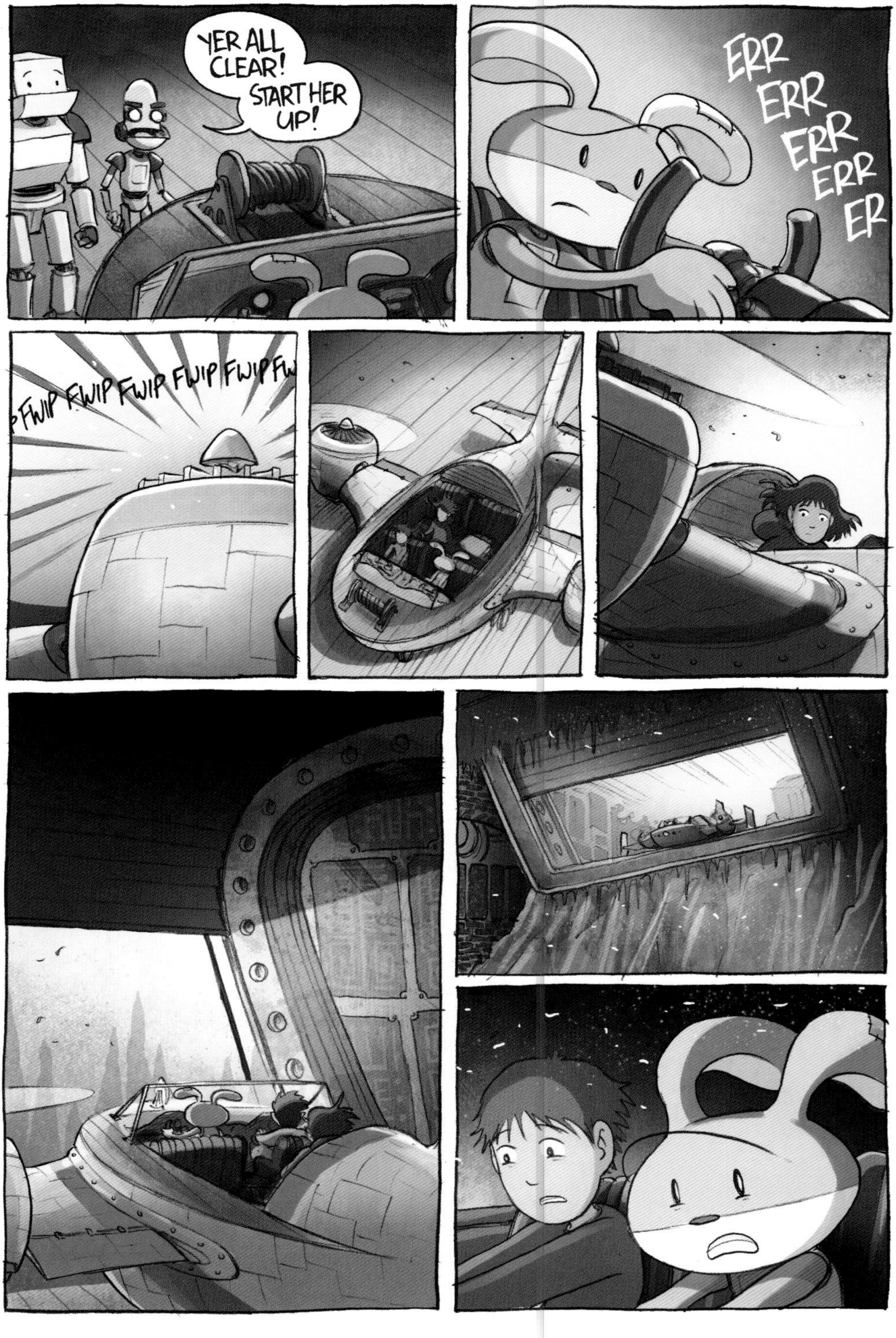
YER ALL CLEAR! START HER UP!
ERR ERR ERR ERR ER
FWIP FWIP FWIP FWIP FWIP FW

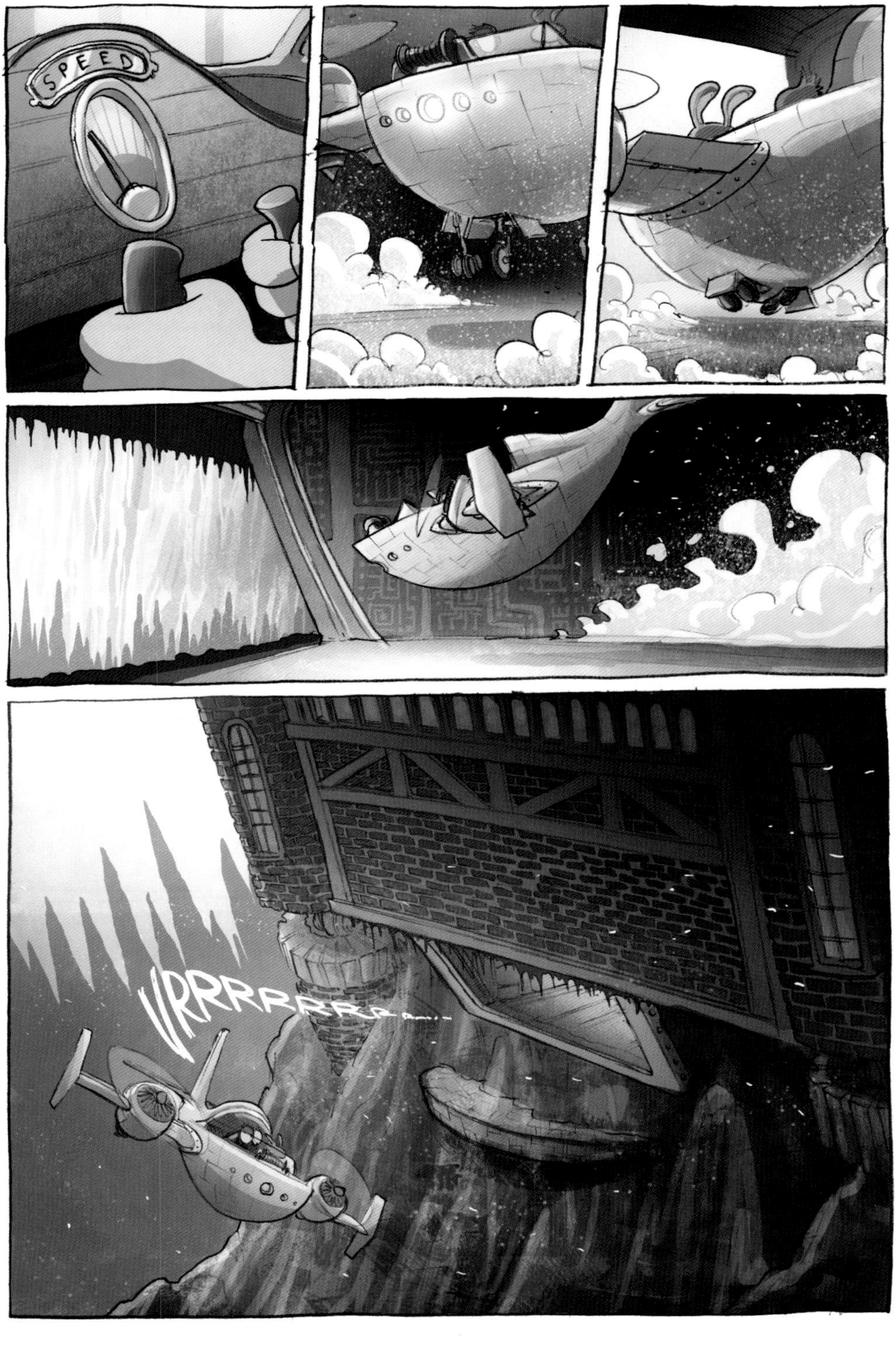
SPEED
URRRRRRRR

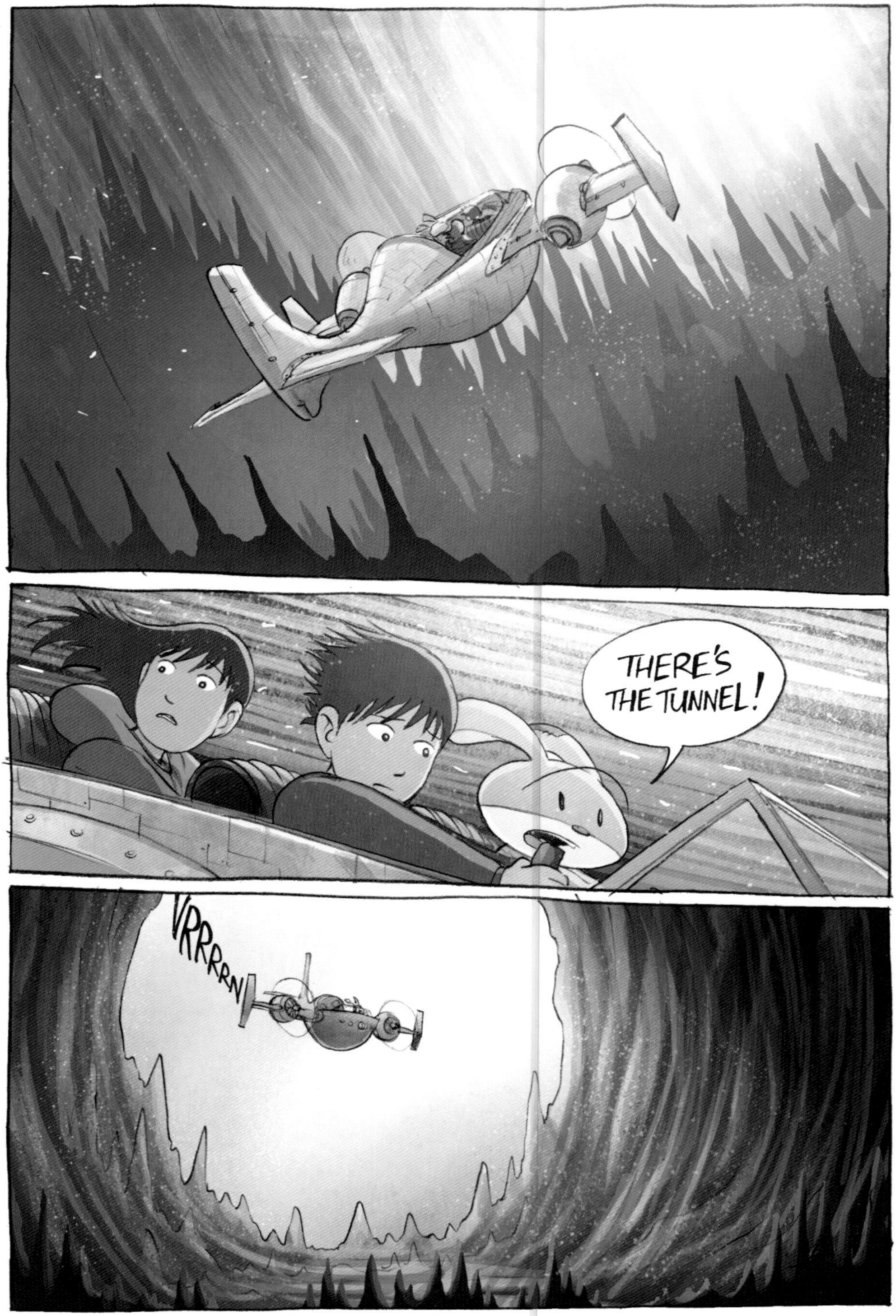
THERE'S THE TUNNEL!
VRRRRRN

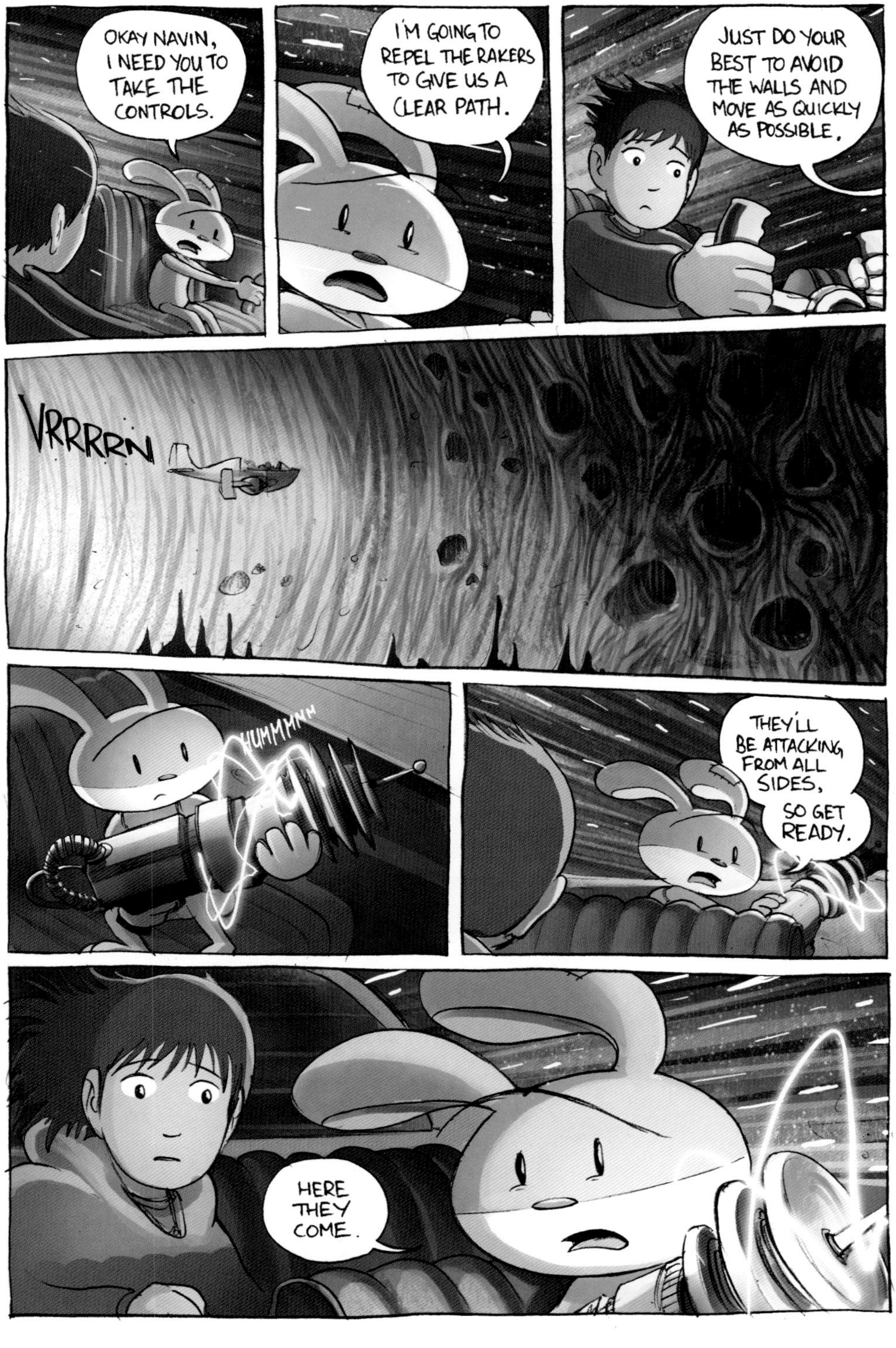
OKAY NAVIN, I NEED YOU TO TAKE THE CONTROLS.
I'M GOING TO REPEL THE RAKERS TO GIVE US A CLEAR PATH.
JUST DO YOUR BEST TO AVOID THE WALLS AND MOVE AS QUICKLY AS POSSIBLE.
VRRRRN
HUMMMM
THEY'LL BE ATTACKING FROM ALL SIDES,
SO GET READY.
HERE THEY COME.

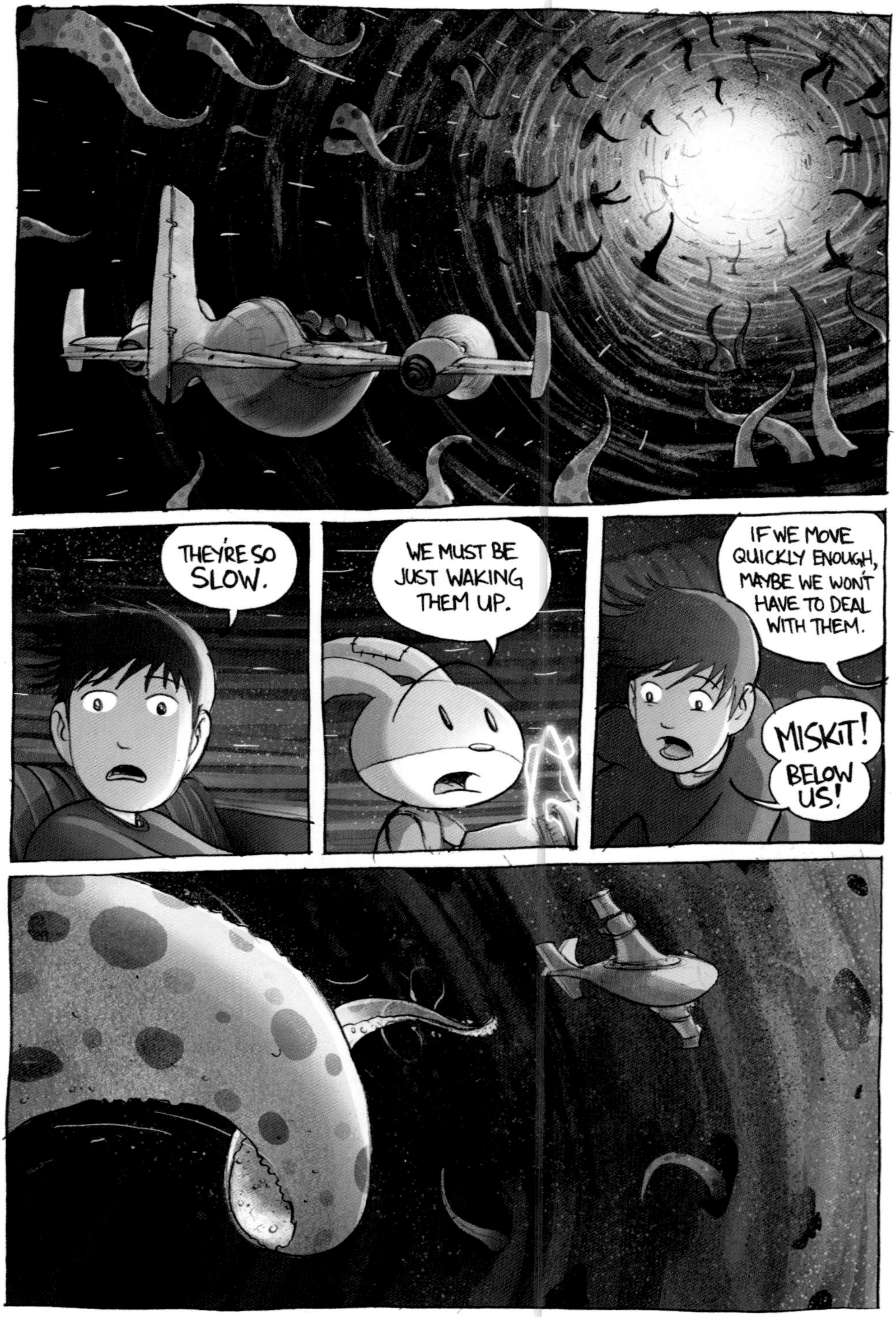
THEY'RE SO SLOW.
WE MUST BE JUST WAKING THEM UP.
IF WE MOVE QUICKLY ENOUGH, MAYBE WE WON'T HAVE TO DEAL WITH THEM.
MISKIT! BELOW US!

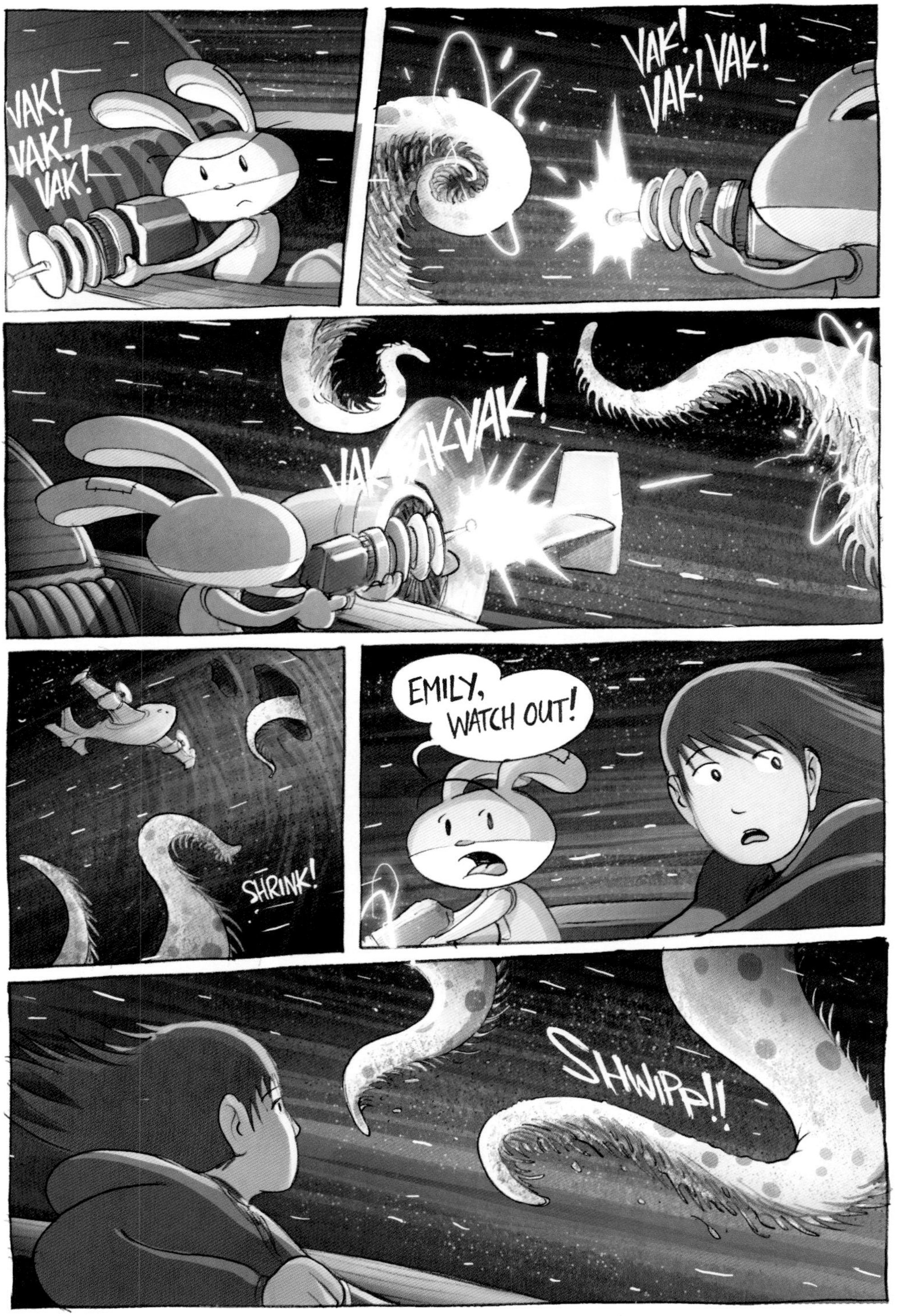
VAK!
VAK!
VAK!
VAK!
VAK! VAK!
VAKVAKVAK!
SHRINK!
EMILY, WATCH OUT!
SHWIPP!!

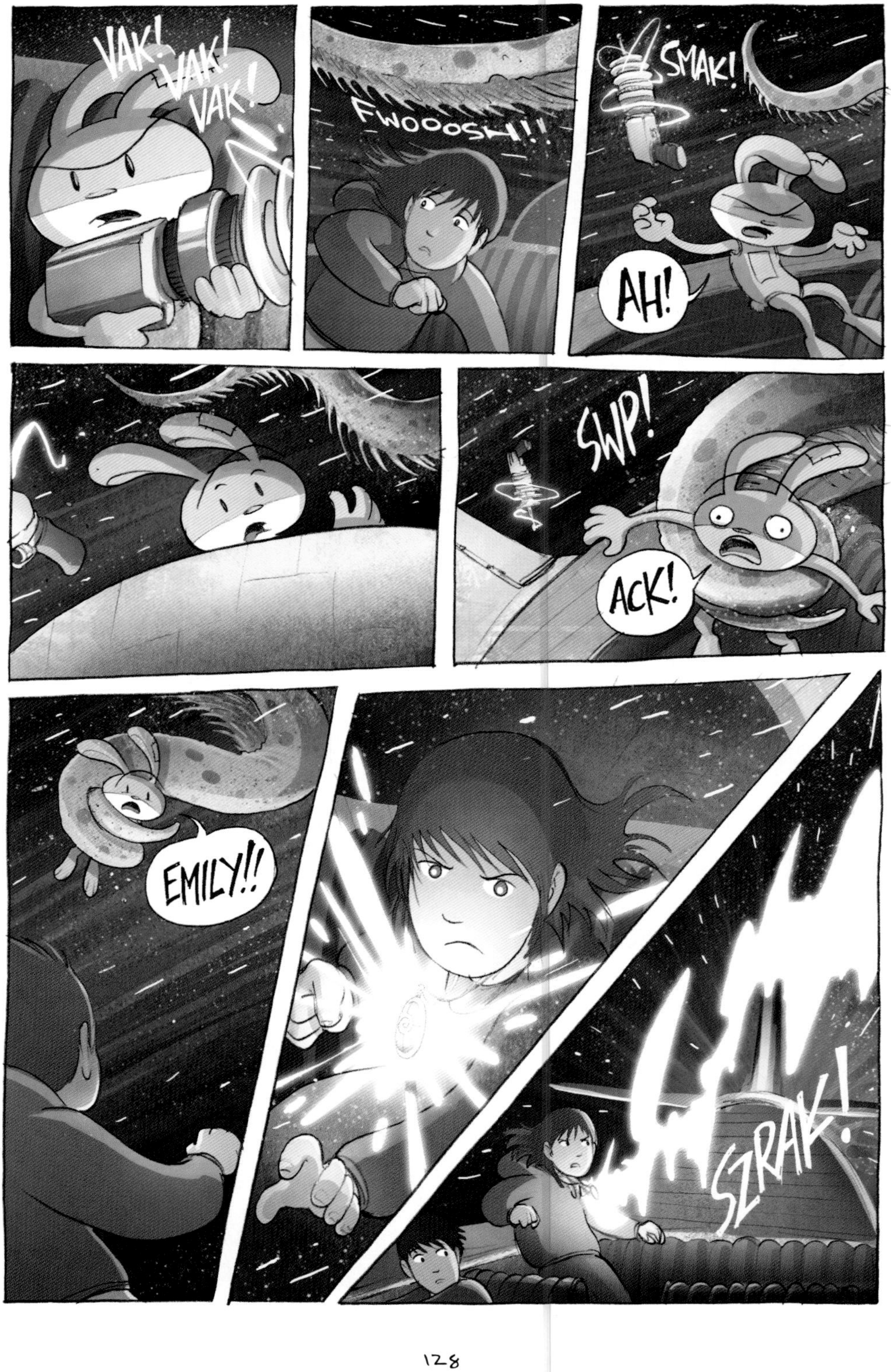
VAK! VAK! VAK!
FWOOOSH!!
SMAK!
AH!
SWP!
ACK!
EMILY!!
SZRAK!

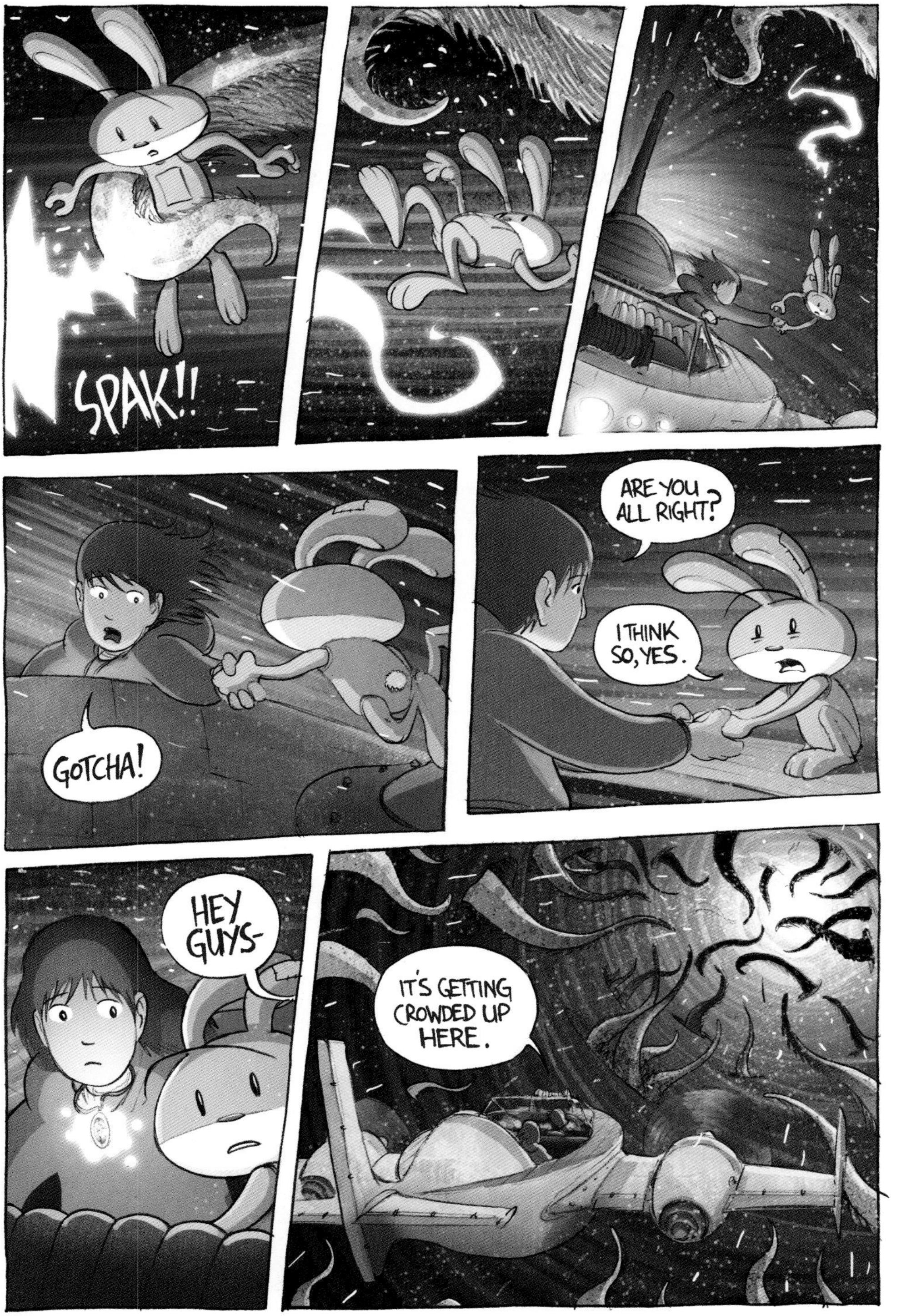
SPAK!!
ARE YOU ALL RIGHT?
GOTCHA!
I THINK SO, YES.
HEY GUYS-
IT'S GETTING CROWDED UP HERE.

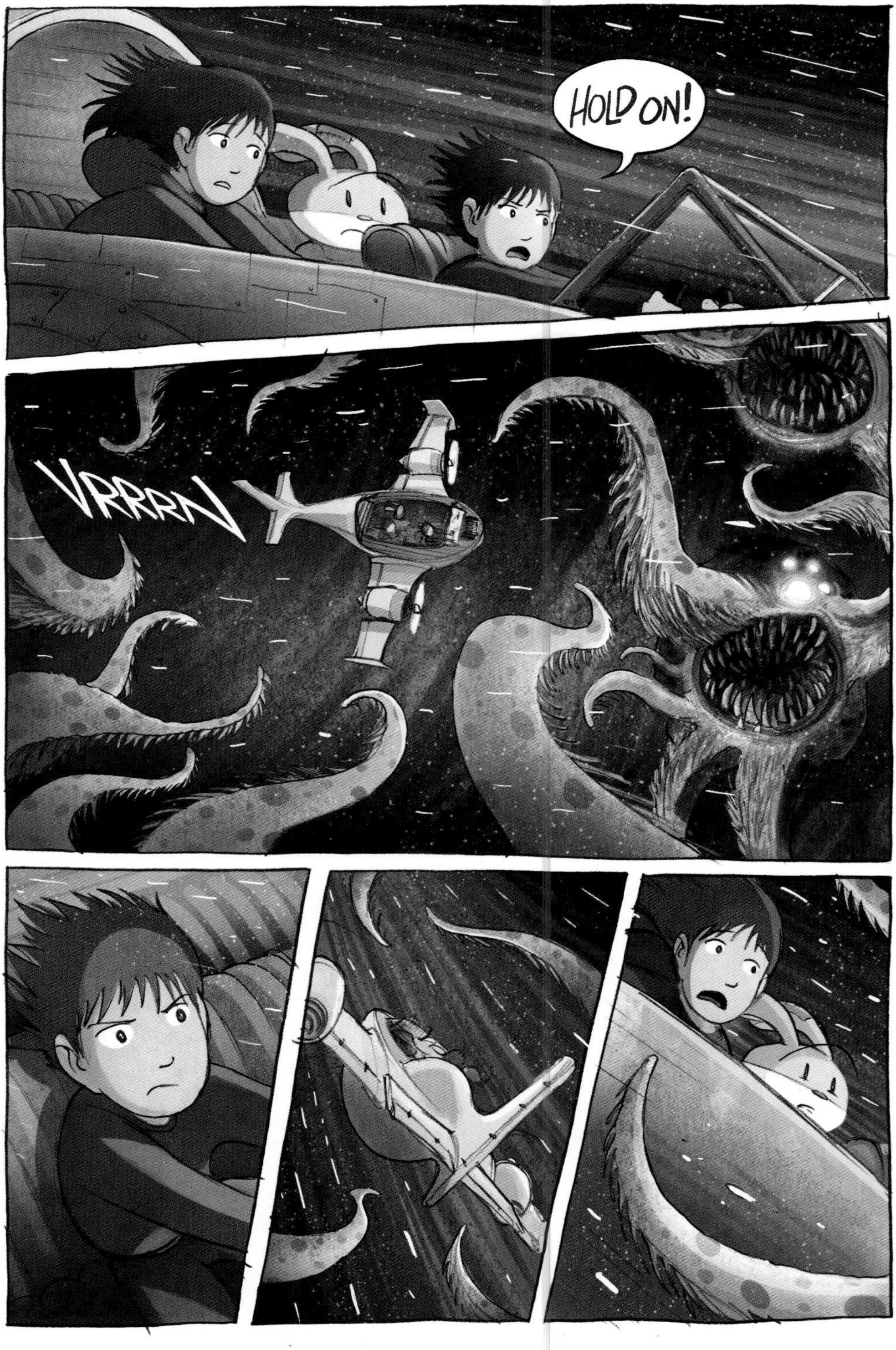
HOLD ON!
VRRRN

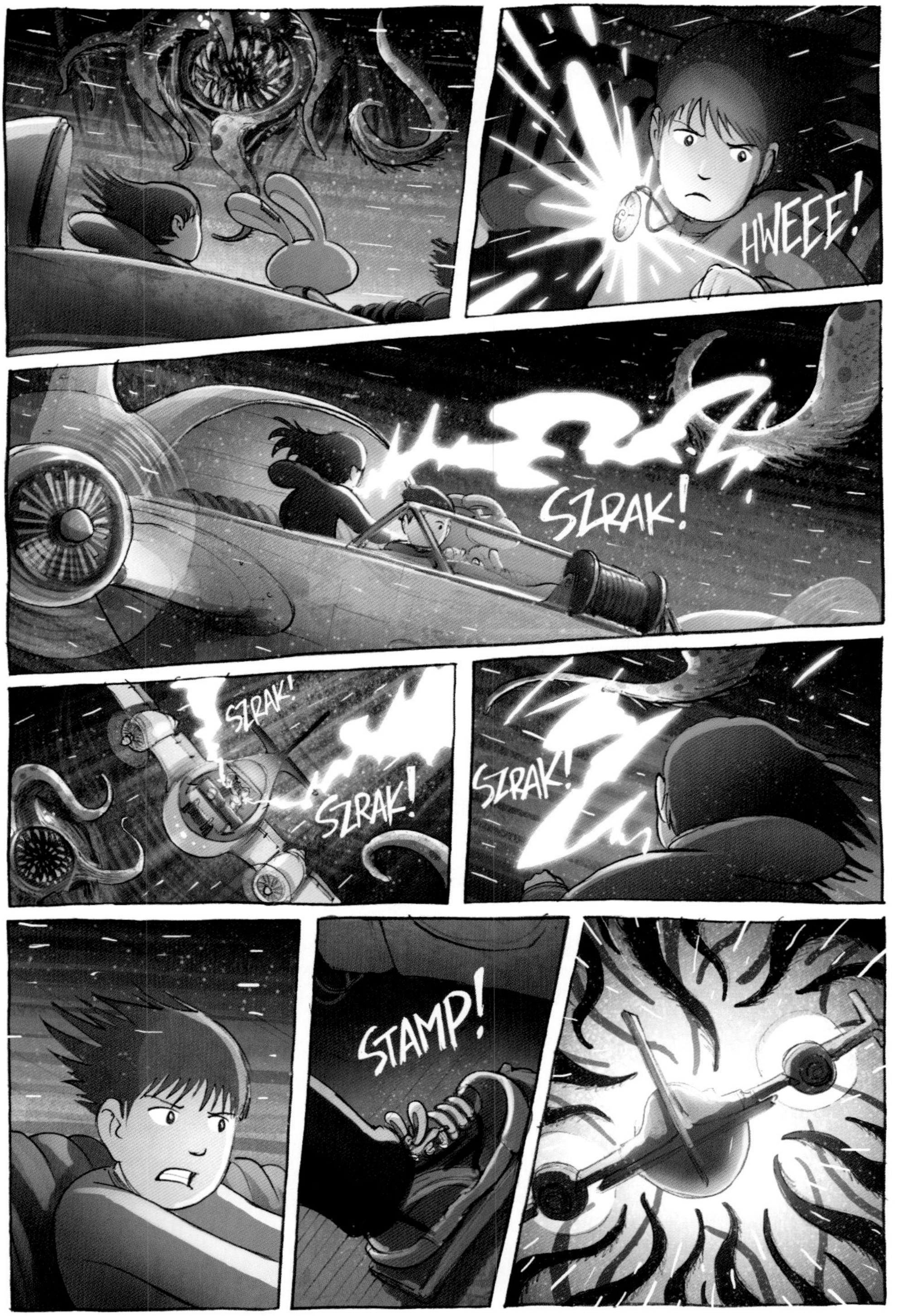
HWEEE!
SZRAK!
SZRAK!
SZRAK!
SZRAK!
STAMP!

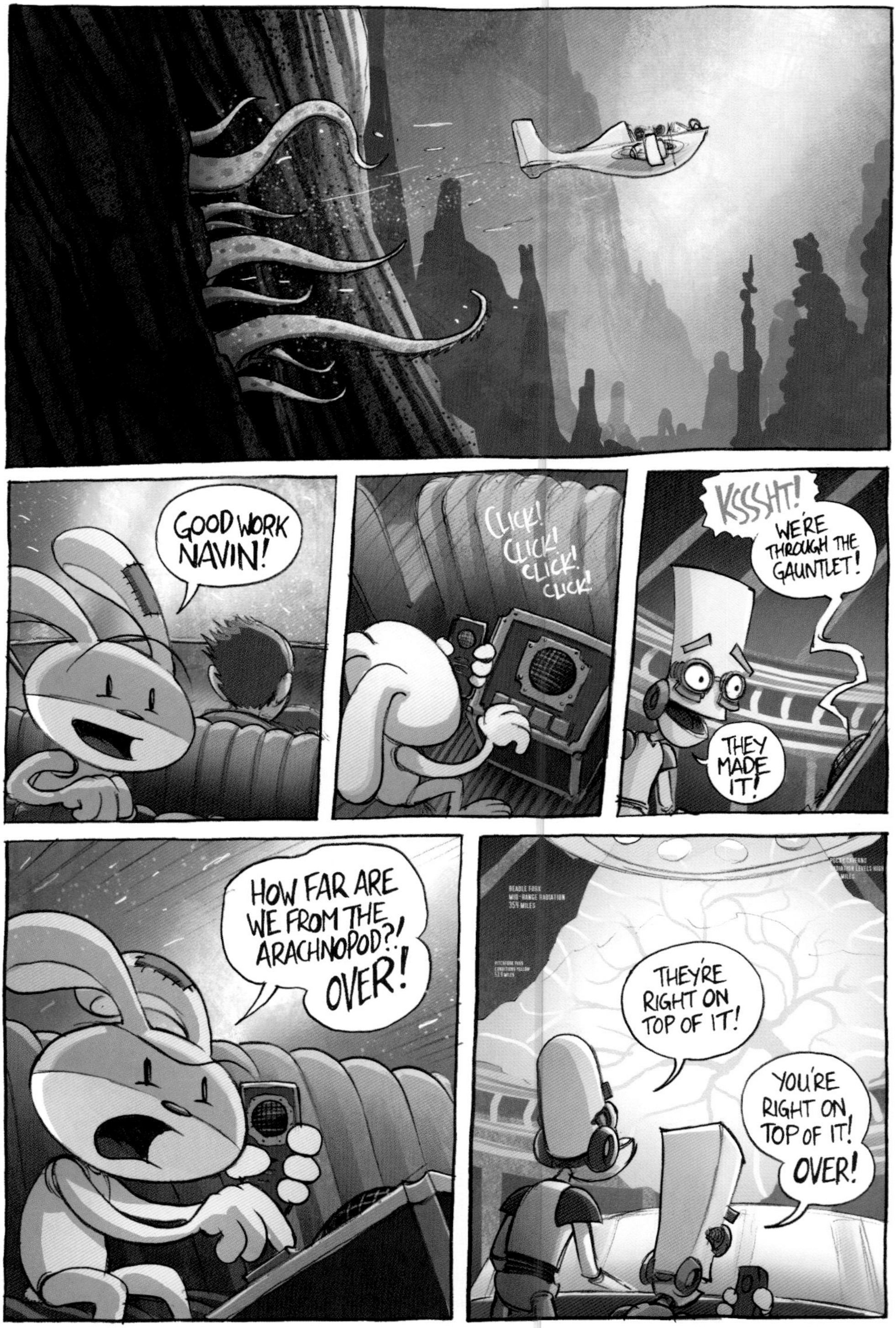
GOOD WORK NAVIN!
CLICK! CLICK! CLICK! CLICK!
KSSSHT!
WE'RE THROUGH THE GAUNTLET!
THEY MADE IT!
HOW FAR ARE WE FROM THE ARACHNOPOD?! OVER!
BEADLE FORK
MID-RANGE RADIATION
354 MILES
THEY'RE RIGHT ON TOP OF IT!
YOU'RE RIGHT ON TOP OF IT! OVER!

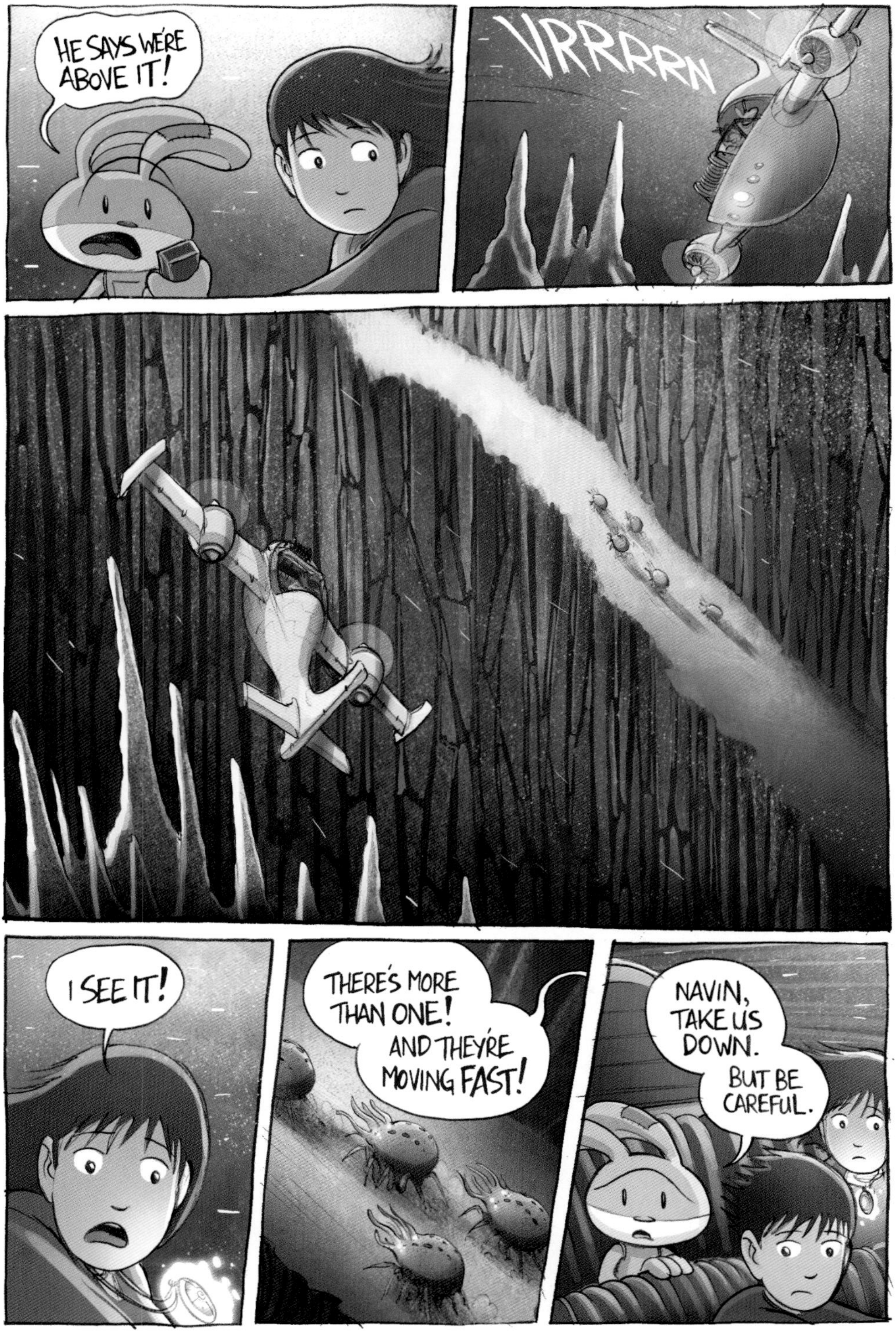
HE SAYS WE'RE ABOVE IT!
VRRRRRN
I SEE IT!
THERE'S MORE THAN ONE!
AND THEY'RE MOVING FAST!
NAVIN, TAKE US DOWN.
BUT BE CAREFUL.

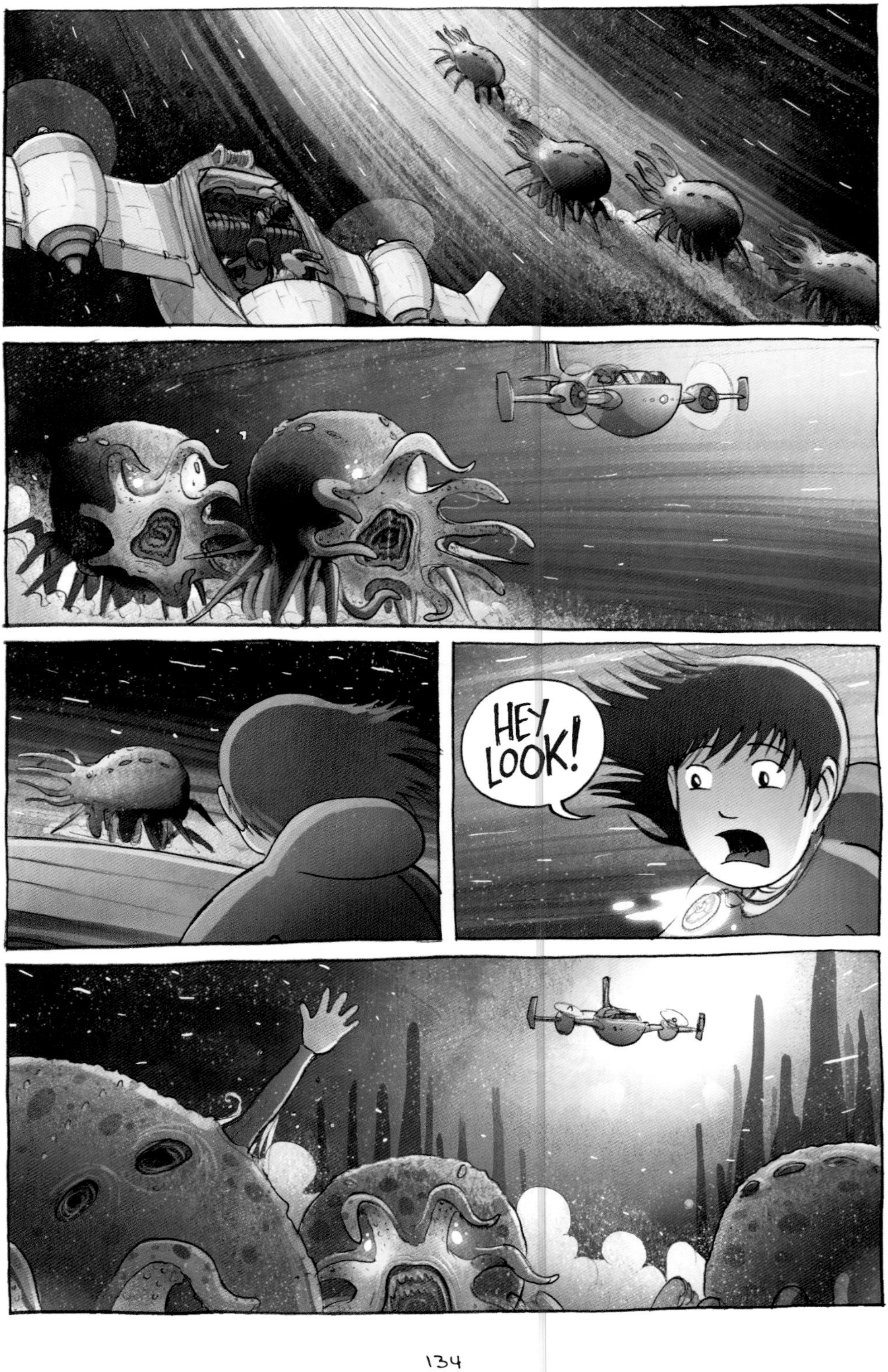
HEY LOOK!

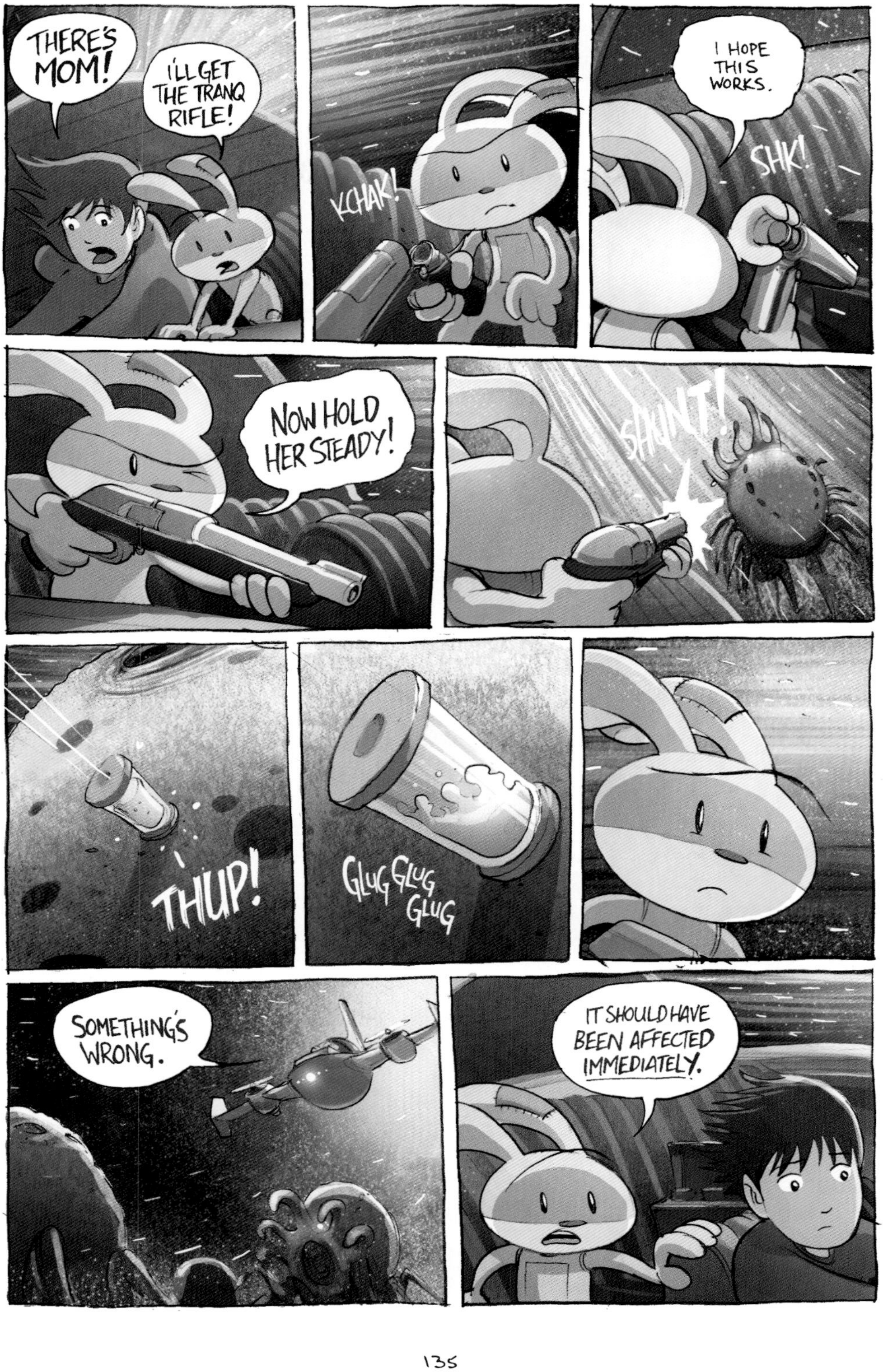
THERE'S MOM!
I'LL GET THE TRANQ RIFLE!
KCHAK!
I HOPE THIS WORKS.
SHK!
NOW HOLD HER STEADY!
SHUNT!
THUP!
GLUG GLUG GLUG
SOMETHING'S WRONG.
IT SHOULD HAVE BEEN AFFECTED IMMEDIATELY.

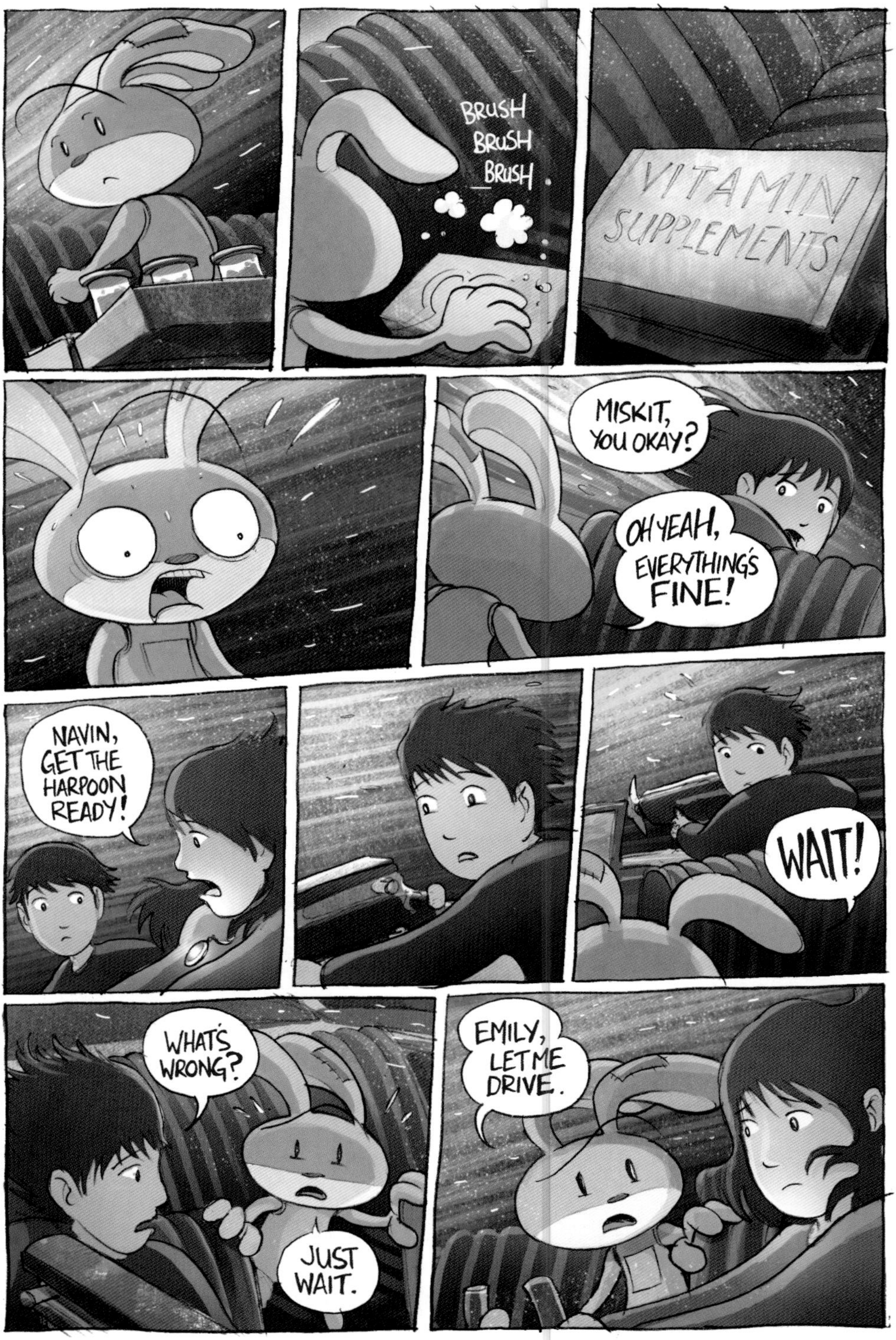
BRUSH
BRUSH
BRUSH
VITAMIN SUPPLEMENTS
MISKIT, YOU OKAY?
OH YEAH, EVERYTHING'S FINE!
NAVIN, GET THE HARPOON READY!
WAIT!
WHAT'S WRONG?
JUST WAIT.
EMILY, LET ME DRIVE.

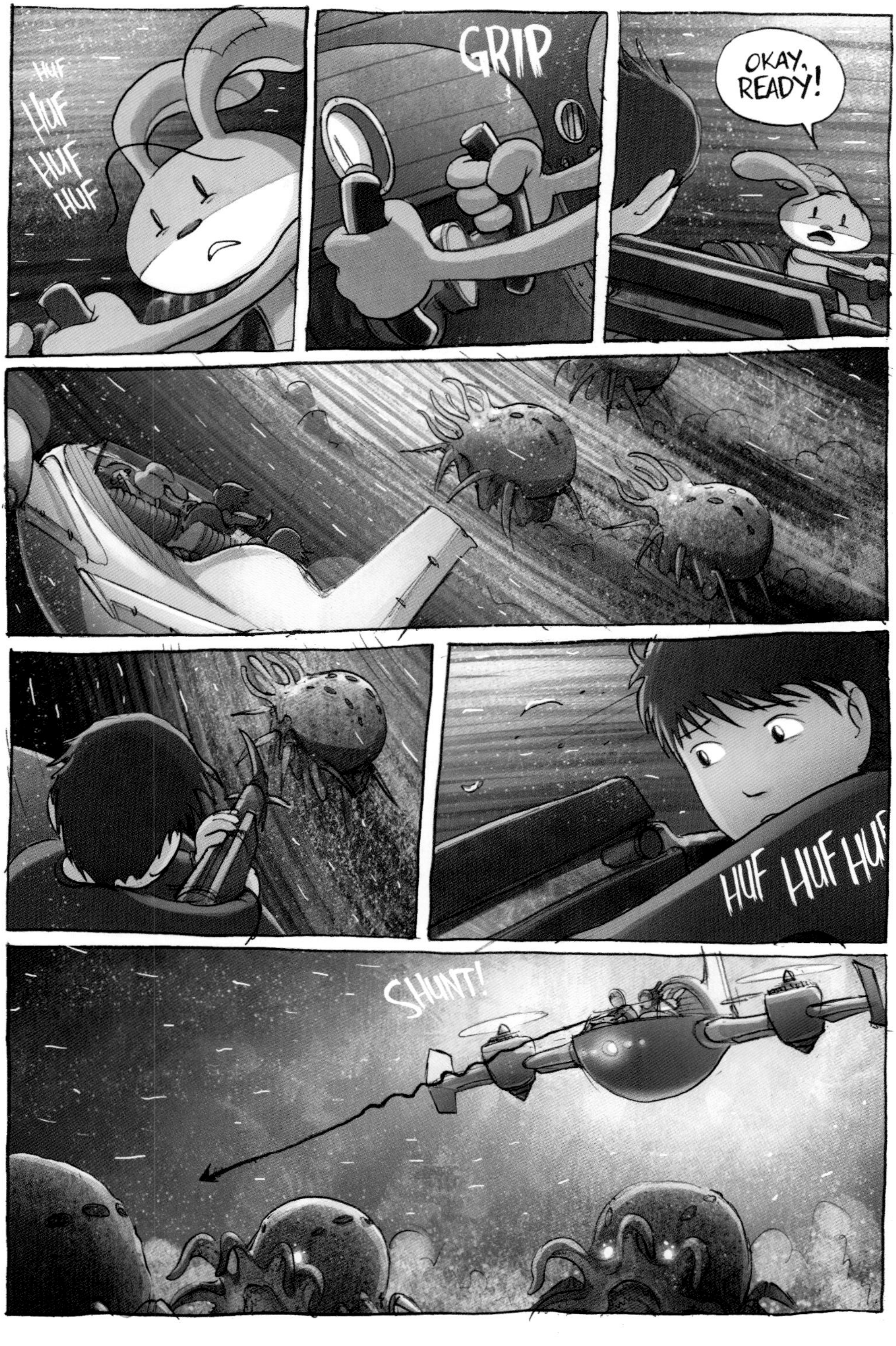
HUF
HUF
HUF
HUF
GRIP
OKAY, READY!
HUF HUF HUF
SHUNT!

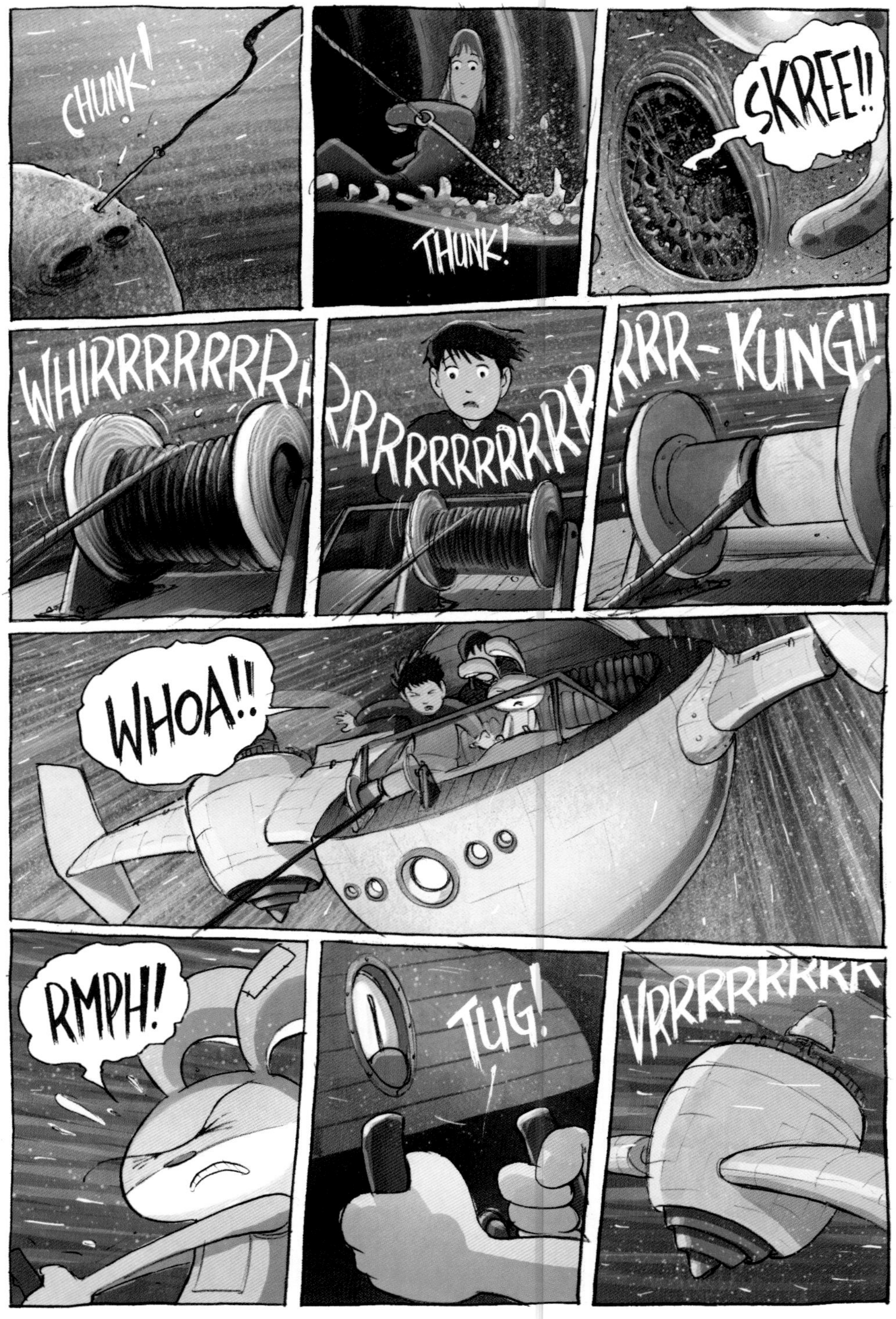
CHUNK!
THUNK!
SKREE!!
WHIRRRRRRRRRRRRRRRRRRRRRRRRRR-KUNG!!
WHOA!!
RMPH!
TUG!
VRRRRKKKK

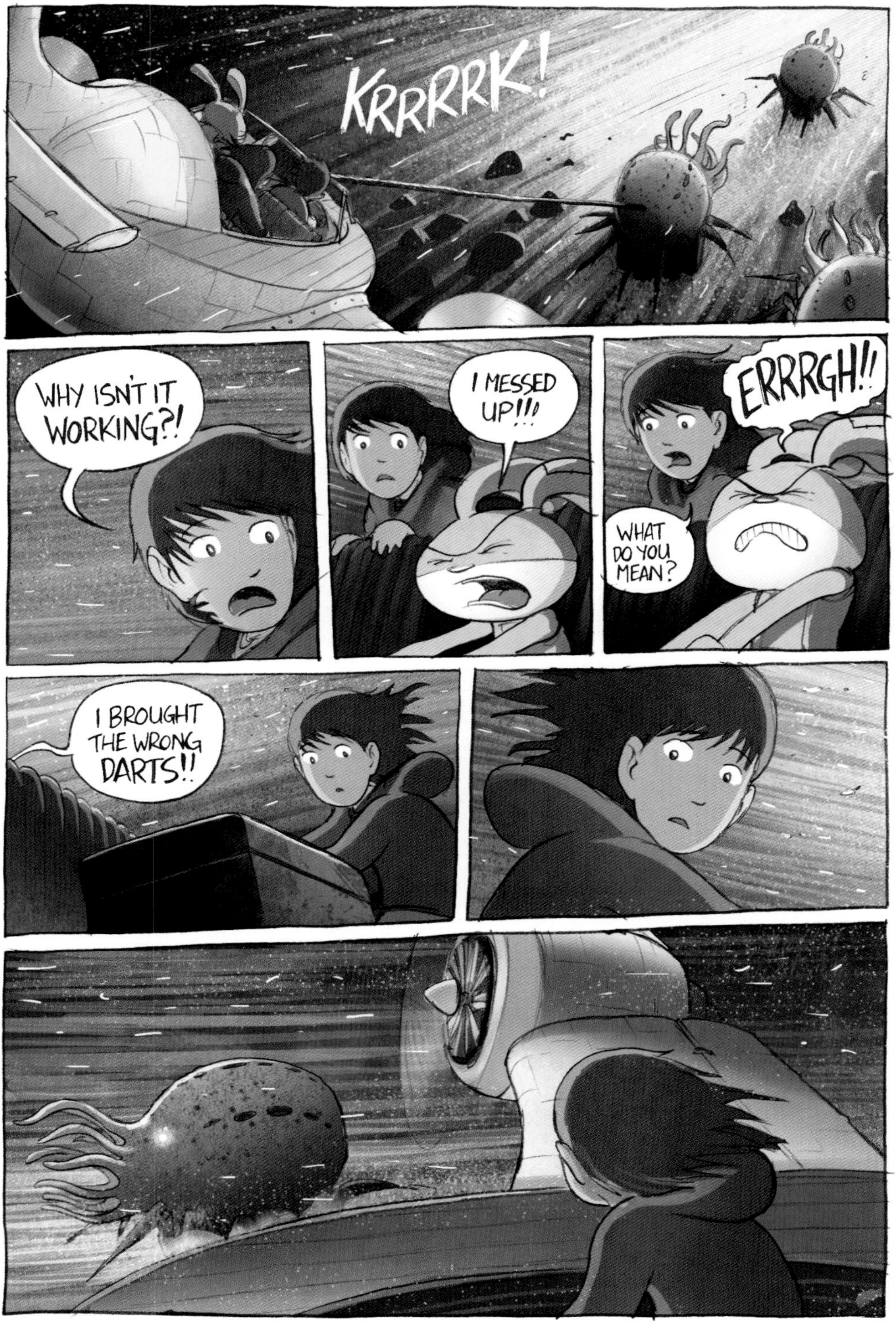
KRRRRK!
WHY ISN'T IT WORKING?!
I MESSED UP!!!
ERRRGH!!
WHAT DO YOU MEAN?
I BROUGHT THE WRONG DARTS!!

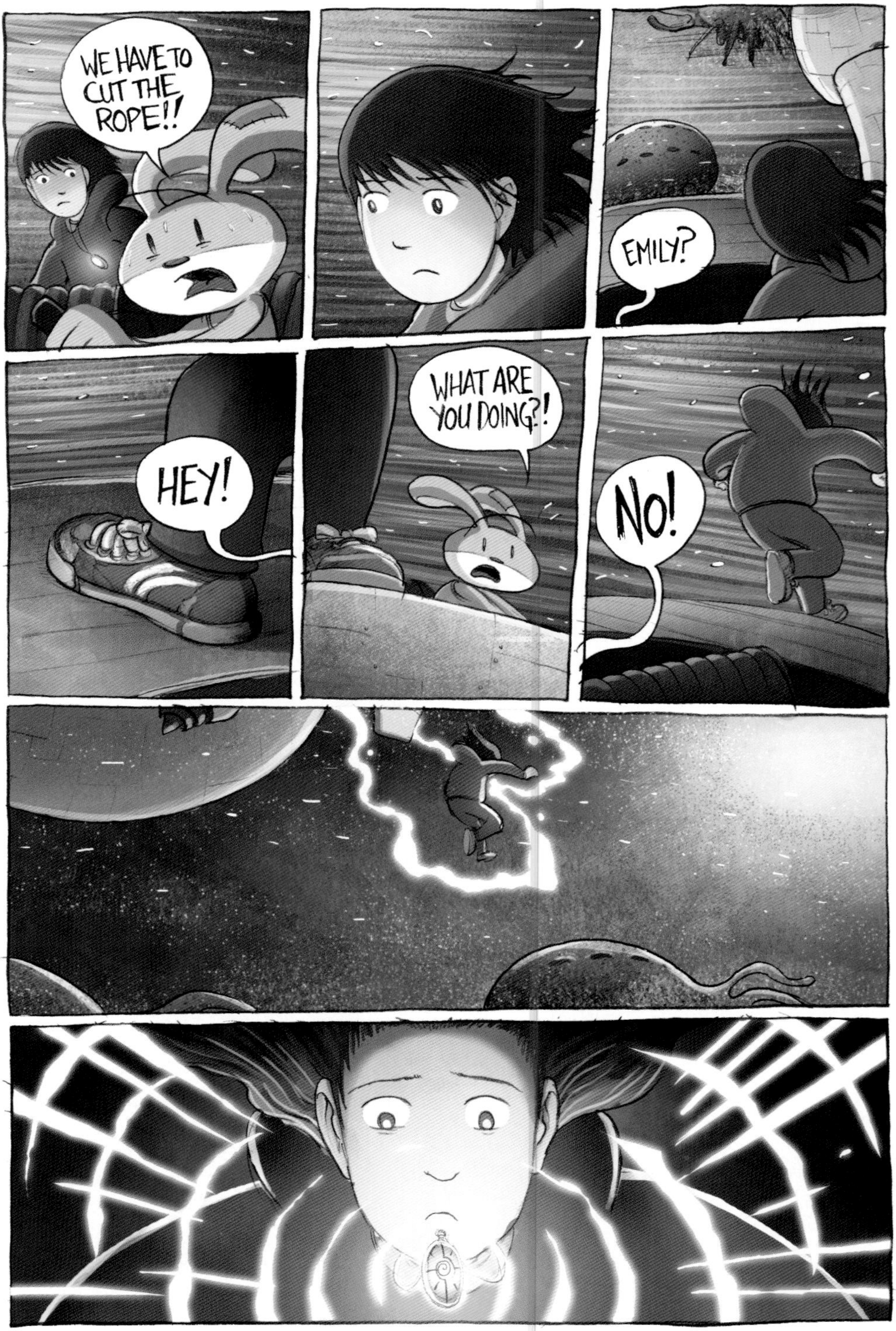
WE HAVE TO CUT THE ROPE!!
EMILY?
HEY!
WHAT ARE YOU DOING?!
NO!

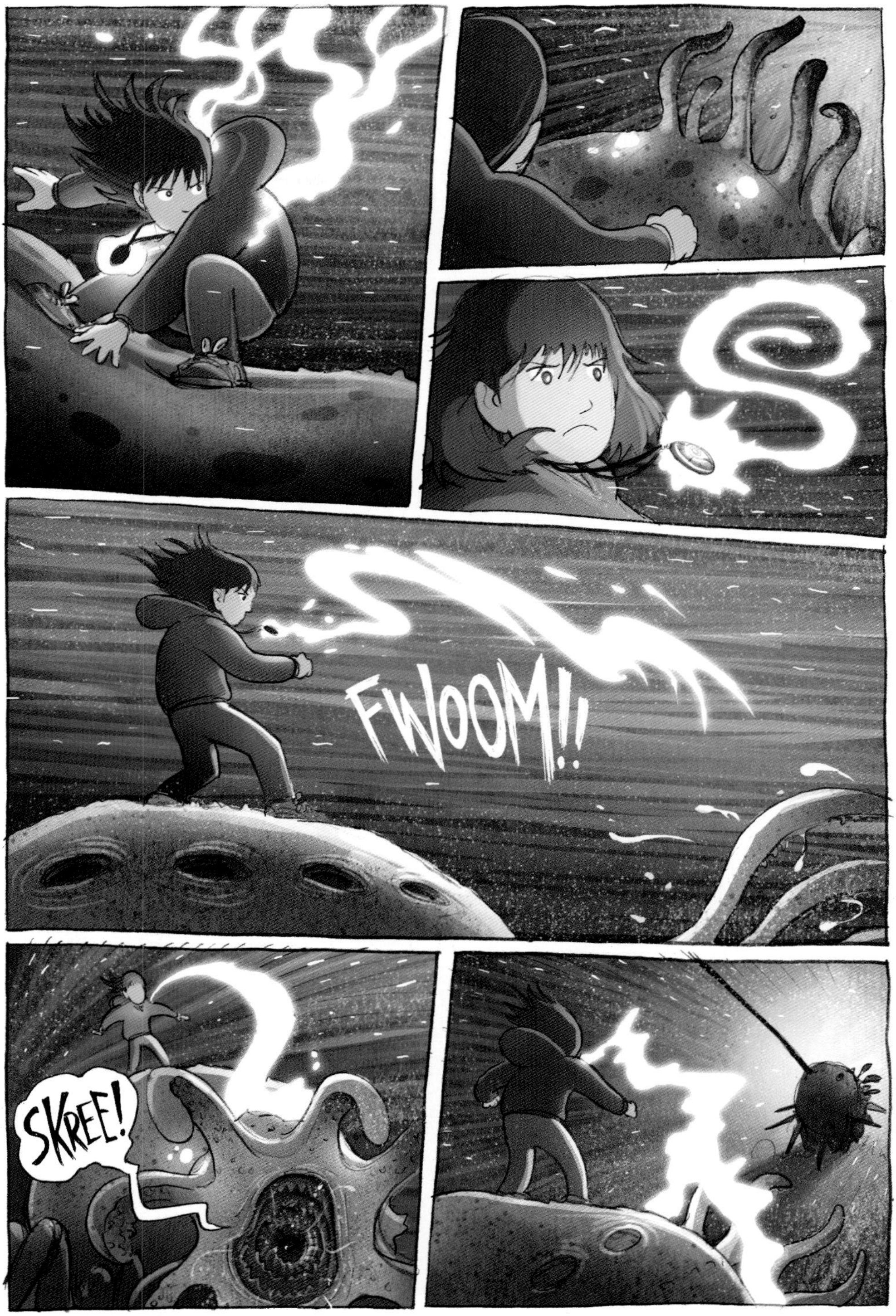
FWOOM!!
SKREE!

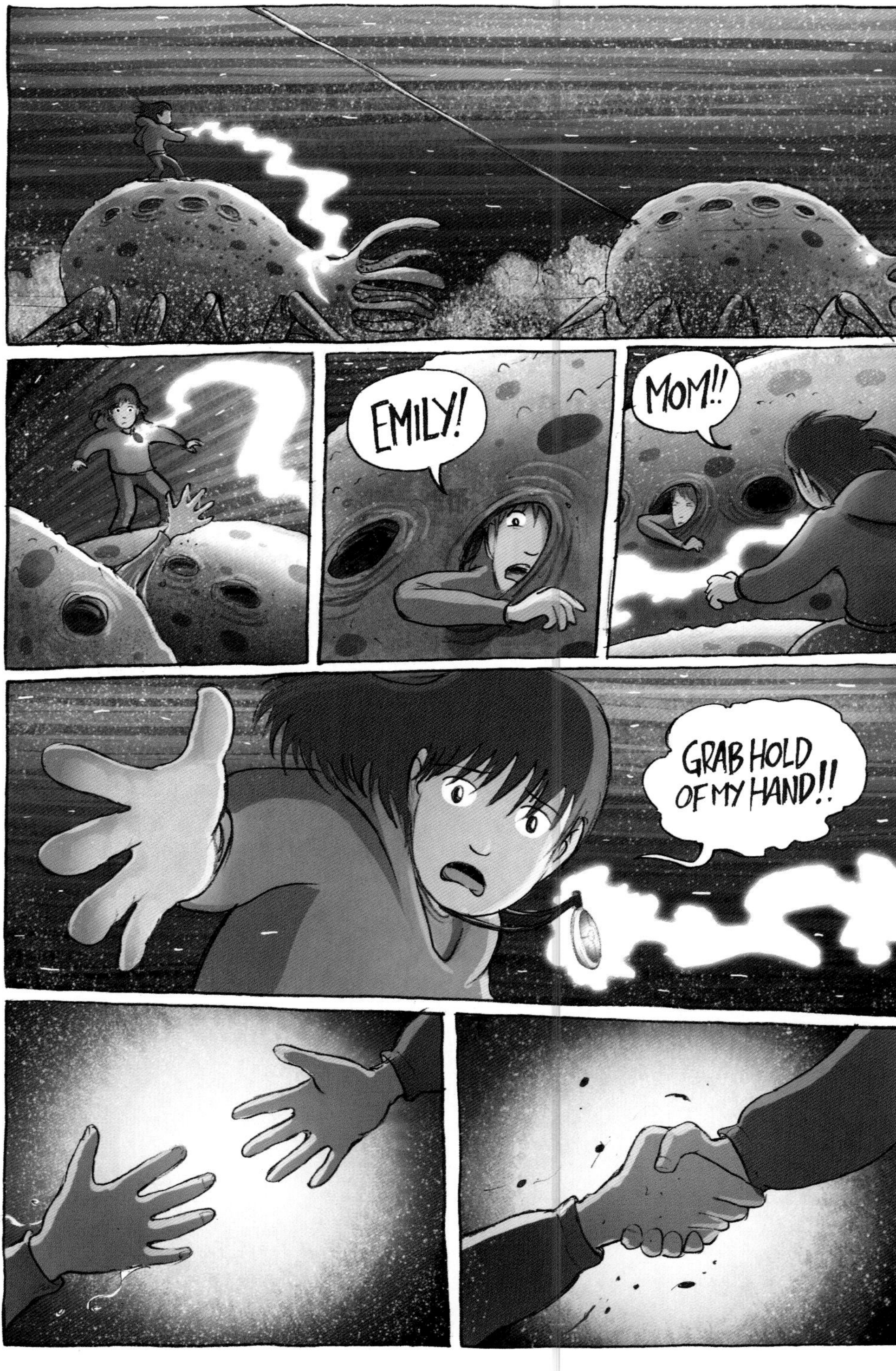
EMILY!
MOM!!
GRAB HOLD OF MY HAND!!

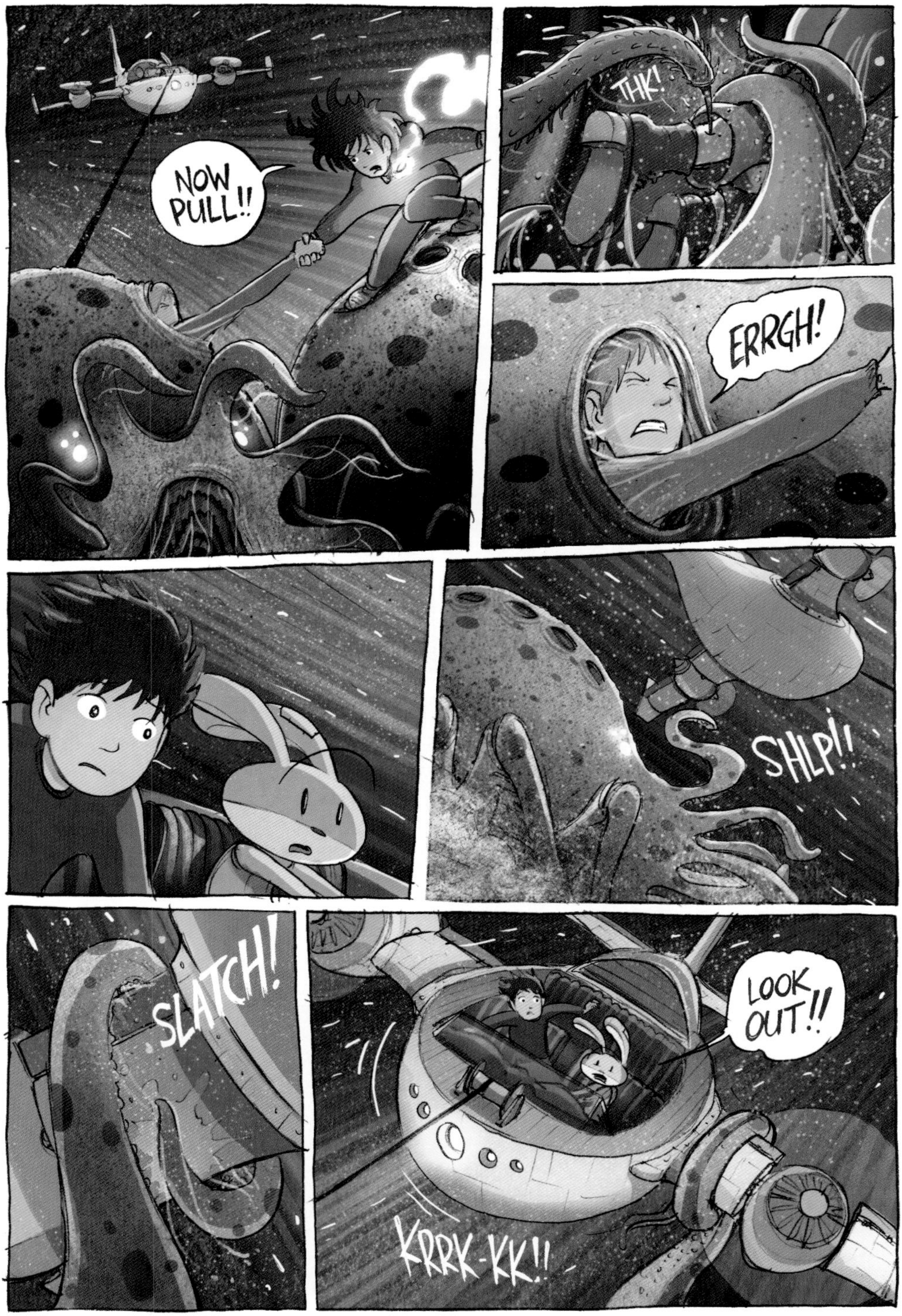
NOW PULL!!
THK!
ERRGH!
SHLP!!
SLATCH!
LOOK OUT!!
KRRK-KK!!

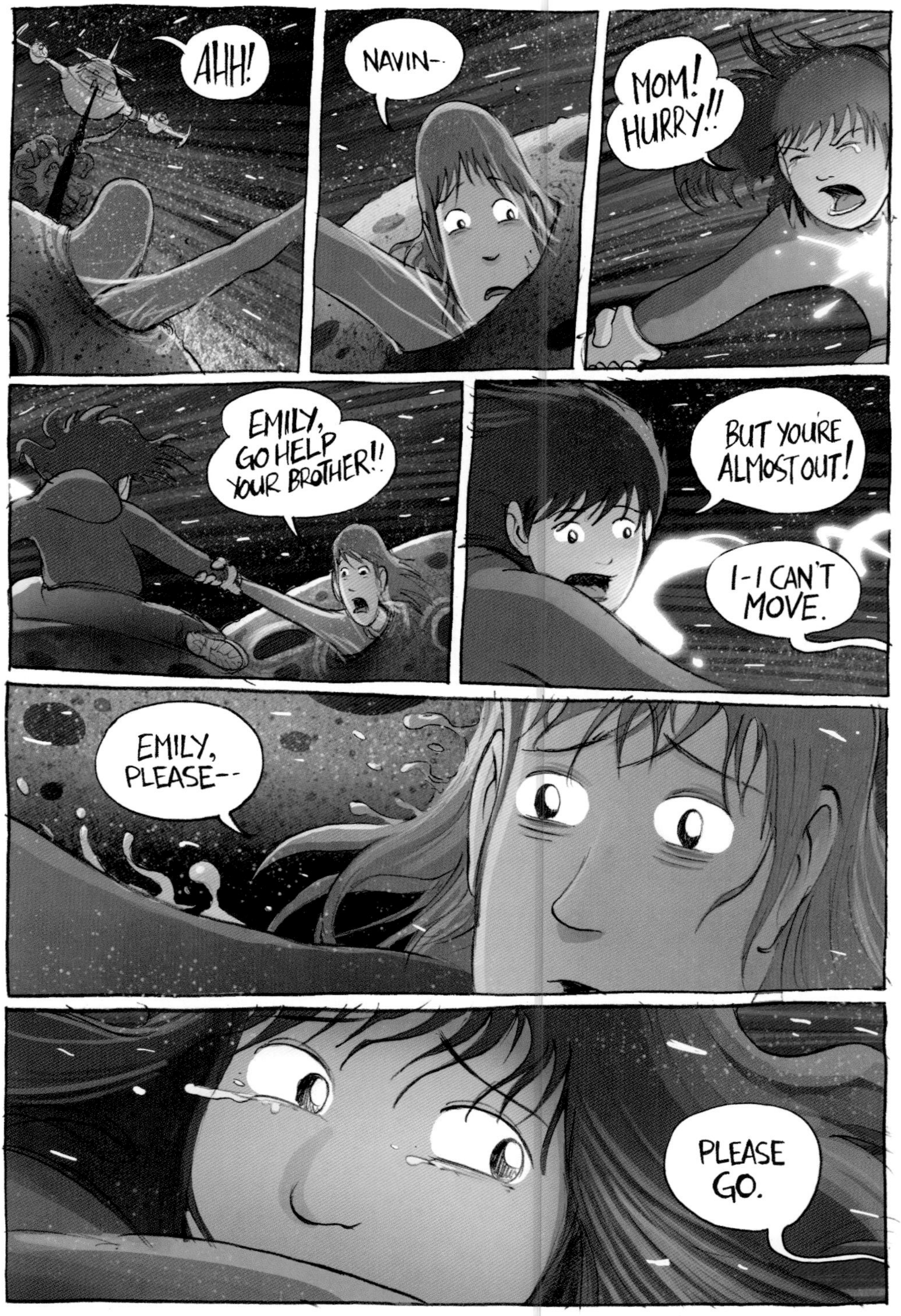
AHH!
NAVIN-
MOM! HURRY!!
EMILY, GO HELP YOUR BROTHER!!
BUT YOU'RE ALMOST OUT!
I-I CAN'T MOVE.
EMILY, PLEASE--
PLEASE GO.

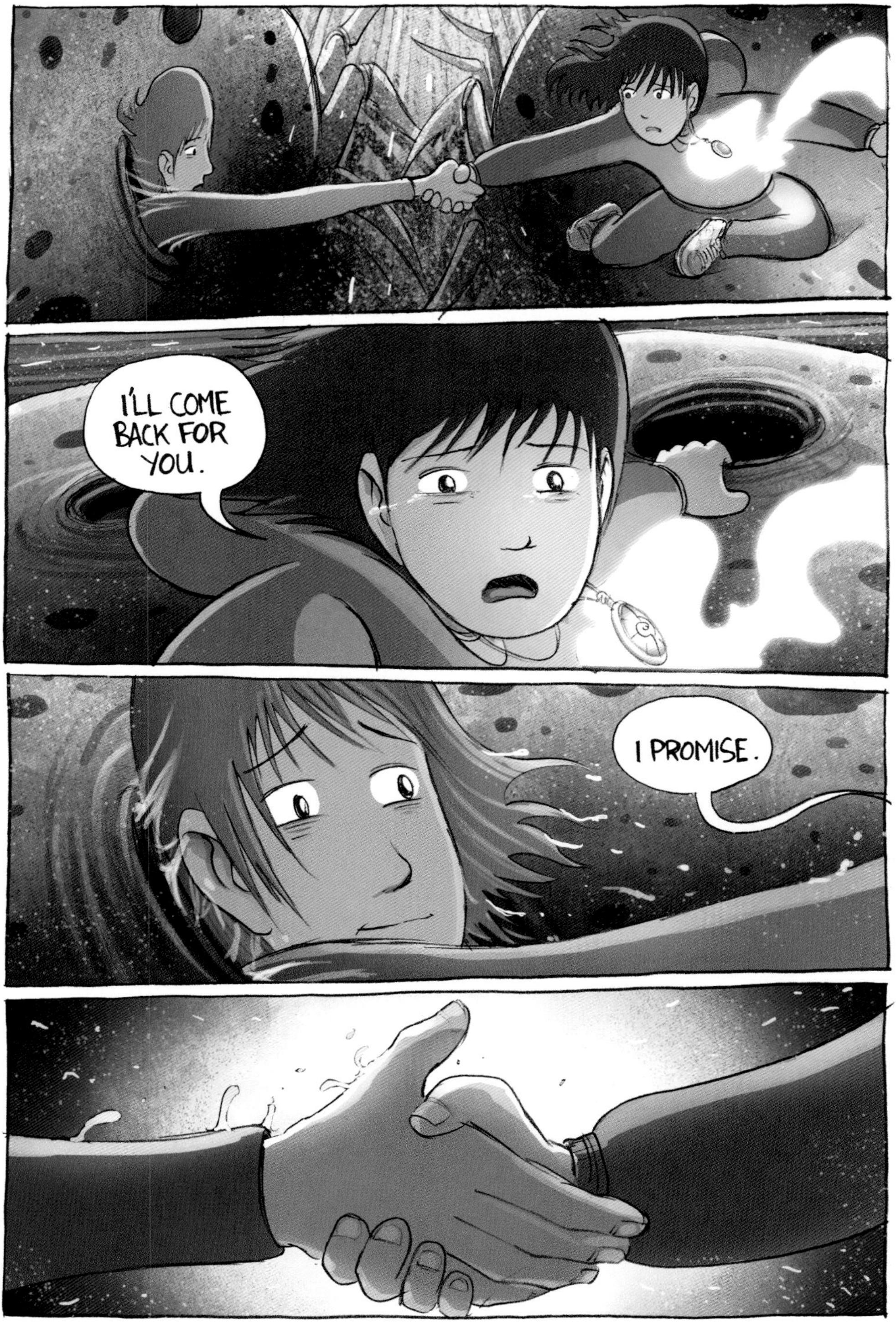
I'LL COME BACK FOR YOU.
I PROMISE.

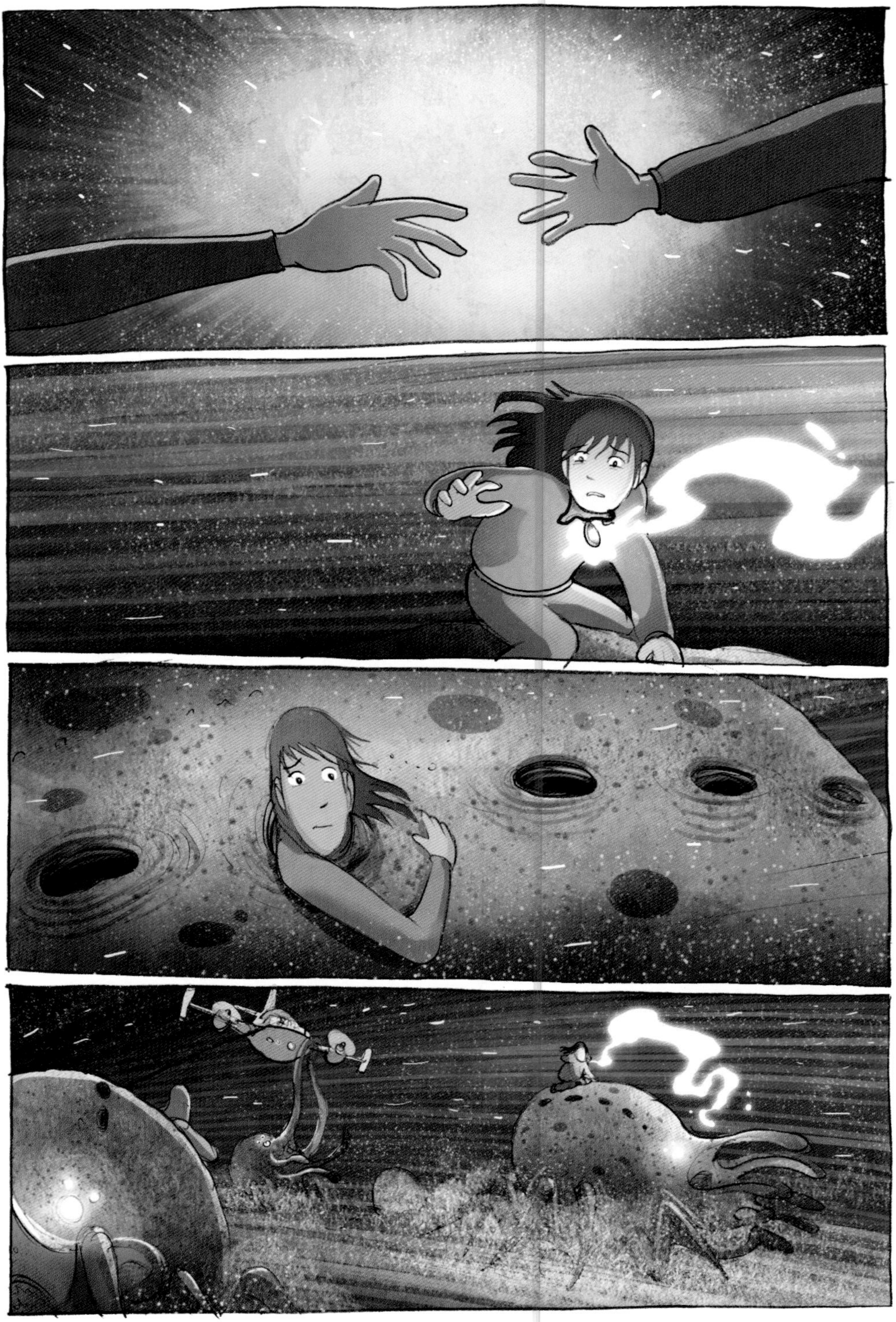

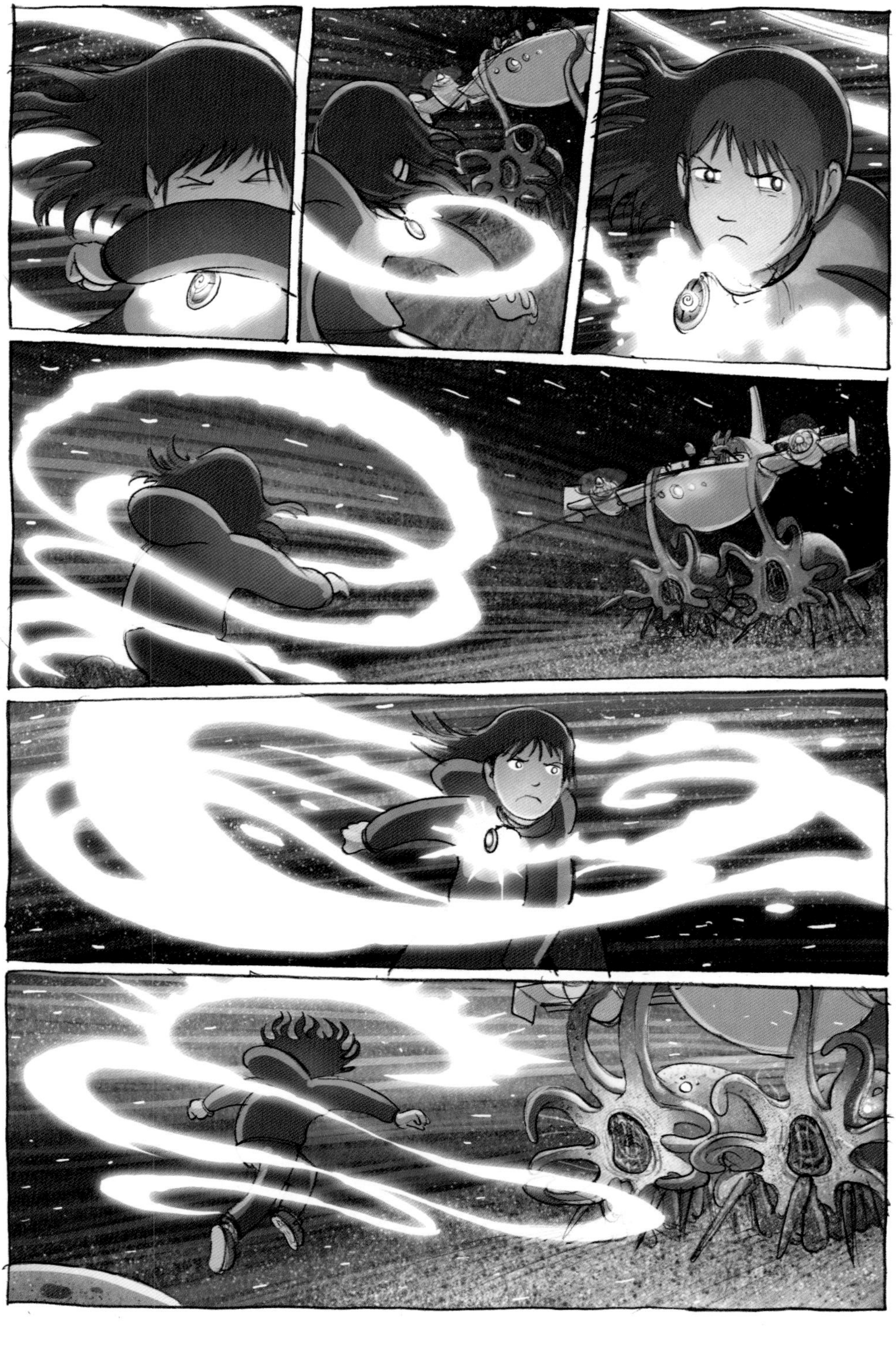

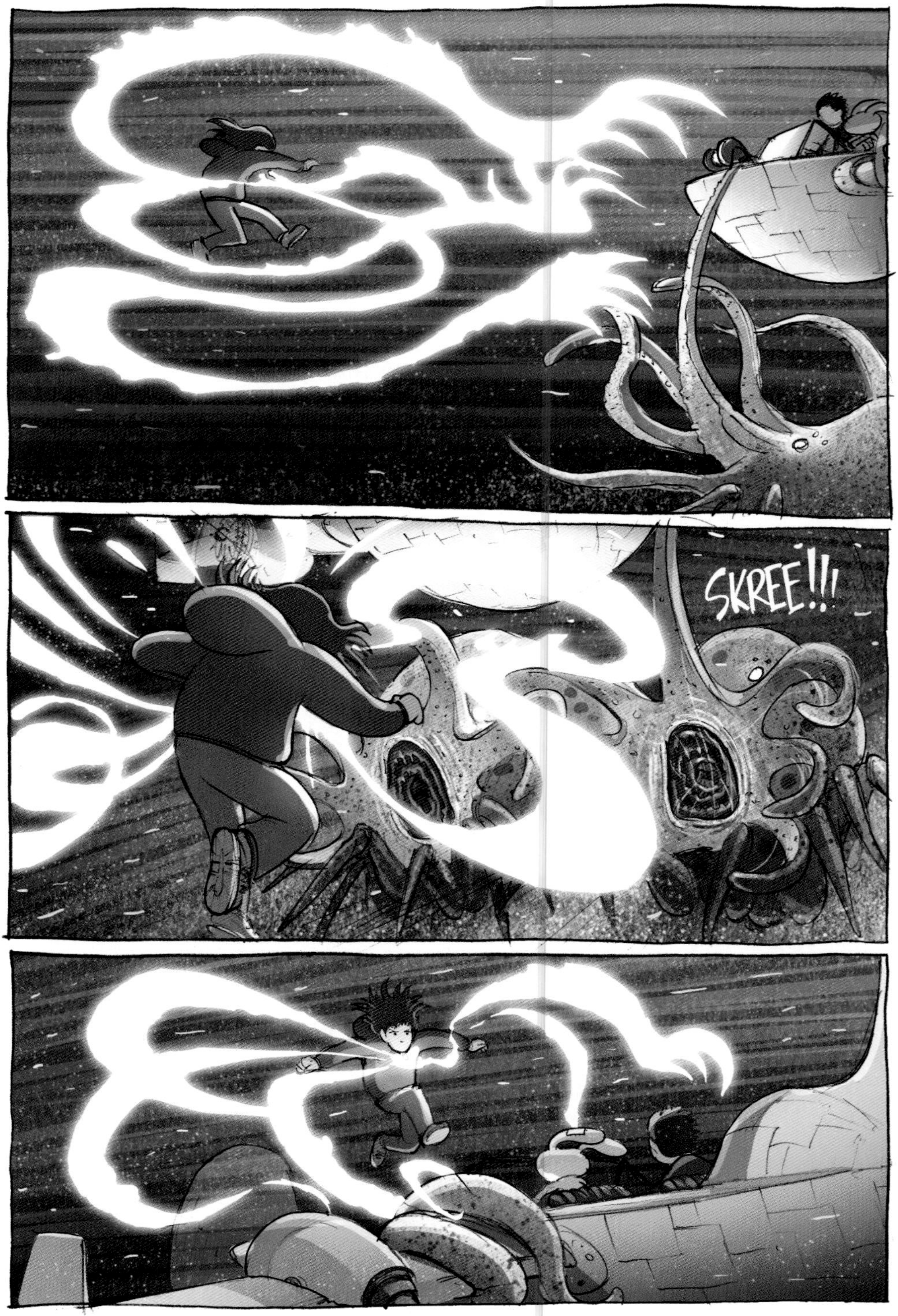
SKREE!!!

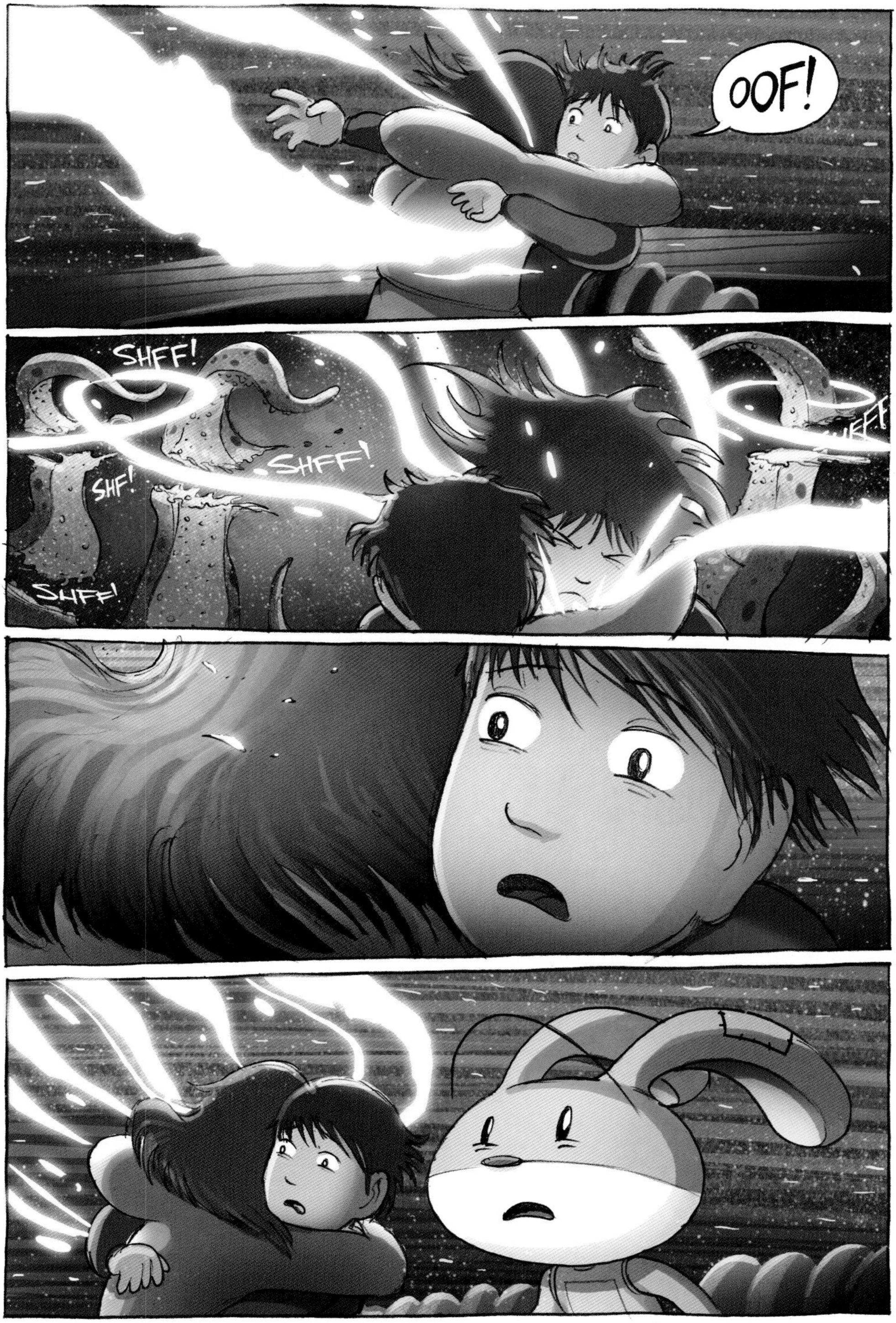
OOF!
SHFF!
SHFF!
SHF!
SHFF!

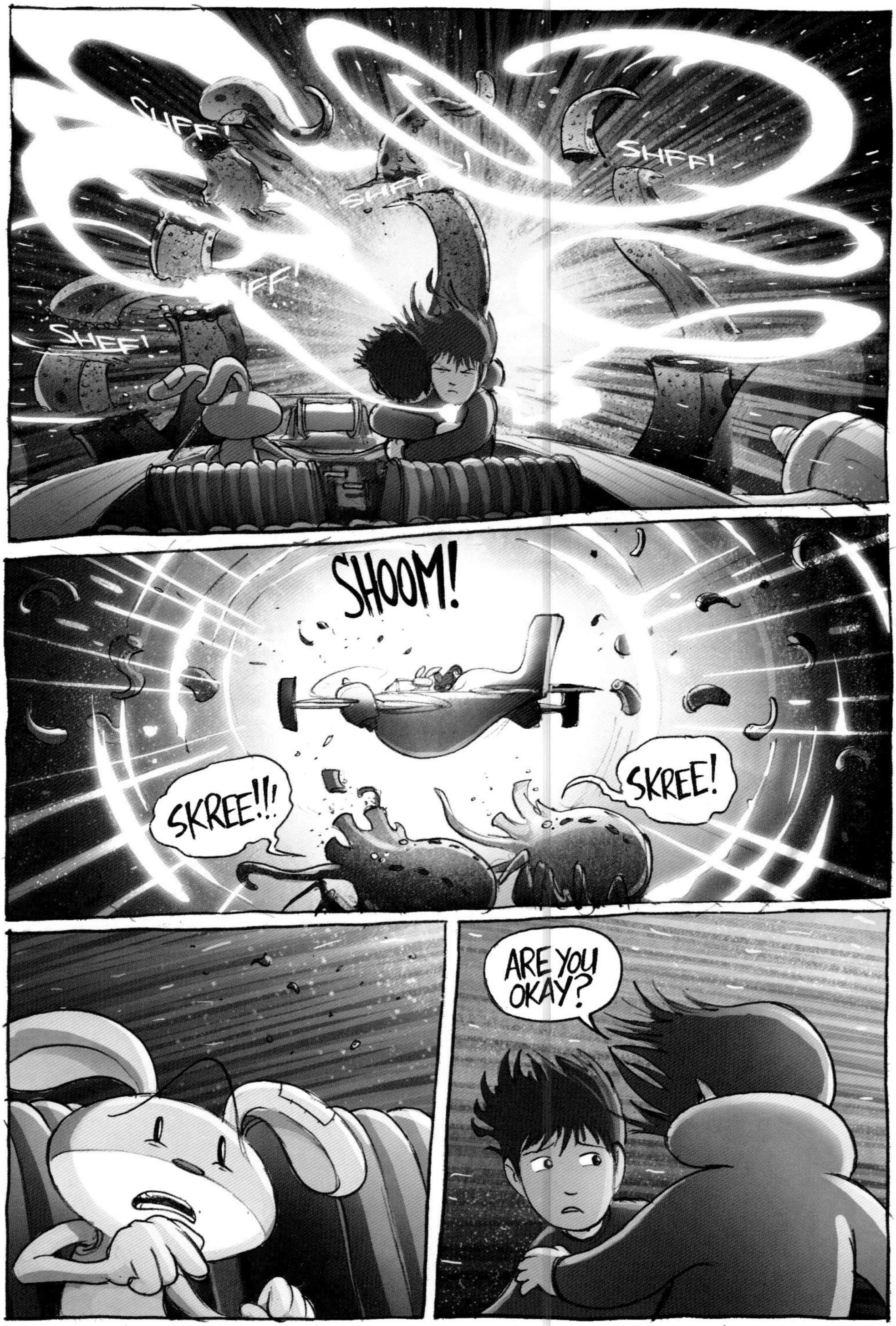

SHFF!
SHFF!
SHFF!
SHFF!
SHFF!
SHOOM!
SKREE!!!
SKREE!
ARE YOU OKAY?

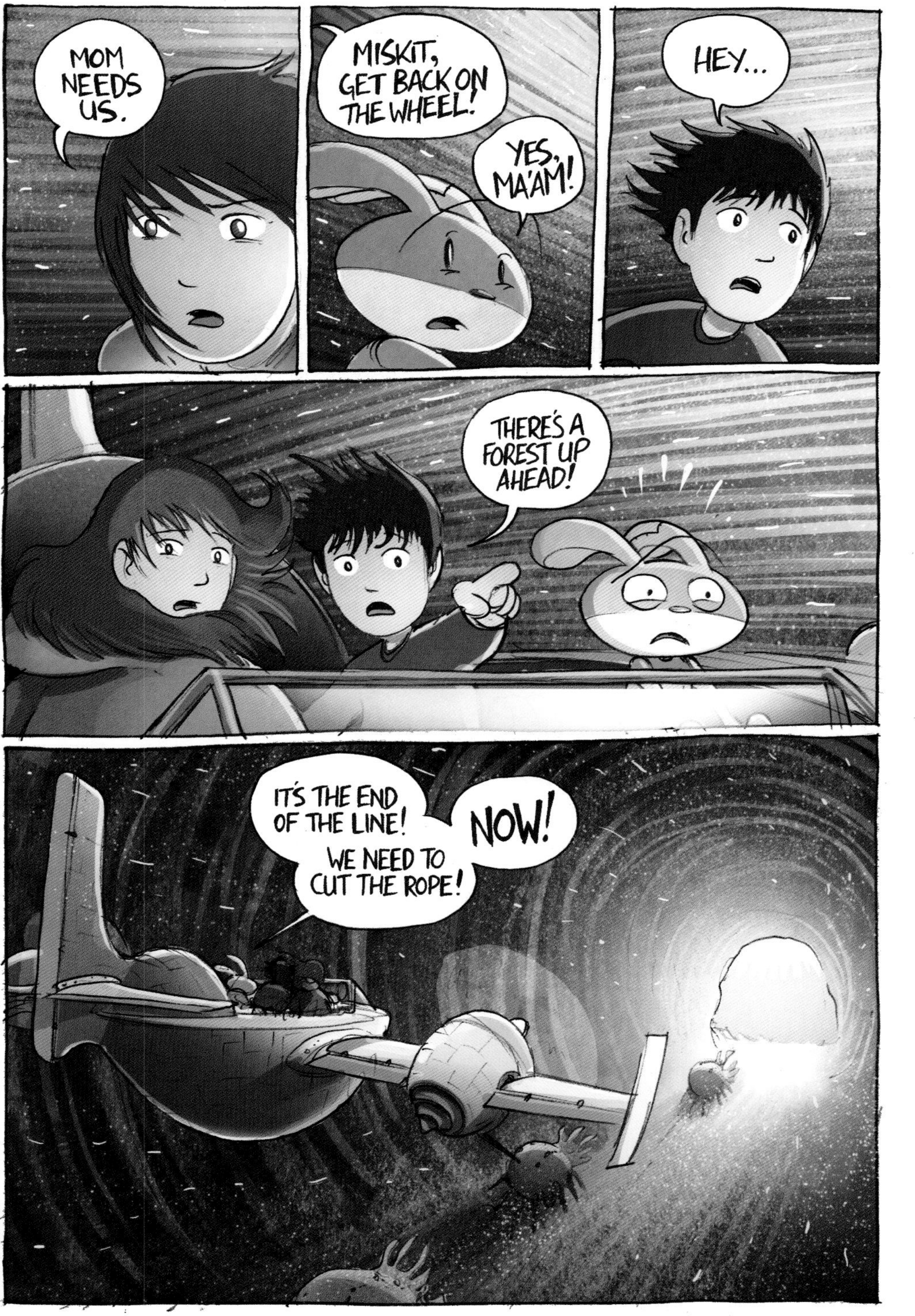
MOM NEEDS US.
MISKIT, GET BACK ON THE WHEEL!
YES, MA'AM!
HEY...
THERE'S A FOREST UP AHEAD!
IT'S THE END OF THE LINE!
WE NEED TO CUT THE ROPE!
NOW!

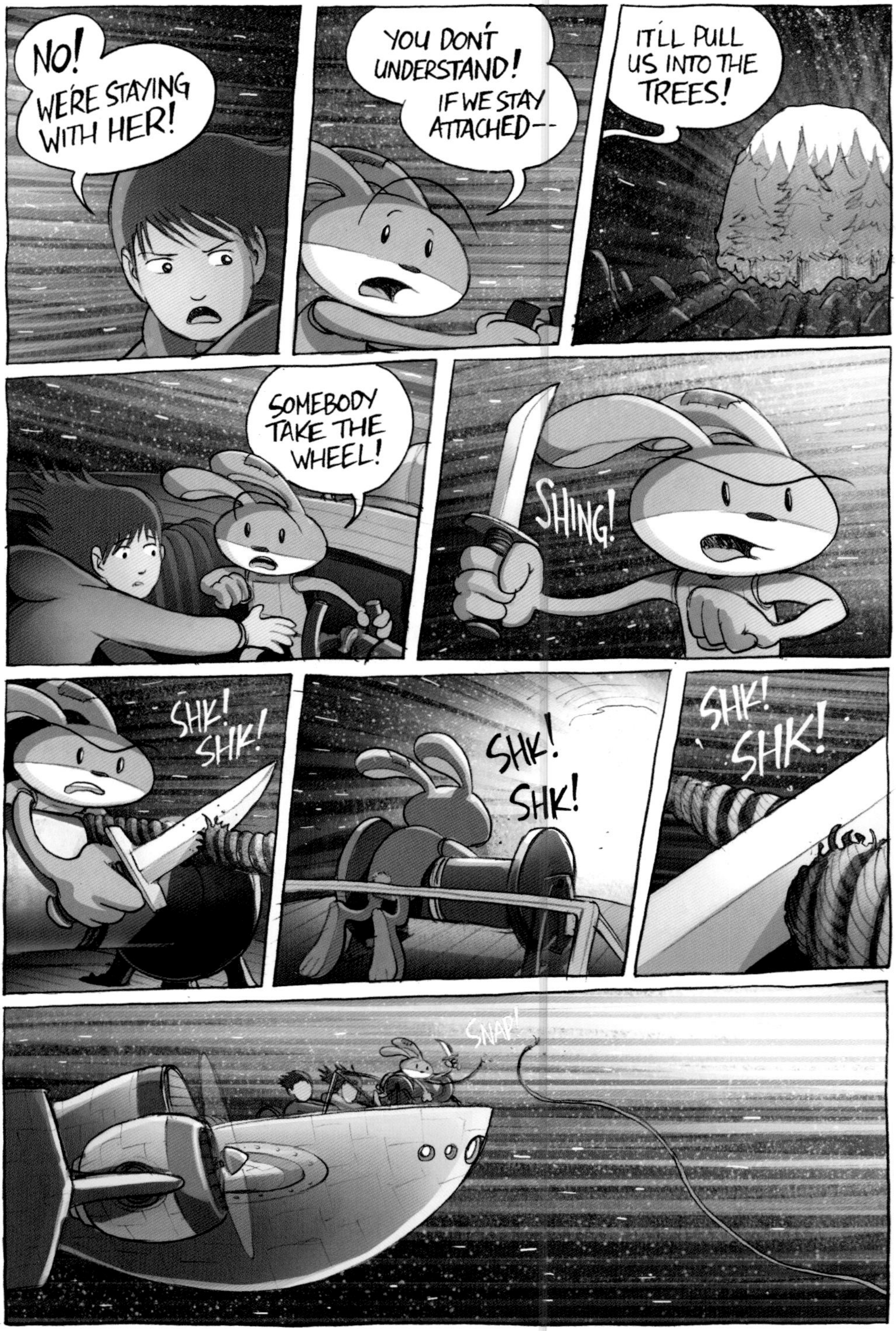
NO!
WE'RE STAYING WITH HER!
YOU DON'T UNDERSTAND!
IF WE STAY ATTACHED--
IT'LL PULL US INTO THE TREES!
SOMEBODY TAKE THE WHEEL!
SHING!
SHK! SHK!
SHK! SHK!
SHK! SHK!
SNAP!

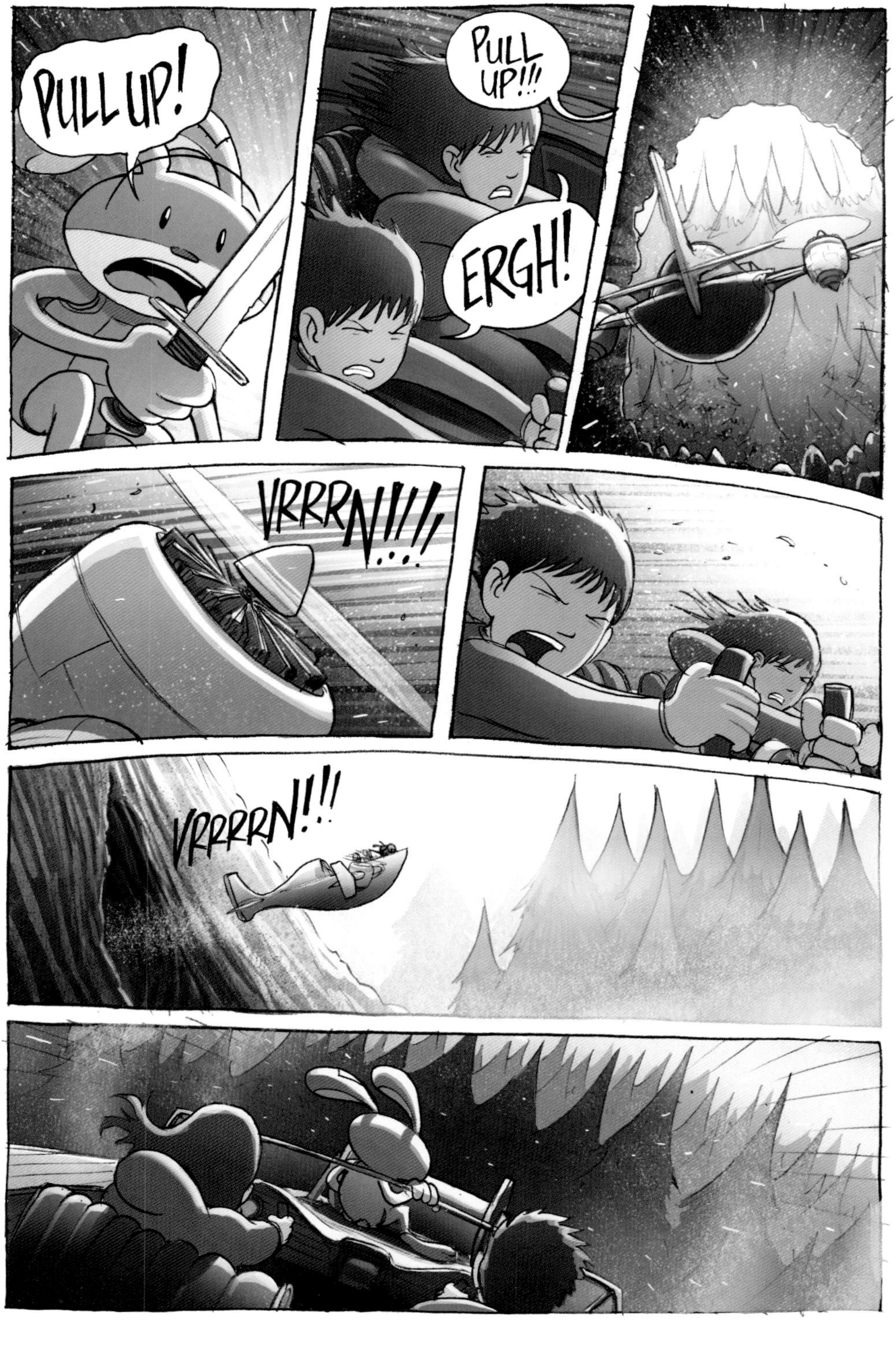
PULL UP!
PULL UP!!!
ERGH!
VRRRN!!!!
VRRRRN!!!

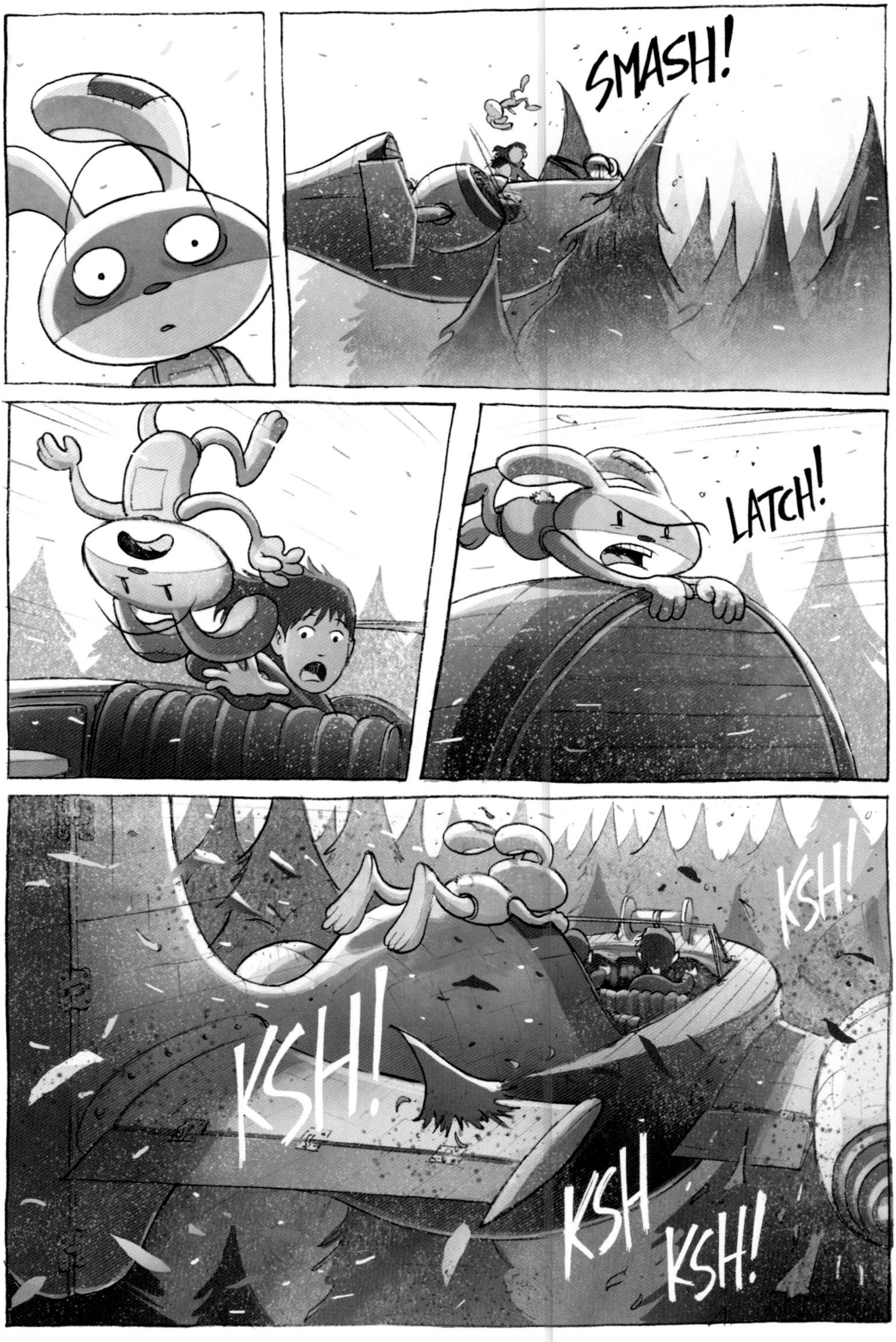
SMASH!
LATCH!
KSH!
KSH!
KSH
KSH!

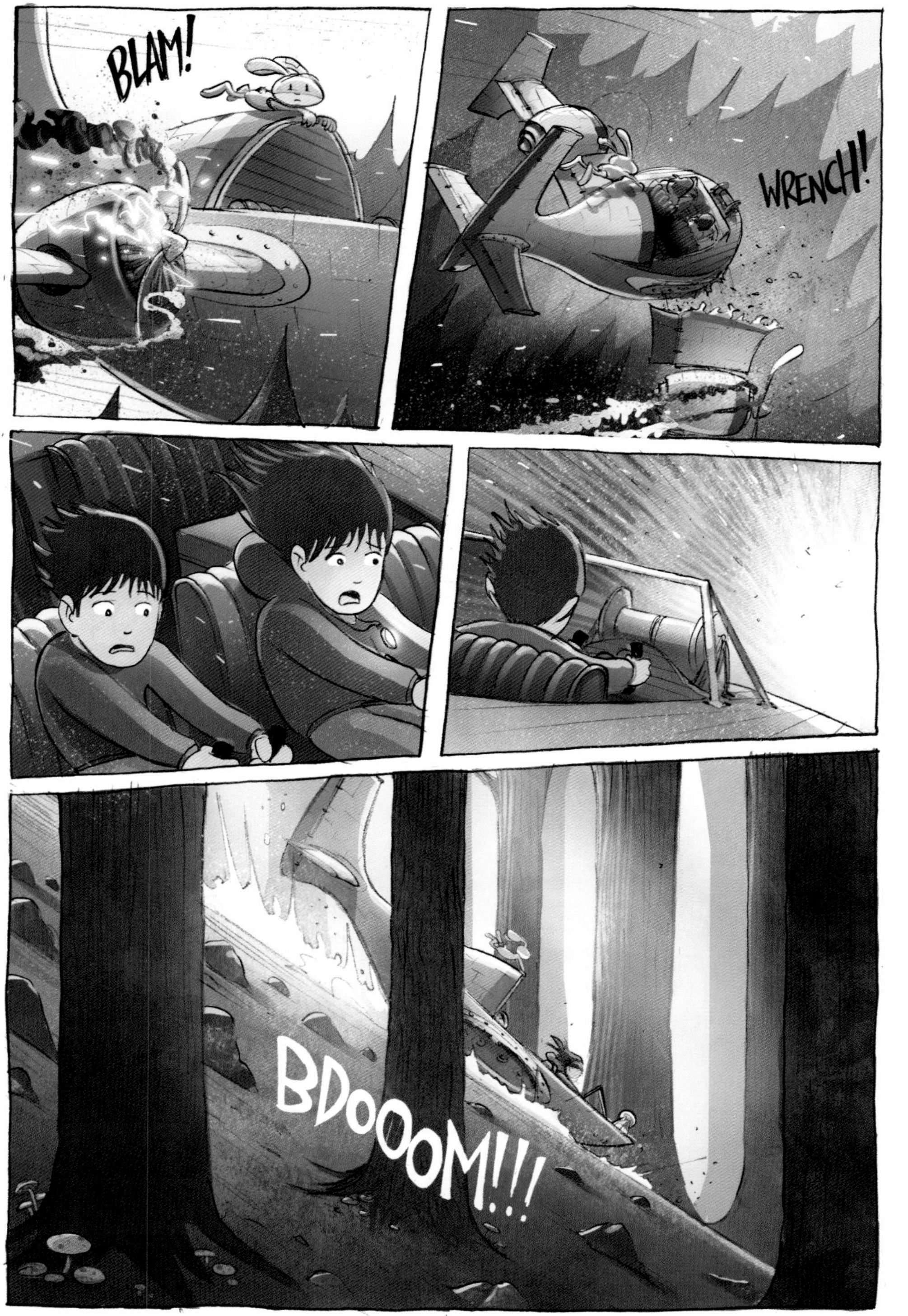
BLAM!
WRENCH!
BDOOOM!!!

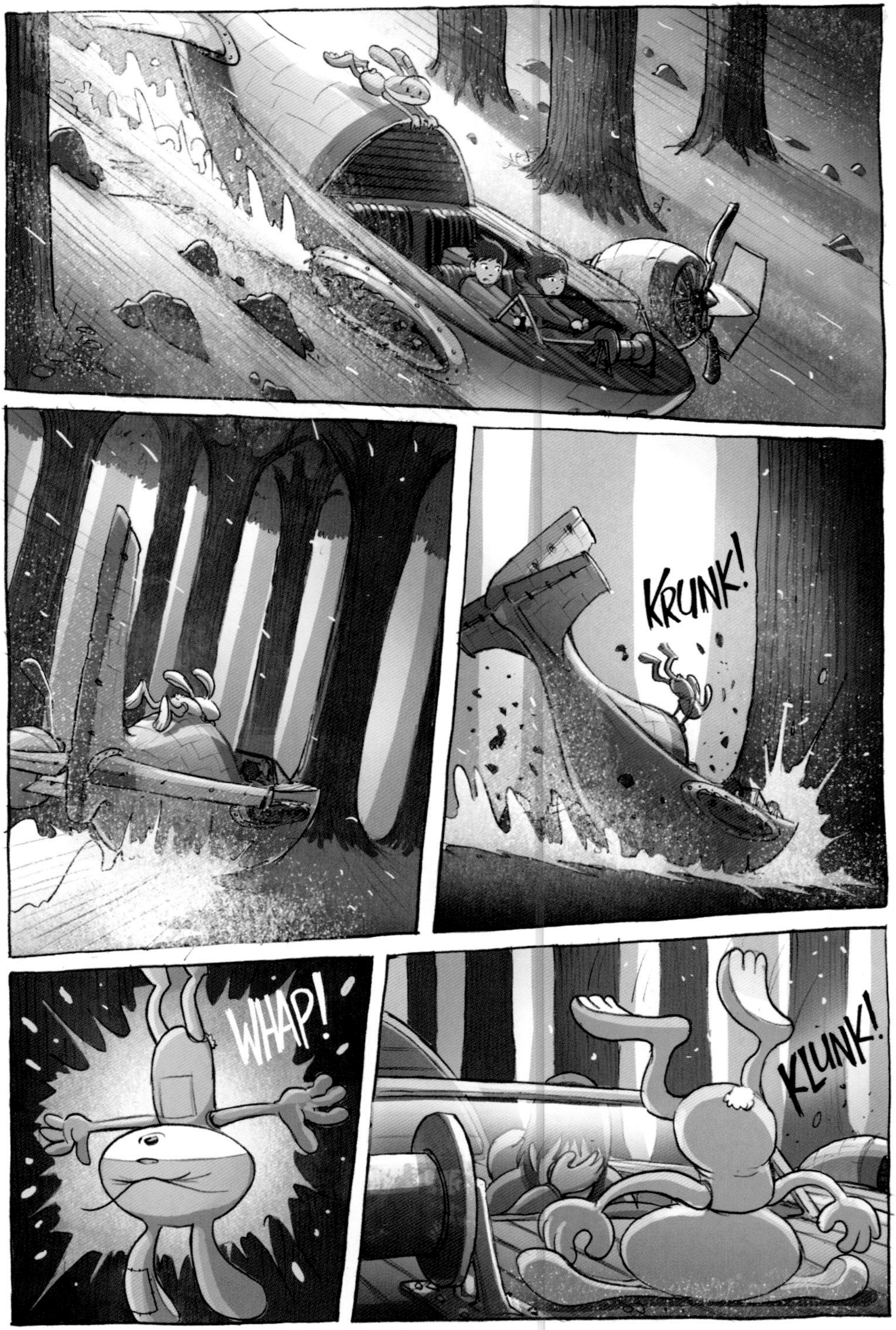
KRUNK!
WHAP!
KLUNK!

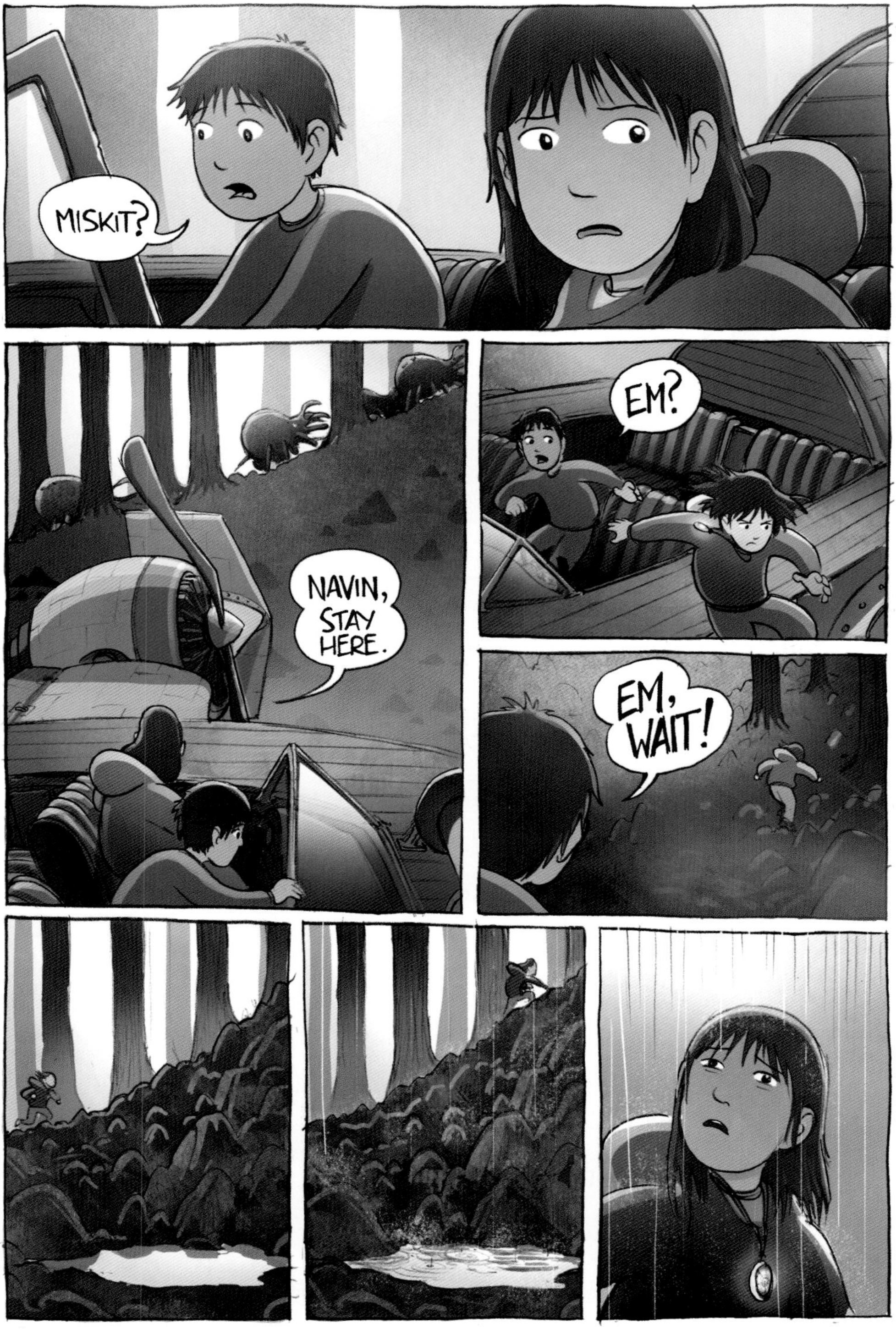
MISKIT?
EM?
NAVIN, STAY HERE.
EM, WAIT!

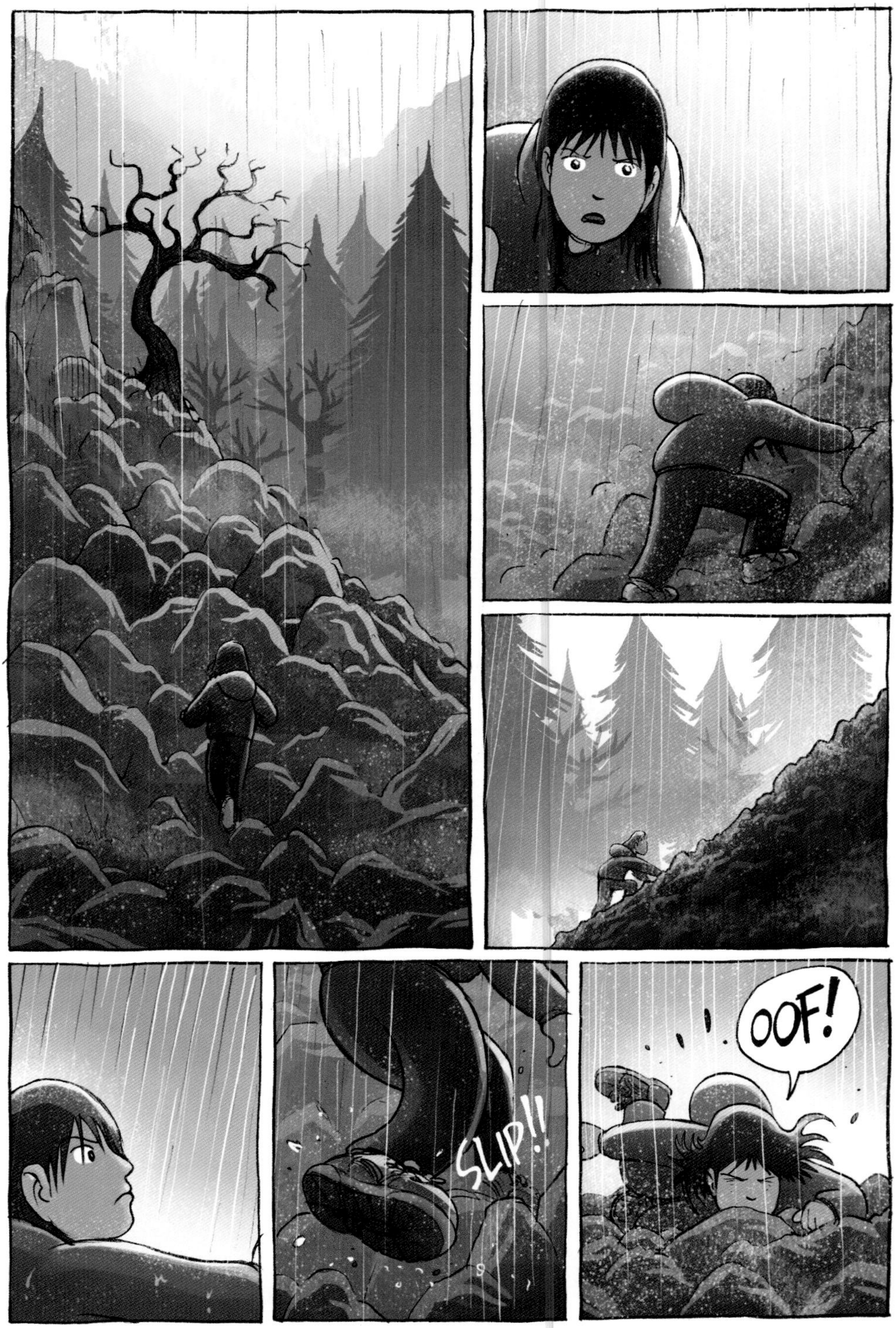
SLIP!!
OOF!

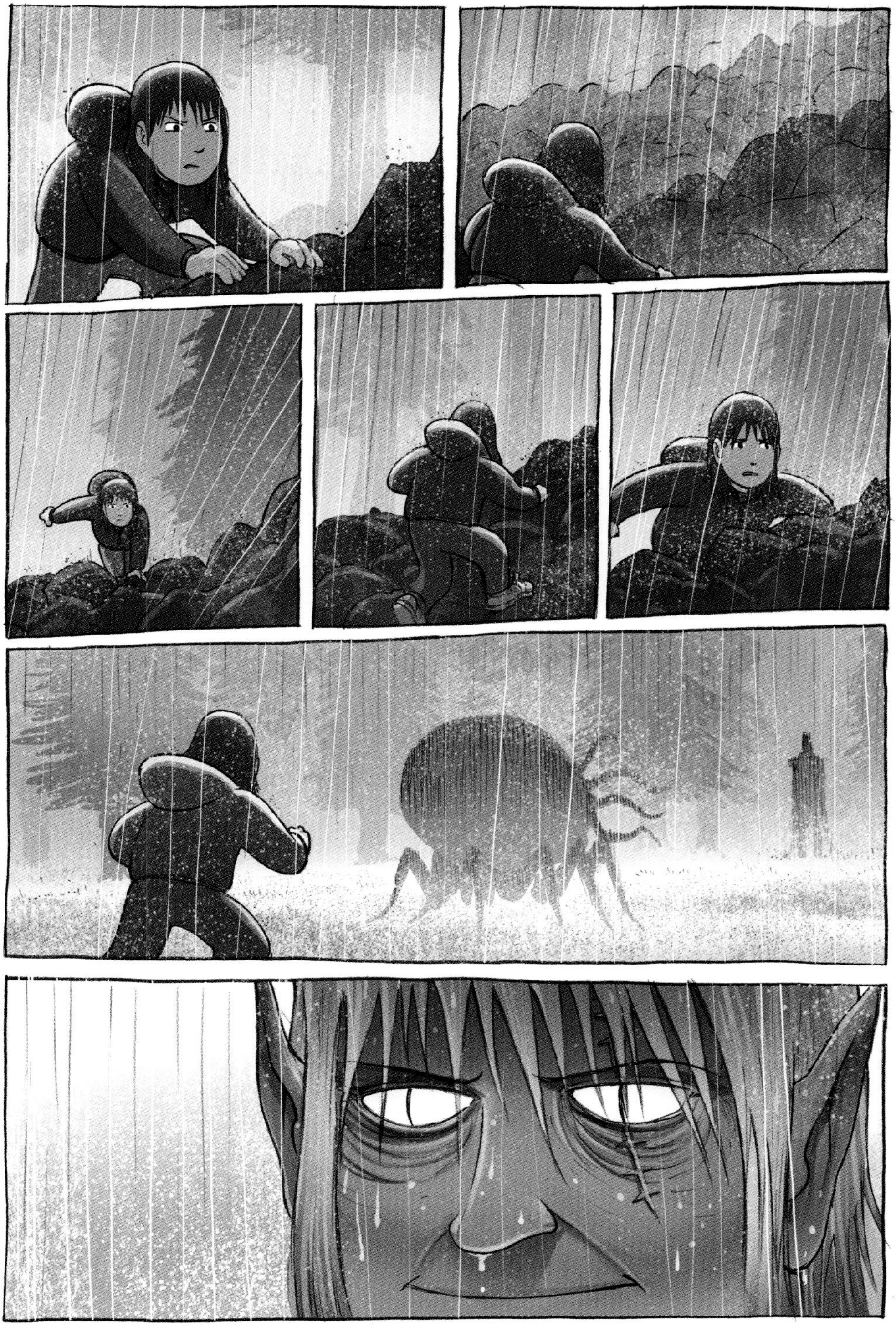

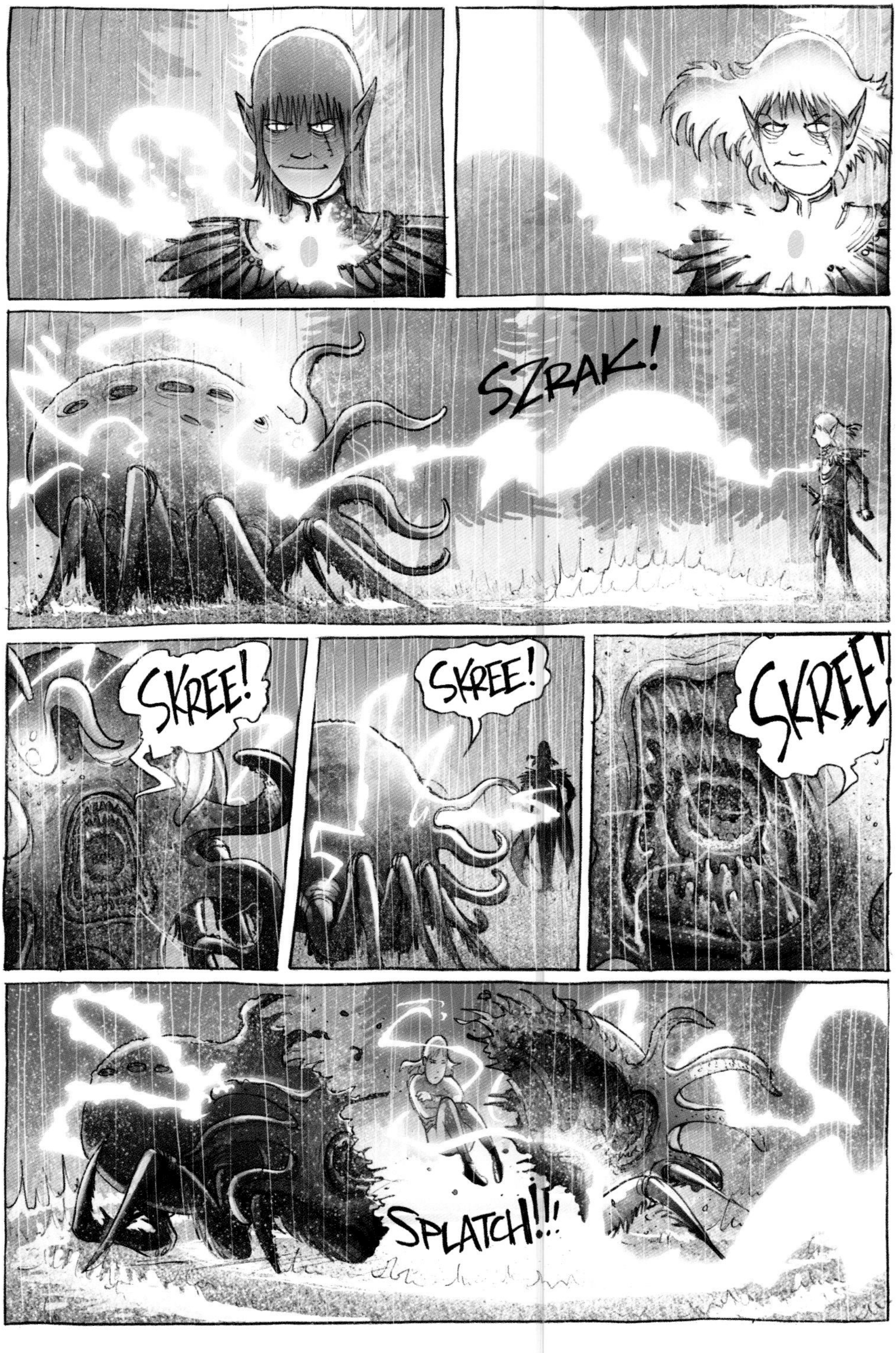
SZRAK!
SKREE!
SKREE!
SKREE!
SPLATCH!!!

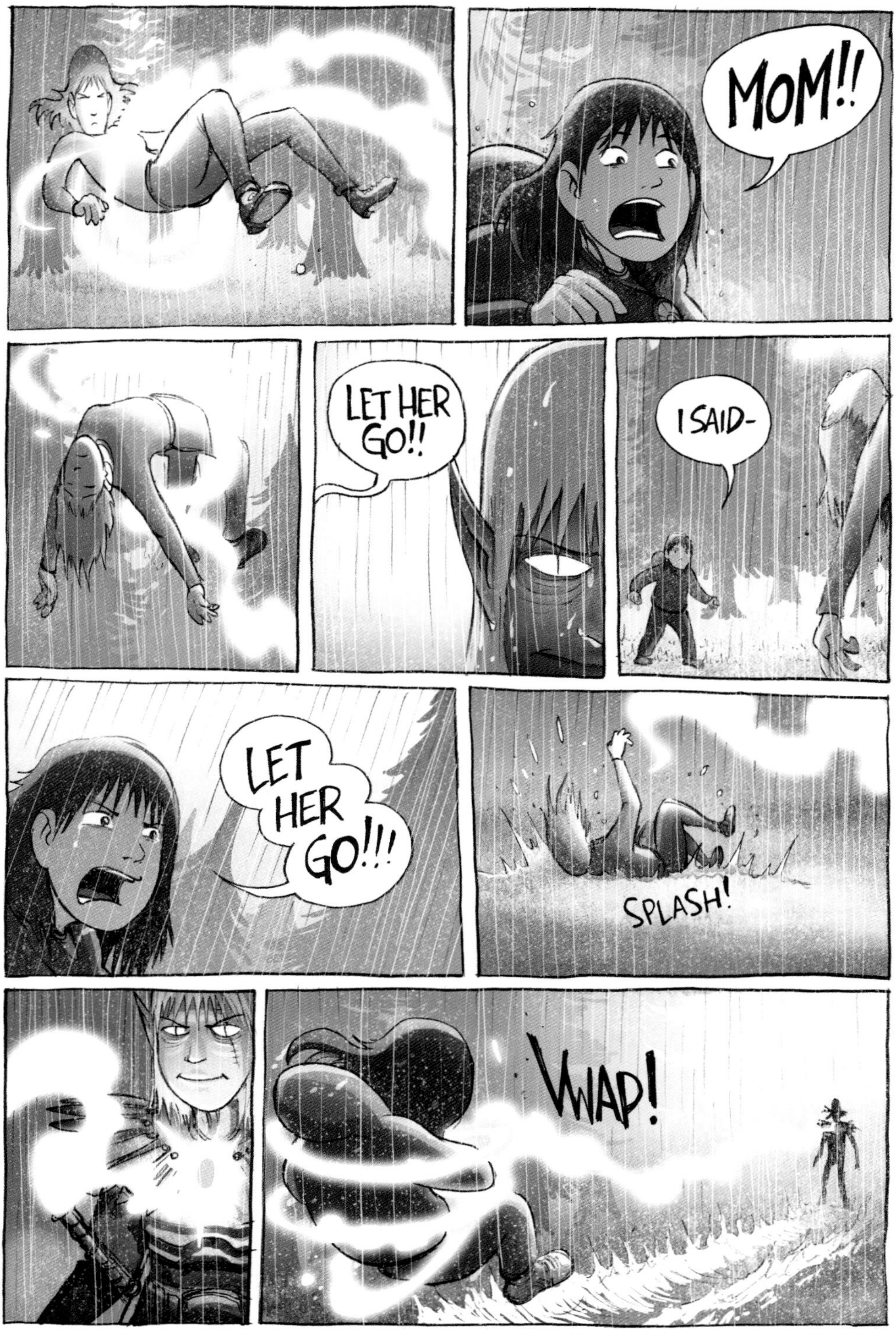
MOM!!
LET HER GO!!
I SAID-
LET HER GO!!!
SPLASH!
WAP!

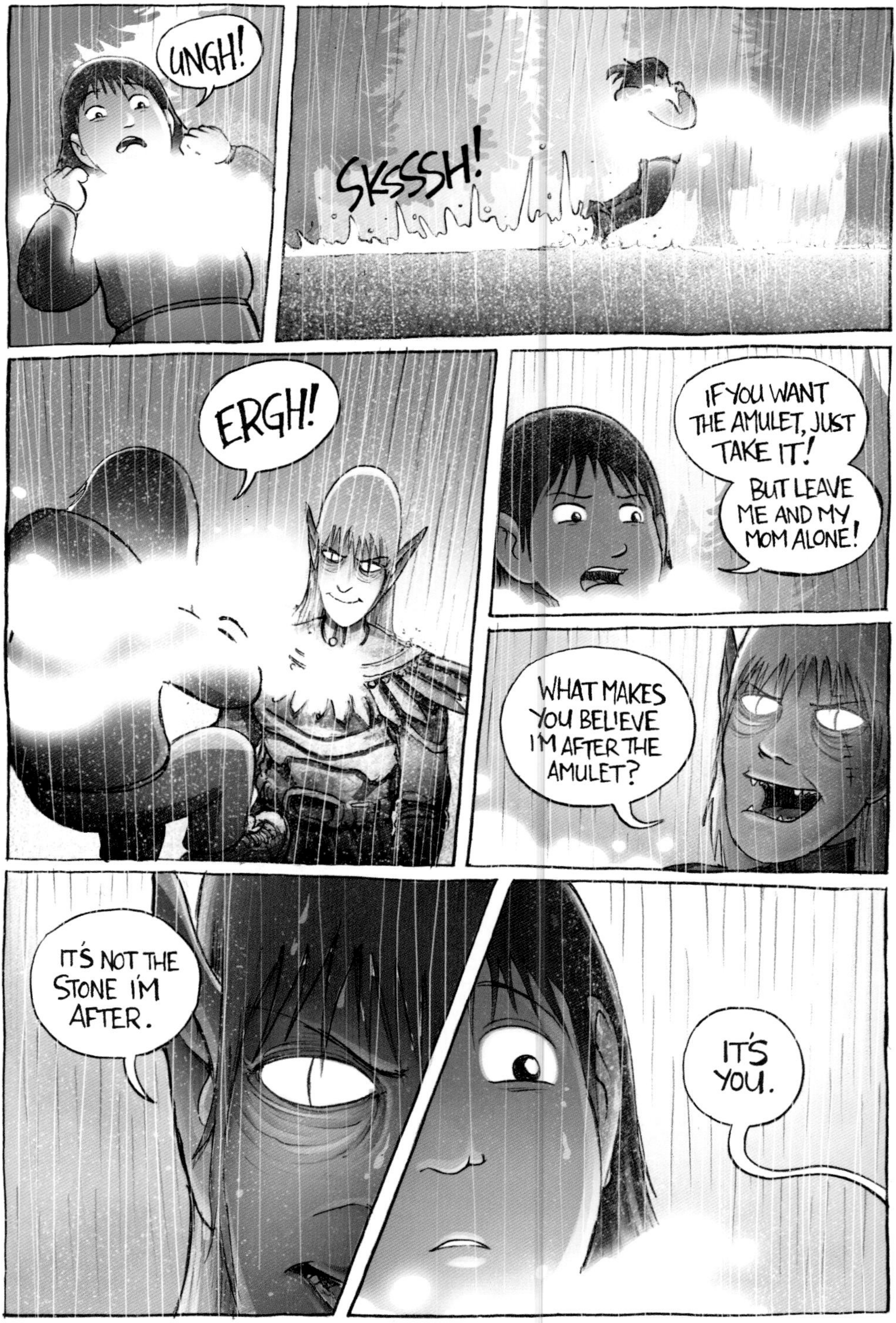
UNGH!
SKSSSH!
ERGH!
IF YOU WANT THE AMULET, JUST TAKE IT!
BUT LEAVE ME AND MY MOM ALONE!
WHAT MAKES YOU BELIEVE I'M AFTER THE AMULET?
IT'S NOT THE STONE I'M AFTER.
IT'S YOU.

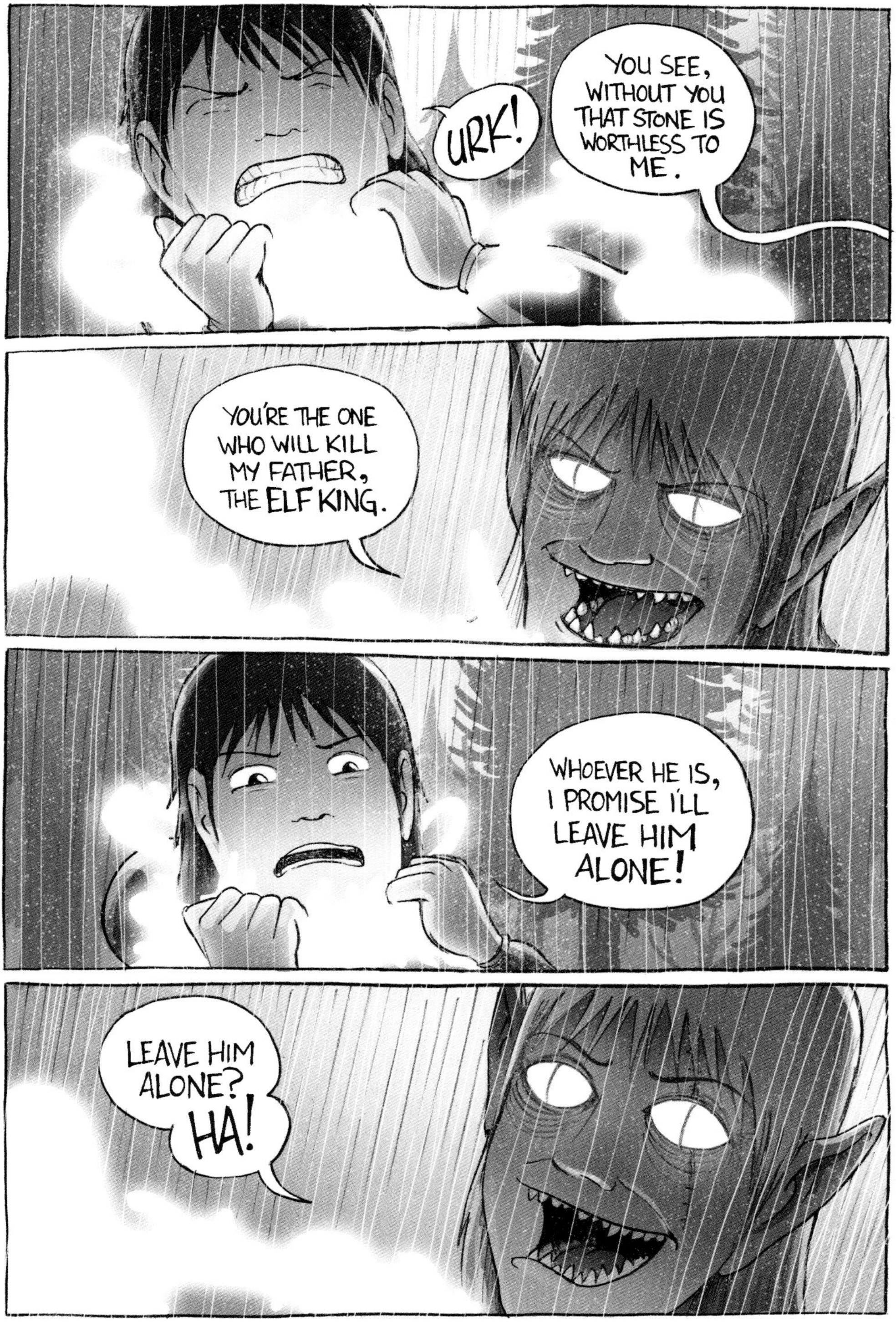
URK!
YOU SEE, WITHOUT YOU THAT STONE IS WORTHLESS TO ME.
YOU'RE THE ONE WHO WILL KILL MY FATHER, THE ELF KING.
WHOEVER HE IS, I PROMISE I'LL LEAVE HIM ALONE!
LEAVE HIM ALONE? HA!

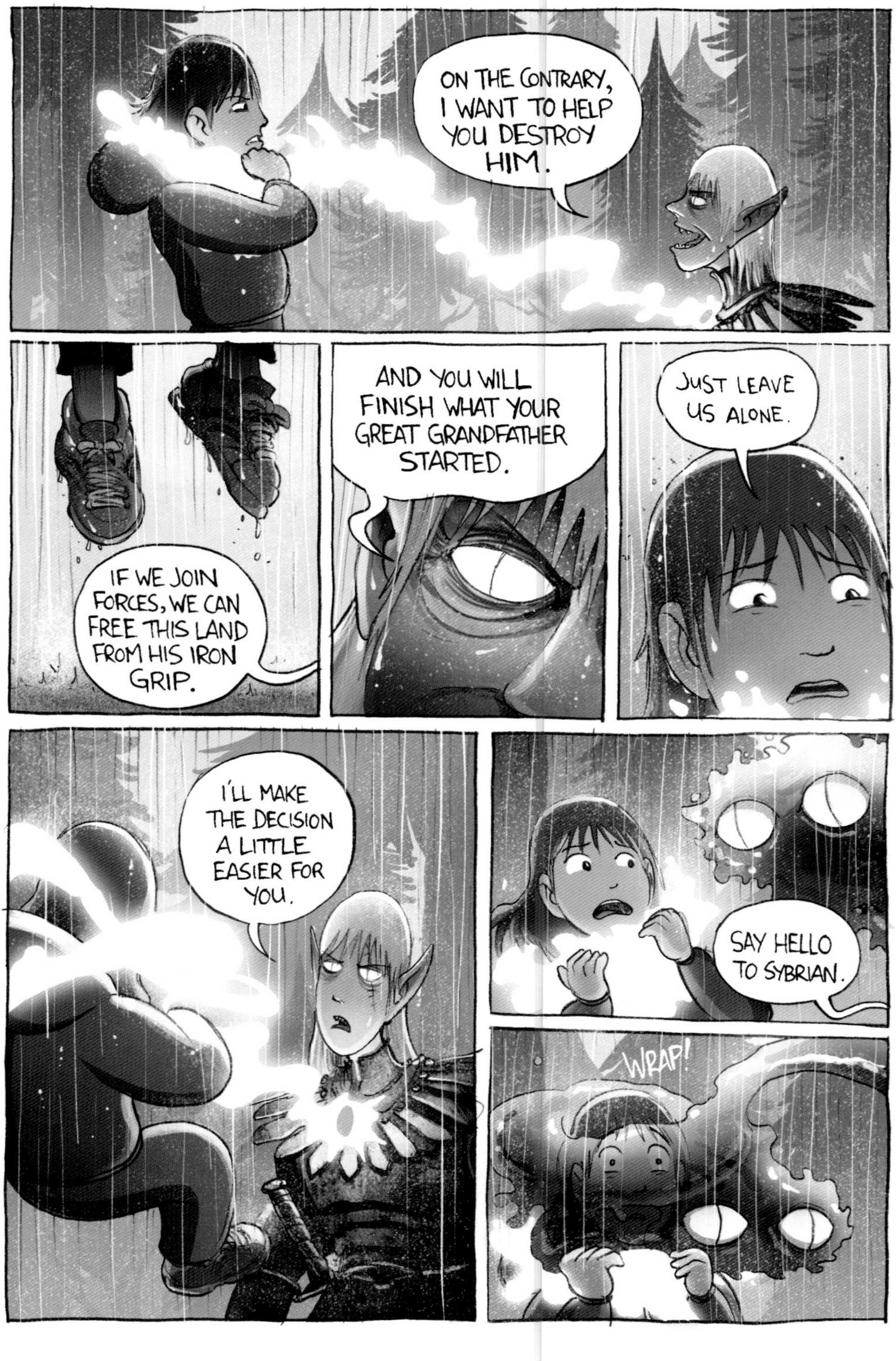
ON THE CONTRARY, I WANT TO HELP YOU DESTROY HIM.
IF WE JOIN FORCES, WE CAN FREE THIS LAND FROM HIS IRON GRIP.
AND YOU WILL FINISH WHAT YOUR GREAT GRANDFATHER STARTED.
JUST LEAVE US ALONE.
I'LL MAKE THE DECISION A LITTLE EASIER FOR YOU.
SAY HELLO TO SYBRIAN.
WRAP!

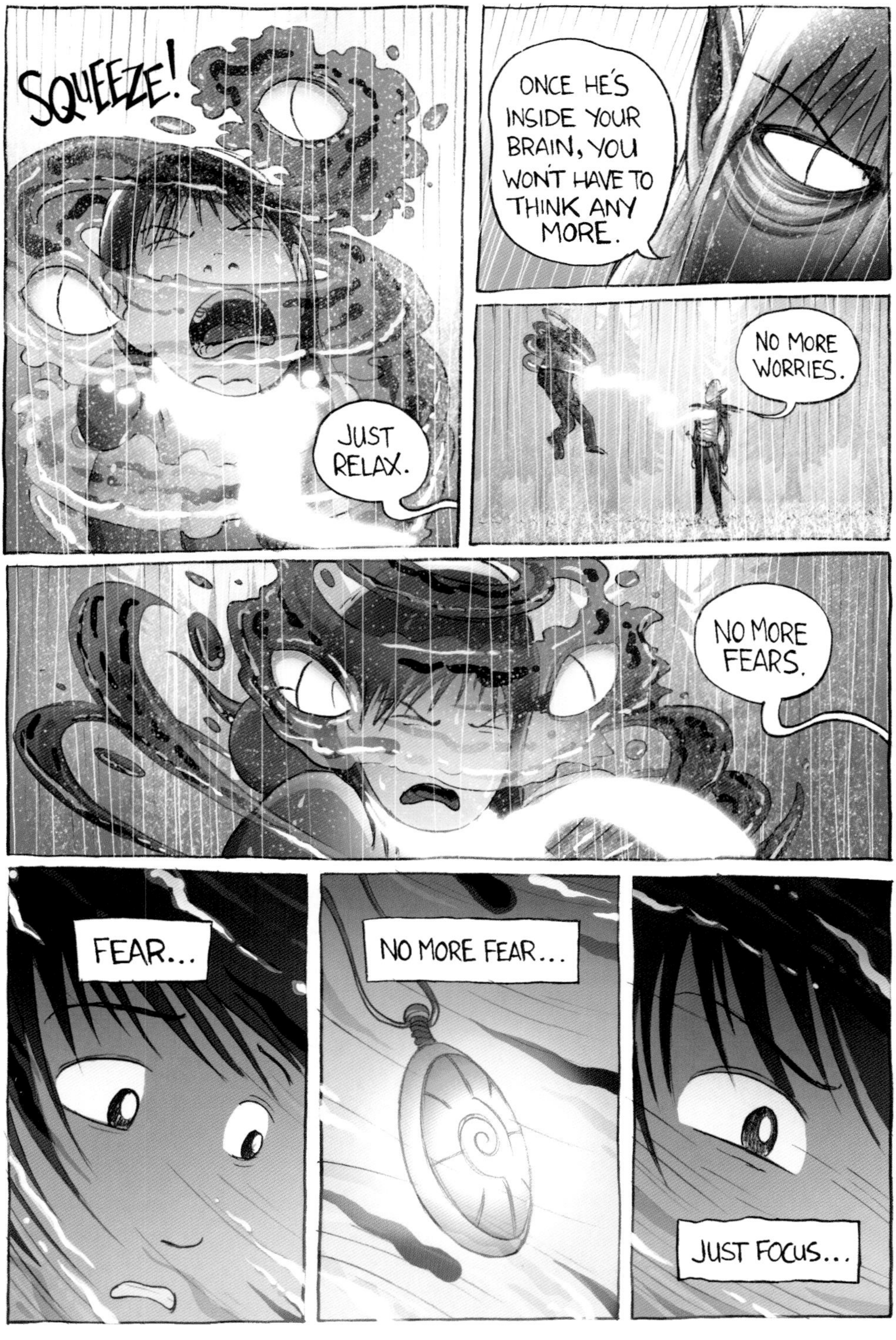
SQUEEZE!
ONCE HE'S INSIDE YOUR BRAIN, YOU WON'T HAVE TO THINK ANY MORE.
JUST RELAX.
NO MORE WORRIES.
NO MORE FEARS.
FEAR...
NO MORE FEAR...
JUST FOCUS...

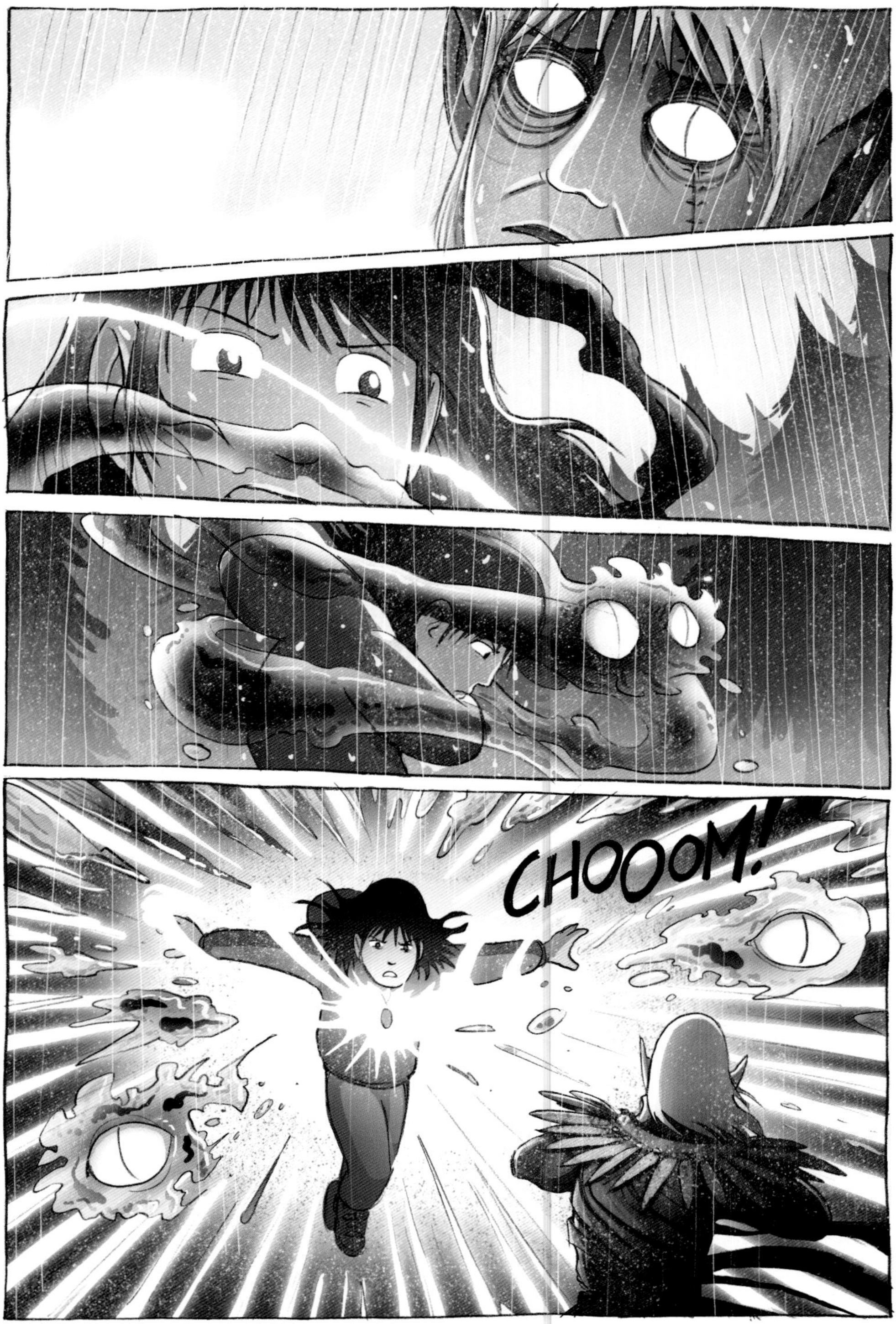
CHOOOM!

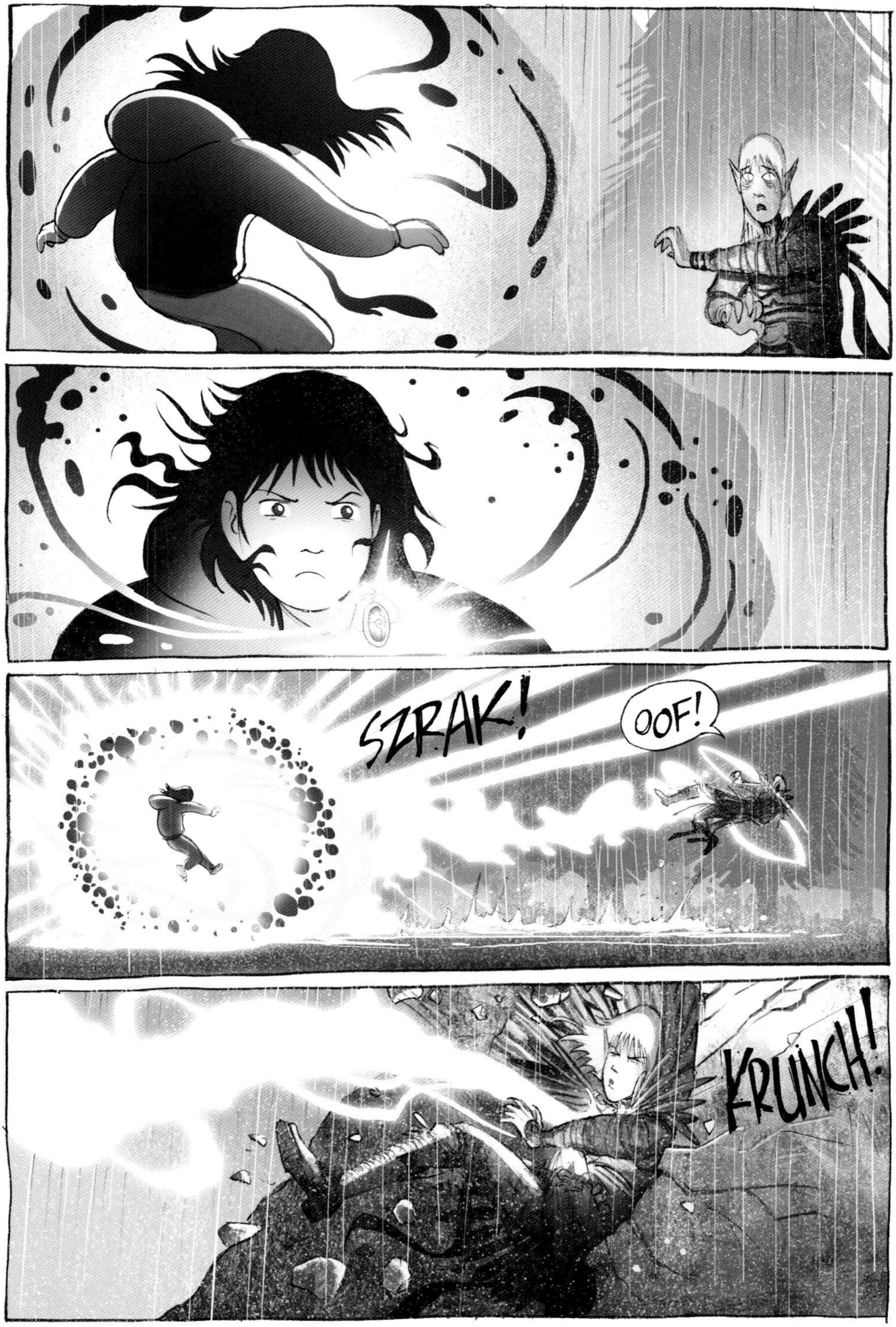
SZRAK!
OOF!
KRUNCH!

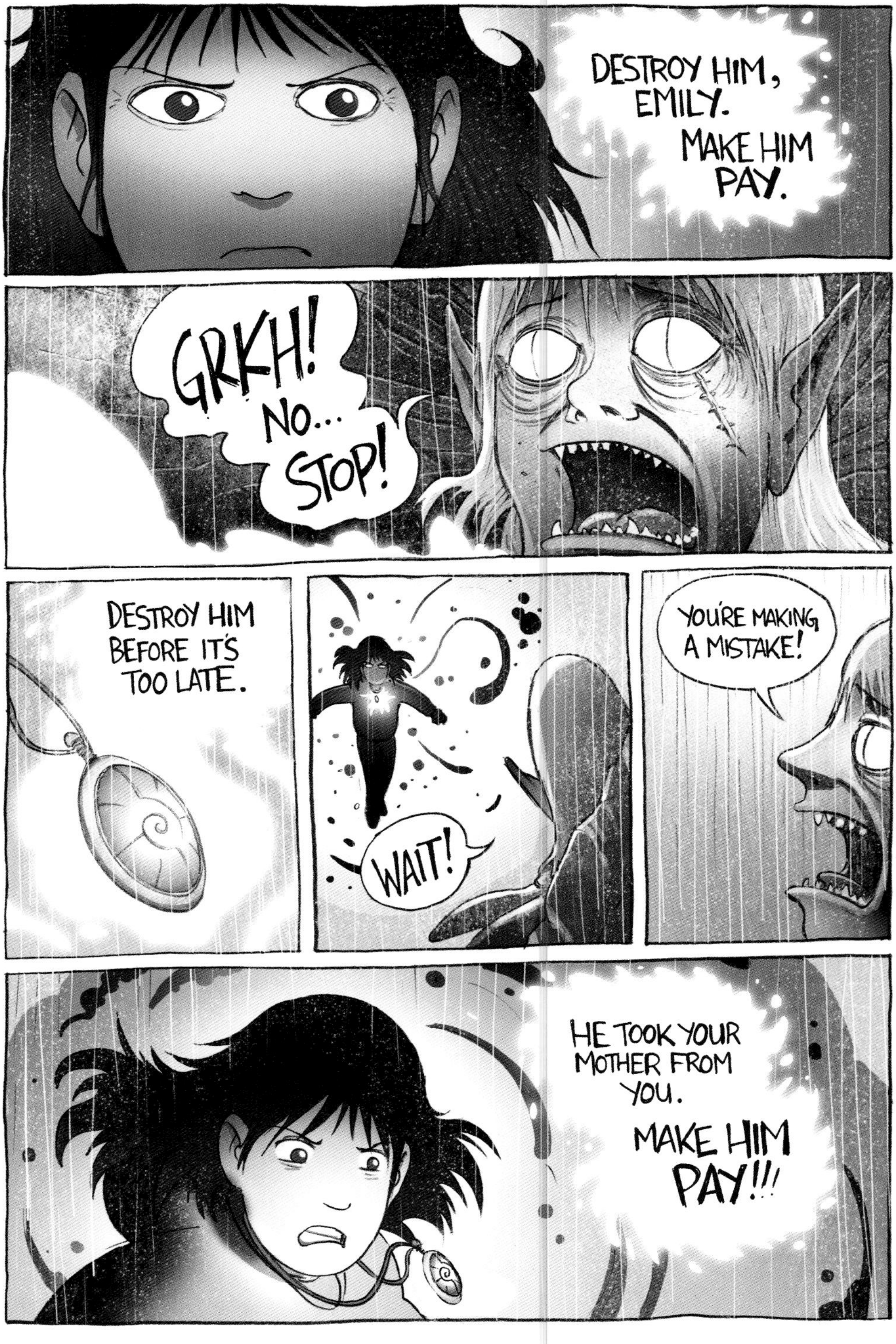
DESTROY HIM, EMILY.
MAKE HIM PAY.
GRKH! NO... STOP!
DESTROY HIM BEFORE IT'S TOO LATE.
WAIT!
YOU'RE MAKING A MISTAKE!
HE TOOK YOUR MOTHER FROM YOU.
MAKE HIM PAY!!!

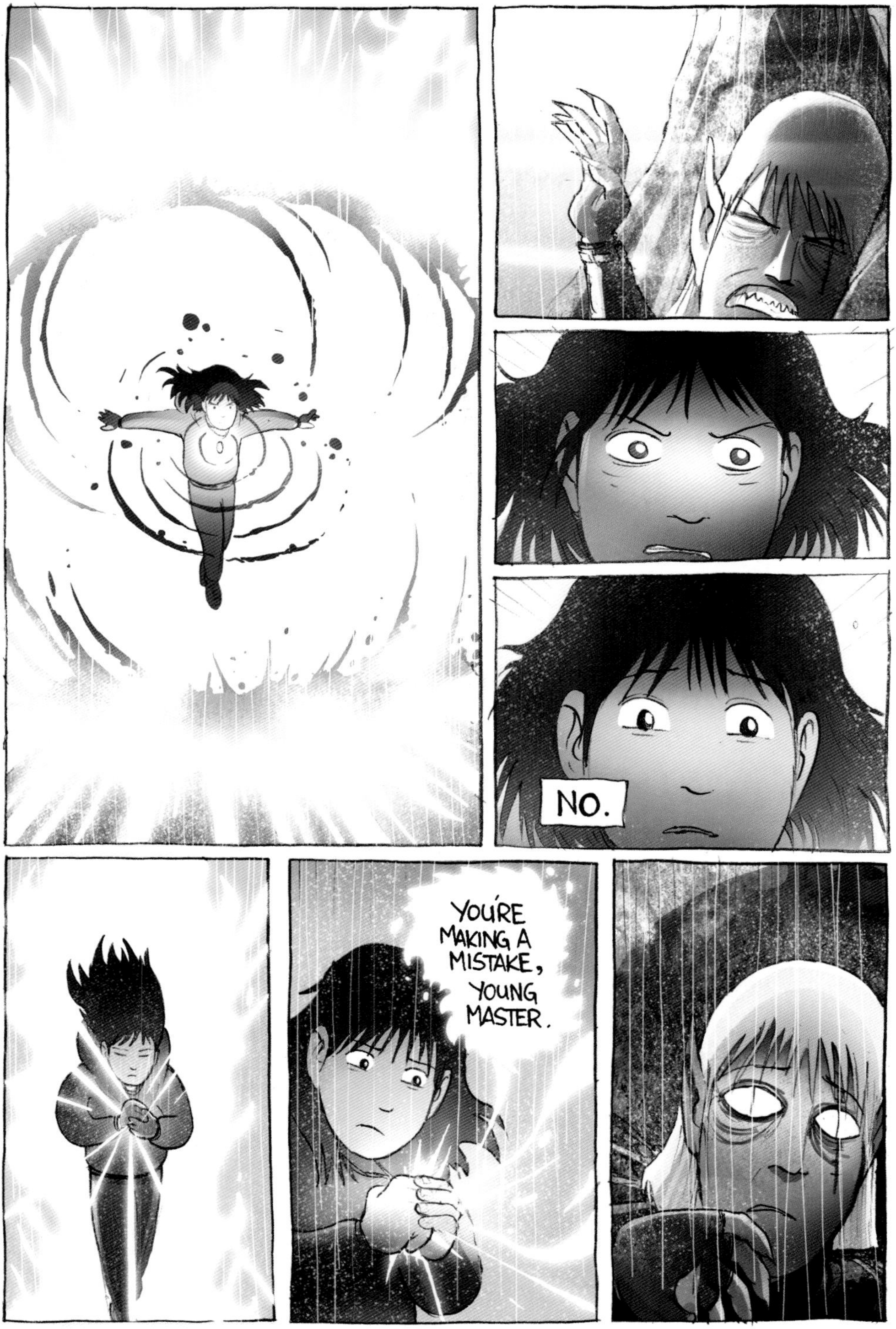
NO.
YOU'RE MAKING A MISTAKE, YOUNG MASTER.

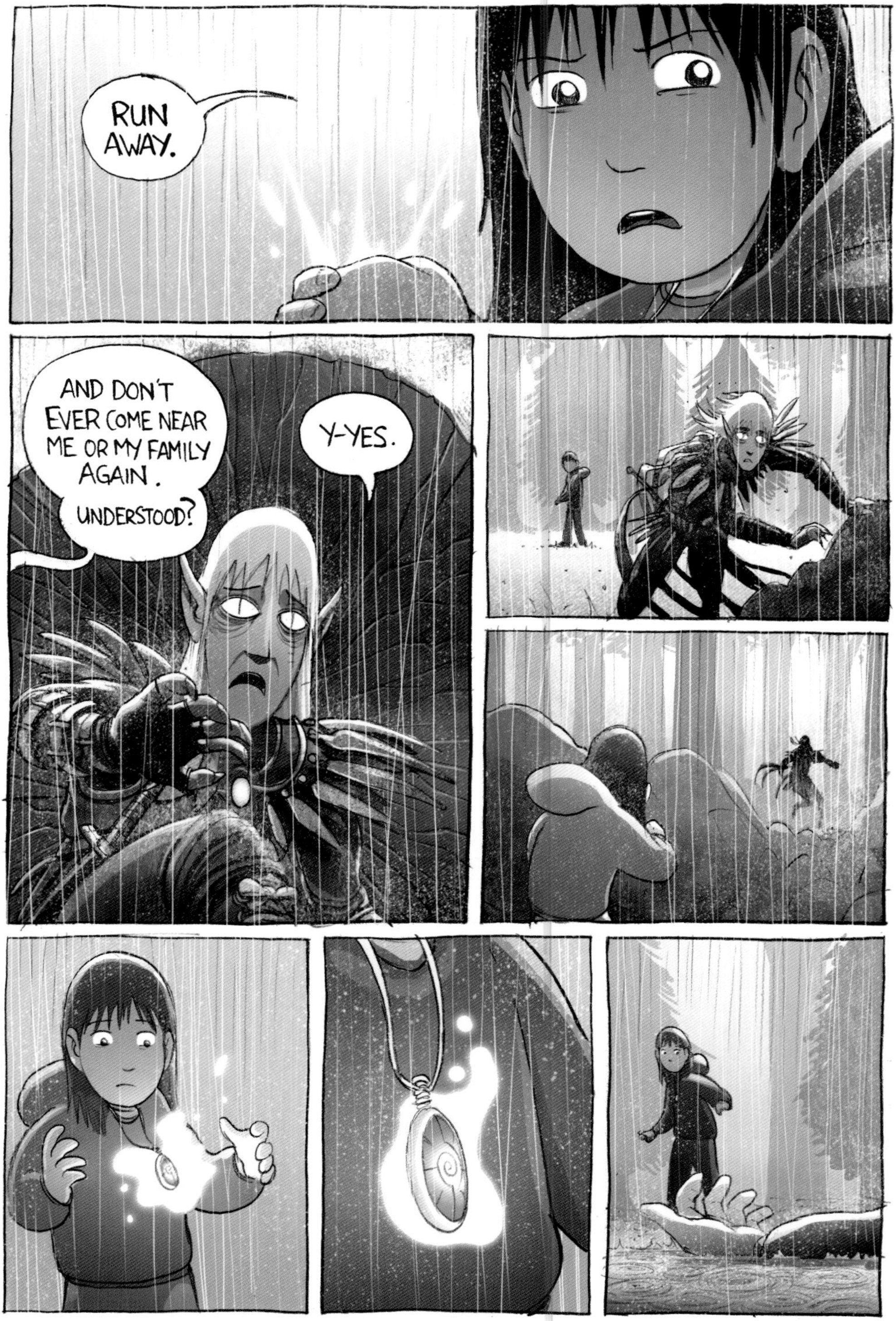
RUN AWAY.
AND DON'T EVER COME NEAR ME OR MY FAMILY AGAIN. UNDERSTOOD?
Y-YES.

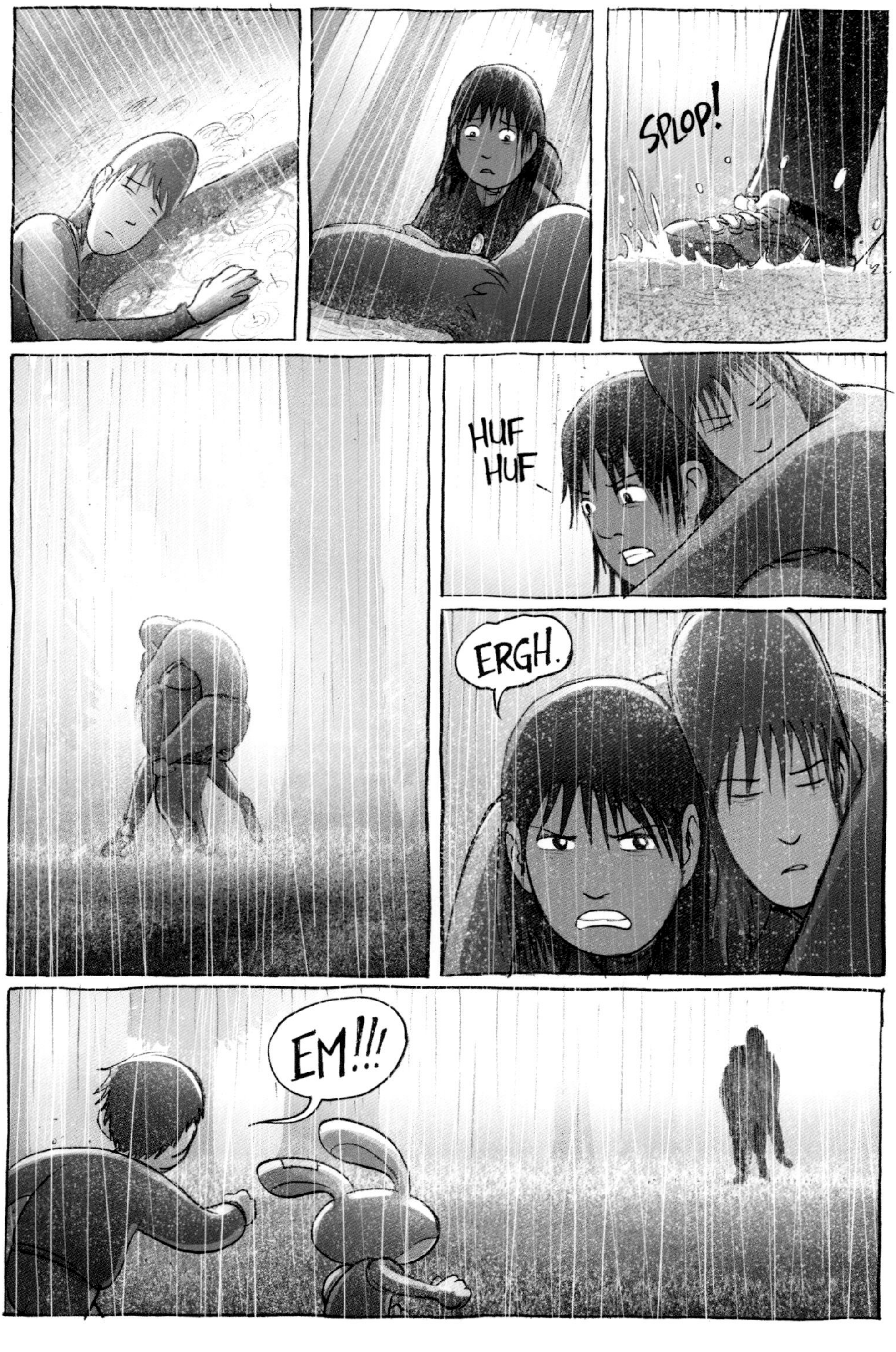
SPLOP!
HUF
HUF
ERGH.
EM!!!

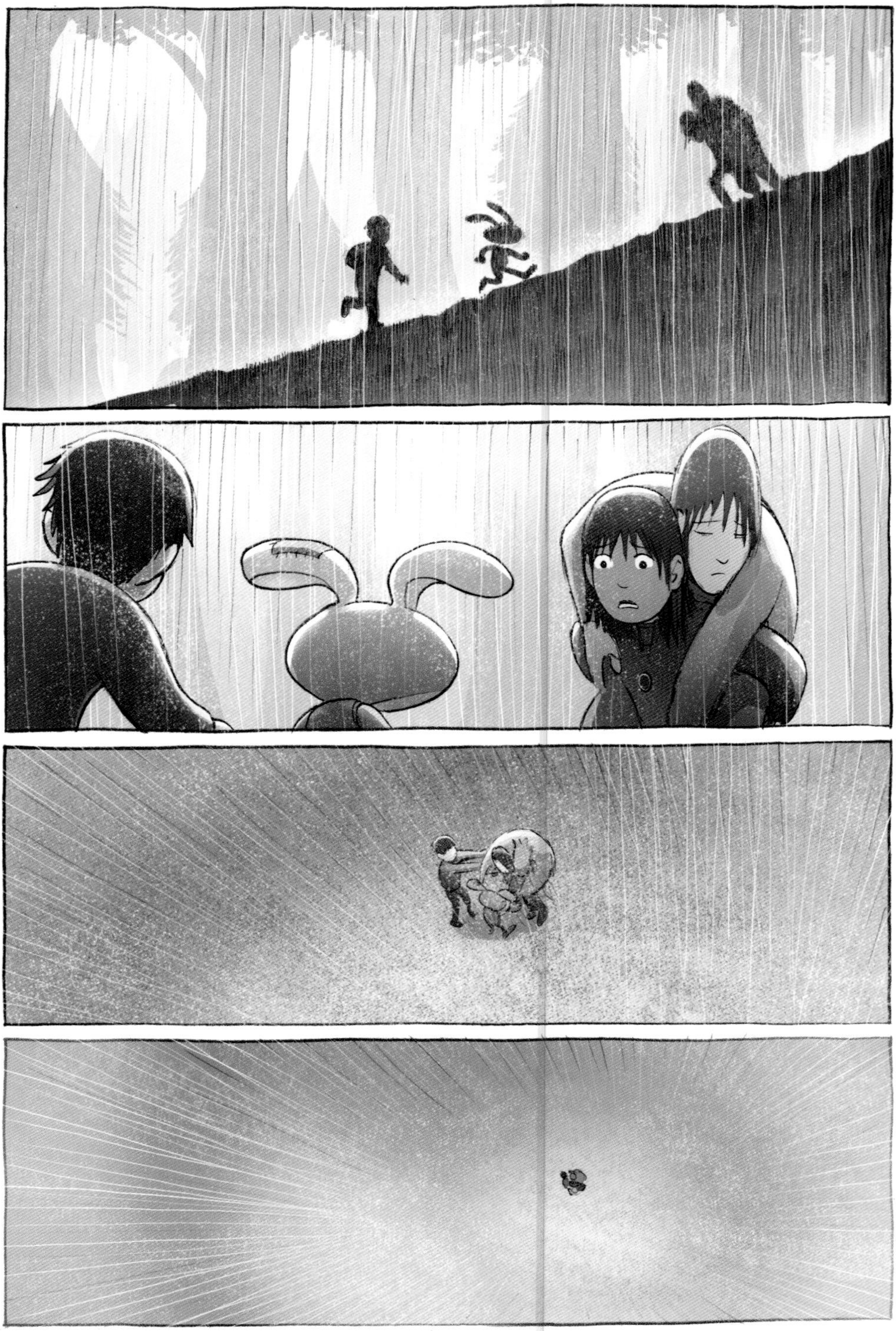

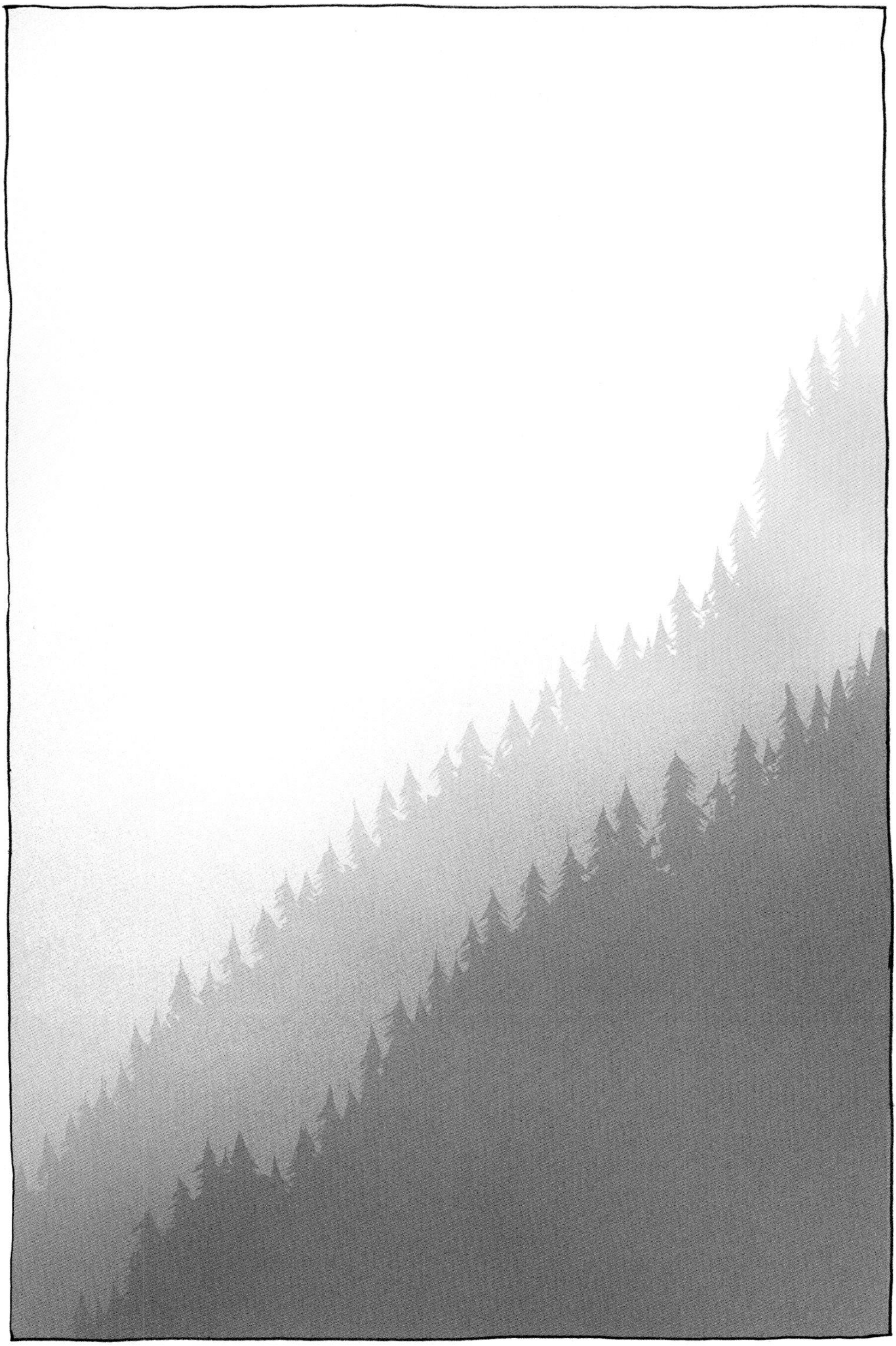

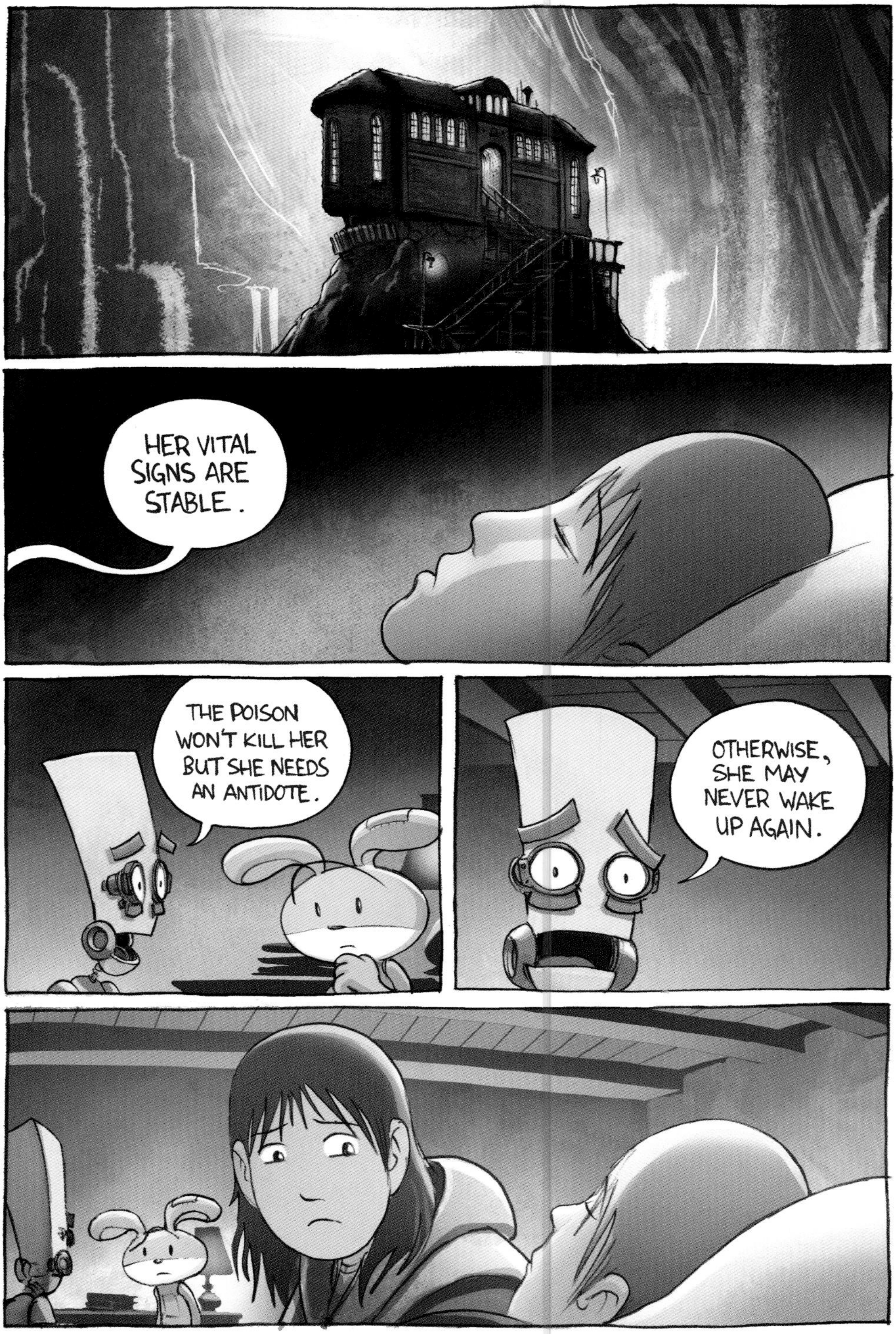
HER VITAL SIGNS ARE STABLE.
THE POISON WON'T KILL HER BUT SHE NEEDS AN ANTIDOTE.
OTHERWISE, SHE MAY NEVER WAKE UP AGAIN.

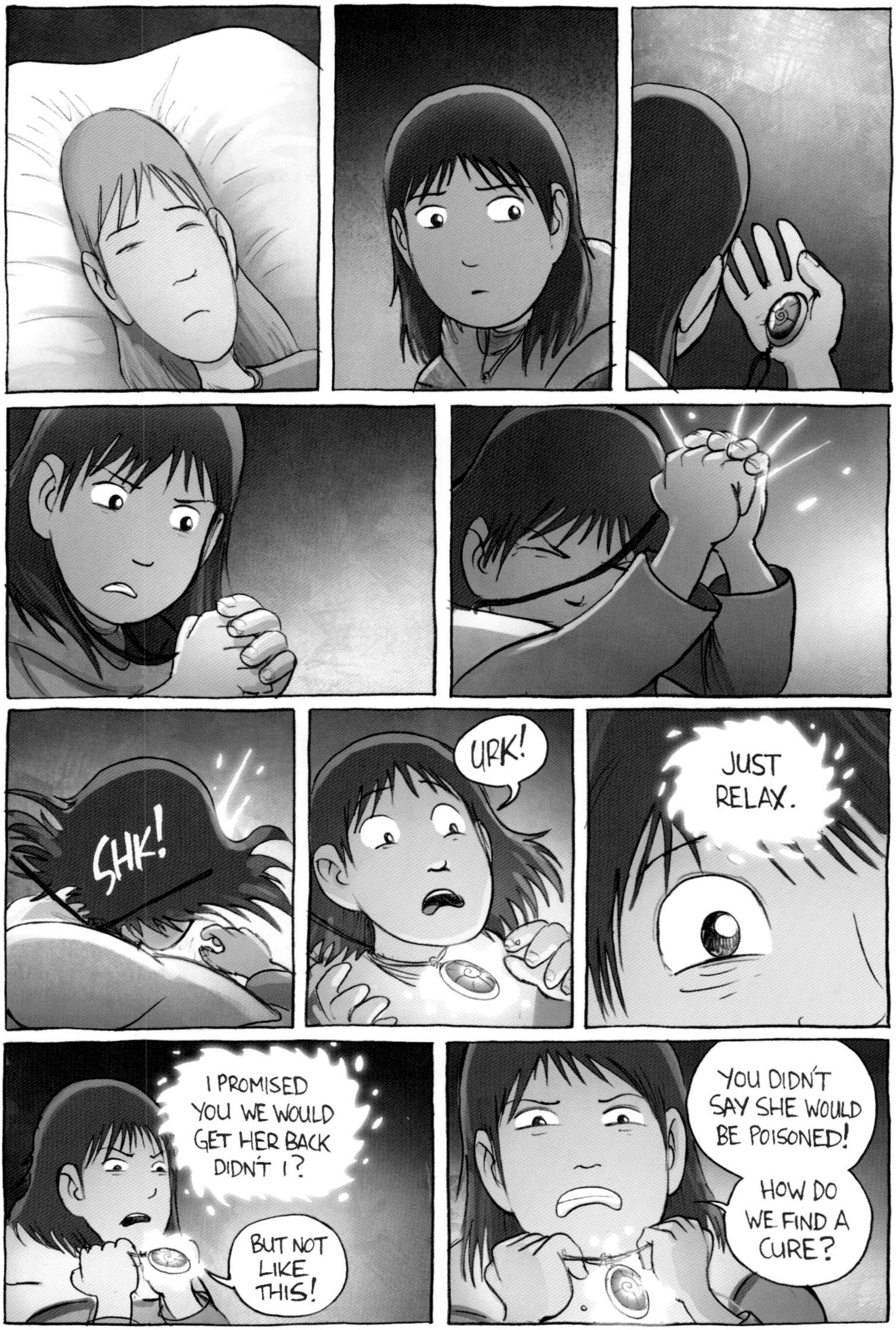
SHK!
URK!
JUST RELAX.
I PROMISED YOU WE WOULD GET HER BACK DIDN'T I?
BUT NOT LIKE THIS!
YOU DIDN'T SAY SHE WOULD BE POISONED!
HOW DO WE FIND A CURE?

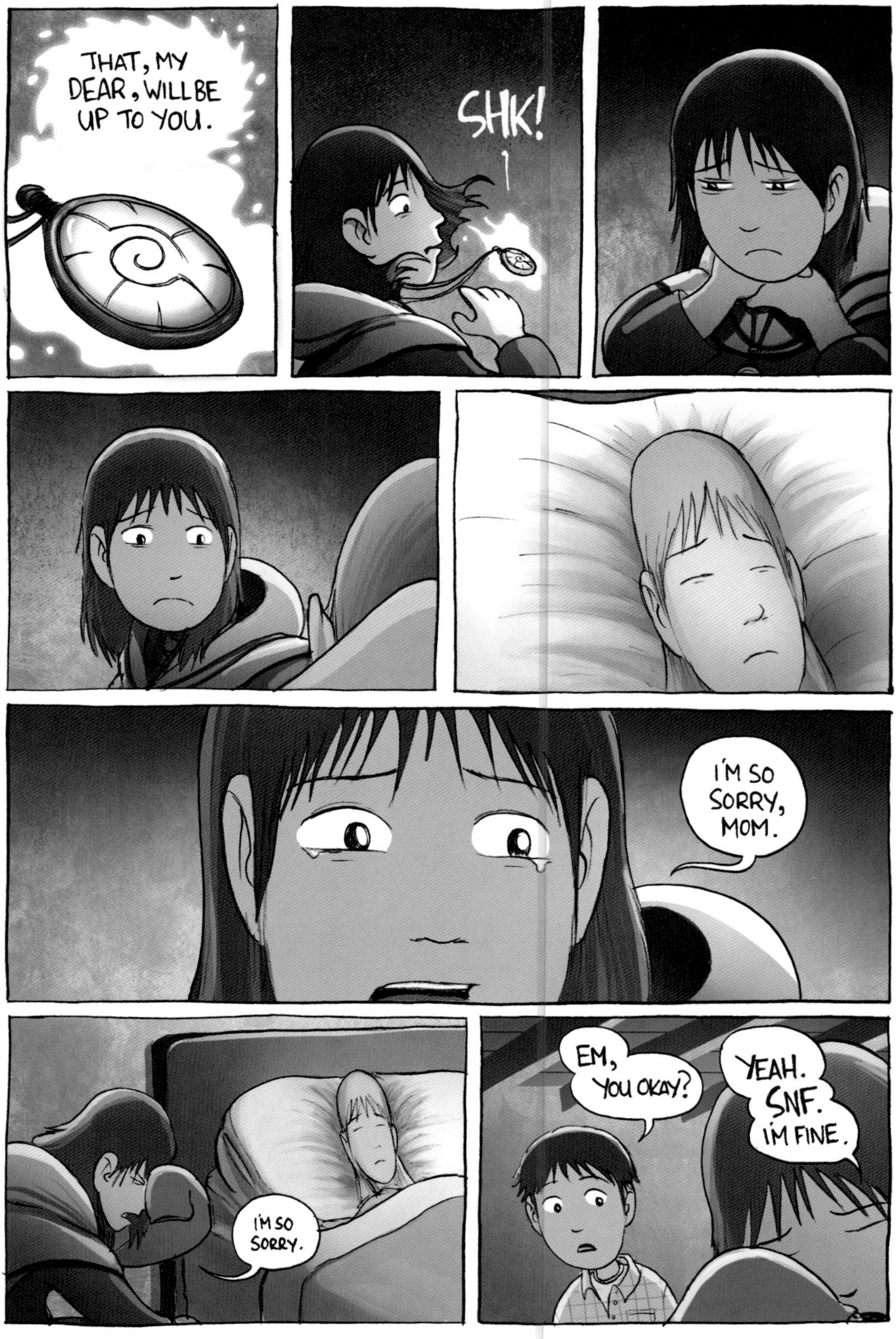
THAT, MY DEAR, WILL BE UP TO YOU.
SHK!
I'M SO SORRY, MOM.
I'M SO SORRY.
EM, YOU OKAY?
YEAH. SNF. I'M FINE.

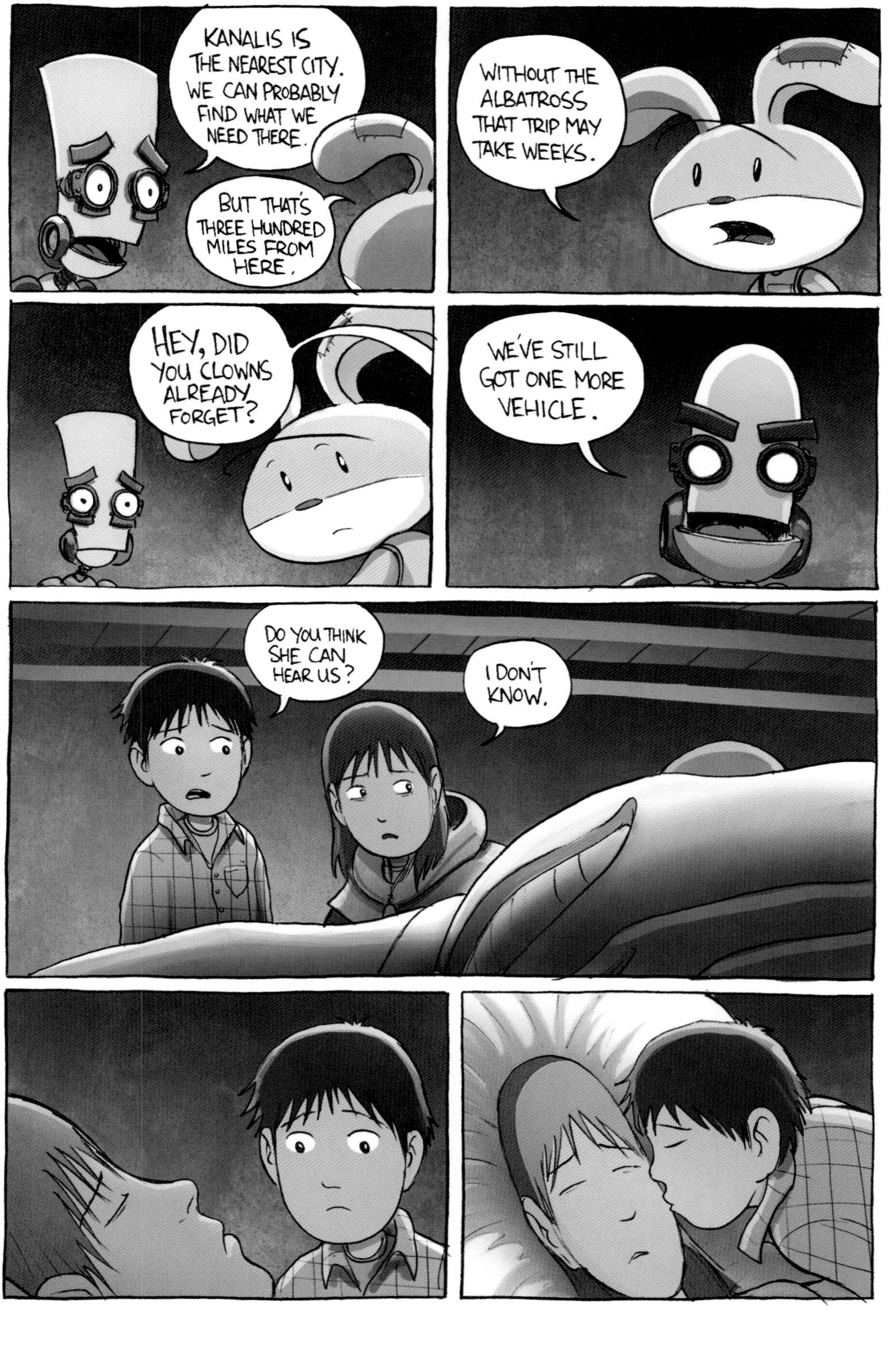
KANALIS IS THE NEAREST CITY. WE CAN PROBABLY FIND WHAT WE NEED THERE.
BUT THAT'S THREE HUNDRED MILES FROM HERE.
WITHOUT THE ALBATROSS THAT TRIP MAY TAKE WEEKS.
HEY, DID YOU CLOWNS ALREADY FORGET?
WE'VE STILL GOT ONE MORE VEHICLE.
DO YOU THINK SHE CAN HEAR US?
I DON'T KNOW.

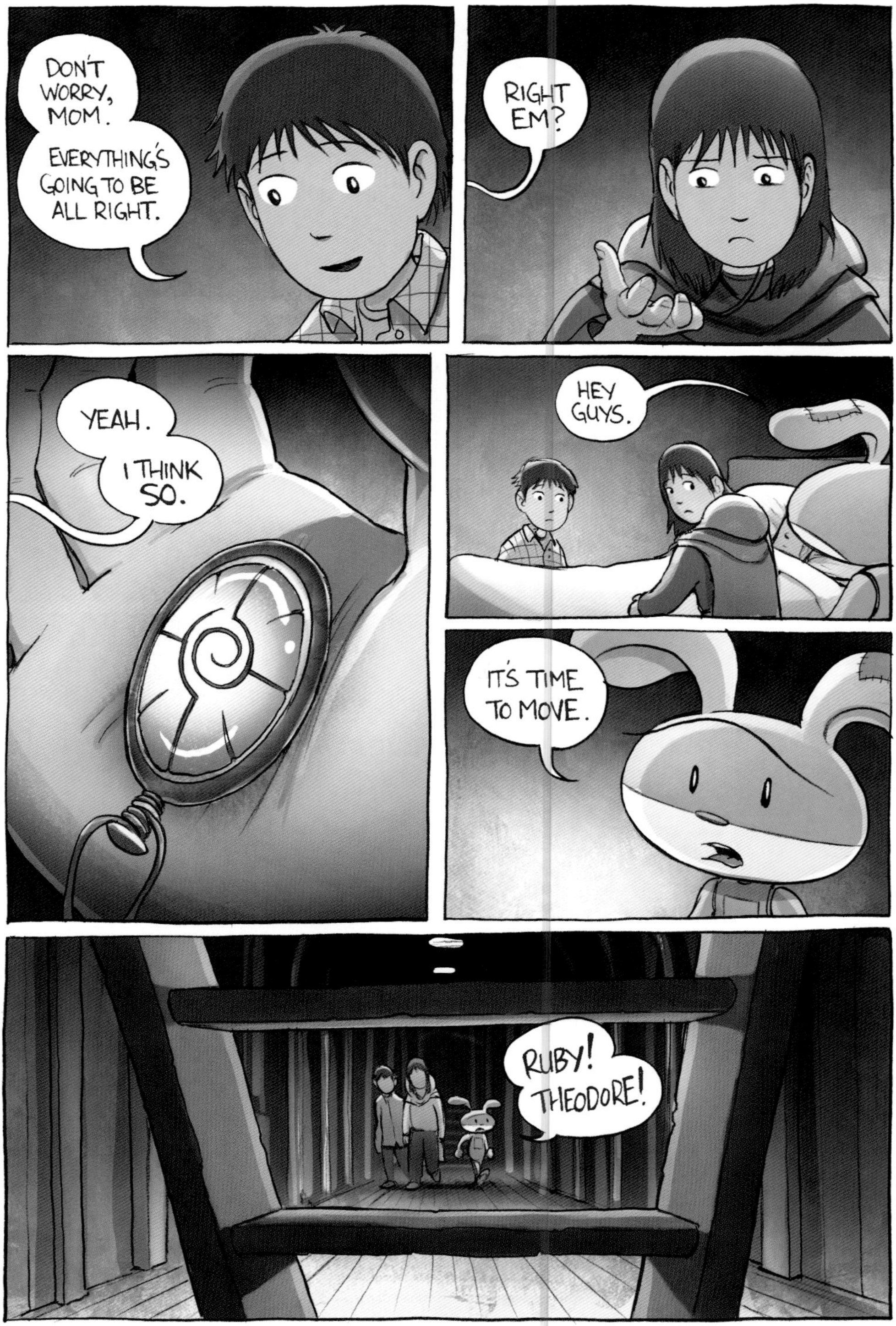
DON'T WORRY, MOM.
EVERYTHING'S GOING TO BE ALL RIGHT.
RIGHT EM?
YEAH.
I THINK SO.
HEY GUYS.
IT'S TIME TO MOVE.
RUBY! THEODORE!

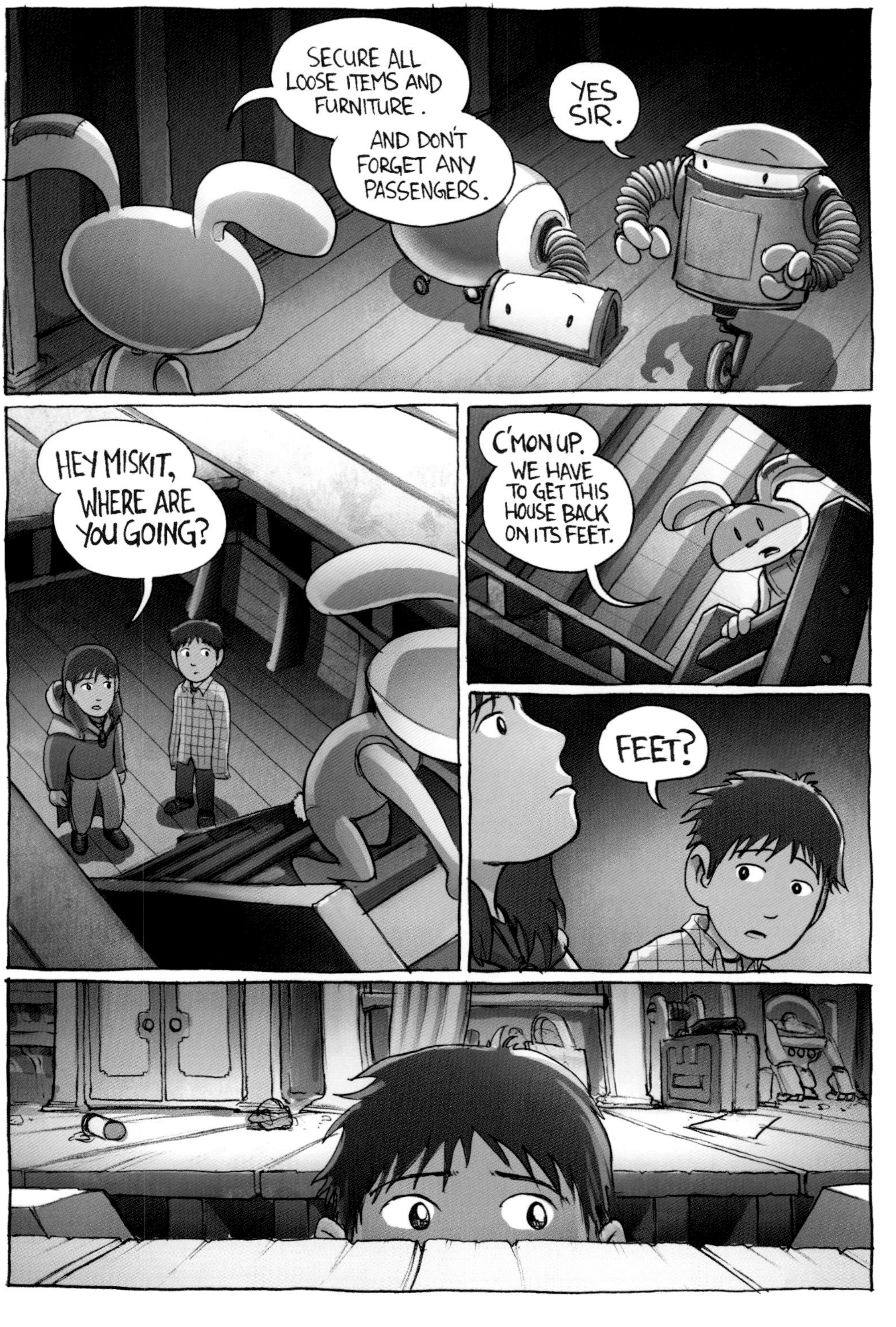
SECURE ALL LOOSE ITEMS AND FURNITURE.
AND DON'T FORGET ANY PASSENGERS.
YES SIR.
HEY MISKIT, WHERE ARE YOU GOING?
C'MON UP.
WE HAVE TO GET THIS HOUSE BACK ON ITS FEET.
FEET?

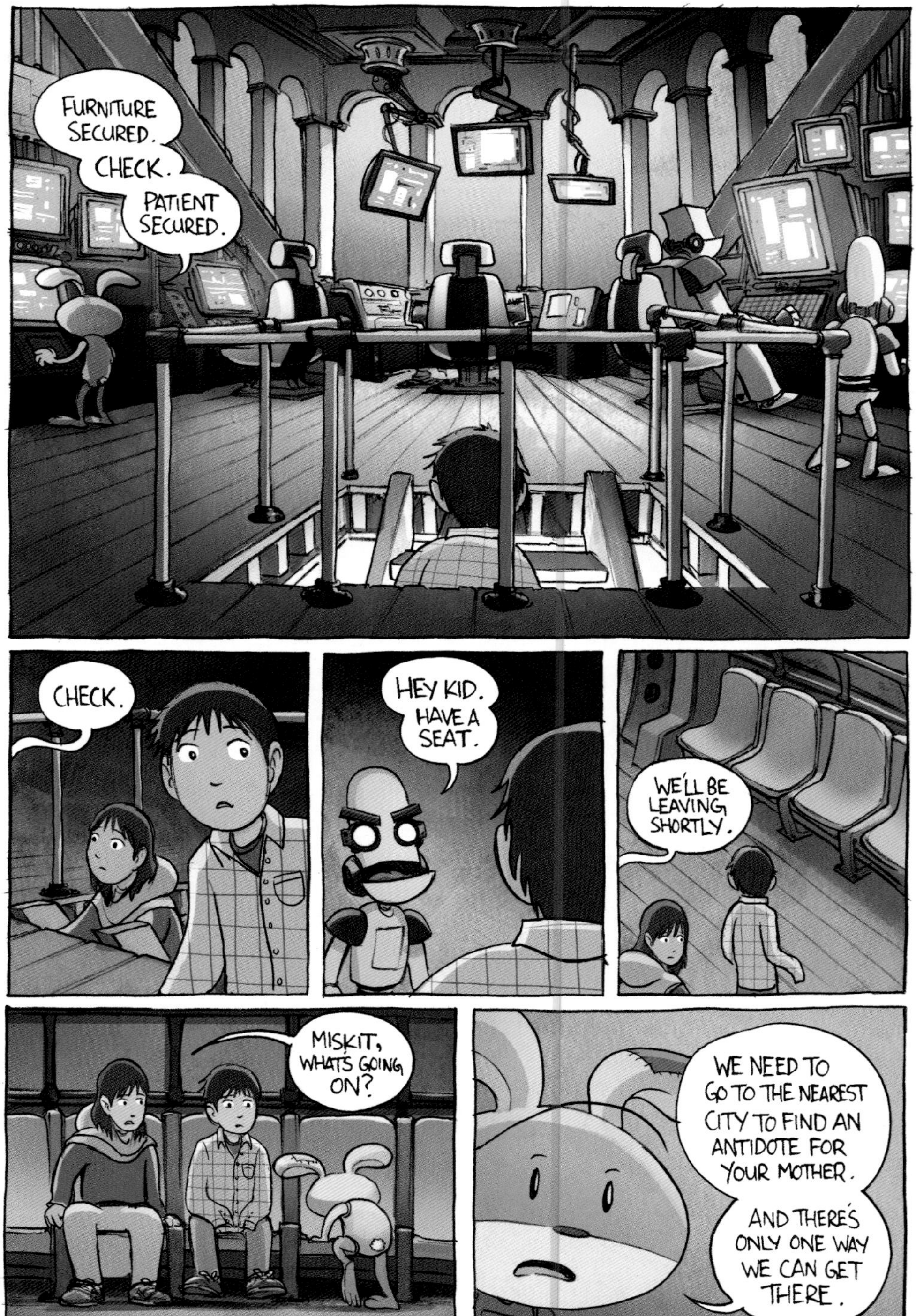
FURNITURE SECURED.
CHECK.
PATIENT SECURED.
CHECK.
HEY KID. HAVE A SEAT.
WE'LL BE LEAVING SHORTLY.
MISKIT, WHAT'S GOING ON?
WE NEED TO GO TO THE NEAREST CITY TO FIND AN ANTIDOTE FOR YOUR MOTHER.
AND THERE'S ONLY ONE WAY WE CAN GET THERE.

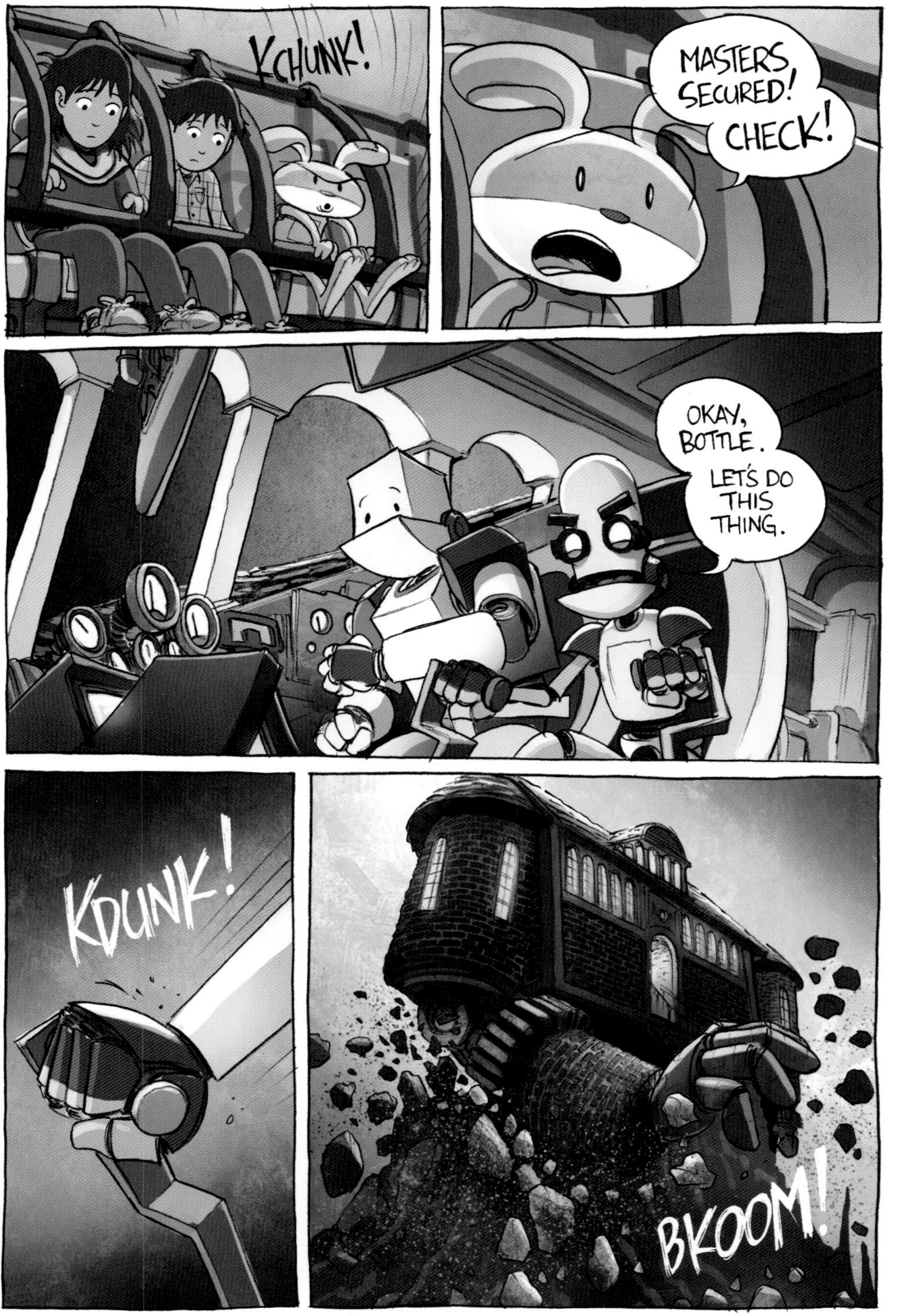
KCHUNK!
MASTERS SECURED!
CHECK!
OKAY, BOTTLE.
LET'S DO THIS THING.
KDUNK!
BKOOM!

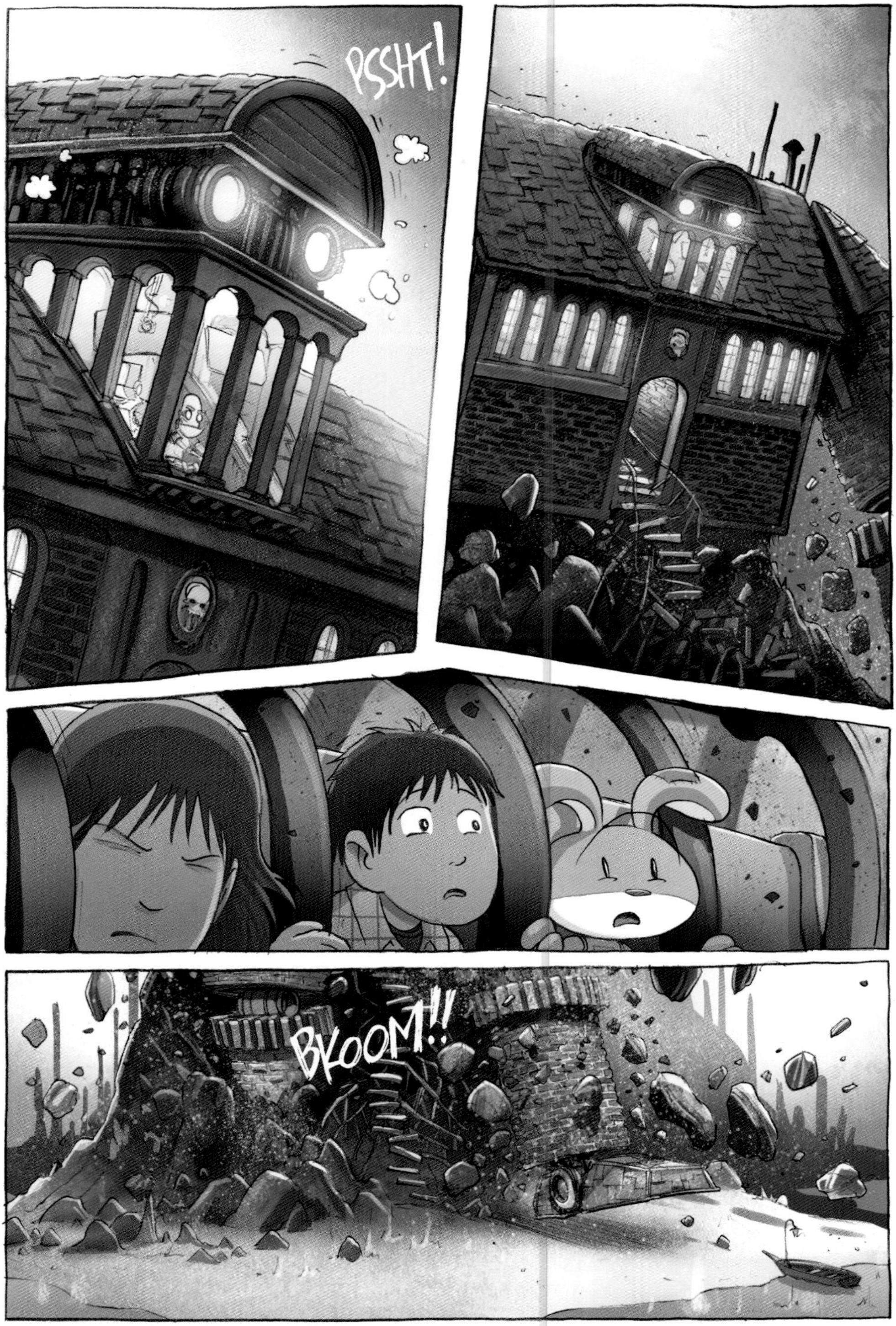
PSSHT!
BKOOM!!

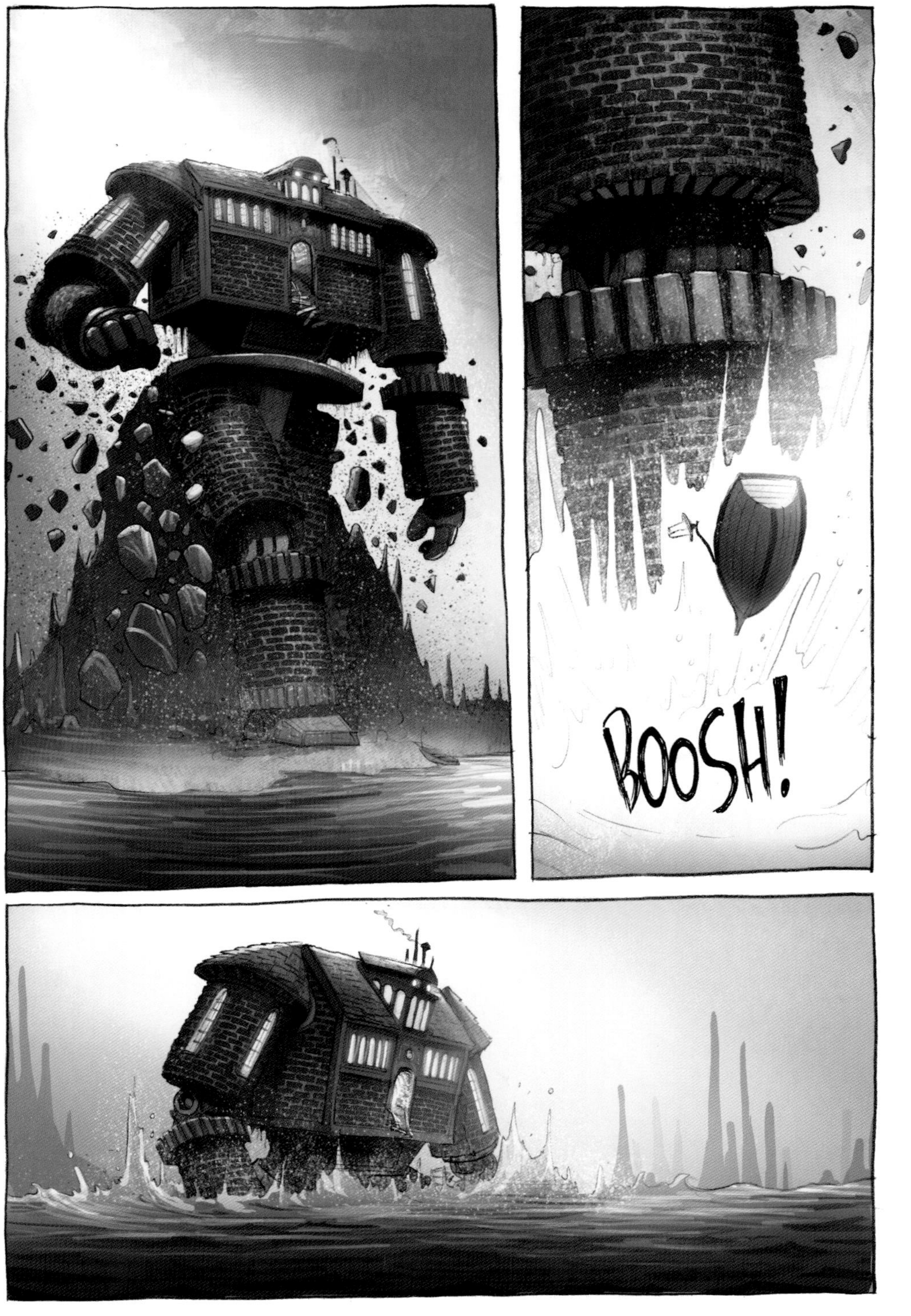
BOOSH!

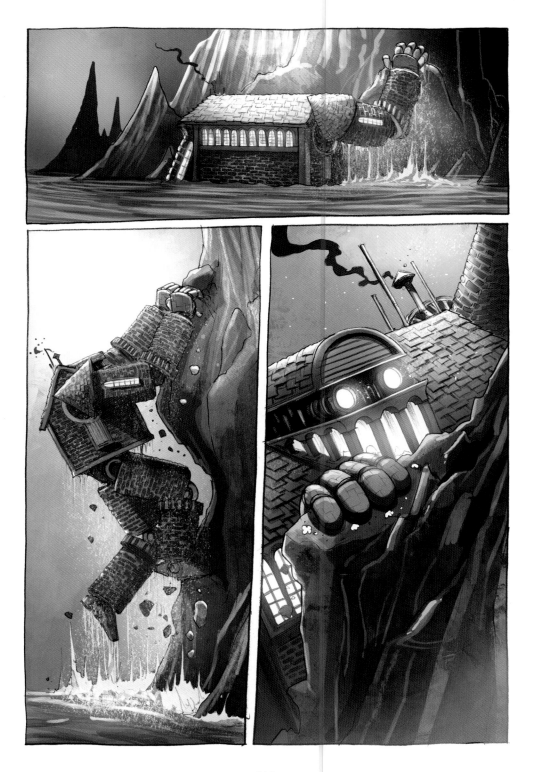

184

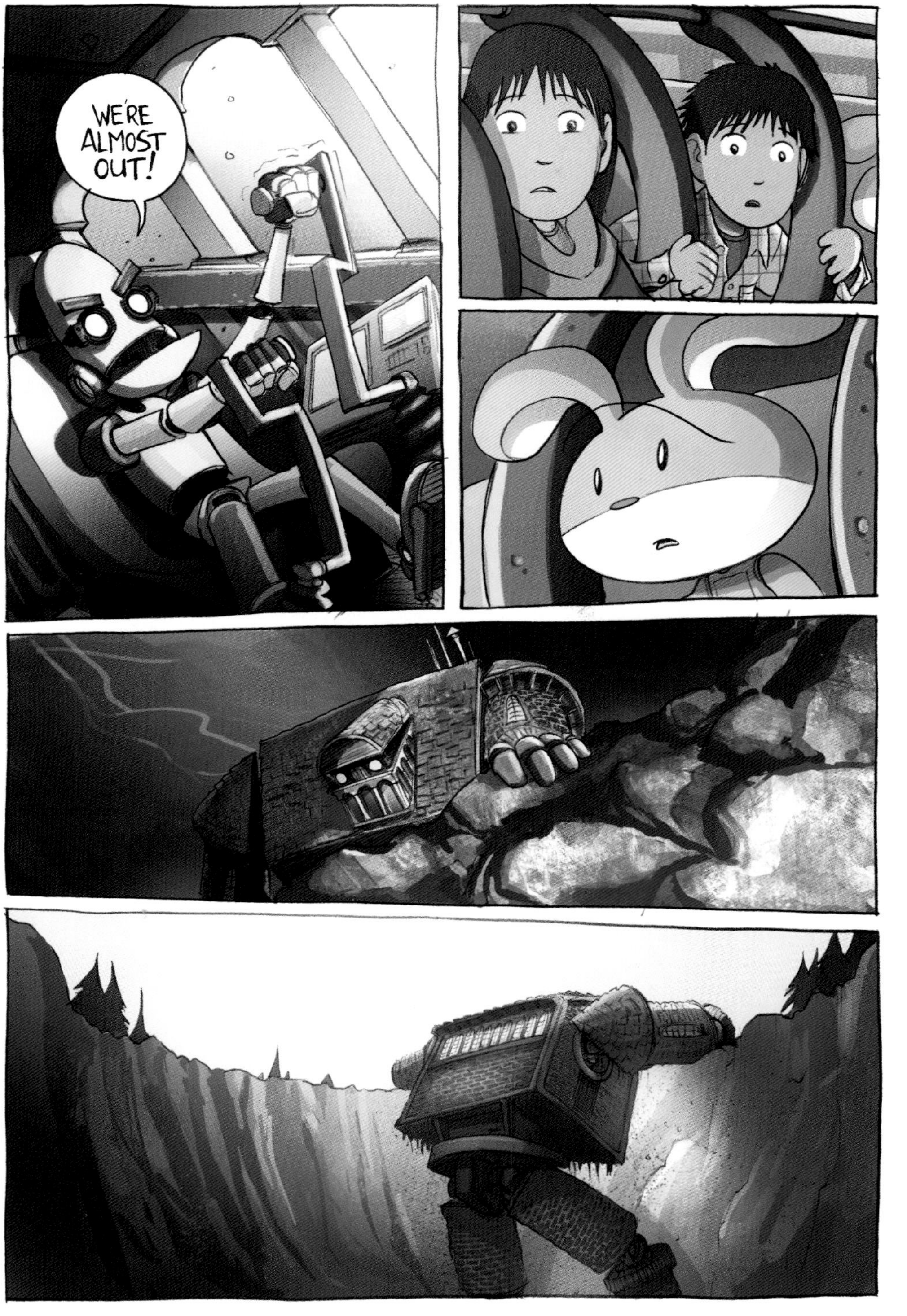
WE'RE ALMOST OUT!

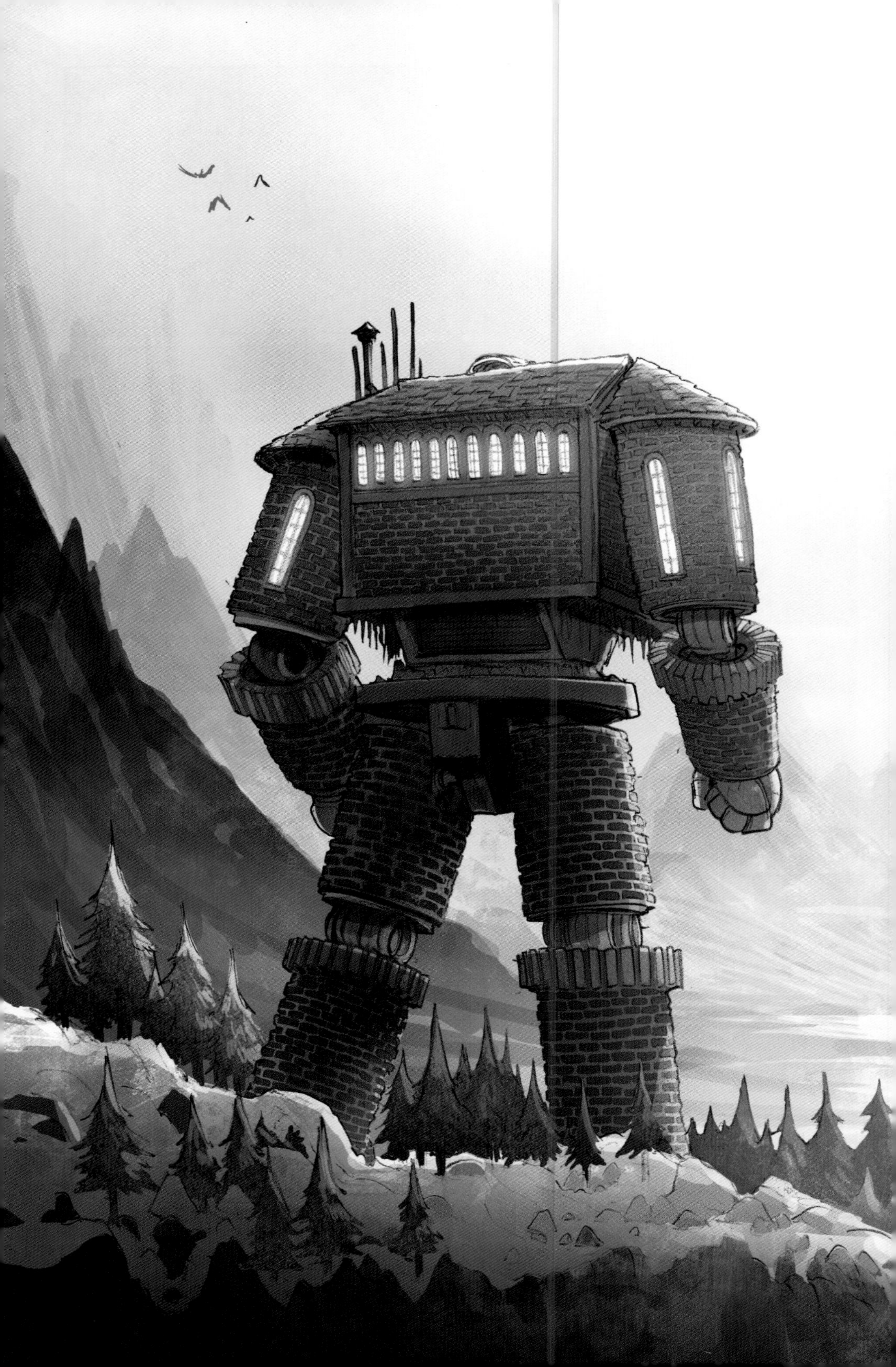

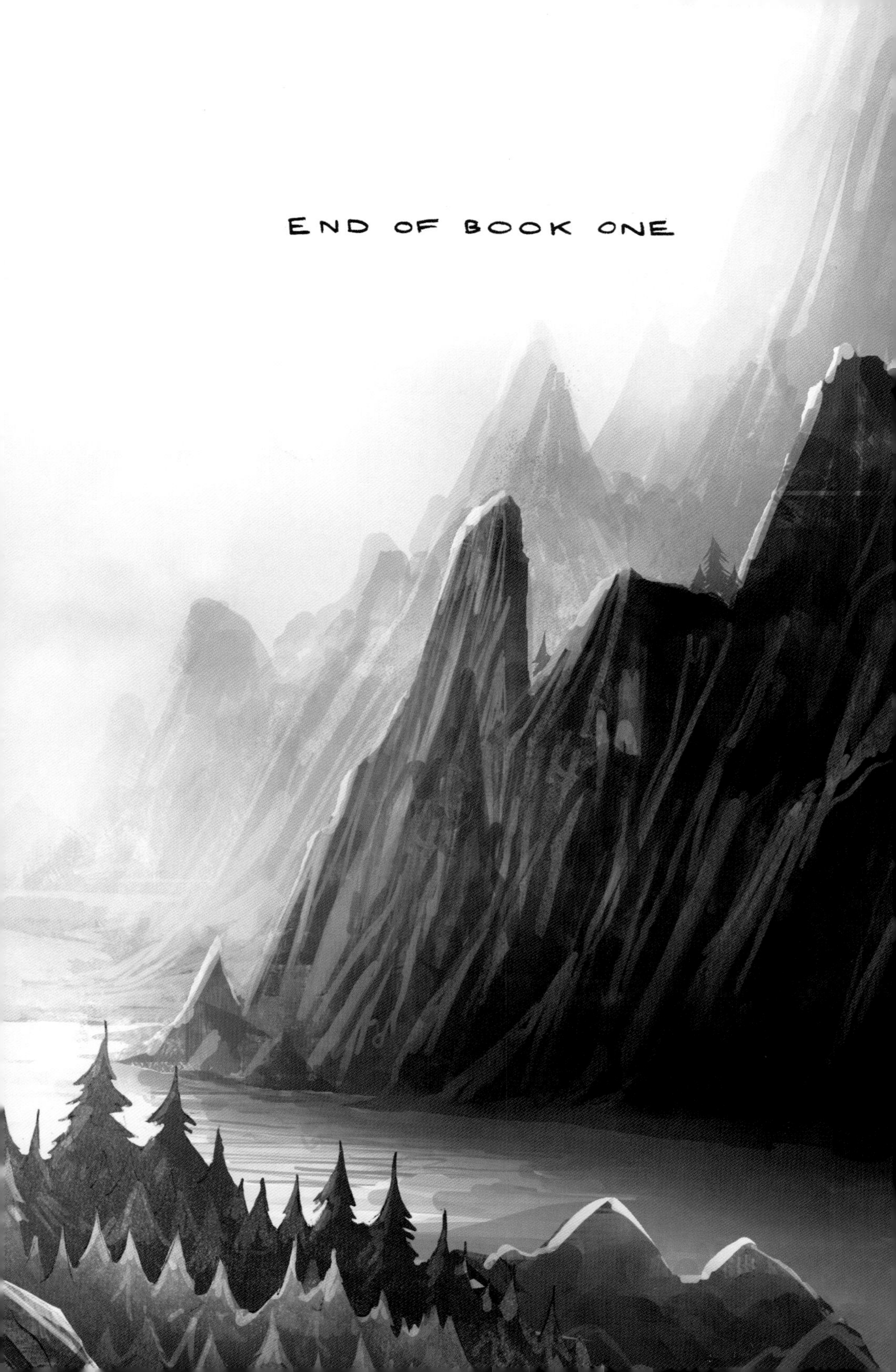
END OF BOOK ONE

ACKNOWLEDGMENTS

The production of this book was a team effort.

A very special thanks to Alan Beadle, Katy Wu, Arree Chung, Erik Martin, Dawn Fujioka, Dave Au, Sho Katayama, Kean Soo, Sarah Mensinga, Matthew Armstrong, Molly Hahn, Shadi Muklashy and Chris Appelhans for lending a hand in the completion of this book. Without these people, I would probably still be toiling away in a little room, trying to finish it. Most of all, I would like to thank my wife Amy, who painted the colors of many of the pages you hold in your hands, and who has been my biggest inspiration in creating this book.

More thanks go to Taka Kibuishi, Judy Hansen, Sheila Keenan, Janna Morishima, Scott McCloud, Jeff Smith, Ben Zhu, Phil Craven, and David Saylor for their support and patience. Thanks everyone!